PENGUIN BOOKS

More Rivals of Sherlock Holmes

After a career in the Thirties as Foreign Correspondent for the *Daily Telegraph* in many European countries, Hugh Greene joined the BBC as Head of the German Service in 1940, a post which he occupied until the end of the war. From 1946 to 1948 he was the controller of Broadcasting in the British Zone of Germany; for eighteen months thereafter he was Head of the BBC East European Service; and from 1950 to 1951 he was Head of the Emergency Information Service in Malaya. In 1960 he became Director-General of the BBC. After his retirement in 1969 he was made a Governor of the BBC and joined The Bodley Head as Chairman. His previous books are *The Spy's Bedside Book*, written in collaboration with his brother, Graham Greene, *The Third Floor Front: A View of Broadcasting in the Sixties* (1969), and *The Rivals of Sherlock Holmes* (1970), also published in Penguins.

More Rivals of
Sherlock Holmes

COSMOPOLITAN
CRIMES

edited and introduced by
Hugh Greene

Penguin Books

Penguin Books Ltd, Harmondsworth, Middlesex, England
Penguin Books Australia Ltd, Ringwood, Victoria, Australia

—

First published by The Bodley Head 1971
Published in Penguin Books 1973

—

Copyright © in the compilation Sir Hugh Greene, 1971

—

Made and printed in Great Britain
by Richard Clay (The Chaucer Press) Ltd
Bungay, Suffolk
Set in Linotype Georgian

For my three musketeers
DONALD, EDWARD *and* STUART
these foreign excursions

Contents

Contents

Acknowledgements

FOR permission to publish some of these stories my thanks are due to: Mrs Dorothy Cheston Bennett for *A Bracelet at Bruges*; Cassell & Co for *The Secret of the* Magnifique; Mills & Boon Ltd for *The Red Silk Scarf*; Gyldendal Forlag of Copenhagen for *A Sensible Course of Action*; Hodder and Stoughton Ltd for *Murder at the Duck Club*. *Arsène Lupin in Prison* was first published in England by Cassell & Co.

It has been by no means easy to trace copyright holders. If in any case I have failed I offer my apologies.

I am grateful to Mrs Dorothy Cheston Bennett and Penguin Ltd for permission to use the extract from Arnold Bennett's Journals in the Introduction.

Mr H. Agerbak, the Counsellor for Press and Cultural Affairs at the Royal Danish Embassy in London, provided me with much interesting information about Baron Palle Rosenkrantz. Miss J. Houlgate, the BBC Reference Librarian, was helpful with other biographical details.

For anyone working on the detective stories of this period there are four indispensable books of reference: *Victorian Detective Fiction* by Graham Greene and Dorothy Glover (Bodley Head, 1966), *Queen's Quorum* by Ellery Queen (Gollancz, 1953), *The Detective Short Story* by Ellery Queen (Boston: Little, Brown & Co, 1942), and *Murder for Pleasure* by Howard Haycraft (New York: D. Appleton-Century Company, 1941).

Introduction

I HAVE limited this collection, as I did *The Rivals of Sherlock Holmes*, to stories published between the first appearance of Sherlock Holmes in the *Strand Magazine* in 1891 and the outbreak of war in 1914. This is a self-contained period with its own character. With the invention of Sherlock Holmes Conan Doyle changed the character of the short detective story, and the First World War changed the character of the world in which the stories were set.

In this collection the connecting link between the stories is that they are all, in some sense, foreign affairs. In one adventure a French detective is at work in London. In the others detectives, agents, and rogues are pursuing their business in France, Switzerland, South Africa, Belgium, the United States, Denmark, Austria, and Canada.

From the time of Edgar Allan Poe onwards the United States, England, and France have produced all the most famous and successful writers of detective stories. Other countries tended to rely, as one can still see on every railway bookstall in Europe, on translations from English and French. I have, however, been able to find for this collection stories by a Danish and an Austro-Hungarian writer which have never appeared before in English.

The literary quality, and the fame, of the writers varies considerably. Of my own favourites, Maurice Leblanc, the

creator of Arsène Lupin, has never been completely forgotten. Grant Allen, Jacques Futrelle, and Robert Barr (the
author of one remarkable story), though they have sunk
into semi-oblivion, seem to me to be among the best of
their kind. Arnold Bennett is not usually thought of as a
writer of detective stories and the book from which I have
taken an episode seems only to have been reprinted once,
more than fifty years ago. About the work of E. Phillips
Oppenheim, still a famous name, there is a strong flavour of
overripe cheese, which appeals to some palates, including, in
small helpings, my own. Reviewers and readers of *The
Rivals of Sherlock Holmes* had different favourites, which
by no means always coincided with my own, and I hope
that will again prove to be the case with this collection.

I begin with two episodes by Grant Allen (1848–99) from
An African Millionaire, one of the most amusing collections of crime stories ever written. It appeared in book form
in 1897 with delightful illustrations by Gordon Browne,
having first seen the light in the *Strand Magazine* in 1896
and 1897. I have included two episodes because space is required for a full appreciation of the long-drawn-out feud
between Sir Charles Vandrift, the South African millionaire, and the ingenious Colonel Clay. Grant Allen was born
in Canada of Irish and French-Canadian ancestry. He won
a classical Postmastership at Merton College, Oxford
(which gives me a certain fellow feeling for him) and he had
a hard time throughout his university career as he had an
invalid wife and little money. After Oxford he was ap-
pointed Professor of Mental and Moral Philosophy in a
newly founded university for Negroes at Spanish Town,
Jamaica. The university soon collapsed for lack of students
and Grant Allen returned to England to make his living by
writing. His output in the twenty-three years of life which
remained to him was extraordinarily varied. It included
poetry, essays, popular science and botany, theology and
fiction. The book which attracted most attention in his lifetime was a novel called *The Woman Who Did* published by

John Lane in 1895 in his Keynotes series with a title-page designed by Aubrey Beardsley. It deals, in the purest language, with the life of a sweet girl graduate from Girton who insisted, on the highest principles, on having a love affair and a child without marriage, and it was condemned by the Mrs Whitehouses of the time as extremely saucy and scandalous. Grant Allen wrote two other excellent books of stories with a semi-detective interest, *Miss Cayley's Adventures* and *Hilda Wade* and two novels in which detectives play a part, *The Scallywag* and *A Splendid Sin*. Perhaps the fact that none of his detective books are mentioned in the American reference book, *British Authors of the Nineteenth Century*, reflects a too modest contemporary estimation of them as compared with his so-called serious work. He died just before completing *Hilda Wade* and the final episode in this book which appeared in the *Strand Magazine* in 1900 (under the appropriate title *The Episode of the Dead Man Who Spoke*) was written, from conversations on his death bed, by his friend and neighbour Dr Conan Doyle.

George Chetwynd Griffith (1859–1906) was one of the best thriller writers of the eighteen-nineties. *The Outlaws of the Air* about a group of anarchists which terrorizes the world from a gigantic airship (New Scotland Yard, the General Post Office, St Paul's, and the Houses of Parliament are all destroyed) and *The Great Pirate Syndicate* about a war between Europe and the Anglo-Saxon Federation still make excellent reading. So far as I can establish he only wrote two books of detective interest and from one of these I have taken a story about I.D.B. on the South African diamond fields. George Griffith, who was the son of a country clergyman, seems to have seen his own short life as one continuous thriller. I need only to reproduce his entry from *Who's Who*. 'Educ. had the advantage of neglected early instruction; got his education wandering about the world; sea-apprentice; sundowner; sailor; stock-rider; butcher; globe-trotter (record round the world in 64½ days); schoolmaster; journalist; story-writer. *Recreations:* loafing, travelling and sailing; went 6½ times round the world; once across the Rockies, thrice over the Andes (treasured a pipe smoked at 19,300 feet above sea-level); three times round the Horn; found the source of the Amazon river-system; flew in a balloon from London to the field of Agincourt, last Englishman who fell there.' Obviously a happy man.

Arnold Bennett (1867–1931) was by no means too modest about his few detective stories and might, I think, have been rather pleased to find himself in a collection like this. About the book of stories from which I have chosen one he wrote in his diary for Friday, 27 November 1903: 'This morning I finished the six *Windsor** stories. They will probably be issued as a book under the title *The Loot of Cities*, and I shall make out of them, first and last, from £200 to £250 – probably the smaller sum. They have occupied less than two months of my time. I began well, languished in the middle, and fired up tremendously towards the end. Indeed I wrote the last three stories in twelve days. And if I had really tried I could have done the whole six in a month. I have learnt a lot about the technique of construction while writing them. And on the whole have not been bored. But once or twice I have been terribly bored.' On 1 December of the same year he noted in his diary that the six stories in *The Loot of Cities* were 'all good on their plane'. Bennett's other excursion into crime fiction was *The Grand Babylon Hotel* which, unlike *The Loot of Cities*, has been reprinted from time to time. About this book he remarked with some pride in his diary on 18 January 1901, that 'the *Graphic* people' before its serialization in a periodical called *The Golden Penny* had issued a circular comparing it with Fergus Hume's famous book *The Mystery of a Hansom Cab*. 'Fancy,' said Bennett, 'writing a story as good as *The Mystery of a Hansom Cab*.' Today it seems much better.

Robert Barr (1850–1912) was a prolific writer of romances

* The reference is to the *Windsor Magazine*, a rival of the *Strand*.

under his own name and the pseudonym Luke Sharp. He owes his survival to one book, *The Triumphs of Eugène Valmont*, and, in fact, to one story in that book, *The Absent-Minded Coterie*, one of the most ingenious detective stories ever written. Otherwise he wrote no detective fiction apart from some short pastiches of Sherlock Holmes (whom he called Sherlaw Kombs) and one very bizarre long short story *From Whose Bourne*, an odd mixture of ghost story and detective story in which a dead man with the aid of some other ghosts investigates his own supposed murder. As was a fairly common publishing practice at the time, *The Triumphs of Eugène ·Valmont* was presented as if it was a full-length novel and not a collection of short stories, and *The Absent-Minded Coterie*, which seems such an intriguing title, is the heading of one of the three chapters into which the story was divided on its first publication. Robert Barr was born in Glasgow and was taken to Canada and the United States as a child. He became headmaster of a school in Windsor, Ontario, when he was barely twenty. He then changed over to journalism and joined the *Detroit Free Press* which sent him as its correspondent to London in 1881. He became a popular writer of magazine stories and launched *The Idler*, with Jerome K. Jerome and John Oxenham. His detective Eugène Valmont, once 'chief detective to the Government of France', was, it has been suggested, the model for Agatha Christie's Hercule Poirot. However that may be, there are certainly marked resemblances.

Jacques Futrelle (1875–1912) went down in the Titanic. If he had lived he might, one feels, have established himself as one of the best American detective-story writers. He was born in Pike County, Georgia, and became a journalist with the *Boston American* and a theatrical manager. His most striking creation was Professor Augustus S. F. X. Van Dusen, known as The Thinking Machine, one of the most original detectives of the period. Professor Van Dusen appeared in three books, first in a rather inferior adventure story called

The Chase of the Golden Plate and then in two volumes of short stories *The Thinking Machine* and *The Thinking Machine on the Case*. *The Thinking Machine*, which was published over here by Chapman & Hall in 1907 and never reprinted in this country, is a very rare book indeed. I have never seen a copy except in the British Museum and even the publisher no longer has a file copy. It is pleasantly illustrated by The Kinneys, whose work is otherwise unknown to me. *The Thinking Machine on the Case* was published in this country under the title *The Professor on the Case* in 1909 as Number 62 in Nelson's splendid red-cloth Sevenpenny Edition, which normally consisted of reprints. That was its first and only appearance in England and anybody fortunate, as I am, to possess a copy is the probably unwitting owner of quite a valuable first edition. My copy cost me one shilling and sixpence at a second-hand bookshop in the Brompton Road, which, like most of the shops at which my collection was assembled, alas no longer exists. Like *The Triumphs of Eugène Valmont*, *The Professor on the Case* was presented by its publisher as if it was a full-length novel. I have included two Futrelle stories in this collection, one from each volume, to show Professor Van Dusen at work in very different settings.

About Maurice Leblanc, the creator of Arsène Lupin, I have been able to discover very little apart from the fact that he was born in Rouen in 1864 and died in Perpignan in 1941. It was thought at one time that he had died in 1926. This was corrected by Howard Haycraft in his invaluable book *Murder for Pleasure* which was published in 1941. At that time nothing had been heard of Maurice Leblanc since the German invasion of France. He had been made a member of the Legion of Honour in 1919. One must assume that he was a quiet man who, in spite of his great success, shunned publicity. It is said that he liked working at café tables in the open air. About his stories there is a unique charm and vivacity (which survives in the contemporary translation) and I make no apology for including two Lupin stories, in both of which Lupin confronts his old antagonist Chief-Inspector Ganimard. Another detective who appears in some Lupin stories is Holmlock Shears. The Leblanc bibliography is complicated by the number of different titles under which his books appeared both in England and America. Between 1909 and 1911 one book appeared under three titles in England (*The Fair-Haired Lady*, *Arsène Lupin versus Holmlock Shears*, and *The Arrest of Arsène Lupin*) and under two more titles in the United States (*The Blonde Lady* and *Arsène Lupin versus Herlock Sholmes*). A nightmare for collectors.

Baron Palle Adam Vilhelm Rosenkrantz (1867–1941), whose story in this collection strikes me as rather charmingly cynical, was descended from the man whose name must have been in Shakespeare's mind when he wrote *Hamlet*. The earlier Palle Rosenkrantz studied at Wittenberg from 1604 to 1606 and afterwards paid several visits to England. On one of these visits, accompanied by another young Danish nobleman called Gyldenstierne, he was an envoy from the King of Denmark to the court of King James I. They did not, however, meet a violent end like their namesakes and went on to give distinguished service in war and peace to the Danish crown. Our Palle Rosenkrantz was regarded when he died as one of Denmark's leading men of letters. He had studied law at Copenhagen University and was then an assistant to a judge, a member of a solicitor's firm and a functionary in a telephone company before he was called to the bar in 1909. He started writing to earn some more money, and his first story, *An Admission*, was inspired by his indignation at a case of police injustice. His concern about police brutality and the need for a reform of the Danish legal system was the basis for his first novels, plays, and detective stories. Later he wrote historical novels, family history, constitutional history, autobiographies, and, in the nineteen-thirties, very successful radio plays. He translated some of Bernard Shaw's plays, including *Pygmalion*, into Danish. One of his full-length detective novels,

The Magistrate's Own Case, was published in English by Methuen in 1908 and is a readable and ingenious story. His short detective stories about Lieutenant Holst of the Copenhagen police have never, until the appearance of one of them in this collection, been translated. Many of his books are still read in Denmark today but most of his detective stories seem to have been forgotten, and even second-hand copies have not been seen in Copenhagen for many years.

Balduin Groller was the pseudonym of Adalbert Goldscheider who was born in 1848 at Arad in Hungary (now Romania) and died in Vienna in 1916. He edited two well-known Vienna papers, the *Neue Illustrierte Zeitung* and the *Neue Wiener Journal*. He published a number of romances and humorous tales from 1880 onwards and between 1910 and 1912 six slim volumes of short stories about the experiences (adventures would be too strong a term) of his detective Dagobert. There is nothing of the professional about Dagobert who moves among the highest social circles of Vienna in an aroma of wine, rich food, cigar smoke, and perfume. The successful Jewish journalist from one of the most eastern provinces of the Austro-Hungarian Empire somehow managed to preserve in his usually rather gay little stories something of the overblown charm of Vienna on the edge of the precipice.

I have already remarked on the somewhat pungent flavour of the writings of Edward Phillips Oppenheim (1866–1946). His first novel was published when he was twenty-one and for more than fifty years he kept up an average of more than three books a year. This puts him in the William Le Queux class. Most of his enormous output comes into the category of diplomatic intrigue and romance rather than crime or detection, and, of the books of short stories he published before 1914, only one, *Mr Laxworthy's Adventures,* can, even with the utmost latitude, be said to qualify for this collection. But one cannot ignore Oppenheim. So here is Mr Laxworthy, and I recommend the opening scene in 'the magnificent buffet of the Gare de Lyons' to connoisseurs of Oppenheim at his ripest. Oppenheim was married to an American and he divided his years between the French Riviera, Guernsey, and Mayfair until the German invasion of France which finally forced him to leave Nice for London. In his autobiography, *The Pool of Memory*, published in November 1941, he gives a peevish, and somehow rather distasteful, account of what he calls the 'hard times' he and other wealthy English inhabitants of the south of France went through in the winter of 1940 to 1941. Still there was always Monsieur Tamme, proprietor of the Montfleuri Hotel, 'among other excellent qualities a born hotelier' who 'was not the sort of man to be caught napping'. He had plenty of coal and coke, wines of the best vintages and 'considerable stores of everything that was necessary for the delectation of his guests'. So, however hard the times, it was not entirely easy to take off for England via Spain and Portugal, and back in London it was disturbing to find that the Minister of Information, Mr Duff Cooper, was 'less curious than I had expected about the French situation'. Alas for the creator of so many secret agents who in their heyday had swayed the fate of governments!

The last story in this collection, by H. Hesketh Prichard (1876–1922), is something of a curiosity. Detectives of fiction usually move in big cities or among the international crowd in Monaco, Switzerland, or the south of France. The hero of Hesketh Prichard's only book of detective stories is November Joe, a Canadian woodsman who is employed under contract by the Quebec provincial police to help them with the investigation of crimes committed in the wilderness. As one of the characters in the book remarks: 'The speciality of a Sherlock Holmes is the everyday routine of a woodsman. Observation and deduction are part and parcel of his daily existence. He literally reads as he runs. The floor of the forest is his page.' So in Hesketh Prichard's book the methods of Baker Street are practised in the Quebec backwoods. Hesketh Prichard, who won the D.S.O. and M.C. as a sniper in France, was a traveller, hunter, cricketer, naturalist and romantic novelist. He lived this extraordinarily active life in spite of a heart defect which led to his being rejected for the army until the outbreak of war. His output of books on sport and travel was considerable, and with his mother he wrote *The Chronicles of Don Q* from which Douglas Fairbanks made a famous silent film.

The Episode of
the Mexican Seer

Grant Allen

My name is Seymour Wilbraham Wentworth. I am brother-in-law and secretary to Sir Charles Vandrift, the South African millionaire and famous financier. Many years ago, when Charlie Vandrift was a small lawyer in Cape Town, I had the (qualified) good fortune to marry his sister. Much later, when the Vandrift estate and farm near Kimberley developed by degrees into the Cloetedorp Golcondas, Limited, my brother-in-law offered me the not unremunerative post of secretary; in which capacity I have ever since been his constant and attached companion.

He is not a man whom any common sharper can take in, is Charles Vandrift. Middle height, square build, firm mouth, keen eyes – the very picture of a sharp and successful business genius. I have only known one rogue impose upon Sir Charles, and that one rogue, as the Commissary of Police at Nice remarked, would doubtless have imposed upon a syndicate of Vidocq, Robert Houdin, and Cagliostro.

We had run across to the Riviera for a few weeks in the season. Our object being strictly rest and recreation from the arduous duties of financial combination, we did not think it necessary to take our wives out with us. Indeed, Lady Vandrift is absolutely wedded to the joys of London, and does not appreciate the rural delights of the Mediterranean littoral. But Sir Charles and I, though immersed in affairs when at home, both thoroughly enjoy the complete change from the City to the charming vegetation and pellucid air on the terrace at Monte Carlo. We *are* so fond of scenery. That delicious view over the rocks of Monaco, with the Maritime Alps in the rear, and the blue sea in front, not to mention the imposing Casino in the foreground, appeals to me as one of the most beautiful prospects in all Europe. Sir Charles has a sentimental attachment for the place. He finds it restores and refreshens him, after the turmoil of London, to win a few hundred at roulette in the course of an afternoon among the palms and cactuses and pure breezes of Monte Carlo. The country, say I, for a jaded intellect! However, we never on any account actually stop in the Principality itself. Sir Charles thinks Monte Carlo is not a sound address for a financier's letters. He prefers a comfortable hotel on the Promenade des Anglais at Nice, where he recovers health and renovates his nervous system by taking daily excursions along the coast to the Casino.

This particular season we were snugly ensconced at the Hotel des Anglais. We had capital quarters on the first floor – salon, study, and bedrooms – and found on the spot a most agreeable cosmopolitan society. All Nice, just then, was ringing with talk about a curious impostor, known to his followers as the Great Mexican Seer, and supposed to be gifted with second sight, as well as with endless other supernatural powers. Now, it is a peculiarity of my able brother-in-law's that, when he meets with a quack, he burns to expose him; he is so keen a man of business himself that it gives him, so to speak, a disinterested pleasure to unmask and detect imposture in others. Many ladies at the hotel, some of whom had met and conversed with the Mexican Seer, were constantly telling us strange stories of his doings. He had disclosed to one the present whereabouts of a runaway husband; he had pointed out to another the numbers that would win at roulette next evening; he had shown a third the image on a screen of the man she had for years adored without his knowledge. Of course, Sir Charles didn't believe a word of it; but his curiosity was roused; he wished to see and judge for himself of the wonderful thought-reader.

'What would be his terms, do you think, for a private *séance*?' he asked of Madame Picardet, the lady to whom the Seer had successfully predicted the winning numbers.

'He does not work for money,' Madame Picardet answered, 'but for the good of humanity. I'm sure he would gladly come and exhibit for nothing his miraculous faculties.'

'Nonsense!' Sir Charles answered. 'The man must live. I'd pay him five guineas, though, to see him alone. What hotel is he stopping at?'

'The Cosmopolitan, I think,' the lady answered. 'Oh no; I remember now, the Westminster.'

Sir Charles turned to me quietly. 'Look here, Seymour,' he whispered. 'Go round to this fellow's place immediately after dinner, and offer him five pounds to give a private *séance* at once in my rooms, without mentioning who I am to him; keep the name quite quiet. Bring him back with you, too, and come straight upstairs with him, so that there may be no collusion. We'll see just how much the fellow can tell us.'

I went as directed. I found the Seer a very remarkable and interesting person. He stood about Sir Charles's own height, but was slimmer and straighter, with an aquiline nose, strangely piercing eyes, very large black pupils, and a finely-chiselled close-shaven face, like the bust of Antinous in our hall in Mayfair. What gave him his most characteristic touch, however, was his odd head of hair, curly and wavy like Paderewski's, standing out in a halo round his high white forehead and his delicate profile. I could see at a glance why he succeeded so well in impressing women; he had the look of a poet, a singer, a prophet.

'I have come round,' I said, 'to ask whether you will consent to give a *séance* at once in a friend's rooms; and my principal wishes me to add that he is prepared to pay five pounds as the price of the entertainment.'

Señor Antonio Herrera – that was what he called himself – bowed to me with impressive Spanish politeness. His dusky olive cheeks were wrinkled with a smile of gentle contempt as he answered gravely –

'I do not sell my gifts; I bestow them freely. If your friend – your anonymous friend – desires to behold the cosmic wonders that are wrought through my hands, I am glad to show them to him. Fortunately, as often happens when it is necessary to convince and confound a sceptic (for that your friend is a sceptic I feel instinctively), I chance to have no engagements at all this evening.' He ran his hand through his fine, long hair reflectively. 'Yes, I go,' he continued, as if addressing some unknown presence that hovered about the ceiling; 'I go; come with me!' Then he put on his broad sombrero, with its crimson ribbon, wrapped a cloak round his shoulders, lighted a cigarette, and strode forth by my side towards the Hotel des Anglais.

He talked little by the way, and that little in curt sentences. He seemed buried in deep thought; indeed, when we reached the door and I turned in, he walked a step or two farther on, as if not noticing to what place I had brought him. Then he drew himself up short, and gazed around him for a moment. 'Ha, the Anglais,' he said – and I may mention in passing that his English, in spite of a slight southern accent, was idiomatic and excellent. 'It is here, then; it is here!' He was addressing once more the unseen presence.

I smiled to think that these childish devices were intended to deceive Sir Charles Vandrift. Not quite the sort of man (as the City of London knows) to be taken in by hocus-pocus. And all this, I saw, was the cheapest and most commonplace conjurer's patter.

We went upstairs to our rooms. Charles had gathered together a few friends to watch the performance. The Seer entered, rapt in thought. He was in evening dress, but a red sash round his waist gave a touch of picturesqueness and a dash of colour. He paused for a moment in the middle of the salon, without letting his eyes rest on anybody or anything. Then he walked straight up to Charles, and held out his dark hand.

'Good evening,' he said. 'You are the host. My soul's sight tells me so.'

'Good shot,' Sir Charles answered. 'These fellows have to be quick-witted, you know, Mrs Mackenzie, or they'd never get on at it.'

The Seer gazed about him, and smiled blankly at a person or two whose faces he seemed to recognize from a previous existence. Then Charles began to ask him a few simple questions, not about himself, but about me, just to test him. He answered most of them with surprising correctness. 'His name? His name begins with an S I think: You call him Seymour.' He paused long between each clause, as if the facts were revealed to him slowly. 'Seymour – Wilbraham – Earl of Strafford. No, not Earl of Strafford! Seymour Wilbraham Wentworth. There seems to be some connection in somebody's mind now present between Wentworth and Strafford. I am not English. I do not know what it means. But they are somehow the same name, Wentworth and Strafford.'

He gazed around, apparently for confirmation. A lady came to his rescue.

'Wentworth was the surname of the great Earl of Strafford,' she murmured gently; 'and I was wondering, as you spoke, whether Mr Wentworth might possibly be descended from him.'

'He is,' the Seer replied instantly, with a flash of those dark eyes. And I thought this curious; for though my father always maintained the reality of the relationship, there was one link wanting to complete the pedigree. He could not make sure that the Hon. Thomas Wilbraham Wentworth was the father of Jonathan Wentworth, the Bristol horse-dealer, from whom we are descended.

'Where was I born?' Sir Charles interrupted, coming suddenly to his own case.

The Seer clapped his two hands to his forehead and held it between them, as if to prevent it from bursting. 'Africa', he said slowly, as the facts narrowed down, so to speak. 'South Africa; Cape of Good Hope; Jansenville; De Witt Street. 1840.'

'By Jove, he's correct,' Sir Charles muttered. 'He seems really to do it. Still, he may have found me out. He may have known where he was coming.'

'I never gave a hint,' I answered; 'till he reached the door, he didn't even know to what hotel I was piloting him.'

The Seer stroked his chin softly. His eye appeared to me to have a furtive gleam in it. 'Would you like me to tell you the number of a bank-note enclosed in an envelope?' he asked casually.

'Go out of the room,' Sir Charles said, 'while I pass it round the company.'

Señor Herrera disappeared. Sir Charles passed it round cautiously, holding it all the time in his own hand, but letting his guests see the number. Then he placed it in an envelope and gummed it down firmly.

The Seer returned. His keen eyes swept the company with a comprehensive glance. He shook his shaggy mane. Then he took the envelope in his hands and gazed at it fixedly. 'AF, 73549,' he answered, in a slow tone. 'A Bank of England note for fifty pounds -- exchanged at the Casino for gold won yesterday at Monte Carlo.'

'I see how he did that,' Sir Charles said triumphantly. 'He must have changed it there himself; and then I changed it back again. In point of fact, I remember seeing a fellow with long hair loafing about. Still, it's capital conjuring.'

'He can see through matter,' one of the ladies interposed. It was Madame Picardet. 'He can see through a box.' She drew a little gold vinaigrette, such as our grandmothers used, from her dress-pocket. 'What is in this?' she inquired, holding it up to him.

26

Señor Herrera gazed through it. 'Three gold coins,' he replied, knitting his brows with the effort of seeing into the box : 'one, an American five dollars; one, a French ten-franc piece; one, twenty marks, German, of the old Emperor William.'

She opened the box and passed it round. Sir Charles smiled a quiet smile.

'Confederacy!' he muttered, half to himself. 'Confederacy!'

The Seer turned to him with a sullen air. 'You want a better sign?' he said, in a very impressive voice. 'A sign that will convince you! Very well: you have a letter in your left waistcoat pocket – a crumpled-up letter. Do you wish me to read it out? I will, if you desire it.'

It may seem to those who know Sir Charles incredible, but, I am bound to admit, my brother-in-law coloured. What that letter contained I cannot say; he only answered, very testily and evasively, 'No, thank you; I won't trouble you. The exhibition you have already given us of your skill in this kind more than amply suffices.' And his fingers strayed nervously to his waistcoat pocket, as if he was half afraid, even then, Señor Herrera would read it.

I fancied too, he glanced somewhat anxiously towards Madame Picardet.

The Seer bowed courteously. 'Your will, señor, is law,' he said. 'I make it a principle, though I can see through all things, invariably to respect the secrecies and sanctities. If it were not so, I might dissolve society. For which of us is there who could bear the whole truth being told about him?' He gazed around the room. An unpleasant thrill supervened. Most of us felt this uncanny Spanish American knew really too much. And some of us were engaged in financial operations.

'For example,' the Seer continued blandly, 'I happened a few weeks ago to travel down here from Paris by train with a very intelligent man, a company promoter. He had in his bag some documents – some confidential documents:' he glanced at Sir Charles. 'You know the kind of thing, my dear sir: reports from experts – from mining engineers. You may have seen some such; marked *strictly private*.'

'They form an element in high finance,' Sir Charles admitted coldly.

'Pre-cisely,' the Seer murmured, his accent for a moment less Spanish than before. 'And, as they were marked *strictly private*, I respect, of course, the seal of confidence. That's all I wish to say. I hold it a duty, being intrusted with such powers, not to use them in a manner which may annoy or incommode my fellow-creatures.'

'Your feeling does you honour,' Sir Charles answered, with some acerbity. Then he whispered in my ear: 'Confounded clever scoundrel, Sey; rather wish we hadn't brought him here.'

Señor Herrera seemed intuitively to divine this wish, for he interposed, in a lighter and gayer tone –

'I will now show you a different and more interesting embodiment of occult power, for which we shall need a somewhat subdued arrangement of surrounding lights. Would you mind, señor host – for I have purposely abstained from reading your name on the brain of any one present – would you mind my turning down this lamp just a little? ... So! That will do. Now, this one; and this one. Exactly! that's right.' He poured a few grains of powder out of a packet into a saucer. 'Next, a match, if you please. Thank you!' It burnt with a strange green light. He drew from his pocket a card, and produced a little ink-bottle. 'Have you a pen?' he asked.

I instantly brought one. He handed it to Sir Charles. 'Oblige me,' he said, 'by writing your name there.' And he indicated a place in the centre of the card, which had an embossed edge, with a small middle square of a different colour.

Sir Charles has a natural disinclination to signing his name without knowing why. 'What do you want with it?' he asked. (A millionaire's signature has so many uses.)

'I want you to put the card in an envelope,' the Seer replied, 'and then to burn it. After that, I shall show you your own name written in letters of blood on my arm, in your own handwriting.'

Sir Charles took the pen. If the signature was to be burned as soon as finished, he didn't mind giving it. He wrote his name in his usual firm clear style – the writing of a man who knows his worth and is not afraid of drawing a cheque for five thousand.

'Look at it long,' the Seer said, from the other side of the room. He had not watched him write it.

Sir Charles stared at it fixedly. The Seer was really beginning to produce an impression.

'Now, put it in that envelope,' the Seer exclaimed.

Sir Charles, like a lamb, placed it as directed.

The Seer strode forward. 'Give me the envelope,' he said. He took it in his hand, walked over towards the fireplace, and solemnly burnt it. 'See – it crumbles into ashes,' he cried. Then he came back to the middle of the room, close to the green light, rolled up his sleeve, and held his arm before Sir Charles. There, in blood-red letters, my brother-in-law read the name, 'Charles Vandrift', in his own handwriting!

'I see how that's done,' Sir Charles murmured, drawing back. 'It's a clever delusion; but still, I see through it. It's like that ghost-book. Your ink was deep green; your light was green; you made me look at it long; and then I saw the same thing written on the skin of your arm in complementary colours.'

'You think so?' the Seer replied, with a curious curl of the lip.

'I'm sure of it,' Sir Charles answered.

Quick as lightning the Seer rolled up his sleeve. 'That's your name,' he cried, in a very clear voice, 'but not your whole name. What do you say, then, to my right? Is this one also a complementary colour?' He held his other arm out. There, in sea-green letters, I read the name, 'Charles

O'Sullivan Vandrift'. It is my brother-in-law's full baptismal designation; but he has dropped the O'Sullivan for many years past, and, to say the truth, doesn't like it. He is a little bit ashamed of his mother's family.

Charles glanced at it hurriedly. 'Quite right,' he said, 'quite right!' But his voice was hollow. I could guess he didn't care to continue the *séance*. He could see through the man, of course; but it was clear the fellow knew too much about us to be entirely pleasant.

'Turn up the lights,' I said, and a servant turned them. 'Shall I say coffee and benedictine?' I whispered to Vandrift.

'By all means,' he answered. 'Anything to keep this fellow from further impertinences! And, I say, don't you think you'd better suggest at the same time that the men should smoke? Even these ladies are not above a cigarette – some of them.'

There was a sigh of relief. The lights burned brightly. The Seer for the moment retired from business, so to speak. He accepted a partaga with a very good grace, sipped his coffee in a corner, and chatted to the lady who had suggested Strafford with marked politeness. He was a polished gentleman.

Next morning, in the hall of the hotel, I saw Madame Picardet again, in a neat tailor-made travelling dress, evidently bound for the railway-station.

'What, off, Madame Picardet?' I cried.

She smiled, and held out her prettily-gloved hand. 'Yes, I'm off,' she answered archly. 'Florence, or Rome, or somewhere. I've drained Nice dry – like a sucked orange. Got all the fun I can out of it. Now I'm away again to my beloved Italy.'

But it struck me as odd that, if Italy was her game, she went by the omnibus which takes down to the *train de luxe* for Paris. However, a man of the world accepts what a lady tells him, no matter how improbable; and I confess, for ten days or so, I thought no more about her, or the Seer either.

At the end of that time our fortnightly pass-book came in from the bank in London. It is part of my duty, as the millionaire's secretary, to make up this book once a fortnight, and to compare the cancelled cheques with Sir Charles's counterfoils. On this particular occasion I happened to observe what I can only describe as a very grave discrepancy – in fact, a discrepancy of £5,000. On the wrong side, too. Sir Charles was debited with £5,000 more than the total amount that was shown on the counterfoils.

I examined the book with care. The source of the error was obvious. It lay in a cheque to Self or Bearer, for £5,000, signed by Sir Charles, and evidently paid across the counter in London, as it bore on its face no stamp or indication of any other office.

I called in my brother-in-law from the salon to the study. 'Look here, Charles,' I said, 'there's a cheque in the book which you haven't entered.' And I handed it to him without comment, for I thought it might have been drawn to settle some little loss on the turf or at cards, or to make up some other affair he didn't desire to mention to me. These things will happen.

He looked at it and stared hard. Then he pursed up his mouth and gave a long low 'Whew!' At last he turned it over and remarked, 'I say, Sey, my boy, we've just been done jolly well brown, haven't we?'

I glanced at the cheque. 'How do you mean?' I inquired.

'Why, the Seer,' he replied, still staring at it ruefully. 'I don't mind the five thou., but to think the fellow should have gammoned the pair of us like that – ignominious, I call it!'

'How do you know it's the Seer?' I asked.

'Look at the green ink,' he answered. 'Besides, I recollect the very shape of the last flourish. I flourished a bit like that in the excitement of the moment, which I don't always do with my regular signature.'

'He's done us,' I answered, recognizing it. 'But how the

dickens did he manage to transfer it to the cheque? This looks like your own handwriting, Charles, not a clever forgery.'

'It is,' he said. 'I admit it – I can't deny it. Only fancy him bamboozling me when I was most on my guard! I wasn't to be taken in by any of his silly occult tricks and catch-words; but it never occurred to me he was going to victimize me financially in this way. I expected attempts at a loan or an extortion; but to collar my signature to a blank cheque – atrocious!'

'How did he manage it?' I asked.

'I haven't the faintest conception. I only know those are the words I wrote. I could swear to them anywhere.'

'Then you can't protest the cheque?'

'Unfortunately, no; it's my own true signature.'

We went that afternoon without delay to see the Chief Commissary of Police at the office. He was a gentlemanly Frenchman, much less formal and red-tapey than usual, and he spoke excellent English with an American accent, having acted, in fact, as a detective in New York for about ten years in his early manhood.

'I guess,' he said slowly, after hearing our story, 'you've been victimized right here by Colonel Clay, gentlemen.'

'Who is Colonel Clay?' Sir Charles asked.

'That's just what I want to know,' the Commissary answered, in his curious American-French-English. 'He is a Colonel, because he occasionally gives himself a commission; he is called Colonel Clay, because he appears to possess an india-rubber face, and he can mould it like clay in the hands of the potter. Real name, unknown. Nationality, equally French and English. Address, usually Europe. Profession, former maker of wax figures to the Musée Grevin. Age, what he chooses. Employs his knowledge to mould his own nose and cheeks, with wax additions, to the character he desires to personate. Aquiline this time, you say. *Hein!* Anything like these photographs?'

He rummaged in his desk and handed us two.

'Not in the least,' Sir Charles answered. 'Except, perhaps, as to the neck, everything here is quite unlike him.'

'Then that's the Colonel!' the Commissary answered, with decision, rubbing his hands in glee. 'Look here,' and he took out a pencil and rapidly sketched the outline of one of the two faces – that of a bland-looking young man, with no expression worth mentioning. 'There's the Colonel in his simple disguise. Very good. Now watch me: figure to yourself that he adds here a tiny patch of wax to his nose – an aquiline bridge – just so; well, you have him right there; and the chin, ah, one touch: now, for hair, a wig: for complexion, nothing easier: that's the profile of your rascal, isn't it?'

'Exactly,' we both murmured. By two curves of the pencil, and a shock of false hair, the face was transmuted.

'He had very large eyes, with very big pupils, though,' I objected, looking close; 'and the man in the photograph here has them small and boiled-fishy.'

'That's so,' the Commissary answered. 'A drop of belladonna expands – and produces the Seer; five grains of opium contract – and give a dead-alive, stupidly-innocent appearance. Well, you leave this affair to me, gentlemen. I'll see the fun out. I don't say I'll catch him for you; nobody ever yet has caught Colonel Clay; but I'll explain how he did the trick; and that ought to be consolation enough to a man of your means for a trifle of five thousand!'

'You are not the conventional French office-holder, M. le Commissaire,' I ventured to interpose.

'You bet!' the Commissary replied, and drew himself up like a captain of infantry. 'Messieurs,' he continued, in French, with the utmost dignity, 'I shall devote the resources of this office to tracing out the crime, and, if possible, to effectuating the arrest of the culpable.'

We telegraphed to London, of course, and we wrote to the bank, with a full description of the suspected person. But I need hardly add that nothing came of it.

Three days later the Commissary called at our hotel.

'Well, gentlemen,' he said, 'I am glad to say I have discovered everything!'

'What? Arrested the Seer?' Sir Charles cried.

The Commissary drew back, almost horrified at the suggestion.

'Arrested Colonel Clay?' he exclaimed. '*Mais*, monsieur, we are only human! Arrested him? No, not quite. But tracked out how he did it. That is already much – to unravel Colonel Clay, gentlemen!'

'Well, what do you make of it?' Sir Charles asked, crestfallen.

The Commissary sat down and gloated over his discovery. It was clear a well-planned crime amused him vastly. 'In the first place, monsieur,' he said, 'disabuse your mind of the idea that when monsieur your secretary went out to fetch Señor Herrera that night, Señor Herrera didn't know to whose rooms he was coming. Quite otherwise, in point of fact. I do not doubt myself that Señor Herrera, or Colonel Clay (call him which you like), came to Nice this winter for no other purpose than just to rob you.'

'But I sent for him,' my brother-in-law interposed.

'Yes; he *meant* you to send for him. He forced a card, so to speak. If he couldn't do that I guess he would be a pretty poor conjurer. He had a lady of his own – his wife, let us say, or his sister – stopping here at this hotel; a certain Madame Picardet. Through her he induced several ladies of your circle to attend his *séances*. She and they spoke to you about him, and aroused your curiosity. You may bet your bottom dollar that when he came to this room he came ready primed and prepared with endless facts about both of you.'

'What fools we have been, Sey,' my brother-in-law exclaimed. 'I see it all now. That designing woman sent round before dinner to say I wanted to meet him; and by the time you got there he was ready for bamboozling me.'

'That's so,' the Commissary answered. 'He had your name

ready painted on both his arms; and he had made other preparations of still greater importance.'

'You mean the cheque. Well, how did he get it?'

The Commissary opened the door. 'Come in,' he said. And a young man entered whom we recognized at once as the chief clerk in the Foreign Department of the Crédit Marseillais, the principal bank all along the Riviera.

'State what you know of this cheque,' the Commissary said, showing it to him, for we had handed it over to the police as a piece of evidence.

'About four weeks since –' the clerk began.

'Say ten days before your *séance*,' the Commissary interposed.

'A gentleman with very long hair and an aquiline nose, dark, strange, and handsome, called in at my department and asked if I could tell him the name of Sir Charles Vandrift's London banker. He said he had a sum to pay in to your credit, and asked if we would forward it for him. I told him it was irregular for us to receive the money, as you had no account with us, but that your London bankers were Darby, Drummond, and Rothenberg, Limited.'

'Quite right,' Sir Charles murmured.

'Two days later a lady, Madame Picardet, who was a customer of ours, brought in a good cheque for three hundred pounds, signed by a first-rate name, and asked us to pay it in on her behalf to Darby, Drummond, and Rothenberg's, and to open a London account with them for her. We did so, and received in reply a cheque-book.'

'From which this cheque was taken, as I learn from the number, by telegram from London,' the Commissary put in. 'Also, that on the same day on which your cheque was cashed, Madame Picardet, in London, withdrew her balance.'

'But how did the fellow get me to sign the cheque?' Sir Charles cried. 'How did he manage the card trick?'

The Commissary produced a similar card from his pocket. 'Was that the sort of thing?' he asked.

'Precisely! A facsimile.'

'I thought so. Well, our Colonel, I find, bought a packet of such cards, intended for admission to a religious function, at a shop in the Quai Masséna. He cut out the centre, and, see here –' The Commissary turned it over, and showed a piece of paper pasted neatly over the back; this he tore off, and there, concealed behind it, lay a folded cheque, with only the place where the signature should be written showing through on the face which the Seer had presented to us. 'I call that a neat trick,' the Commissary remarked, with professional enjoyment of a really good deception.

'But he burnt the envelope before my eyes,' Sir Charles exclaimed.

'Pooh!' the Commissary answered. 'What would he be worth as a conjurer, anyway, if he couldn't substitute one envelope for another between the table and the fireplace without your noticing it? And Colonel Clay, you must remember, is a prince among conjurers.'

'Well, it's a comfort to know we've identified our man, and the woman who was with him,' Sir Charles said, with a slight sigh of relief. 'The next thing will be, of course, you'll follow them up on these clues in England and arrest them?'

The Commissary shrugged his shoulders. 'Arrest them!' he exclaimed, much amused. 'Ah, monsieur, but you are sanguine! No officer of justice has ever succeeded in arresting le Colonel Caoutchouc, as we call him in French. He is as slippery as an eel, that man. He wriggles through our fingers. Suppose even we caught him, what could we prove? I ask you. Nobody who has seen him once can ever swear to him again in his next impersonation. He is *impayable*, this good Colonel. On the day when I arrest him, I assure you, monsieur, I shall consider myself the smartest police-officer in Europe.'

'Well, I shall catch him yet,' Sir Charles answered, and relapsed into silence.

The Episode of the Diamond Links

Grant Allen

'LET us take a trip to Switzerland,' said Lady Vandrift. And any one who knows Amelia will not be surprised to learn that we *did* take a trip to Switzerland accordingly. Nobody can drive Sir Charles, except his wife. And nobody at all can drive Amelia.

There were difficulties at the outset, because we had not ordered rooms at the hotels beforehand, and it was well on in the season; but they were overcome at last by the usual application of a golden key; and we found ourselves in due time pleasantly quartered in Lucerne, at that most comfortable of European hostelries, the Schweitzerhof.

We were a square party of four – Sir Charles and Amelia, myself and Isabel. We had nice big rooms, on the first floor, overlooking the lake; and as none of us was possessed with the faintest symptom of that incipient mania which shows itself in the form of an insane desire to climb mountain heights of disagreeable steepness and unnecessary snowiness, I will venture to assert we all enjoyed ourselves. We spent most of our time sensibly in lounging about the lake on the jolly little steamers; and when we did a mountain climb, it was on the Rigi or Pilatus – where an engine undertook all the muscular work for us.

As usual, at the hotel, a great many miscellaneous people showed a burning desire to be specially nice to us. If you wish to see how friendly and charming humanity is, just try being a well-known millionaire for a week, and you'll learn a thing or two. Wherever Sir Charles goes he is surrounded by charming and disinterested people, all eager to make his distinguished acquaintance, and all familiar with several excellent investments, or several deserving objects of Christian charity. It is my business in life, as his brother-in-law and secretary, to decline with thanks the excellent investments, and to throw judicious cold water on the objects of charity. Even I myself, as the great man's almoner, am very much sought after. People casually allude before me to artless stories of 'poor curates in Cumberland, you know, Mr Wentworth', or widows in Cornwall, penniless poets with epics in their desks, and young painters who need but the breath of a patron to open to them the doors of an admiring Academy. I smile and look wise, while I administer cold water in minute doses; but I never report one of these cases to Sir Charles, except in the rare or almost unheard-of event where I think there is really something in them.

Ever since our little adventure with the Seer at Nice, Sir Charles, who is constitutionally cautious, had been even more careful than usual about possible sharpers. And, as chance would have it, there sat just opposite us at *table d'hôte* at the Schweitzerhof – 'tis a fad of Amelia's to dine at *table d'hôte*; she says she can't bear to be boxed up all day in private rooms with 'too much family' – a sinister-looking man with dark hair and eyes, conspicuous by his bushy overhanging eyebrows. My attention was first called to the eyebrows in question by a nice little parson who sat at our side, and who observed that they were made up of certain large and bristly hairs, which (he told us) had been traced by Darwin to our monkey ancestors. Very pleasant little fellow, this fresh-faced young parson, on his honeymoon tour with a nice wee wife, a bonnie Scotch lassie with a charming accent.

I looked at the eyebrows close. Then a sudden thought struck me. 'Do you believe they're his own?' I asked of the curate; 'or are they only stuck on – a make-up disguise? They really almost look like it.'

'You don't suppose –' Charles began, and checked himself suddenly.

'Yes, I do,' I answered; 'the Seer!' Then I recollected my blunder, and looked down sheepishly. For, to say the truth, Vandrift had straightly enjoined on me long before to say nothing of our painful little episode at Nice to Amelia; he was afraid if *she* once heard of it, *he* would hear of it for ever after.

'What Seer?' the little parson inquired, with parsonical curiosity.

I noticed the man with the overhanging eyebrows give a queer sort of start. Charles's glance was fixed upon me. I hardly knew what to answer.

'Oh, a man who was at Nice with us last year,' I stammered out, trying hard to look unconcerned. 'A fellow they talked about, that's all.' And I turned the subject.

But the curate, like a donkey, wouldn't let me turn it.

'Had he eyebrows like that?' he inquired, in an undertone. I was really angry. If this *was* Colonel Clay, the curate was obviously giving him the cue, and making it much more difficult for us to catch him, now we might possibly have lighted on the chance to do so.

'No, he hadn't,' I answered testily; 'it was a passing expression. But this is not the man. I was mistaken, no doubt.' And I nudged him gently.

The little curate was too innocent for anything. 'Oh, I see,' he replied, nodding hard and looking wise. Then he turned to his wife and made an obvious face, which the man with the eyebrows couldn't fail to notice.

Fortunately, a political discussion going on a few places farther down the table spread up to us and diverted attention for a moment. The magical name of Gladstone saved us. Sir Charles flared up. I was truly pleased, for I could see Amelia was boiling over with curiosity by this time.

After dinner, in the billiard-room, however, the man with

the big eyebrows sidled up and began to talk to me. If he *was* Colonel Clay, it was evident he bore us no grudge at all for the five thousand pounds he had done us out of. On the contrary, he seemed quite prepared to do us out of five thousand more when opportunity offered; for he introduced himself at once as Dr Hector Macpherson, the exclusive grantee of extensive concessions from the Brazilian Government on the Upper Amazons. He dived into conversation with me at once as to the splendid mineral resources of his Brazilian estate – the silver, the platinum, the actual rubies, the possible diamonds. I listened and smiled; I knew what was coming. All he needed to develop this magnificent concession was a little more capital. It was sad to see thousands of pounds' worth of platinum and car-loads of rubies just crumbling in the soil or carried away by the river, for want of a few hundreds to work them with properly. If he knew of anybody, now, with money to invest, he could recommend him – nay, offer him – a unique opportunity of earning, say, forty per cent on his capital, on unimpeachable security.

'I wouldn't do it for every man,' Dr Hector Macpherson remarked, drawing himself up: 'but if I took a fancy to a fellow who had command of ready cash, I might choose to put him in the way of feathering his nest with unexampled rapidity.'

'Exceedingly disinterested of you,' I answered drily, fixing my eyes on his eyebrows.

The little curate, meanwhile, was playing billiards with Sir Charles. His glance followed mine as it rested for a moment on the monkey-like hairs.

'False, obviously false,' he remarked with his lips; and I'm bound to confess I never saw any man speak so well by movement alone; you could follow every word though not a sound escaped him.

During the rest of that evening Dr Hector Macpherson stuck to me as close as a mustard-plaster. And he was almost as irritating. I got heartily sick of the Upper Amazons.

I have positively waded in my time through ruby mines (in prospectuses, I mean) till the mere sight of a ruby absolutely sickens me. When Charles, in an unwonted fit of generosity, once gave his sister Isabel (whom I had the honour to marry) a ruby necklet (inferior stones), I made Isabel change it for sapphires and amethysts, on the judicious plea that they suited her complexion better. (I scored one, incidentally, for having considered Isabel's complexion.) By the time I went to bed I was prepared to sink the Upper Amazons in the sea, and to stab, shoot, poison, or otherwise seriously damage the man with the concession and false eyebrows.

For the next three days, at intervals, he returned to the charge. He bored me to death with his platinum and his rubies. He didn't want a capitalist who would personally exploit the thing; he would prefer to do it all on his own account, giving the capitalist preference debentures of his bogus company, and a lien on the concession. I listened and smiled; I listened and yawned; I listened and was rude; I ceased to listen at all; but still he droned on with it. I fell asleep on the steamer one day, and woke up in ten minutes to hear him droning yet, 'And the yield of platinum per ton was certified to be –' I forget how many pounds, or ounces, or pennyweights. These details of assays have ceased to interest me: like the man who 'didn't believe in ghosts', I have seen too many of them.

The fresh-faced little curate and his wife, however, were quite different people. He was a cricketing Oxford man: she was a breezy Scotch lass, with a wholesome breath of the Highlands about her. I called her 'White Heather'. Their name was Brabazon. Millionaires are so accustomed to being beset by harpies of every description, that when they come across a young couple who are simple and natural, they delight in the purely human relation. We picnicked and went excursions a great deal with the honeymooners. They were frank in their young love, and so proof against chaff, that we all really liked them. But whenever I called the pretty girl 'White Heather', she looked so shocked, and cried: 'Oh, Mr Wentworth!' Still, we were the best of friends. The curate offered to row us in a boat on the lake one day, while the Scotch lassie assured us she could take an oar almost as well as he did. However, we did not accept their offer, as row-boats exert an unfavourable influence upon Amelia's digestive organs.

'Nice young fellow, that man Brabazon,' Sir Charles said to me one day, as we lounged together along the quay; 'never talks about advowsons or next presentations. Doesn't seem to me to care two pins about promotion. Says he's quite content in his country curacy; enough to live upon, and needs no more; and his wife has a little, a very little, money. I asked him about his poor today, on purpose to test him: these parsons are always trying to screw something out of one for their poor; men in my position know the truth of the saying that we have that class of the population always with us. Would you believe it, he says he hasn't any poor at all in his parish! They're all well-to-do farmers or else able-bodied labourers, and his one terror is that somebody will come and try to pauperize them. "If a philanthropist were to give me fifty pounds today for use at Empingham," he said, "I assure you, Sir Charles, I shouldn't know what to do with it. I think I should buy new dresses for Jessie, who wants them about as much as anybody else in the village – that is to say, not at all." There's a parson for you, Sey, my boy. Only wish we had one of his sort at Seldon.'

'He certainly doesn't want to get anything out of you,' I answered.

That evening at dinner a queer little episode happened. The man with the eyebrows began talking to me across the table in his usual fashion, full of his wearisome concession on the Upper Amazons. I was trying to squash him as politely as possible, when I caught Amelia's eye. Her look amused me. She was engaged in making signals to Charles at her side to observe the little curate's curious sleeve-links.

I glanced at them, and saw at once they were a singular possession for so unobtrusive a person. They consisted each of a short gold bar for one arm of the link, fastened by a tiny chain of the same material to what seemed to my tolerably experienced eye – a first-rate diamond. Pretty big diamonds, too, and of remarkable shape, brilliancy, and cutting. In a moment I knew what Amelia meant. She owned a diamond *rivière*, said to be of Indian origin, but short by two stones for the circumference of her tolerably ample neck. Now, she had long been wanting two diamonds like these to match her set; but owing to the unusual shape and antiquated cutting of her own gems, she had never been able to complete the necklet, at least without removing an extravagant amount from a much larger stone of the first water.

The Scotch lassie's eyes caught Amelia's at the same time, and she broke into a pretty smile of good-humoured amusement. 'Taken in another person, Dick, dear!' she exclaimed, in her breezy way, turning to her husband. 'Lady Vandrift is observing your diamond sleeve-links.'

'They're very fine gems,' Amelia observed incautiously. (A most unwise admission if she desired to buy them.)

But the pleasant little curate was too transparently simple a soul to take advantage of her slip of judgement. 'They *are* good stones,' he replied; 'very good stones – considering. They're not diamonds at all, to tell you the truth. They're best old-fashioned Oriental paste. My great-grandfather bought them, after the siege of Seringapatam, for a few rupees, from a Sepoy who had looted them from Tippoo Sultan's palace. He thought, like you, he had got a good thing. But it turned out, when they came to be examined by experts, they were only paste – very wonderful paste; it is supposed they had even imposed upon Tippoo himself, so fine is the imitation. But they are worth – well, say, fifty shillings at the utmost.'

While he spoke Charles looked at Amelia, and Amelia looked at Charles. Their eyes spoke volumes. The *rivière* was also supposed to have come from Tippoo's collection. Both drew at once an identical conclusion. These were two of the same stones, very likely torn apart and disengaged from the rest in the *mêlée* at the capture of the Indian palace.

'Can you take them off?' Sir Charles asked blandly. He spoke in the tone that indicates business.

'Certainly,' the little curate answered, smiling. 'I'm accustomed to taking them off. They're always noticed. They've been kept in the family ever since the siege, as a sort of valueless heirloom, for the sake of the picturesqueness of the story, you know; and nobody ever sees them without asking, as you do, to examine them closely. They deceive even experts at first. But they're paste, all the same; unmitigated Oriental paste, for all that.'

He took them both off, and handed them to Charles. No man in England is a finer judge of gems than my brother-in-law. I watched him narrowly. He examined them close, first with the naked eye, then with the little pocket-lens which he always carries. 'Admirable imitation,' he muttered, passing them on to Amelia. 'I'm not surprised they should impose upon inexperienced observers.'

But from the tone in which he said it, I could see at once he had satisfied himself they were real gems of unusual value. I know Charles's way of doing business so well. His glance to Amelia meant, 'These are the very stones you have so long been in search of.'

The Scotch lassie laughed a merry laugh. 'He sees through them now, Dick,' she cried. 'I felt sure Sir Charles would be a judge of diamonds.'

Amelia turned them over. I know Amelia, too; and I knew from the way Amelia looked at them that she meant to have them. And when Amelia means to have anything, people who stand in the way may just as well spare themselves the trouble of opposing her.

They were beautiful diamonds. We found out afterwards the little curate's account was quite correct: these stones *had* come from the same necklet as Amelia's *rivière*, made for a favourite wife of Tippoo's who had presumably as expansive personal charms as our beloved sister-in-law's. More perfect diamonds have seldom been seen. They have excited the universal admiration of thieves and connoisseurs. Amelia told me afterwards that, according to legend, a Sepoy stole the necklet at the sack of the palace, and then fought with another for it. It was believed that two stones got spilt in the scuffle, and were picked up and sold by a third person – a looker-on – who had no idea of the value of his booty. Amelia had been hunting for them for several years to complete her necklet.

'They are excellent paste,' Sir Charles observed, handing them back. 'It takes a first-rate judge to detect them from the reality. Lady Vandrift has a necklet much the same in character, but composed of genuine stones; and as these are so much like them, and would complete her set, to all outer appearance, I wouldn't mind giving you, say, £10 for the pair of them.'

Mrs Brabazon looked delighted. 'Oh, sell them to him, Dick,' she cried, 'and buy me a brooch with the money! A pair of common links would do for you just as well. Ten pounds for two paste stones! It's quite a lot of money.'

She said it so sweetly, with her pretty Scotch accent, that I couldn't imagine how Dick had the heart to refuse her. But he did, all the same.

'No, Jess, darling,' he answered. 'They're worthless, I know; but they have for me a certain sentimental value, as I've often told you. My dear mother wore them, while she lived, as ear-rings; and as soon as she died I had them set as links in order that I might always keep them about me. Besides, they have historical and family interest. Even a worthless heirloom, after all, *is* an heirloom.'

Dr Hector Macpherson looked across and intervened. 'There is a part of my concession,' he said, 'where we have reason to believe a perfect new Kimberley will soon be discovered. If at any time you would care, Sir Charles, to look at my diamonds – when I get them – it would afford me the

greatest pleasure in life to submit them to your consideration.'

Sir Charles could stand it no longer. 'Sir,' he said, gazing
across at him with his sternest air, 'if your concession were as
full of diamonds as Sindbad the Sailor's valley, I would not
care to turn my head to look at them. I am acquainted with
the nature and practice of salting.' And he glared at the
man with the overhanging eyebrows as if he would devour
him raw. Poor Dr Hector Macpherson subsided instantly.
We learnt a little later that he was a harmless lunatic, who
went about the world with successive concessions for ruby
mines and platinum reefs, because he had been ruined and
driven mad by speculations in the two, and now recouped
himself by imaginary grants in Burmah and Brazil, or
anywhere else that turned up handy. And his eyebrows,
after all, were of Nature's handicraft. We were sorry for
the incident; but a man in Sir Charles's position is such
a mark for rogues that, if he did not take means to
protect himself promptly, he would be for ever overrun by
them.

When we went up to our *salon* that evening, Amelia
flung herself on the sofa. 'Charles,' she broke out in the
voice of a tragedy queen, 'those are real diamonds, and I
shall never be happy again till I get them.'

'They are real diamonds,' Charles echoed. 'And you shall
have them, Amelia. They're worth not less than three thousand pounds. But I shall bid them up gently.'

So, next day, Charles set to work to higgle with the
curate. Brabazon, however, didn't care to part with them.
He was no money-grubber, he said. He cared more for his
mother's gift and a family tradition than for a hundred
pounds, if Sir Charles were to offer it. Charles's eye
gleamed. 'But if I give you *two* hundred!' he said insinuat-
ingly. 'What opportunities for good! You could build a new
wing to your village school-house!'

'We have ample accommodation,' the curate answered,
'No, I don't think I'll sell them.'

Still, his voice faltered somewhat, and he looked down at them inquiringly.

Charles was too precipitate.

'A hundred pounds more or less matters little to me,' he said; 'and my wife has set her heart on them. It's every man's duty to please his wife – isn't it, Mrs Brabazon? – I offer you three hundred.'

The little Scotch girl clasped her hands.

'Three hundred pounds! Oh, Dick, just think what fun we could have, and what good we could do with it! Do let him have them.'

Her accent was irresistible. But the curate shook his head.

'Impossible,' he answered. 'My dear mother's ear-rings! Uncle Aubrey would be so angry if he knew I'd sold them. I daren't face Uncle Aubrey.'

'Has he expectations from Uncle Aubrey?' Sir Charles asked of White Heather.

Mrs Brabazon laughed. 'Uncle Aubrey! Oh dear, no. Poor dear old Uncle Aubrey! Why, the darling old soul hasn't a penny to bless himself with, except his pension. He's a retired post captain.' And she laughed melodiously. She was a charming woman.

'Then I should disregard Uncle Aubrey's feelings,' Sir Charles said decisively.

'No, no,' the curate answered. 'Poor dear old Uncle Aubrey! I wouldn't do anything for the world to annoy him. And he'd be sure to notice it.'

We went back to Amelia. 'Well, have you got them?' she asked.

'No,' Sir Charles answered. 'Not yet. But he's coming round, I think. He's hesitating now. Would rather like to sell them himself, but is afraid what "Uncle Aubrey" would say about the matter. His wife will talk him out of his needless considerations for Uncle Aubrey's feelings; and to-morrow we'll finally clench the bargain.'

Next morning we stayed late in our *salon*, where we always breakfasted, and did not come down to the public rooms till just before *déjeuner*, Sir Charles being busy with me over arrears of correspondence. When we *did* come down the *concierge* stepped forward with a twisted little feminine note for Amelia. She took it and read it. Her countenance fell. 'There, Charles,' she cried, handing it to him, 'you've let the chance slip. I shall *never* be happy now! They've gone off with the diamonds.'

Charles seized the note and read it. Then he passed it on to me. It was short, but final:

Thursday, 6 a.m.

Dear Lady Vandrift — Will you kindly excuse our having gone off hurriedly without bidding you good-bye? We have just had a horrid telegram to say that Dick's favourite sister is *dangerously* ill of fever in Paris. I wanted to shake hands with you before we left — you have all been so sweet to us — but we go by the morning train, absurdly early, and I wouldn't for worlds disturb you. Perhaps some day we may meet again — though buried as we are in a North-country village, it isn't likely; but in any case, you have secured the grateful recollection of Yours very cordially,

Jessie Brabazon

P.S. — Kindest regards to Sir Charles and those dear Went-worths, and a kiss for yourself, if I may venture to send you one.

'She doesn't even mention where they've gone,' Amelia exclaimed in a very bad humour.

'The *concierge* may know,' Isabel suggested, looking over my shoulder.

We asked at his office.

Yes, the gentleman's address was the Rev. Richard Peploe Brabazon, Holme Bush Cottage, Empingham, Northum-berland.

Any address where letters might be sent at once, in Paris?

For the next ten days, or till further notice, Hôtel des Deux Mondes, Avenue de l'Opéra.

Amelia's mind was made up at once.

'Strike while the iron's hot,' she cried. 'This sudden ill-ness, coming at the end of their honeymoon, and involving ten days' more stay at an expensive hotel, will probably upset the curate's budget. He'll be glad to sell now. You'll get them for three hundred. It was absurd of Charles to offer so much at first; but offered once, of course we must stick to it.'

'What do you propose to do?' Charles asked. 'Write, or telegraph?'

'Oh, how silly men are!' Amelia cried. 'Is this the sort of business to be arranged by letter, still less by telegram? No. Seymour must start off at once, taking the night train to Paris; and the moment he gets there, he must interview the curate or Mrs Brabazon. Mrs Brabazon's the best. She has none of this stupid, sentimental nonsense about Uncle Aubrey.'

It is no part of a secretary's duties to act as a diamond broker. But when Amelia puts her foot down, she puts her foot down – a fact which she is unnecessarily fond of emphasizing in that identical proposition. So the self-same evening saw me safe in the train on my way to Paris; and next morning I turned out of my comfortable sleeping-car at the Gare de Strasbourg. My orders were to bring back those diamonds, alive or dead, so to speak, in my pocket to Lucerne; and to offer any needful sum, up to two thousand five hundred pounds, for their immediate purchase.

When I arrived at the Deux Mondes I found the poor little curate and his wife both greatly agitated. They had sat up all night, they said, with their invalid sister; and the sleeplessness and suspense had certainly told upon them after their long railway journey. They were pale and tired, Mrs Brabazon, in particular, looking ill and worried – too much like White Heather. I was more than half ashamed of bothering them about the diamonds at such a moment, but it occurred to me that Amelia was probably right – they would now have reached the end of the sum set apart for their Continental trip, and a little ready cash might be far from unwelcome.

I broached the subject delicately. It was a fad of Lady Vandrift's, I said. She had set her heart upon those useless trinkets. And she wouldn't go without them. She must and would have them. But the curate was obdurate. He threw Uncle Aubrey still in my teeth. Three hundred? – no, never! A mother's present; impossible, dear Jessie! Jessie begged and prayed; she had grown really attached to Lady Vandrift, she said; but the curate wouldn't hear of it. I went up tentatively to four hundred. He shook his head gloomily. It wasn't a question of money, he said. It was a question of affection. I saw it was no use trying that tack any longer. I struck out a new line. 'These stones,' I said, 'I think I ought to inform you, are really diamonds. Sir Charles is certain of it. Now, is it right for a man of your profession and position to be wearing a pair of big gems like those, worth several hundred pounds, as ordinary sleeve-links? A woman? – yes, I grant you. But for a man, is it manly? And you a cricketer!'

He looked at me and laughed. 'Will nothing convince you?' he cried. 'They have been examined and tested by half a dozen jewellers, and we know them to be paste. It wouldn't be right of me to sell them to you under false pretences, however unwilling on my side. I *couldn't* do it.'

'Well, then,' I said, going up a bit in my bids to meet him, 'I'll put it like this. These gems are paste. But Lady Vandrift has an unconquerable and unaccountable desire to possess them. Money doesn't matter to her. She is a friend of your wife's. As a personal favour, won't you sell them to her for a thousand?'

He shook his head. 'It would be wrong,' he said, 'I might even add, criminal.'

'But we take all risk,' I cried.

He was absolute adamant. 'As a clergyman,' he answered, 'I feel I cannot do it.'

'Will *you* try, Mrs Brabazon?' I asked.

The pretty little Scotchwoman leant over and whispered. She coaxed and cajoled him. Her ways were winsome. I couldn't hear what she said, but he seemed to give way at last. 'I should love Lady Vandrift to have them,' she murmured turning to me. 'She *is* such a dear!' And she took out the links from her husband's cuffs and handed them across to me.

'How much?' I asked.

'Two thousand?' she answered interrogatively. It was a big rise, all at once; but such are the ways of women.

'Done!' I replied. 'Do you consent?'

The curate looked up as if ashamed of himself.

'I consent,' he said slowly, 'since Jessie wishes it. But as a clergyman, and to prevent any future misunderstanding, I should like you to give me a statement in writing that you buy them on my distinct and positive declaration that they are made of paste – old Oriental paste – not genuine stones, and that I do not claim any other qualities for them.'

I popped the gems into my purse, well pleased.

'Certainly,' I said, pulling out a paper. Charles, with his unerring business instinct, had anticipated the request, and given me a signed agreement to that effect.

'You will take a cheque?' I inquired.

He hesitated.

'Notes of the Bank of France would suit me better,' he answered.

'Very well,' I replied. 'I will go out and get them.'

How very unsuspicious some are! He allowed me to go off – with the stones in my pocket!

Sir Charles had given me a blank cheque, not exceeding two thousand five hundred pounds. I took it to our agents and cashed it for notes of the Bank of France. The curate clasped them with pleasure. And right glad I was to go back to Lucerne that night, feeling that I had got those diamonds into my hands for about a thousand pounds under their real value!

At Lucerne railway station Amelia met me. She was positively agitated.

'Have you brought them, Seymour?' she asked.

'Yes,' I answered, producing my spoils in triumph.

'Oh, how dreadful!' she cried, drawing back. 'Do you think they're real? Are you sure he hasn't cheated you?'

'Certain of it,' I replied, examining them. 'No one can take me in, in the matter of diamonds. Why on earth should you doubt them?'

'Because I've been talking to Mrs O'Hagan, at the hotel, and she says there's a well-known trick just like that – she's read of it in a book. A swindler has two sets – one real, one false; and he makes you buy the false ones by showing you the real, and pretending he sells them as a special favour.'

'You needn't be alarmed,' I answered. 'I am a judge of diamonds.'

'I shan't be satisfied,' Amelia murmured, 'till Charles has seen them.'

We went up to the hotel. For the first time in her life I saw Amelia really nervous as I handed the stones to Charles to examine. Her doubt was contagious. I half feared, myself, he might break out into a deep monosyllabic interjection, losing his temper in haste, as he often does when things go wrong. But he looked at them with a smile, while I told him the price.

'Eight hundred pounds less than their value,' he answered, well satisfied.

'You have no doubt of their reality?' I asked.

'Not the slightest,' he replied, gazing at them. 'They are genuine stones, precisely the same in quality and type as Amelia's necklet.'

Amelia drew a sigh of relief. 'I'll go upstairs,' she said slowly, 'and bring down my own for you both to compare with them.'

One minute later she rushed down again, breathless. Amelia is far from slim, and I never before knew her exert herself so actively.

'Charles, Charles!' she cried. 'Do you know what dreadful thing has happened? Two of my own stones are gone. He's stolen a couple of diamonds from my necklet, and sold them back to me.'

She held out the *rivière*. It was all too true. Two gems were missing – and these two just fitted the empty places!

A light broke in upon me. I clapped my hand to my head. 'By Jove,' I exclaimed, 'the little curate is – Colonel Clay!'

Charles clapped his own hand to his brow in turn. 'And Jessie,' he cried, 'White Heather – that innocent little Scotchwoman! I often detected a familiar ring in her voice, in spite of the charming Highland accent. Jessie is – Madame Picardet!'

We had absolutely no evidence; but, like the Commissary at Nice, we felt instinctively sure of it.

Sir Charles was determined to catch the rogue. This second deception put him on his mettle. 'The worst of the man is,' he said, 'he has a method. He doesn't go out of his way to cheat us; he makes us go out of ours to be cheated. He lays a trap, and we tumble headlong into it. Tomorrow, Sey, we must follow him on to Paris.'

Amelia explained to him what Mrs O'Hagan had said. Charles took it all in at once, with his usual sagacity. 'That explains,' he said, 'why the rascal used this particular trick to draw us on by. If we had suspected him he could have shown the diamonds were real, and so escaped detection. It was a blind to draw us off from the fact of the robbery. He went to Paris to be out of the way when the discovery was made, and to get a clear day's start of us. What a consummate rogue! And to do me twice running!'

'How did they get at my jewel-case, though?' Amelia exclaimed.

'That's the question,' Charles answered. 'You *do* leave it about so!'

'And why didn't he steal the whole *rivière* at once, and sell the gems?' I inquired.

'Too cunning,' Charles replied. 'This was much better business. It isn't easy to dispose of a big thing like that. In the first place, the stones are large and valuable; in the second place, they're well known – every dealer has heard of the Vandrift *rivière*, and seen pictures of the shape of them.

They're marked gems, so to speak. No, he played a better game – took a couple of them off, and offered them to the only person on earth who was likely to buy them without suspicion. He came here, meaning to work this very trick; he had the links made right to the shape beforehand, and then he stole the stones and slipped them into their places. It's a wonderfully clever trick. Upon my soul, I almost admire the fellow.'

For Charles is a businessman himself, and can appreciate business capacity in others.

How Colonel Clay came to know about that necklet, and to appropriate two of the stones, we only discovered much later. I will not here anticipate that disclosure. One thing at a time is a good rule in life. For the moment he succeeded in baffling us altogether.

However, we followed him on to Paris, telegraphing beforehand to the Bank of France to stop the notes. It was all in vain. They had been cashed within half an hour of my paying them. The curate and his wife, we found, quitted the Hôtel des Deux Mondes for parts unknown that same afternoon. And, as usual with Colonel Clay, they vanished into space, leaving no clue behind them. In other words, they changed their disguise, no doubt, and reappeared somewhere else that night in altered characters. At any rate, no such person as the Reverend Richard Peploe Brabazon was ever afterwards heard of – and, for the matter of that no such village exists as Empingham, Northumberland.

We communicated the matter to the Parisian police. They were *most* unsympathetic. 'It is no doubt Colonel Clay,' said the official whom we saw; 'but you seem to have little just ground of complaint against him. As far as I can see, messieurs, there is not much to choose between you. You, Monsieur le Chevalier, desired to buy diamonds at the price of paste. You, madame, feared you had bought paste at the price of diamonds. You, monsieur the secretary, tried to get the stones from an unsuspecting person for half their

value. He took you all in, that brave Colonel Caoutchouc –
it was diamond cut diamond.'

Which was true, no doubt, but by no means consoling.

We returned to the Grand Hotel. Charles was fuming
with indignation. 'This is really too much,' he exclaimed.
'What an audacious rascal! But he will never again take me
in, my dear Sey. I only hope he'll try it on. I should love to
catch him. I'd know him another time, I'm sure, in spite of
his disguises. It's absurd my being tricked twice running
like this. But never again while I live! Never again, I de-
clare to you!'

'*Jamais de la vie!*' a courier in the hall close by murmured responsively. We stood under the verandah of the
Grand Hotel, in the big glass courtyard. And I verily believe that courier was really Colonel Clay himself in one of
his disguises.

But perhaps we were beginning to suspect him everywhere.

3

Five Hundred Carats

George Griffith

I t was several months after the brilliant if somewhat mysterious recovery of the £15,000 parcel from the notorious but now vanished Seth Salter* that I had the pleasure, and I think I may fairly add the privilege, of making the acquaintance of Inspector Lipinzki.

I can say without hesitation that in the course of wanderings which have led me over a considerable portion of the lands and seas of the world I have never met a more interesting man than he was. I say 'was', poor fellow, for he is now no longer anything but a memory of bitterness to the I.D.B. – but that is a yarn with another twist.

There is no need for further explanation of the all too brief intimacy which followed our introduction, than the statement of the fact that the greatest South African detective of his day was after all a man as well as a detective, and hence not only justifiably proud of the many brilliant achievements which illustrated his career, but also by no means loth that some day the story of them should, with all due and proper precautions and reservations, be told to a wider and possibly less prejudiced audience than the motley and migratory population of the Camp as it was in his day.

I had not been five minutes in the cosy, tastily-furnished

* The reference is to an earlier case of Inspector Lipinzki.

sanctum of his low, broad-roofed bungalow in New De Beers Road before I saw it was a museum as well as a study. Specimens of all sorts of queer apparatus employed by the I.D.B.'s for smuggling diamonds were scattered over the tables and mantelpiece.

There were massive, handsomely-carved briar and meerschaum pipes which seemed to hold wonderfully little tobacco for their size; rough sticks of firewood ingeniously hollowed out, which must have been worth a good round sum in their time; hollow handles of travelling trunks; ladies' boot heels of the fashion affected on a memorable occasion by Mrs Michael Mosenstein; and novels, hymnbooks, church-services, and bibles, with cavities cut out of the centre of their leaves which had once held thousands of pounds' worth of illicit stones on their unsuspected passage through the book-post.

But none of these interested, or, indeed, puzzled me so much as did a couple of curiously assorted articles which lay under a little glass case on a wall bracket. One was an ordinary piece of heavy lead tubing, about three inches long and an inch in diameter, sealed by fusing at both ends, and having a little brass tap fused into one end. The other was a small ragged piece of dirty red sheet – indiarubber, very thin – in fact almost transparent – and, roughly speaking, four or five inches square.

I was looking at these things, wondering what on earth could be the connection between them, and what manner of strange story might be connected with them, when the Inspector came in.

'Good evening. Glad to see you!' he said, in his quiet and almost gentle voice, and without a trace of foreign accent, as we shook hands. 'Well, what do you think of my museum? I daresay you've guessed already that if some of these things could speak they could keep your readers entertained for some little time, eh?'

'Well, there is no reason why their owner shouldn't speak for them,' I said, making the obvious reply, 'provided always, of course, that it wouldn't be giving away too many secrets of state.'

'My dear sir,' he said, with a smile which curled up the ends of his little, black, carefully-trimmed moustache ever so slightly, 'I should not have made you the promise I did at the club the other night if I had not been prepared to rely absolutely on your discretion – and my own. Now, there's whiskey-and-soda or brandy; which do you prefer? You smoke, of course, and I think you'll find these pretty good, and that chair I can recommend. I have unravelled many a knotty problem in it, I can tell you.'

'And now,' he went on when we were at last comfortably settled, 'may I ask which of my relics has most aroused your professional curiosity?'

It was already on the tip of my tongue to ask for the story of the gas-pipe and piece of indiarubber, but the Inspector forestalled me by saying:

'But perhaps that is hardly a fair question, as they will all probably seem pretty strange to you. Now, for instance, I saw you looking at two of my curios when I came in. You would hardly expect them to be associated, and very intimately too, with about the most daring and skilfully planned diamond robbery that ever took place on the Fields, or off them, for the matter of that, would you?'

'Hardly,' I said. 'And yet I think I have learned enough of the devious ways of the I.D.B. to be prepared for a perfectly logical explanation of the fact.'

'As logical as I think I may fairly say romantic,' replied the Inspector as he set his glass down. 'In one sense it was the most ticklish problem that I've ever had to tackle. Of course you've heard some version or other of the disappearance of the Great De Beers' Diamond?'

'I should rather think I had!' I said, with a decided thrill of pleasurable anticipation, for I felt sure that now, if ever, I was going to get to the bottom of the great mystery. 'Everybody in Camp seems to have a different version of it, and, of course, everyone seems to think that if he had only had the management of the case the mystery would have been solved long ago.'

'It is invariably the case,' said the Inspector, with another of his quiet, pleasant smiles, 'that everyone can do work better than those whose reputation depends upon the doing of it. We are not altogether fools at the Department, and yet I have to confess that I myself was in ignorance as to just how that diamond disappeared, or where it got to, until twelve hours ago.

'Now, I am going to tell you the facts exactly as they are, but under the condition that you will alter all the names except, if you choose, my own, and that you will not publish the story for at least twelve months to come. There are personal and private reasons for this which you will probably understand without my stating them. Of course it will, in time, leak out into the papers, although there has been, and will be, no prosecution; but anything in the newspapers will of necessity be garbled and incorrect, and – well, I may as well confess that I am sufficiently vain to wish that my share in the transaction shall not be left altogether to the tender mercies of the imaginative penny-a-liner.'

I acknowledged the compliment with a bow as graceful as the easiness of the Inspector's chair would allow me to make, but I said nothing, as I wanted to get to the story.

'I had better begin at the beginning,' the Inspector went on, as he meditatively snipped the end of a fresh cigar. 'As I suppose you already know, the largest and most valuable diamond ever found on these fields was a really magnificent stone, a perfect octahedron, pure white, without a flaw, and weighing close on 500 carats. There's a photograph of it there on the mantelpiece. I've got another one by me; I'll give it you before you leave Kimberley.

'Well, this stone was found about six months ago in one of the drives on the 800-foot level of Kimberley Mine. It was taken by the overseer straight to the De Beers' offices and placed on the Secretary's desk – you know where he sits, on the right hand side as you go into the Board

Room through the green baize doors. There were several of the Directors present at the time, and, as you may imagine, they were pretty well pleased at the find, for the stone, without any exaggeration, was worth a prince's ransom.

'Of course, I needn't tell you that the value per carat of a diamond which is perfect and of a good colour increases in a sort of geometrical progression with the size. I dare say that stone was worth anywhere between one and two millions, according to the depth of the purchaser's purse. It was worthy to adorn the proudest crown in the world instead of – but there, you'll think me a very poor story-teller if I anticipate.

'Well, the diamond, after being duly admired, was taken upstairs to the Diamond Room by the Secretary himself, accompanied by two of the Directors. Of course, you have been through the new offices of De Beers, but still, perhaps I had better just run over the ground, as the locality is rather important.

'You know that when you get upstairs and turn to the right on the landing from the top of the staircase there is a door with a little grille in it. You knock, a trap-door is raised and, if you are recognized and your business warrants it, you are admitted. Then you go along a little passage out of which a room opens on the left, and in front of you is another door leading into the Diamond Rooms themselves.

'You know, too, that in the main room fronting Stockdale Street and Jones Street the diamond tables run round the two sides under the windows, and are railed off from the rest of the room by a single light wooden rail. There is a table in the middle of the room, and on your right hand as you go in there is a big safe standing against the wall. You will remember, too, that in the corner exactly facing the door stands the glass case containing the diamond scales. I want you particularly to recall the fact that these scales stand diagonally across the corner by the window. The secondary room, as you know, opens out on to the left, but that is not of much consequence.'

I signified my remembrance of these details and the Inspector went on.

'The diamond was first put in the scale and weighed in the presence of the Secretary and the two Directors by one of the higher officials, a licensed diamond broker and a most trusted employee of De Beers, whom you may call Philip Marsden when you come to write the story. The weight, as I told you, in round figures was 500 carats. The stone was then photographed, partly for purposes of identification and partly as a reminder of the biggest stone ever found in Kimberley in its rough state.

'The gem was then handed over to Mr Marsden's care pending the departure of the Diamond Post to Vryburg on the following Monday – this was a Tuesday. The Secretary saw it locked up in the big safe by Mr Marsden, who, as usual, was accompanied by another official, a younger man than himself, whom you can call Henry Lomas, a connection of his, and also one of the most trusted members of the staff.

'Every day, and sometimes two or three times a day, either the Secretary or one or other of the Directors came up and had a look at the big stone, either for their own satisfaction or to show it to some of their more intimate friends. I ought, perhaps, to have told you before that the whole Diamond Room staff were practically sworn to secrecy on the subject, because, as you will readily understand, it was not considered desirable for such an exceedingly valuable find to be made public property in a place like this. When Saturday came it was decided not to send it down to Cape Town, for some reasons connected with the state of the market. When the safe was opened on Monday morning the stone was gone.

'I needn't attempt to describe the absolute panic which followed. It had been seen two or three times in the safe on the Saturday, and the Secretary himself was positive that it was there at closing time, because he saw it just as the safe was being locked for the night. In fact, he actually saw it put in, for it had been taken out to show to a friend of his a few minutes before.

'The safe had not been tampered with, nor could it have been unlocked, because when it is closed for the night it cannot be opened again unless either the Secretary or the Managing Director is present, as they each have a master-key without which the key used during the day is of no use.

'Of course I was sent for immediately, and I admit I was fairly staggered. If the Secretary had not been so positive that the stone was locked up when he saw the safe closed on the Saturday I should have worked upon the theory -- the only possible one, as it seemed – that the stone had been abstracted from the safe during the day, concealed in the room, and somehow or other smuggled out, although even that would have been almost impossible in consequence of the strictness of the searching system and the almost certain discovery which must have followed an attempt to get it out of the town.

'Both the rooms were searched in every nook and cranny. The whole staff, naturally feeling that every one of them must be suspected, immediately volunteered to submit to any process of search that I might think satisfactory, and I can assure you the search was a very thorough one.

'Nothing was found, and when we had done there wasn't a scintilla of evidence to warrant us in suspecting anybody. It is true that the diamond was last actually seen by the Secretary in charge of Mr Marsden and Mr Lomas. Mr Marsden opened the safe, Mr Lomas put the tray containing the big stone and several other fine ones into its usual compartment, and the safe door was locked. Therefore that fact went for nothing.

'You know, I suppose, that one of the Diamond Room staff always remains all night in the room; there is at least one night-watchman on every landing; and the frontages are patrolled all night by armed men of the special police. Lomas was on duty on the Saturday night. He was searched as usual when he came off duty on Sunday morning. Nothing was found, and I recognized that it was absolutely impossible that he could have brought the diamond out of the room or passed it to any confederate in the street without being discovered. Therefore, though at first sight suspicion might have pointed to him as being the one who was apparently last in the room with the diamond, there was absolutely no reason to connect that fact with its disappearance.'

'I must say that that is a great deal plainer and more matter-of-fact than any of the other stories that I have heard of the mysterious disappearance,' I said, as the Inspector paused to re-fill his glass and ask me to do likewise.

'Yes,' he said drily, 'the truth *is* more commonplace up to a certain point than the sort of stories that a stranger will find floating about Kimberley, but still I daresay you have found in your own profession that it sometimes has a way of – to put it in sporting language – giving Fiction a seven-pound handicap and beating it in a canter.'

'For my own part,' I answered with an affirmative nod, 'my money would go on Fact every time. Therefore it would go on now if I were betting. At any rate, I may say that none of the fiction that I have so far heard has offered even a reasonable explanation of the disappearance of that diamond, given the conditions which you have just stated, and, as far as I can see, I admit that I couldn't give the remotest guess at the solution of the mystery.'

'That's exactly what I said to myself after I had been worrying day and night for more than a week over it,' said the Inspector. 'And then,' he went on, suddenly getting up from his seat and beginning to walk up and down the room with quick, irregular strides, 'all of a sudden in the middle of a very much smaller puzzle, just one of the common I.D.B. cases we have almost every week, the whole of the work that I was engaged upon vanished from my mind, leaving it for a moment a perfect blank. Then, like a light-ning flash out of a black cloud, there came a momentary ray of light which showed me the clue to the mystery. That was the idea. These,' he said, stopping in front of the mantel-piece and putting his finger on the glass case which covered the two relics that had started the story, 'these were the materialization of it.'

'And yet, my dear Inspector,' I ventured to interrupt, 'you will perhaps pardon me for saying that your ray of light leaves me just as much in the dark as ever.'

'But your darkness shall be made day all in good course,' he said with a smile. I could see that he had an eye for dramatic effect, and so I thought it was better to let him tell the story uninterrupted and in his own way, so I simply assured him of my ever-increasing interest and waited for him to go on. He took a couple of turns up and down the room in silence, as though he were considering in what form he should spring the solution of the mystery upon me, then he stopped and said abruptly :

'I didn't tell you that the next morning – that is to say, Sunday – Mr Marsden went out on horseback, shooting in the veld up towards that range of hills which lies over yonder to the north-westward between here and Barkly West. I can see by your face that you are already asking yourself what that has got to do with spiriting a million or so's worth of crystalized carbon out of the safe at De Beers'. Well, a little patience, and you shall see.

'Early that same Sunday morning, I was walking down Stockdale Street, in front of the De Beers' offices, smoking a cigar, and, of course, worrying my brains about the dia-mond. I took a long draw at my weed, and quite involun-tarily put my head back and blew it up into the air – there, just like that – and the cloud drifted diagonally across the street dead in the direction of the hills on which Mr Philip Marsden would just then be hunting buck. At the same instant the revelation which had scattered my thoughts about the other little case that I mentioned just now came back to me. I saw, with my mind's eye, of course – well, now, what do you think I saw!'

'If it wouldn't spoil an incomparable detective,' I said, somewhat irrelevantly, 'I should say that you would make an excellent story-teller. Never mind what I think. I'm in the plastic condition just now. I am receiving impressions, not making them. Now, what did you see?'

'I saw the Great De Beers' Diamond – say from ten to fifteen hundred thousand pounds' worth of concentrated capital – floating from the upper storey of the De Beers' Consolidated Mines, rising over the housetops, and drifting down the wind to Mr Philip Marsden's hunting-ground.'

To say that I stared in the silence of blank amazement at the Inspector, who made this astounding assertion with a dramatic gesture and inflection which naturally cannot be reproduced in print, would be to utter the merest commonplace. He seemed to take my stare for one of incredulity rather than wonder, for he said almost sharply:

'Ah, I see you are beginning to think that I am talking fiction now; but never mind, we will see about that later on. You have followed me, I have no doubt, closely enough to understand that, having exhausted all the resources of my experience and such native wit as the Fates have given me, and having made the most minute analysis of the circumstances of the case, I had come to the fixed conclusion that the great diamond had not been carried out of the room on the person of a human being, nor had it been dropped or thrown from the windows to the street – yet it was equally undeniable that it had got out of the safe and out of the room.'

'And therefore it flew out, I suppose!' I could not help interrupting, nor, I am afraid, could I quite avoid a suggestion of incredulity in my tone.

'Yes, my dear sir!' replied the Inspector, with an emphasis which he increased by slapping the four fingers of his right hand on the palm of his left. 'Yes, it flew out. It flew some seventeen or eighteen miles before it returned to the earth in which it was born, if we may accept the theory of the terrestrial origin of diamonds. So far, as the event proved, I was absolutely correct, wild and all as you may naturally think my hypothesis to have been.

'But,' he continued, stopping in his walk and making an eloquent gesture of apology, 'being only human, I almost instantly deviated from truth into error. In fact, I freely confess to you that there and then I made what I consider to be the greatest and most fatal mistake of my career.

'Absolutely certain as I was that the diamond had been conveyed through the air to the Barkly Hills, and that Mr Philip Marsden's shooting expedition had been undertaken with the object of recovering it, I had all the approaches to the town watched till he came back. He came in by the Old Transvaal Road about an hour after dark. I had him arrested, took him into the house of one of my men who happened to live out that way, searched him, as I might say, from the roots of his hair to the soles of his feet, and found – nothing.

'Of course he was indignant, and of course I looked a very considerable fool. In fact, nothing would pacify him but that I should meet him the next morning in the Board Room at De Beers', and, in the presence of the Secretary and at least three Directors, apologize to him for my unfounded suspicions and the outrage that they had led me to make upon him. I was, of course, as you might say, between the devil and the deep sea. I had to do it, and I did it; but my convictions and my suspicions remained exactly what they were before.

'Then there began a very strange, and, although you may think the term curious, a very pathetic, waiting game between us. He knew that in spite of his temporary victory I had really solved the mystery and was on the right track. I knew that the great diamond was out yonder somewhere among the hills or on the veld, and I knew, too, that he was only waiting for my vigilance to relax to go out and get it.

'Day after day, week after week, and month after month the game went on in silence. We met almost every day. His credit had been completely restored at De Beers'. Lomas, his connection and, as I firmly believed, his confederate, had been, through his influence, sent on a mission to England, and when he went I confess to you that I thought the game was up – that Marsden had somehow managed to recover the diamond, and that Lomas had taken it beyond our reach.

'Still I watched and waited, and as time went on I saw that my fears were groundless and that the gem was still on the veld or in the hills. He kept up bravely for weeks, but at last the strain began to tell upon him. Picture to yourself the pitiable position of a man of good family in the Old Country, of expensive tastes and very considerable ambition, living here in Kimberley on a salary of some £12 a week, worth about £5 in England, and knowing that within a few miles of him, in a spot that he alone knew of, there lay a concrete fortune of say, fifteen hundred thousand pounds, which was his for the picking up if he only dared to go and take it, and yet he dared not do so.

'Yes, it is a pitiless trade this of ours, and professional thief-catchers can't afford to have much to do with mercy, and yet I tell you that as I watched that man day after day, with the fever growing hotter in his blood and the unbearable anxiety tearing ever harder and harder at his nerves, I pitied him – yes, I pitied him so much that I even found myself growing impatient for the end to come. Fancy that, a detective, a thief-catcher getting impatient to see his victim out of his misery!

'Well, I had to wait six months – that is to say, I had to wait until five o'clock this morning – for the end. Soon after four one of my men came and knocked me up; he brought a note into my bedroom and I read it in bed. It was from Philip Marsden asking me to go and see him at once and alone. I went, as you may be sure, with as little delay as possible. I found him in his sitting-room. The lights were burning. He was fully dressed, and had evidently been up all night.

'Even I, who have seen the despair that comes of crime in most of its worst forms, was shocked at the look of him. Still he greeted me politely and with perfect composure. He affected not to see the hand that I held out to him, but asked me quite kindly to sit down and have a chat with him. I sat down, and when I looked up I saw him standing in front of me, covering me with a brace of revolvers. My life, of course, was absolutely at his mercy, and whatever I might have thought of myself or the situation, there was obviously nothing to do but to sit still and wait for developments.

'He began very quietly to tell me why he had sent for me. He said: "I wanted to see you, Mr Lipinzki, to clear up this matter about the big diamond. I have seen for a long time – in fact from that Sunday night – that you had worked out a pretty correct notion as to the way that diamond vanished. You are quite right; it did fly across the veld to the Barkly Hills. I am a bit of a chemist you know, and when I had once made up my mind to steal it – for there is no use in mincing words now – I saw that it would be perfectly absurd to attempt to smuggle such a stone out by any of the ordinary methods.

' "I daresay you wonder what these revolvers are for. They are to keep you there in that chair till I've done, for one thing. If you attempt to get out of it or utter a sound I shall shoot you. If you hear me out you will not be injured, so you may as well sit still and keep your ears open.

' "To have any chance of success I must have had a confederate, and I made young Lomas one. If you look on that little table beside your chair you will see a bit of closed lead piping with a tap in it and a piece of thin sheet indiarubber. That is the remains of the apparatus that I used. I make them a present to you; you may like to add them to your collection.

' "Lomas, when he went on duty that Saturday night,

took the bit of tube charged with compressed hydrogen and an empty child's toy balloon with him. You will remember that that night was very dark, and that the wind had been blowing very steadily all day towards the Barkly Hills. Well, when everything was quiet he filled the balloon with gas, tied the diamond –"

' "But how did he get the diamond out of the safe? The Secretary saw it locked up that evening!" I exclaimed, my curiosity getting the better of my prudence.

' "It was not locked up in the safe at all that night," he answered, smiling with a sort of ghastly satisfaction. "Lomas and I, as you know, took the tray of diamonds to the safe, and, as far as the Secretary could see, put them in, but as he put the tray into its compartment he palmed the big diamond as I had taught him to do in a good many lessons before. At the moment that I shut the safe and locked it, the diamond was in his pocket.

' "The Secretary and his friends left the room, Lomas and I went back to the table, and I told him to clean the scales as I wanted to test them. While he was doing so he slipped the diamond behind the box, and there it lay between the box and the corner of the wall until it was wanted.

' "We all left the room as usual, and, as you know, we were searched. When Lomas went on night-duty there was the diamond ready for its balloon voyage. He filled the balloon just so that it lifted the diamond and no more. The lead pipe he just put where the diamond had been – the only place you never looked in. When the row was over on the Monday I locked it up in the safe. We were all searched that day; the next I brought it away and now you may have it.

' "Two of the windows were open on account of the heat. He watched his opportunity, and committed it to the air about two hours before dawn. You know what a sudden fall there is in the temperature here just before daybreak. I calculated upon that to contract the volume of the gas sufficiently to destroy the balance and bring the balloon to the ground, and I knew that, if Lomas had obeyed my instructions, it would fall either on the veld or on this side of the hills.

' "The balloon was a bright red, and, to make a long story short, I started out before daybreak that morning, as you know, to look for buck. When I got outside the camp I took compass bearings and rode straight down the wind towards the hills. By good luck or good calculation, or both, I must have followed the course of the balloon almost exactly, for in three hours after I left the camp I saw the little red speck ahead of me up among the stones on the hillside.

' "I dodged about for a bit as though I were really after buck, in case anybody was watching me. I worked round to the red spot, put my foot on the balloon, and burst it. I folded the indiarubber up, as I didn't like to leave it there, and put it in my pocket-book. You remember that when you searched me you didn't open my pocket-book, as, of course, it was perfectly flat, and the diamond couldn't possibly have been in it. That's how you missed your clue, though I don't suppose it would have been much use to you as you'd already guessed it. However, there it is at your service now."

' "And the diamond?"

'As I said these three words his whole manner suddenly changed. So far he had spoken quietly and deliberately, and without even a trace of anger in his voice, but now his white, sunken cheeks suddenly flushed a bright fever red and his eyes literally blazed at me. His voice sank to a low, hissing tone that was really horrible to hear.

' "The diamond!" he said. "Yes, curse it, and curse you, Mr Inspector Lipinzki – for it and you have been a curse to me! Day and night I have seen the spot where I buried it, and day and night you have kept your nets spread about my feet so that I could not move a step to go and take it. I can bear the suspense no longer. Between you – you and that infernal stone – you have wrecked my health and driven me mad. If I had all the wealth of De Beers' now it wouldn't be any use to me, and tonight a new fear came to me – that if this goes on much longer I shall go mad, really mad, and in my delirium rob myself of my revenge on you by letting out where I hid it.

' "Now listen. Lomas has gone. He is beyond your reach. He has changed his name – his very identity. I have sent him by different posts, and to different names and addresses, two letters. One is a plan and the other is a key to it. With those two pieces of paper he can find the diamond. Without them you can hunt for a century and never go near it.

' "And now that you know that – that your incomparable stone, which should have been mine, is out yonder somewhere where you can never find it, you and the De Beers' people will be able to guess at the tortures of Tantalus that you have made me endure. That is all you have got by your smartness. That is my legacy to you – curse you! If I had my way I would send you all out there to hunt for it without food or drink till you died of hunger and thirst of body, as you have made me die a living death of hunger and thirst of mind."

'As he said this, he covered me with one revolver, and put the muzzle of the other into his mouth. With an ungovernable impulse, I sprang to my feet. He pulled both triggers at once. One bullet passed between my arm and my body, ripping a piece out of my coat sleeve; the other – well, I can spare you the details. He dropped dead instantly.'

'And the diamond?' I said.

'The reward is £20,000, and it is at your service,' replied the Inspector, in his suavest manner, 'provided that you can find the stone – or Mr Lomas and his plans.'

4

A Bracelet at Bruges

Arnold Bennett

THE bracelet had fallen into the canal.

And the fact that the canal was the most picturesque canal in the old Flemish city of Bruges, and that the ripples caused by the splash of the bracelet had disturbed reflections of wondrous belfries, towers, steeples, and other unique examples of Gothic architecture, did nothing whatever to assuage the sudden agony of that disappearance. For the bracelet had been given to Kitty Sartorius by her grateful and lordly manager, Lionel Belmont (U.S.A.), upon the completion of the unexampled run of *The Delminico Doll*, at the Regency Theatre, London. And its diamonds were worth five hundred pounds, to say nothing of the gold.

The beautiful Kitty, and her friend Eve Fincastle, the journalist, having exhausted Ostend, had duly arrived at Bruges in the course of their holiday tour. The question of Kitty's jewellery had arisen at the start. Kitty had insisted that she must travel with all her jewels, according to the custom of theatrical stars of great magnitude. Eve had equally insisted that Kitty must travel without jewels, and had exhorted her to remember the days of her simplicity. They compromised. Kitty was allowed to bring the bracelet, but nothing else save the usual half-dozen rings. The ravishing creature could not have persuaded herself to leave the bracelet behind, because it was so recent a gift and still new and strange and heavenly to her. But, since prudence forbade even Kitty to let the trifle lie about in hotel bedrooms, she was obliged always to wear it. And she had been wearing it this bright afternoon in early October, when the girls, during a stroll, had met one of their new friends, Madame Lawrence, on the world-famous Quai du Rosaire, just at the back of the Hôtel de Ville and the Halles.

Madame Lawrence resided permanently in Bruges. She was between twenty-five and forty-five, dark, with the air of continually subduing a natural instinct to dash, and well dressed in black. Equally interested in the peerage and in the poor, she had made the acquaintance of Eve and Kitty at the Hôtel de la Grande Place, where she called from time to time to induce English travellers to buy genuine Bruges lace, wrought under her own supervision by her own paupers. She was Belgian by birth, and when complimented on her fluent and correct English, she gave all the praise to her deceased husband, an English barrister. She had settled in Bruges like many people settle there, because Bruges is inexpensive, picturesque, and inordinately respectable. Besides an English church and chaplain, it has two cathedrals and an episcopal palace, with a real bishop in it.

'What an exquisite bracelet! May I look at it?'

It was these simple but ecstatic words, spoken with Madame Lawrence's charming foreign accent, which had begun the tragedy. The three women had stopped to admire the always admirable view from the little quay, and they were leaning over the rails when Kitty unclasped the bracelet for the inspection of the widow. The next instant there was a *plop*, an affrighted exclamation from Madame Lawrence in her native tongue, and the bracelet was engulfed before the very eyes of all three.

The three looked at each other non-plussed. Then they looked around, but not a single person was in sight. Then, for some reason which, doubtless, psychology can explain, they stared hard at the water, though the water there was just as black and foul as it is everywhere else in the canal system of Bruges.

'Surely you've not dropped it!' Eve Fincastle exclaimed in a voice of horror. Yet she knew positively that Madame Lawrence had.

The delinquent took a handkerchief from her muff and sobbed into it. And between her sobs she murmured. 'We must inform the police.'

'Yes, of course,' said Kitty, with the lightness of one to whom a five-hundred-pound bracelet is a bagatelle. 'They'll fish it up in no time.'

'Well,' Eve decided, 'you go to the police at once, Kitty; and Madame Lawrence will go with you, because she speaks French and I'll stay here to mark the exact spot.'

The other two started, but Madame Lawrence, after a few steps, put her hand to her side. 'I can't,' she sighed, pale. 'I am too upset. I cannot walk. You go with Miss Sartorius,' she said to Eve, 'and I will stay,' and she leaned heavily against the railings.

Eve and Kitty ran off, just as if it was an affair of seconds, and the bracelet had to be saved from drowning. But they had scarcely turned the corner, thirty yards away, when they reappeared in company with a high official of police, whom, by the most lucky chance in the world, they had encountered in the covered passage leading to the Place du Borg. This official, instantly enslaved by Kitty's beauty, proved to be the very mirror of politeness and optimism. He took their names and addresses, and a full description of the bracelet, and informed them that at that place the canal was nine feet deep. He said that the bracelet should undoubtedly be recovered on the morrow, but that, as dusk was imminent, it would be futile to commence angling that night. In the meantime the loss should be kept secret; and to make all sure, a succession of gendarmes should guard the spot during the night.

Kitty grew radiant, and rewarded the gallant officer with

smiles; Eve was satisfied, and the face of Madame Lawrence wore a less mournful hue.

'And now,' said Kitty to Madame, when everything had been arranged, and the first of the gendarmes was duly installed at the exact spot against the railings, 'you must come and take tea with us in our winter garden; and be gay! Smile: I insist. And I insist that you don't worry.'

Madame Lawrence tried feebly to smile.

'You are very good-natured,' she stammered.

Which was decidedly true.

2

The winter-garden of the Hôtel de la Grande Place, referred to in all the hotel's advertisements, was merely the inner court of the hotel, roofed in by glass at the height of the first storey. Cane flourished there, in the shape of lounge-chairs, but no other plant. One of the lounge-chairs was occupied when, just as the carillon in the belfry at the other end of the Place began to play Gounod's 'Nazareth', indicating the hour of five o'clock, the three ladies entered the winter-garden. Apparently the toilettes of two of them had been adjusted and embellished as for a somewhat ceremonious occasion.

'Lo!' cried Kitty Sartorius, when she perceived the occupant of the chair, 'the millionaire! Mr Thorold, how charming of you to reappear like this! I invite you to tea.'

Cecil Thorold rose with appropriate eagerness.

'Delighted!' he said, smiling, and then explained that he had arrived from Ostend about two hours before and had taken rooms in the hotel.

'You knew we were staying here?' Eve asked as he shook hands with her.

'No,' he replied; 'but I am glad to find you again.'

'Are you?' She spoke languidly, but her colour heightened and those eyes of hers sparkled.

'Madame Lawrence,' Kitty chirruped, 'let me present Mr

Cecil Thorold. He is appallingly rich, but we mustn't let that frighten us.'

From a mouth less adorable than the mouth of Miss Sartorius such an introduction might have been judged lacking in the elements of good form, but for more than two years now Kitty had known that whatever she did or said was perfectly correct because she did or said it. The new acquaintances laughed amiably and a certain intimacy was at once established.

'Shall I order tea, dear?' Eve suggested.

'No, dear,' said Kitty quietly. 'We will wait for the Count.'

'The Count?' demanded Cecil Thorold.

'The Comte d'Avrec,' Kitty explained. 'He is staying here.'

'A French nobleman, doubtless?'

'Yes,' said Kitty; and she added, 'you will like him. He is an archaeologist, and a musician – oh, and lots of things!'

'If I am one minute late, I entreat pardon,' said a fine tenor voice at the door.

It was the Count. After he had been introduced to Madame Lawrence, and Cecil Thorold had been introduced to him, tea was served.

Now, the Comte d'Avrec was everything that a French count ought to be. As dark as Cecil Thorold, and even handsomer, he was a little older and a little taller than the millionaire, and a short, pointed, black beard, exquisitely trimmed, gave him an appearance of staid reliability which Cecil lacked. His bow was a vertebrate poem, his smile a consolation for all misfortunes, and he managed his hat, stick, gloves, and cup with the dazzling assurance of a conjurer. To observe him at afternoon tea was to be convinced that he had been specially created to shine gloriously in drawing-rooms, winter-gardens, and *tables d'hôte*. He was one of those men who always do the right thing at the right moment, who are capable of speaking an indefinite number of languages with absolute purity of accent (he spoke English much better than Madame Lawrence), and who can and do discourse with *verve* and accuracy on all sciences, arts, sports, and religions. In short, he was a phoenix of a count; and this was certainly the opinion of Miss Kitty Sartorius and of Miss Eve Fincastle, both of whom reckoned that what they did not know about men might be ignored. Kitty and the Count, it soon became evident, were mutually attracted; their souls were approaching each other with a velocity which increased inversely as the square of the lessening distance between them. And Eve was watching this approximation with undisguised interest and relish.

Nothing of the least importance occurred, save the Count's marvellous exhibition of how to behave at afternoon tea, until the refection was nearly over; and then, during a brief pause in the talk, Cecil, who was sitting to the left of Madame Lawrence, looked sharply round at the right shoulder of his tweed coat; he repeated the gesture a second and yet a third time.

'What is the matter with the man?' asked Eve Fincastle. Both she and Kitty were extremely bright, animated, and even excited.

'Nothing. I thought I saw something on my shoulder, that's all,' said Cecil. 'Ah! It's only a bit of thread.' And he picked off the thread with his left hand and held it before Madame Lawrence. 'See! It's a piece of thin black silk, knotted. At first I took it for an insect – you know how queer things look out of the corner of your eye. Pardon!' He had dropped the fragment on to Madame Lawrence's black silk dress. 'Now it's lost.'

'If you will excuse me, kind friends,' said Madame Lawrence, 'I will go.' She spoke hurriedly, and as though in mental distress.

'Poor thing!' Kitty Sartorius exclaimed when the widow had gone. 'She's still dreadfully upset'; and Kitty and Eve proceeded jointly to relate the story of the diamond bracelet, upon which hitherto they had kept silence (though with difficulty), out of regard for Madame Lawrence's feelings.

Cecil made almost no comment.

The Count, with the sympathetic excitability of his race, walked up and down the winter-garden, asseverating earnestly that such clumsiness amounted to a crime; then he grew calm and confessed that he shared the optimism of the police as to the recovery of the bracelet; lastly he complimented Kitty on her equable demeanour under this affliction.

'Do you know, Count,' said Cecil Thorold, later, after they had all four ascended to the drawing-room overlooking the Grande Place, 'I was quite surprised when I saw at tea that you had to be introduced to Madame Lawrence.'

'Why so, my dear Mr Thorold?' the Count inquired suavely.

'I thought I had seen you together in Ostend a few days ago.'

The Count shook his wonderful head.

'Perhaps you have a brother –?' Cecil paused.

'No,' said the Count. 'But it is a favourite theory of mine that everyone has his double somewhere in the world.' Previously the Count had been discussing Planchette – he was a great authority on the supernatural, the sub-conscious, and the subliminal. He now deviated gracefully to the discussion of the theory of doubles.

'I suppose you aren't going out for a walk, dear, before dinner?' said Eve to Kitty.

'No, dear,' said Kitty, positively.

'I think I shall,' said Eve.

And her glance at Cecil Thorold intimated in the plainest possible manner that she wished not only to have a companion for a stroll, but to leave Kitty and the Count in dual solitude.

'I shouldn't, if I were you, Miss Fincastle,' Cecil remarked, with calm and studied blindness. 'It's risky here in the evenings – with these canals exhaling miasma and mosquitoes and bracelets and all sorts of things.'

'I will take the risk, thank you,' said Eve, in an icy tone, and she haughtily departed; she would not cower before Cecil's millions. As for Cecil, he joined in the discussion of the theory of doubles.

3

On the next afternoon but one, policemen were still fishing, without success, for the bracelet, and raising from the ancient duct long-buried odours which threatened to destroy the inhabitants of the quay. (When Kitty Sartorius had hinted that perhaps the authorities might see their way to drawing off the water from the canal, the authorities had intimated that the death-rate of Bruges was already as high as convenient.) Nevertheless, though nothing had happened, the situation had somehow developed, and in such a manner that the bracelet itself was in danger of being partially forgotten; and of all places in Bruges, the situation had developed on the top of the renowned Belfry which dominates the Grande Place in particular and the city in general.

The summit of the Belfry is three hundred and fifty feet high, and it is reached by four hundred and two winding stone steps, each a separate menace to life and limb. Eve Fincastle had climbed those steps alone, perhaps in quest of the view at the top, perhaps in quest of spiritual calm. She had not been leaning over the parapet more than a minute before Cecil Thorold had appeared, his field-glasses slung over his shoulder. They had begun to talk a little, but nervously and only in snatches. The wind blew free up there among the forty-eight bells, but the social atmosphere was oppressive.

'The Count is a most charming man,' Eve was saying, as if in defence of the Count.

'He is,' said Cecil; 'I agree with you.'

'Oh no, you don't, Mr Thorold! Oh no, you don't!'

Then there was a pause, and the twain looked down upon Bruges, with its venerable streets, its grass-grown squares, its waterways, and its innumerable monuments, spread out maplike beneath them in the mellow October sunshine. Citizens passed along the thoroughfare in the semblance of tiny dwarfs.

'If you didn't hate him,' said Eve, 'you wouldn't behave as you do.'

'How do I behave, then?'

Eve schooled her voice to an imitation of jocularity –

'All Tuesday evening, and all day yesterday, you couldn't leave them alone. You know you couldn't.'

Five minutes later the conversation had shifted.

'You actually saw the bracelet fall into the canal?' said Cecil.

'I actually saw the bracelet fall into the canal. And no one could have got it out while Kitty and I were away, because we weren't away half a minute.'

But they could not dismiss the subject of the Count, and presently he was again the topic.

'Naturally it would be a good match for the Count – for *any* man,' said Eve; 'but then it would also be a good match for Kitty. Of course, he is not so rich as some people, but he is rich.'

Cecil examined the horizon with his glasses, and then the streets near the Grande Place.

'Rich, is he? I'm glad of it. By the by, he's gone to Ghent for the day, hasn't he?'

'Yes, he went by the 9.27, and returns by the 4.38.'

Another pause.

'Well,' said Cecil at length, handing the glasses to Eve Fincastle, 'kindly glance down there. Follow the line of the Rue St Nicholas. You see the cream-coloured house with the enclosed courtyard? Now, do you see two figures standing together near a door – a man and a woman, the woman on the steps? Who are they?'

'I can't see very well,' said Eve.

'Oh yes, my dear lady, you can,' said Cecil. 'These glasses are the very best. Try again.'

'They look like the Comte d'Avrec and Madame Law-rence,' Eve murmured.

'But the Count is on his way from Ghent! I see the steam of the 4.38 over there. The curious thing is that the Count entered the house of Madame Lawrence, to whom he was introduced for the first time the day before yesterday, at ten o'clock this morning. Yes, it would be a very good match for the Count. When one comes to think of it, it usually is that sort of man that contrives to marry a brilliant and successful actress. There! He's just leaving, isn't he? Now let us descend and listen to the recital of his day's doings in Ghent – shall we?'

'You mean to insinuate,' Eve burst out in sudden wrath, 'that the Count is an – an *adventurer*, and that Madame Lawrence ... Oh! Mr Thorold!' She laughed condescend-ingly. 'This jealousy is too absurd. Do you suppose I haven't noticed how impressed you were with Kitty at the Devon-shire Mansion that night, and again at Ostend, and again here? You're simply carried away by jealousy; and you think because you are a millionaire you must have all you want. I haven't the slightest doubt that the Count...'

'Anyhow,' said Cecil, 'let us go down and hear about Ghent.'

His eyes made a number of remarks (indulgent, angry, amused, protective, admiring, perspicacious, puzzled), too subtle for the medium of words.

They groped their way down to earth in silence, and it was in silence that they crossed the Grande Place. The Count was seated on the *terrasse* in front of the hotel, with a liqueur glass before him, and he was making graceful and expressive signs to Kitty Sartorius, who leaned her marvel-lous beauty out of a first-storey window. He greeted Cecil Thorold and Eve with an equal grace.

'And how is Ghent?' Cecil inquired.

'Did you go to Ghent, after all, Count?' Eve put in. The Comte d'Avrec looked from one to another, and then, in-stead of replying, he sipped at his glass. 'No,' he said, 'I didn't go. The rather curious fact is that I happened to meet Madame Lawrence, who offered to show me her collection of lace. I have been an amateur of lace for some years, and really Madame Lawrence's collection is amazing. You have seen it? No? You should do so. I'm afraid I have spent most of the day there.'

When the Count had gone to join Kitty in the drawing-room, Eve Fincastle looked victoriously at Cecil, as if to demand of him. 'Will you apologize?'

'My dear journalist,' Cecil remarked simply, 'you gave the show away.'

That evening the continued obstinacy of the bracelet, which still refused to be caught, began at last to disturb the birdlike mind of Kitty Sartorius. Moreover, the secret was out, and the whole town of Bruges was discussing the episode and the chances of success.

'Let us consult Planchette,' said the Count. The proposal was received with enthusiasm by Kitty. Eve had disappeared.

Planchette was produced; and when asked if the bracelet would be recovered, it wrote, under the hands of Kitty and the Count, a trembling 'Yes'. When asked 'By whom?' it wrote a word that faintly resembled 'Avrec'.

The Count stated that he should personally commence dragging operations at sunrise. 'You will see,' he said, 'I shall succeed.'

'Let me try this toy, may I?' Cecil asked blandly, and, upon Kitty agreeing, he addressed Planchette in a clear voice, 'Now, Planchette, who will restore the bracelet to its owner?'

And Planchette wrote 'Thorold', but in characters as firm and regular as those of a copy-book.

'Mr Thorold is laughing at us,' observed the Count, imperturbably bland.

'How horrid you are, Mr Thorold!' Kitty exclaimed.

4

Of the four persons more or less interested in the affair, three were secretly active that night, in and out of the hotel. Only Kitty Sartorius, chief mourner for the bracelet, slept placidly in her bed. It was towards three o'clock in the morning that a sort of preliminary crisis was reached.

From a multiplicity of doors which ventilate its rooms, one would imagine that the average foreign hotel must have been designed immediately after its architect had been to see a Palais Royal farce, in which every room opens into every other room in every act. The Hôtel de la Grande Place was not peculiar in this respect; it abounded in doors. All the chambers on the second storey, over the public rooms, fronting the Place, communicated one with the next, but naturally most of the communicating doors were locked. Cecil Thorold and the Comte d'Avrec had each a bedroom and a sitting-room on that floor. The Count's sitting-room adjoined Cecil's; and the door between was locked, and the key in the possession of the landlord.

Nevertheless, at three a.m. this particular door opened noiselessly from Cecil's side, and Cecil entered the domain of the Count. The moon shone, and Cecil could plainly see not only the silhouette of the Belfry across the Place, but also the principal objects within the room. He noticed the table in the middle, the large easy-chair turned towards the hearth, the old-fashioned sofa; but not a single article did he perceive which might have been the personal property of the Count. He cautiously passed across the room through the moonlight to the door of the Count's bedroom, which apparently, to his immense surprise, was not only shut, but locked, and the key in the lock on the sitting-room side. Silently unlocking it, he entered the bedroom and disappeared...

In less than five minutes he crept back into the Count's sitting-room, closed the door and locked it.

'Odd!' he murmured reflectively; but he seemed quite happy.

There was a sudden movement in the region of the hearth, and a form rose from the armchair. Cecil rushed to the switch and turned on the electric light. Eve Fincastle stood before him. They faced each other.

'What are you doing here at this time, Miss Fincastle?' he asked, sternly. 'You can talk freely; the Count will not waken.'

'I may ask you the same question,' Eve replied, with cold bitterness.

'Excuse me. You may not. You are a woman. This is the Count's room –'

'You are in error,' she interrupted him. 'It is not the Count's room. It is mine. Last night I told the Count I had some important writing to do, and I asked him as a favour to relinquish this room to me for twenty-four hours. He very kindly consented. He removed his belongings, handed me the key of that door, and the transfer was made in the hotel books. And now,' she added, 'may I inquire, Mr Thorold, what you are doing in my room?'

'I – I thought it was the Count's,' Cecil faltered, decidedly at a loss for a moment. 'In offering my humblest apologies, permit me to say that I admire you, Miss Fincastle.'

'I wish I could return the compliment,' Eve exclaimed, and she repeated with almost plaintive sincerity: 'I do wish I could.'

Cecil raised his arms and let them fall to his side.

'You meant to catch me,' he said. 'You suspected something, then? The "important writing" was an invention.' And he added, with a faint smile: 'You really ought not to have fallen asleep. Suppose I had not wakened you?'

'Please don't laugh, Mr Thorold. Yes, I did suspect. There was something in the demeanour of your servant Lecky that gave me the idea ... I did mean to catch you. Why you, a millionaire, should be a burglar, I cannot understand. I never understood that incident at the Devonshire

Mansion; it was beyond me. I am by no means sure that you didn't have a great deal to do with the Rainshore affair at Ostend. But that you should have stooped to slander is the worst. I confess you are a mystery. I confess that I can make no guess at the nature of your present scheme. And what I shall do, now that I have caught you, I don't know. I can't decide; I must think. If, however, anything is missing to-morrow morning, I shall be bound in any case to denounce you. You grasp that?'

'I grasp it perfectly, my dear journalist,' Cecil replied. 'And something will not improbably be missing. But take the advice of a burglar and a mystery, and go to bed, it is half past three.'

And Eve went. And Cecil bowed her out and then retired to his own rooms. And the Count's apartment was left to the moonlight.

5

'Planchette is a very safe prophet,' said Cecil to Kitty Sartorius the next morning, 'provided it has firm guidance.'

They were at breakfast.

'What do you mean?'

'I mean that Planchette prophesied last night that I should restore to you your bracelet. I do.'

He took the lovely gewgaw from his pocket and handed it to Kitty.

'Ho-ow did you find it, you dear thing?' Kitty stammered, trembling under the shock of joy.

'I fished it up out – out of the mire by a contrivance of my own.'

'But when?'

'Oh! Very early. At three o'clock a.m. You see, I was determined to be first.'

'In the dark, then?'

'I had a light. Don't you think I'm rather clever?'

Kitty's scene of ecstatic gratitude does not come into the

story. Suffice it to say that not until the moment of its restoration did she realize how precious the bracelet was to her.

It was ten o'clock before Eve descended. She had breakfasted in her room, and Kitty had already exhibited to her the prodigal bracelet.

'I particularly want you to go up the Belfry with me, Miss Fincastle,' Cecil greeted her; and his tone was so serious and so urgent that she consented. They left Kitty playing waltzes on the piano in the drawing-room.

'And now, O man of mystery?' Eve questioned, when they had toiled to the summit, and saw the city and its dwarfs beneath them.

'We are in no danger of being disturbed here,' Cecil began; 'but I will make my explanation – the explanation which I certainly owe you – as brief as possible. Your Comte d'Avrec is an adventurer (please don't be angry), and your Madame Lawrence is an adventuress. I knew that I had seen them together. They work in concert, and for the most part make a living on the gaming-tables of Europe. Madame Lawrence was expelled from Monte Carlo last year for being too intimate with a croupier. You may be aware that at a roulette-table one can do a great deal with the aid of the croupier. Madame Lawrence appropriated the bracelet 'on her own', as it were. The Count (he may be a real Count, for anything I know) heard first of that enterprise from the lips of Miss Sartorius. He was annoyed, angry – because he was really a little in love with your friend, and he saw golden prospects. It is just this fact – the Count's genuine passion for Miss Sartorius – that renders the case psychologically interesting. To proceed, Madame Lawrence became jealous. The Count spent six hours yesterday in trying to get the bracelet from her, and failed. He tried again last night, and succeeded, but not too easily, for he did not re-enter the hotel till after one o'clock. At first I thought he had succeeded in the daytime, and I had arranged accordingly, for I did not see why he should have the honour and glory of restoring the bracelet to its owner. Lecky and I fixed up a sleeping-draught for him. The minor details were simple. When you caught me this morning, the bracelet was in my pocket, and in its stead I had left a brief note for the perusal of the Count, which has had the singular effect of inducing him to decamp; probably he has not gone alone. But isn't it amusing that, since you so elaborately took his sitting-room, he will be convinced that you are a party to his undoing – you, his staunchest defender?'

Eve's face gradually broke into an embarrassed smile.

'You haven't explained,' she said, 'how Madame Lawrence got the bracelet.'

'Come over here,' Cecil answered. 'Take these glasses and look down at the Quai du Rosaire. You see everything plainly?' Eve could, in fact, see on the quay the little mounds of mud which had been extracted from the canal in the quest of the bracelet. Cecil continued: 'On my arrival in Bruges on Monday, I had a fancy to climb the Belfry at once. I witnessed the whole scene between you and Miss Sartorius and Madame Lawrence, through my glasses. Immediately your backs were turned, Madame Lawrence, her hands behind her, and her back against the railing, began to make a sort of rapid, drawing up motion with her forearms. Then I saw a momentary glitter ... Considerably mystified, I visited the spot after you had left it, chatted with the gendarme on duty and got round him, and then it dawned on me that a robbery had been planned, prepared, and executed with extraordinary originality and ingenuity. A long, thin thread of black silk must have been ready tied to the railing, with perhaps a hook at the other end. As soon as Madame Lawrence held the bracelet, she attached the hook to it and dropped it. The silk, especially as it was the last thing in the world you would look for, would be as good as invisible. When you went for the police, Madame retrieved the bracelet, hid it in her muff, and broke off the silk. Only, in her haste, she left a bit of silk tied to the railing. That fragment I carried to the hotel. All along she must have been a little uneasy about me ... And that's all. Except that I wonder you thought I was jealous of the Count's attentions to your friend.' He gazed at her admiringly.

'I'm glad you are not a thief, Mr Thorold,' said Eve.

'Well,' Cecil smiled, 'as for that, I left him a couple of louis for fares, and I shall pay his hotel bill.'

'Why?'

'There were notes for nearly ten thousand francs with the bracelet. Ill-gotten gains, I am sure. A trifle, but the only reward I shall have for my trouble. I shall put them to good use.' He laughed, serenely gay.

The Absent-Minded Coterie

Robert Barr

I WELL remember the November day when I first heard of the Summertrees case, because there hung over London a fog so thick that two or three times I lost my way, and no cab was to be had at any price. The few cabmen then in the streets were leading their animals slowly along, making for their stables. It was one of those depressing London days which filled me with ennui and a yearning for my own clear city of Paris, where, if we are ever visited by a slight mist, it is at least clean, white vapour, and not this horrible London mixture saturated with suffocating carbon. The fog was too thick for any passer to read the content bills of the newspapers plastered on the pavement, and as there were probably no races that day the newsboys were shouting what they considered the next most important event – the election of an American President. I bought a paper and thrust it into my pocket. It was late when I reached my flat, and, after dining there, which was an unusual thing for me to do, I put on my slippers, took an easy-chair before the fire, and began to read my evening journal. I was distressed to learn that the eloquent Mr Bryan had been defeated. I knew little about the silver question, but the man's oratorical power had appealed to me, and my sympathy was aroused because he owned many silver mines, and yet the price of the metal was so low that apparently he could not make a living through the operation of them. But, of course, the cry that he was a plutocrat, and a reputed millionaire over and over again, was bound to defeat him in a democracy where the average voter is exceedingly poor and not comfortably well-to-do as is the case with our peasants in France. I always took great interest in the affairs of the huge republic to the west, having been at some pains to inform myself accurately regarding its politics, and although, as my readers know, I seldom quote anything complimentary that is said of me, nevertheless, an American client of mine once admitted that he never knew the true inwardness – I think that was the phrase he used – of American politics until he heard me discourse upon them. But then, he added, he had been a very busy man all his life.

I had allowed my paper to slip to the floor, for in very truth the fog was penetrating even into my flat, and it was becoming difficult to read, notwithstanding the electric light. My man came in, and announced that Mr Spenser Hale wished to see me, and, indeed, any night, but especially when there is rain or fog outside, I am more pleased to talk with a friend than to read a newspaper.

'*Mon Dieu*, my dear Monsieur Hale, it is a brave man you are to venture out in such a fog as is abroad tonight.'

'Ah, Monsieur Valmont,' said Hale with pride, 'you cannot raise a fog like this in Paris!'

'No. There you are supreme,' I admitted, rising and saluting my visitor, then offering him a chair.

'I see you are reading the latest news,' he said, indicating my newspaper. 'I am very glad that man Bryan is defeated. Now we shall have better times.'

I waved my hand as I took my chair again. I will discuss many things with Spenser Hale, but not American politics; he does not understand them. It is a common defect of the English to suffer complete ignorance regarding the internal affairs of other countries.

'It is surely an important thing that brought you out on

such a night as this. The fog must be very thick in Scotland Yard.'

This delicate shaft of fancy completely missed him, and he answered stolidly,

'It's thick all over London, and, indeed, throughout most of England.'

'Yes, it is,' I agreed, but he did not see that either.

Still a moment later he made a remark which, if it had come from some people I know, might have indicated a glimmer of comprehension.

'You are a very, very clever man, Monsieur Valmont, so all I need say is that the question which brought me here is the same as that on which the American election was fought. Now, to a countryman, I should be compelled to give further explanation, but to you, monsieur, that will not be necessary.'

There are times when I dislike the crafty smile and partial closing of the eyes which always distinguishes Spenser Hale when he places on the table a problem which he expects will baffle me. If I said he never did baffle me, I would be wrong, of course, for sometimes the utter simplicity of the puzzles which trouble him leads me into an intricate involution entirely unnecessary in the circumstances.

I pressed my finger-tips together, and gazed for a few moments at the ceiling. Hale had lit his black pipe, and my silent servant placed at his elbow the whisky and soda, then tip-toed out of the room. As the door closed my eyes came from the ceiling to the level of Hale's expansive countenance.

'Have they eluded you?' I asked quietly.

'Who?'

'The coiners.'

Hale's pipe dropped from his jaw, but he managed to catch it before it reached the floor. Then he took a gulp from the tumbler.

'That was just a lucky shot,' he said.

'*Parfaitement*,' I replied carelessly.

'Now, own up, Valmont, wasn't it?'

I shrugged my shoulders. A man cannot contradict a guest in his own house.

'Oh, stow that!' cried Hale impolitely. He is a trifle prone to strong and even slangy expressions when puzzled. 'Tell me how you guessed it.'

'It is very simple, *mon ami*. The question on which the American election was fought is the price of silver, which is so low that it has ruined Mr Bryan, and threatens to ruin all the farmers of the west who possess silver mines on their farms. Silver troubled America, ergo silver troubles Scotland Yard.

'Very well, the natural inference is that someone has stolen bars of silver. But such a theft happened three months ago, when the metal was being unloaded from a German steamer at Southampton, and my dear friend Spenser Hale ran down the thieves very cleverly as they were trying to dissolve the marks off the bars with acid. Now crimes do not run in series, like the numbers in roulette at Monte Carlo. The thieves are men of brains. They say to themselves, "What chance is there successfully to steal bars of silver while Mr Hale is at Scotland Yard?" Eh, my good friend?'

'Really, Valmont,' said Hale taking another sip, 'sometimes you almost persuade me that you have reasoning powers.'

'Thanks, comrade. Then it is not a *theft* of silver we have now to deal with. But the American election was fought on the *price* of silver. If silver had been high in cost, there would have been no silver question. So the crime that is bothering you arises through the low price of silver, and this suggests that it must be a case of illicit coinage, for there the low price of the metal comes in. You have, perhaps, found a more subtle illegitimate act going forward than heretofore. Someone is making your shillings and your half-crowns from real silver, instead of from baser metal, and yet there is a large profit which has not hitherto

92

been possible through the high price of silver. With the old conditions you were familiar, but this new element sets at nought all your previous formulae. That is how I reasoned the matter out.'

'Well, Valmont, you have hit it. I'll say that for you; you have hit it. There is a gang of expert coiners who are putting out real silver money, and making a clear shilling on the half-crown. We can find no trace of the coiners, but we know the man who is shoving the stuff.'

'That ought to be sufficient,' I suggested.

'Yes, it should, but it hasn't proved so up to date. Now I came tonight to see if you would do one of your French tricks for us, right on the quiet.'

'What French trick, Monsieur Spenser Hale?' I inquired with some asperity, forgetting for the moment that the man invariably became impolite when he grew excited.

'No offence intended,' said this blundering officer, who really is a good-natured fellow, but always puts his foot in it, and then apologizes. 'I want someone to go through a man's house without a search warrant, spot the evidence, let me know, and then we'll rush the place before he has time to hide his tracks.'

'Who is this man and where does he live?'

'His name is Ralph Summertrees, and he lives in a very natty little bijou residence, as the advertisements call it, situated in no less a fashionable street than Park Lane.'

'I see. What has aroused your suspicions against him?'

'Well, you know, that's an expensive district to live in; it takes a bit of money to do the trick. This Summertrees has no ostensible business, yet every Friday he goes to the United Capital Bank in Piccadilly, and deposits a bag of swag, usually all silver coins.'

'Yes, and this money?'

'This money, so far as we can learn, contains a good many of these new pieces which never saw the British Mint.'

'It's not all the new coinage, then?'

'Oh no, he's a bit too artful for that. You see, a man can go round London, his pockets filled with new coinage five-shilling pieces, buy this, that, and the other, and come home with his change in legitimate coins of the realm – half-crowns, florins, shillings, sixpences, and all that.'

'I see. Then why don't you nab him one day when his pockets are stuffed with illegitimate five-shilling pieces?'

'That could be done, of course, and I've thought of it, but, you see, we want to land the whole gang. Once we arrest him, without knowing where the money came from, the real coiners would take flight.'

'How do you know he is not the real coiner himself?'

Now poor Hale is as easy to read as a book. He hesitated before answering this question, and looked confused as a culprit caught in some dishonest act.

'You need not be afraid to tell me,' I said soothingly after a pause. 'You have had one of your men in Mr Summertrees's house, and so learned that he is not the coiner. But your man has not succeeded in getting you evidence to incriminate other people.'

'You've about hit it again, Monsieur Valmont. One of my men has been Summertrees's butler for two weeks, but, as you say, he has found no evidence.'

'Is he still butler?'

'Yes.'

'Now tell me how far you have got. You know that Summertrees deposits a bag of coin every Friday in the Piccadilly bank, and I suppose the bank has allowed you to examine one or two of the bags.'

'Yes, sir, they have, but, you see, banks are very difficult to treat with. They don't like detectives bothering round, and while they do not stand out against the law, still they never answer any more questions than they're asked, and Mr Summertrees has been a good customer at the United Capital for many years.'

'Haven't you found out where the money comes from?'

'Yes, we have; it is brought there night after night by a

man who looks like a respectable city clerk and he puts it into a large safe, of which he holds the key, this safe being on the ground floor, in the dining-room.'

'Haven't you followed the clerk?'

'Yes. He sleeps in the Park Lane house every night, and goes up in the morning to an old curiosity shop in Tottenham Court Road, where he stays all day, returning with his bag of money in the evening.'

'Why don't you arrest and question him?'

'Well, Monsieur Valmont, there is just the same objection to his arrest as to that of Summertrees himself. We could easily arrest both, but we have not the slightest evidence against either of them, and then, although we put the go-betweens in clink, the worst criminals of the lot would escape.'

'Nothing suspicious about the old curiosity shop?'

'No. It appears to be perfectly regular.'

'This game has been going on under your noses for how long?'

'For about six weeks.'

'Is Summertrees a married man?'

'No.'

'Are there any women servants in the house?'

'No, except that three charwomen come in every morning to do up the rooms.'

'Of what is his household comprised?'

'There is the butler, then the valet, and last, the French cook.'

'Ah,' cried I, 'the French cook! This case interests me. So Summertrees has succeeded in completely disconcerting your man? Has he prevented him going from top to bottom of the house?'

'Oh no, he has rather assisted him than otherwise. On one occasion he went to the safe, took out the money, had Podgers – that's my chap's name – help him to count it, and then actually sent Podgers to the bank with the bag of coin.'

'And Podgers has been all over the place?'

'Yes.'

'Saw no signs of a coining establishment?'

'No. It is absolutely impossible that any coining can be done there. Besides, as I tell you, that respectable clerk brings him the money.'

'I suppose you want me to take Podgers' position?'

'Well, Monsieur Valmont, to tell you the truth, I would rather you didn't. Podgers has done everything a man can do, but I thought if you got into the house, Podgers assisting, you might go through it night after night at your leisure.'

'I see. That's just a little dangerous in England. I think I should prefer to assure myself the legitimate standing of being the amiable Podgers' successor. You say that Summertrees has no business?'

'Well, sir, not what you might call a business. He is by way of being an author, but I don't count that any business.'

'Oh, an author, is he? When does he do his writing?'

'He locks himself up most of the day in his study.'

'Does he come out for lunch?'

'No; he lights a little spirit lamp inside, Podgers tells me, and makes himself a cup of coffee, which he takes with a sandwich or two.'

'That's rather frugal fare for Park Lane.'

'Yes, Monsieur Valmont, it is, but he makes it up in the evening, when he has a long dinner with all them foreign kickshaws you people like, done by his French cook.'

'Sensible man! Well, Hale, I see I shall look forward with pleasure to making the acquaintance of Mr Summertrees. Is there any restriction on the going and coming of your man Podgers?'

'None in the least. He can get away either night or day.'

'Very good, friend Hale, bring him here tomorrow, as soon as our author locks himself up in his study, or rather, I should say, as soon as the respectable clerk leaves for Tottenham Court Road, which I should guess, as you put it, is about half an hour after his master turns the key of the room in which he writes.'

'You are quite right in that guess, Valmont. How did you hit it?'

'Merely a surmise, Hale. There is a good deal of oddity about that Park Lane house, so it doesn't surprise me in the least that the master gets to work earlier in the morning than the man. I have also a suspicion that Ralph Summertrees knows perfectly well what the estimable Podgers is there for.'

'What makes you think that?'

'I can give no reason except that my opinion of the acuteness of Summertrees has been gradually rising all the while you were speaking, and at the same time my estimate of Podgers' craft has been as steadily declining. However, bring the man here tomorrow, that I may ask him a few questions.'

*

Next day, about eleven o'clock, the ponderous Podgers, hat in hand, followed his chief into my room. His broad, impassive, immobile smooth face gave him rather more the air of a genuine butler than I had expected, and this appearance, of course, was enhanced by his livery. His replies to my questions were those of a well-trained servant who will not say too much unless it is made worth his while. All in all, Podgers exceeded my expectations, and really my friend Hale had some justification for regarding him, as he evidently did, as a triumph in his line.

'Sit down, Mr Hale, and you, Podgers.'

The man disregarded my invitation, standing like a statue until his chief made a motion; then he dropped into a chair. The English are great on discipline.

'Now, Mr Hale, I must first congratulate you on the make-up of Podgers. It is excellent. You depend less on artificial assistance than we do in France, and in that I think you are right.'

'Oh, we know a bit over here, Monsieur Valmont,' said Hale, with pardonable pride.

'Now then, Podgers, I want to ask you about this clerk. What time does he arrive in the evening?'

'At prompt six, sir.'

'Does he ring, or let himself in with a latchkey?'

'With a latchkey, sir.'

'How does he carry the money?'

'In a little locked leather satchel, sir, flung over his shoulder.'

'Does he go direct to the dining-room?'

'Yes, sir.'

'Have you seen him unlock the safe and put in the money?'

'Yes, sir.'

'Does the safe unlock with a word or a key?'

'With a key, sir. It's one of the old-fashioned kind.'

'Then the clerk unlocks his leather money bag?'

'Yes, sir.'

'That's three keys used within as many minutes. Are they separate or in a bunch?'

'In a bunch, sir.'

'Did you ever see your master with this bunch of keys?'

'No, sir.'

'You saw him open the safe once, I am told?'

'Yes, sir.'

'Did he use a separate key, or one of a bunch?'

Podgers slowly scratched his head, then said,

'I don't just remember, sir.'

'Ah, Podgers, you are neglecting the big things in that house. Sure you can't remember?'

'No, sir.'

'Once the money is in and the safe locked up, what does the clerk do?'

'Goes to his room, sir.'

'Where is this room?'

'On the third floor, sir.'

'Where do you sleep?'

'On the fourth floor with the rest of the servants, sir.'

'Where does the master sleep?'

'On the second floor, adjoining his study.'

'The house consists of four storeys and a basement, does it?'

'Yes, sir.'

'I have somehow arrived at the suspicion that it is a very narrow house. Is that true?'

'Yes, sir.'

'Does the clerk ever dine with your master?'

'No, sir. The clerk don't eat in the house at all, sir.'

'Does he go away before breakfast?'

'No, sir.'

'No one takes breakfast to his room?'

'No, sir.'

'What time does he leave the house?'

'At ten o'clock, sir.'

'When is breakfast served?'

'At nine o'clock, sir.'

'At what hour does your master retire to his study?'

'At half past nine, sir.'

'Locks the door on the inside?'

'Yes, sir.'

'Never rings for anything during the day?'

'Not that I know of, sir.'

'What sort of a man is he?'

Here Podgers was on familiar ground, and he rattled off a description minute in every particular.

'What I meant was, Podgers, is he silent, or talkative, or does he get angry? Does he seem furtive, suspicious, anxious, terrorized, calm, excitable, or what?'

'Well, sir, he is by way of being very quiet, never has much to say for himself; never saw him angry, or excited.'

'Now, Podgers, you've been at Park Lane for a fortnight

or more. You are a sharp, alert, observant man. What happens there that strikes you as unusual?'

'Well, I can't exactly say, sir,' replied Podgers, looking rather helplessly from his chief to myself, and back again.

'Your professional duties have often compelled you to enact the part of butler before, otherwise you wouldn't do it so well. Isn't that the case?'

Podgers did not reply, but glanced at his chief. This was evidently a question pertaining to the service, which a subordinate was not allowed to answer. However, Hale said at once,

'Certainly. Podgers has been in dozens of places.'

'Well, Podgers, just call to mind some of the other households where you have been employed, and tell me any particulars in which Mr Summertrees's establishment differs from them.'

Podgers pondered a long time.

'Well, sir, he do stick to writing pretty close.'

'Ah, that's his profession, you see, Podgers. Hard at it from half past nine till towards seven, I imagine?'

'Yes, sir.'

'Anything else, Podgers? No matter how trivial.'

'Well, sir, he's fond of reading too; leastways he's fond of newspapers.'

'When does he read?'

'I've never seen him read 'em, sir; indeed, so far as I can tell, I never knew the papers to be opened, but he takes them all in, sir.'

'What, all the morning papers?'

'Yes, sir, and all the evening papers too.'

'Where are the morning papers placed?'

'On the table in his study, sir.'

'And the evening papers?'

'Well, sir, when the evening papers come, the study is locked. They are put on a side table in the dining-room, and he takes them upstairs with him to his study.'

'This has happened every day since you've been there?'

'Yes, sir.'

'You reported that very striking fact to your chief, of course?'

'No, sir, I don't think I did,' said Podgers, confused.

'You should have done so. Mr Hale would have known how to make the most of a point so vital.'

'Oh, come now, Valmont,' interrupted Hale, 'you're chaffing us. Plenty of people take in all the papers!'

'I think not. Even clubs and hotels subscribe to the leading journals only. You said *all*, I think, Podgers?'

'Well, *nearly* all, sir.'

'But which is it? There's a vast difference.'

'He takes a good many, sir.'

'How many?'

'I don't just know, sir.'

'That's easily found out, Valmont,' cried Hale, with some impatience, 'if you think it really important.'

'I think it so important that I'm going back with Podgers myself. You can take me into the house, I suppose, when you return?'

'Oh yes, sir.'

'Coming back to these newspapers for a moment, Podgers. What is done with them?'

'They are sold to the ragman, sir, once a week.'

'Who takes them from the study?'

'I do, sir.'

'Do they appear to have been read very carefully?'

'Well, no, sir; leastways, some of them seem never to have been opened, or else folded up very carefully again.'

'Did you notice that extracts have been clipped from any of them?'

'No, sir.'

'Does Mr Summertrees keep a scrapbook?'

'Not that I know of, sir.'

'Oh, the case is perfectly plain,' said I, leaning back in my chair, and regarding the puzzled Hale with that cherubic expression of self-satisfaction which I know is so annoying to him.

'*What's* perfectly plain?' he demanded, more gruffly perhaps than etiquette would have sanctioned.

'Summertrees is no coiner, nor is he linked with any band of coiners.'

'What is he, then?'

'Ah, that opens another avenue of inquiry. For all I know to the contrary, he may be the most honest of men. On the surface it would appear that he is a reasonably industrious tradesman in Tottenham Court Road, who is anxious that there should be no visible connection between a plebeian employment and so aristocratic a residence as that in Park Lane.'

At this point Spenser Hale gave expression to one of those rare flashes of reason which are always an astonishment to his friends.

'That is nonsense, Monsieur Valmont,' he said, 'the man who is ashamed of the connection between his business and his house is one who is trying to get into Society, or else the women of his family are trying it, as is usually the case. Now Summertrees has no family. He himself goes nowhere, gives no entertainments, and accepts no invitations. He belongs to no club, therefore to say that he is ashamed of his connection with the Tottenham Court Road shop is absurd. He is concealing the connection for some other reason that will bear looking into.'

'My dear Hale, the goddess of Wisdom herself could not have made a more sensible series of remarks. Now, *mon ami*, do you want my assistance, or have you enough to go on with?'

'Enough to go on with? We have nothing more than we had when I called on you last night.'

'Last night, my dear Hale, you supposed this man was in league with coiners. Today you know he is not.'

'I know you *say* he is not.'

I shrugged my shoulders, and raised my eyebrows, smiling at him.

'It is the same thing, Monsieur Hale.'

'Well, of all the conceited –' and the good Hale could go no further.

'If you wish my assistance, it is yours.'

'Very good. Not to put too fine a point upon it, I do.'

'In that case, my dear Podgers, you will return to the residence of our friend Summertrees, and get together for me in a bundle all of yesterday's morning and evening papers, that were delivered to the house. Can you do that, or are they mixed up in a heap in the coal cellar?'

'I can do it, sir. I have instructions to place each day's papers in a pile by itself in case they should be wanted again. There is always one week's supply in the cellar and we sell the papers of the week before to the ragman.'

'Excellent. Well, take the risk of abstracting one day's journals, and have them ready for me. I will call upon you at half past three o'clock exactly, and then I want you to take me upstairs to the clerk's bedroom in the third storey, which I suppose is not locked during the daytime?'

'No, sir, it is not.'

With this the patient Podgers took his departure. Spenser Hale rose when his assistant left.

'Anything further I can do?' he asked.

'Yes; give me the address of the shop in Tottenham Court Road. Do you happen to have about you one of those new five-shilling pieces which you believe to be illegally coined?'

He opened his pocket-book, took out the bit of white metal, and handed it to me.

'I'm going to pass this off before evening,' I said, putting it in my pocket, 'and I hope none of your men will arrest me.'

'That's all right,' laughed Hale as he took his leave.

At half past three Podgers was waiting for me, and opened the front door as I came up the steps, thus saving me the necessity of ringing. The house seemed strangely quiet. The French cook was evidently down in the basement, and we had probably all the upper part to ourselves, unless Summertrees was in his study, which I doubted. Podgers led me directly upstairs to the clerk's room on the third floor, walking on tip-toe, with an elephantine air of silence and secrecy combined, which struck me as unnecessary.

'I will make an examination of this room,' I said. 'Kindly wait for me down by the door of the study.'

The bedroom proved to be of respectable size when one considers the smallness of the house. The bed was all nicely made up, and there were two chairs in the room, but the usual washstand and swing-mirror were not visible. However, seeing a curtain at the farther end of the room, I drew it aside, and found, as I expected, a fixed lavatory in an alcove of perhaps four feet deep by five in width. As the room was about fifteen feet wide, this left two thirds of the space unaccounted for. A moment later, I opened a door which exhibited a closet filled with clothes hanging on hooks. This left a space of five feet between the clothes closet and the lavatory. I thought at first that the entrance to the secret stairway must have issued from the lavatory, but examining the boards closely, although they sounded hollow to the knuckles, they were quite evidently plain matchboarding, and not a concealed door. The entrance to the stairway, therefore, must issue from the clothes closet. The right-hand wall proved similar to the matchboarding of the lavatory as far as the casual eye or touch was concerned, but I saw at once it was a door. The latch turned out to be somewhat ingeniously operated by one of the hooks which held a pair of old trousers. I found that the hook, if pressed upward, allowed the door to swing outward, over the stairhead. Descending to the second floor, a similar latch let me in to a similar clothes closet in the room beneath. The two rooms were identical in size, one directly above the other, the only difference being that the lower room door gave into the study, instead of into the hall, as was the case with the upper chamber.

The study was extremely neat, either not much used, or the abode of a very methodical man. There was nothing on the table except a pile of that morning's papers. I walked to the farther end, turned the key in the lock, and came out upon the astonished Podgers.

'Well, I'm blowed!' exclaimed he.

'Quite so,' I rejoined, 'you've been tip-toeing past an empty room for the last two weeks. Now, if you'll come with me, Podgers, I'll show you how the trick is done.'

When he entered the study, I locked the door once more, and led the assumed butler, still tip-toeing through force of habit, up the stair into the top bedroom, and so out again, leaving everything exactly as we found it. We went down the main stair to the front hall, and there Podgers had my parcel of papers all neatly wrapped up. This bundle I carried to my flat, gave one of my assistants some instructions, and left him at work on the papers.

*

I took a cab to the foot of Tottenham Court Road, and walked up that street till I came to J. Simpson's old curiosity shop. After gazing at the well-filled windows for some time, I stepped inside, having selected a little iron crucifix displayed behind the pane; the work of some ancient craftsman.

I knew at once from Podgers' description that I was waited upon by the veritable respectable clerk who brought the bag of money each night to Park Lane, and who I was certain was no other than Ralph Summertrees himself.

There was nothing in his manner differing from that of any other quiet salesman. The price of the crucifix proved to be seven-and-six, and I threw down a sovereign to pay for it.

'Do you mind the change being all in silver, sir?' he asked, and I answered without any eagerness, although the question aroused a suspicion that had begun to be allayed.

'Not in the least.'

He gave me half-a-crown, three two-shilling pieces, and four separate shillings, all the coins being well-worn silver of the realm, the undoubted inartistic product of the reputable British Mint. This seemed to dispose of the theory that he was palming off illegitimate money. He asked me if I were interested in any particular branch of antiquity, and I replied that my curiosity was merely general, and exceedingly amateurish, whereupon he invited me to look around. This I proceeded to do, while he resumed the addressing and stamping of some wrapped-up pamphlets which I surmised to be copies of his catalogue.

He made no attempt either to watch me or to press his wares upon me. I selected at random a little ink-stand, and asked its price. It was two shillings, he said, whereupon I produced my fraudulent five-shilling piece. He took it, gave me the change without comment, and the last doubt about his connection with coiners flickered from my mind.

At this moment a young man came in, who, I saw at once, was not a customer. He walked briskly to the farther end of the shop, and disappeared behind a partition which had one pane of glass in it that gave an outlook towards the front door.

'Excuse me a moment,' said the shopkeeper, and he followed the young man into the private office.

As I examined the curious heterogeneous collection of things for sale, I heard the clink of coins being poured out on the lid of a desk or an uncovered table, and the murmur of voices floated out to me. I was now near the entrance of the shop, and by a sleight-of-hand trick, keeping the corner of my eye on the glass pane of the private office, I removed the key of the front door without a sound, and took an impression of it in wax, returning the key to its place unobserved. At this moment another young man came in, and walked straight past me into the private office. I heard him say,

'Oh, I beg pardon, Mr Simpson. How are you, Rogers?'

'Hallo, Macpherson,' saluted Rogers, who then came out, bidding good night to Mr Simpson, and departed whistling down the street, but not before he had repeated his phrase to another young man entering, to whom he gave the name of Tyrrel.

I noted these three names in my mind. Two others came in together, but I was compelled to content myself with memorizing their features, for I did not learn their names. These men were evidently collectors, for I heard the rattle of money in every case; yet here was a small shop, doing apparently very little business, for I had been within it for more than half an hour, and yet remained the only customer. If credit were given, one collector would certainly have been sufficient, yet five had come in, and had poured their contributions into the pile Summertrees was to take home with him that night.

I determined to secure one of the pamphlets which the man had been addressing. They were piled on a shelf behind the counter, but I had no difficulty in reaching across and taking the top one, which I slipped into my pocket. When the fifth young man went down the street Summertrees himself emerged, and this time he carried in his hand the well-filled locked leather satchel, with the straps dangling. It was now approaching half past five, and I saw he was eager to close up and get away.

'Anything else you fancy, sir?' he asked me.

'No, or rather yes and no. You have a very interesting collection here, but it's getting so dark I can hardly see.'

'I close at half past five, sir.'

'Ah, in that case,' I said, consulting my watch, 'I shall be pleased to call some other time.'

'Thank you, sir,' replied Summertrees quietly, and with that I took my leave.

From the corner of an alley on the other side of the street – I saw him put up the shutters with his own hands, then he emerged with overcoat on, and the money satchel slung across his shoulder. He locked the door, tested it with his knuckles, and walked down the street, carrying under one arm the pamphlets he had been addressing. I followed him some distance, saw him drop the pamphlets into the box at the first post office he passed, and walk rapidly towards his house in Park Lane.

When I returned to my flat and called in my assistant, he said,

'After putting to one side the regular advertisements of pills, soap, and what not, here is the only one common to all the newspapers, morning and evening alike. The advertisements are not identical, sir, but they have two points of similarity, or perhaps I should say three. They all profess to furnish a cure for absent-mindedness; they all ask that the applicant's chief hobby will be stated, and they all bear the same address: Dr Willoughby, in Tottenham Court Road.'

'Thank you,' said I, as he placed the scissored advertisements before me.

I read several of the announcements. They were all small, and perhaps that is why I had never noticed one of them in the newspapers, for certainly they were odd enough. Some asked for lists of absent-minded men, with the hobbies of each, and for these lists, prices of from one shilling to six were offered. In other clippings Dr Willoughby professed to be able to cure absent-mindedness. There were no fees, and no treatment, but a pamphlet would be sent, which, if it did not benefit the receiver, could do no harm. The doctor was unable to meet patients personally, nor could he enter into correspondence with them. The address was the same as that of the old curiosity shop in Tottenham Court Road. At this juncture I pulled the pamphlet from my pocket, and saw it was entitled *Christian Science and Absent Mindedness*, by Dr Stamford Willoughby, and at the end of the article was the statement contained in the advertisements, that Dr Willoughby would neither see patients nor hold any correspondence with them.

I drew a sheet of paper towards me, wrote to Dr Willoughby alleging that I was a very absent-minded man, and would be glad of his pamphlet, adding that my special hobby was the collecting of first editions. I then signed myself, 'Alport Webster, Imperial Flats, London, W.'

I may here explain that it is often necessary for me to see people under some other name than the well-known appellation of Eugène Valmont. There are two doors to my flat, and on one of these is painted, 'Eugène Valmont'; on the other there is a receptacle, into which can be slipped a sliding panel bearing any *nom de guerre* I choose. The same device is arranged on the ground floor, where the names of all the occupants of the building appear on the right-hand wall.

I sealed, addressed, and stamped my letter, then told my man to put out the name of Alport Webster, and if I did not happen to be in when anyone called upon that mythical person, he was to make an appointment for me.

It was nearly six o'clock next afternoon when the card of Angus Macpherson was brought in to Mr Alport Webster. I recognized the young man at once as the second who had entered the little shop carrying his tribute to Mr Simpson the day before. He held three volumes under his arm, and spoke in such a pleasant, insinuating sort of way, that I knew at once he was an adept at his profession of canvasser.

'Will you be seated, Mr Macpherson? In what can I serve you?'

He placed the three volumes, backs upward, on my table.

'Are you interested at all in first editions, Mr Webster?'

'It is the one thing I am interested in,' I replied; 'but unfortunately they often run into a lot of money.'

'That is true,' said Macpherson sympathetically, 'and I have here three books, one of which is an exemplification of what you say. This one costs a hundred pounds. The last copy that was sold by auction in London brought a hundred and twenty-three pounds. This next one is forty pounds, and the third ten pounds. At these prices I am certain you could not duplicate three such treasures in any book shop in Britain.'

I examined them critically, and saw at once that what he said was true. He was still standing on the opposite side of the table.

'Please take a chair, Mr Macpherson. Do you mean to say you go round London with a hundred and fifty pounds worth of goods under your arm in this careless way?'

The young man laughed.

'I run very little risk, Mr Webster. I don't suppose anyone I meet imagines for a moment there is more under my arm than perhaps a trio of volumes I have picked up in the fourpenny box to take home with me.'

I lingered over the volume for which he asked a hundred pounds, then said, looking across at him,

'How came you to be possessed of this book, for instance?'

He turned upon me a fine, open countenance, and answered without hesitation in the frankest possible manner,

'I am not in actual possession of it, Mr Webster. I am by way of being a connoisseur in rare and valuable books myself, although, of course I have little money with which to indulge in the collection of them. I am acquainted, however, with the lovers of desirable books in different quarters of London. These three volumes, for instance, are from the library of a private gentleman in the West End. I have sold many books to him, and he knows I am trustworthy. He wishes to dispose of them at something under their real value, and has kindly allowed me to conduct the negotiation. I make it my business to find out those who are interested in rare books, and by such trading I add considerably to my income.'

'How, for instance, did you learn that I was a bibliophile?'

Mr Macpherson laughed genially.

'Well, Mr Webster, I must confess that I chanced it. I do that very often. I take a flat like this, and send in my card to the name on the door. If I am invited in, I ask the occupant the question I asked you just now: "Are you interested in rare editions?" If he says no, I simply beg pardon and retire. If he says yes, then I show my wares.'

'I see,' said I, nodding. What a glib young liar he was, with that innocent face of his, and yet my next question brought forth the truth.

'As this is the first time you have called upon me, Mr Macpherson, you have no objection to my making some further inquiry, I suppose. Would you mind telling me the name of the owner of these books in the West End?'

'His name is Mr Ralph Summertrees, of Park Lane.'

'Of Park Lane? Ah, indeed.'

'I shall be glad to leave the books with you, Mr Webster, and if you care to make an appointment with Mr Summertrees, I am sure he will not object to say a word in my favour.'

'Oh, I do not in the least doubt it, and should not think of troubling the gentleman.'

'I was going to tell you,' went on the young man, 'that I have a friend, a capitalist, who, in a way, is my supporter; for, as I said, I have little money of my own. I find it is often inconvenient for people to pay down any considerable sum. When, however, I strike a bargain, my capitalist buys the books, and I make an arrangement with my customer to pay a certain amount each week, and so even a large purchase is not felt, as I make the instalments small enough to suit my client.'

'You are employed during the day, I take it?'

'Yes, I am a clerk in the City.'

Again we were in the blissful realms of fiction!

'Suppose I take this book at ten pounds, what instalment should I have to pay each week?'

'Oh, what you like, sir. Would five shillings be too much?'

'I think not.'

'Very well, sir, if you pay me five shillings now, I will

leave the book with you, and shall have pleasure in calling this day week for the next instalment.'

I put my hand into my pocket, and drew out two half-crowns, which I passed over to him.

'Do I need to sign any form or undertaking to pay the rest?'

The young man laughed cordially.

'Oh no, sir, there is no formality necessary. You see, sir, this is largely a labour of love with me, although I don't deny I have my eye on the future. I am getting together what I hope will be a very valuable connection with gentlemen like yourself who are fond of books, and I trust some day that I may be able to resign my place with the insurance company and set up a choice little business of my own, where my knowledge of values in literature will prove useful.'

And then, after making a note in a little book he took from his pocket, he bade me a most graceful good-bye and departed, leaving me cogitating over what it all meant.

Next morning two articles were handed to me. The first came by post and was a pamphlet on *Christian Science and Absent Mindedness*, exactly similar to the one I had taken away from the old curiosity shop; the second was a small key made from my wax impression that would fit the front door of the same shop – a key fashioned by an excellent anarchist friend of mine in an obscure street near Holborn.

That night at ten o'clock I was inside the old curiosity shop, with a small storage battery in my pocket, and a little electric glow lamp at my buttonhole, a most useful instrument for either burglar or detective.

I had expected to find the books of the establishment in a safe, which, if it was similar to the one in Park Lane, I was prepared to open with the false keys in my possession or to take an impression of the keyhole and trust to my anarchist friend for the rest. But to my amazement I discovered all the papers pertaining to the concern in a desk which was not even locked. The books, three in number, were the ordinary day book, journal, and ledger referring to the shop; book-keeping of the older fashion; but in a portfolio lay half a dozen foolscap sheets, headed 'Mr Rogers's List', 'Mr Macpherson's', 'Mr Tyrrel's', the names I had already learned, and three others. These lists contained in the first column, names; in the second column, addresses; in the third, sums of money; and then in the small, square places following were amounts ranging from two-and-sixpence to a pound. At the bottom of Mr Macpherson's list was the name Alport Webster, Imperial Flats, £10; then in the small, square place, five shillings. These six sheets, each headed by a canvasser's name, were evidently the record of current collections, and the innocence of the whole thing was so apparent that if it were not for my fixed rule never to believe that I am at the bottom of any case until I have come on something suspicious, I would have gone out as empty-handed as I came in.

The six sheets were loose in a thin portfolio, but standing on a shelf above the desk were a number of fat volumes, one of which I took down, and saw that it contained similar lists running back several years. I noticed on Mr Macpherson's current list the name of Lord Semptam, an eccentric old nobleman whom I knew slightly. Then turning to the list immediately before the current one the name was still there; I traced it back through list after list until I found the first entry, which was no less than three years previous, and there Lord Semptam was down for a piece of furniture costing fifty pounds, and on that account he had paid a pound a week for more than three years, totalling a hundred and seventy pounds at the least, and instantly the glorious simplicity of the scheme dawned upon me, and I became so interested in the swindle that I lit the gas, fearing my little lamp would be exhausted before my investigation ended, for it promised to be a long one.

In several instances the intended victim proved shrewder than old Simpson had counted upon and the word 'Settled' had been written on the line carrying the name when the exact number of instalments was paid. But as these shrewd persons dropped out, others took their places, and Simpson's dependence on their absent-mindedness seemed to be justified in nine cases out of ten. His collectors were collecting long after the debt had been paid. In Lord Semptam's case, the payment had evidently become chronic, and the old man was giving away his pound a week to the suave Macpherson two years after his debt had been liquidated.

From the big volume I detached the loose leaf, dated 1893, which recorded Lord Semptam's purchase of a carved table for fifty pounds, and on which he had been paying a pound a week from that time to the date of which I am writing, which was November 1896. This single document taken from the file of three years previous, was not likely to be missed, as would have been the case if I had selected a current sheet. I nevertheless made a copy of the names and addresses of Macpherson's present clients; then, carefully placing everything exactly as I had found it, I extinguished the gas, and went out of the shop, locking the door behind me. With the 1893 sheet in my pocket I resolved to prepare a pleasant little surprise for my suave friend Macpherson when he called to get his next instalment of five shillings.

Late as was the hour when I reached Trafalgar Square, I could not deprive myself of the felicity of calling on Mr Spenser Hale, who I knew was then on duty. He never appeared at his best during office hours, because officialism stiffened his stalwart frame. Mentally he was impressed with the importance of his position, and added to this he was not then allowed to smoke his big, black pipe and terrible tobacco. He received me with the curtness I had been taught to expect when I inflicted myself upon him at his office. He greeted me abruptly with,

'I say, Valmont, how long do you expect to be on this job?'

'What job?' I asked mildly.

'Oh, you know what I mean : the Summertrees affair.'

'Oh, *that*!' I exclaimed, with surprise. 'The Summertrees case is already completed, of course. If I had known you were in a hurry, I should have finished up everything yesterday, but as you and Podgers, and I don't know how many more, have been at it sixteen or seventeen days, if not longer, I thought I might venture to take as many hours, as I am working entirely alone. You said nothing about haste, you know.'

'Oh, come now, Valmont, that's a bit thick. Do you mean to say you have already got evidence against the man?'

'Evidence absolute and complete.'

'Then who are the coiners?'

'My most estimable friend, how often have I told you not to jump at conclusions? I informed you when you first spoke to me about the matter that Summertrees was neither a coiner nor a confederate of coiners. I secured evidence sufficient to convict him of quite another offence, which is probably unique in the annals of crime. I have penetrated the mystery of the shop, and discovered the reason for all those suspicious actions which quite properly set you on his trail. Now I wish you to come to my flat next Wednesday night at a quarter to six, prepared to make an arrest.'

'I must know who I am to arrest, and on what counts.'

'Quite so, *mon ami* Hale; I did not say you were to make an arrest, but merely warned you to be prepared. If you have time now to listen to the disclosures, I am quite at your service. I promise you there are some original features in the case. If, however, the present moment is inopportune, drop in on me at your convenience, previously telephoning so that you may know whether I am there or not, and thus your valuable time will not be expended purposelessly.'

With this I presented to him my most courteous bow, and although his mystified expression hinted a suspicion that he thought I was chaffing him, as he would call it, official dignity dissolved somewhat, and he intimated his desire to hear all about it then and there. I had succeeded in arousing my friend Hale's curiosity. He listened to the evidence with perplexed brow, and at last ejaculated he would be blessed.

'This young man,' I said, in conclusion, 'will call upon me at six on Wednesday afternoon, to receive his second five shillings. I propose that you, in your uniform, shall be seated there with me to receive him, and I am anxious to study Mr Macpherson's countenance when he realizes he has walked in to confront a policeman. If you will then allow me to cross-examine him for a few moments, not after the manner of Scotland Yard, with a warning lest he incriminate himself, but in the free and easy fashion we adopt in Paris, I shall afterwards turn the case over to you to be dealt with at your discretion.'

'You have a wonderful flow of language, Monsieur Valmont,' was the officer's tribute to me. 'I shall be on hand at a quarter to six on Wednesday.'

'Meanwhile,' said I, 'kindly say nothing of this to anyone. We must arrange a complete surprise for Macpherson. That is essential. Please make no move in the matter at all until Wednesday night.'

Spenser Hale, much impressed, nodded acquiescence, and I took a polite leave of him.

*

The question of lighting is an important one in a room such as mine, and electricity offers a good deal of scope to the ingenious. Of this fact I have taken full advantage. I can manipulate the lighting of my room so that any particular spot is bathed in brilliancy, while the rest of the space remains in comparative gloom, and I arranged the lamps so that the full force of their rays impinged against the door that Wednesday evening, while I sat on one side of the table in semi-darkness and Hale sat on the other, with a light beating down on him from above which gave him the odd, sculptured look of a living statue of Justice, stern and triumphant. Anyone entering the room would first be dazzled by the light, and next would see the gigantic form of Hale in the full uniform of his order.

When Angus Macpherson was shown into this room he was quite visibly taken aback, and paused abruptly on the threshold, his gaze riveted on the huge policeman. I think his first purpose was to turn and run, but the door closed behind him, and he doubtless heard, as we all did, the sound of the bolt being thrust in its place, thus locking him in.

'I – I beg your pardon,' he stammered, 'I expected to meet Mr Webster.'

As he said this, I pressed the button under my table, and was instantly enshrouded with light. A sickly smile overspread the countenance of Macpherson as he caught sight of me, and he made a very creditable attempt to carry off the situation with nonchalance.

'Oh, there you are, Mr Webster; I did not notice you at first.'

It was a tense moment. I spoke slowly and impressively.

'Sir, perhaps you are not unacquainted with the name of Eugène Valmont.'

He replied brazenly,

'I am sorry to say, sir, I never heard of the gentleman before.'

At this came a most inopportune 'Haw-haw' from that blockhead Spenser Hale, completely spoiling the dramatic situation I had elaborated with such thought and care. It is little wonder the English possess no drama, for they show scant appreciation of the sensational moments in life.

'Haw-haw,' brayed Spenser Hale, and at once reduced the emotional atmosphere to a fog of commonplace. However, what is a man to do? He must handle the tools with which it pleases Providence to provide him. I ignored Hale's untimely laughter.

'Sit down, sir,' I said to Macpherson, and he obeyed.

'You have called on Lord Semptam this week,' I continued sternly.

'Yes, sir.'

'And collected a pound from him?'

'Yes, sir.'

'In October 1893 you sold Lord Semptam a carved antique table for fifty pounds?'

'Quite right, sir.'

'When you were here last week you gave me Ralph Summertrees as the name of a gentleman living in Park Lane. You knew at the time that this man was your employer?'

Macpherson was now looking fixedly at me, and on this occasion made no reply. I went on calmly,

'You also knew that Summertrees, of Park Lane, was identical with Simpson, of Tottenham Court Road?'

'Well, sir,' said Macpherson, 'I don't exactly see what you're driving at, but it's quite usual for a man to carry on a business under an assumed name. There is nothing illegal about that.'

'We will come to the illegality in a moment, Mr Macpherson. You, and Rogers, and Tyrrel, and three others, are confederates of this man Simpson.'

'We are in his employ; yes, sir, but no more confederates than clerks usually are.'

'I think, Mr Macpherson, I have said enough to show you that the game is, what you call, up. You are now in the presence of Mr Spenser Hale, from Scotland Yard, who is waiting to hear your confession.'

Here the stupid Hale broke in with his –

'And remember, sir, that anything you say will be –'

'Excuse me, Mr Hale,' I interrupted hastily, 'I shall turn over the case to you in a very few moments, but I ask you to remember our compact, and to leave it for the present entirely in my hands. Now, Mr Macpherson, I want your confession, and I want it at once.'

'Confession? Confederates?' protested Macpherson with admirably simulated surprise. 'I must say you use extraordinary terms, Mr – Mr – What did you say the name was?'

'Haw-haw,' roared Hale. 'His name is Monsieur Valmont.'

'I implore you, Mr Hale, to leave this man to me for a very few moments. Now, Macpherson, what have you to say in your defence?'

'Where nothing criminal has been alleged, Monsieur Valmont, I see no necessity for defence. If you wish me to admit that somehow you have acquired a number of details regarding our business, I am perfectly willing to do so, and to subscribe to their accuracy. If you will be good enough to let me know of what you complain, I shall endeavour to make the point clear to you if I can. There has evidently been some misapprehension, but for the life of me, without further explanation, I am as much in a fog as I was on my way coming here, for it is getting a little thick outside.'

Macpherson certainly was conducting himself with great discretion, and presented, quite unconsciously, a much more diplomatic figure than my friend, Spenser Hale, sitting stiffly opposite me. His tone was one of mild expostulation, mitigated by the intimation that all misunderstanding speedily would be cleared away. To outward view he offered a perfect picture of innocence, neither protesting too much nor too little. I had, however, another surprise in store for him, a trump card, as it were, and I played it down on the table.

'There!' I cried with vim, 'have you ever seen that sheet before!'

He glanced at it without offering to take it in his hand.

'Oh yes,' he said, 'that has been abstracted from our file. It is what I call my visiting list.'

'Come, come, sir,' I cried sternly, 'you refuse to confess, but I warn you we know all about it. You never heard of Dr Willoughby, I suppose?'

'Yes, he is the author of the silly pamphlet on Christian Science.'

'You are in the right, Mr Macpherson; on Christian Science and Absent Mindedness.'

'Possibly. I haven't read it for a long while.'

119

'Have you ever met this learned doctor, Mr Macpherson?'

'Oh yes. Dr Willoughby is the pen-name of Mr Summertrees. He believes in Christian Science and that sort of thing, and writes about it.'

'Ah, really. We are getting your confession bit by bit, Mr Macpherson. I think it would be better to be quite frank with us.'

'I was just going to make the same suggestion to you, Monsieur Valmont. If you will tell me in a few words exactly what is your charge against either Mr Summertrees or myself, I will know then what to say.'

'We charge you, sir, with obtaining money under false pretences, which is a crime that has landed more than one distinguished financier in prison.'

Spenser Hale shook his fat forefinger at me, and said,

'Tut, tut, Valmont; we mustn't threaten, we mustn't threaten, you know;' but I went on without heeding him.

'Take for instance, Lord Semptam. You sold him a table for fifty pounds, on the instalment plan. He was to pay a pound a week, and in less than a year the debt was liquidated. But he is an absent-minded man, as all your clients are. That is why you came to me. I had answered the bogus Willoughby's advertisement. And so you kept on collecting and collecting for something more than three years. Now do you understand the charge?'

Mr Macpherson's head during this accusation was held slightly inclined to one side. At first his face was clouded by the most clever imitation of anxious concentration of mind I had ever seen, and this was gradually cleared away by the dawn of awakening perception. When I had finished, an ingratiating smile hovered about his lips.

'Really, you know,' he said, 'that is rather a capital scheme. The absent-minded league, as one might call them. Most ingenious. Summertrees, if he had any sense of humour, which he hasn't, would be rather taken by the idea that his innocent fad for Christian Science had led him to be suspected of obtaining money under false pretences. But, really, there are no pretensions about the matter at all. As I understand it, I simply call and receive the money through the forgetfulness of the persons on my list, but where I think you would have both Summertrees and myself, if there was anything in your audacious theory, would be an indictment for conspiracy. Still, I quite see how the mistake arises. You have jumped to the conclusion that we sold nothing to Lord Semptam except that carved table three years ago. I have pleasure in pointing out to you that his lordship is a frequent customer of ours, and has had many things from us at one time or another. Sometimes he is in our debt; sometimes we are in his. We keep a sort of running contract with him by which he pays us a pound a week. He and several other customers deal on the same plan, and in return for an income that we can count upon, they get the first offer of anything in which they are supposed to be interested. As I have told you, we call these sheets in the office our visiting lists, but to make the visiting lists complete you need what we term our encyclopaedia. We call it that because it is in so many volumes; a volume for each year, running back I don't know how long. You will notice little figures here from time to time above the amount stated on this visiting list. These figures refer to the page of the encyclopaedia for the current year, and on that page is noted the new sale, and the amount of it, as it might be set down, say, in a ledger.'

'That is a very entertaining explanation, Mr Macpherson. I suppose this encyclopaedia, as you call it, is in the shop at Tottenham Court Road?'

'Oh no, sir. Each volume of the encyclopaedia is self-locking. These books contain the real secret of our business, and they are kept in the safe at Mr Summertrees's house in Park Lane. Take Lord Semptam's account, for instance. You will find in faint figures under a certain date, 102. If you turn to page 102 of the encyclopaedia for that year, you will then see a list of what Lord Semptam has bought, and the prices he was charged for them. It is really a very simple matter. If you will allow me to use your telephone for a moment, I will ask Mr Summertrees, who has not yet begun dinner, to bring with him here the volume for 1893, and, within a quarter of an hour, you will be perfectly satisfied that everything is quite legitimate.'

I confess that the young man's naturalness and confidence staggered me, the more so as I saw by the sarcastic smile on Hale's lips that he did not believe a single word spoken. A portable telephone stood on the table, and as Macpherson finished his explanation, he reached over and drew it towards him. Then Spenser Hale interfered.

'Excuse *me*,' he said. 'I'll do the telephoning. What is the call number of Mr Summertrees?'

'140 Hyde Park.'

Hale at once called up Central, and presently was answered from Park Lane. We heard him say.

'Is that the residence of Mr Summertrees? Oh, is that you, Podgers? Is Mr Summertrees in? Very well. This is Hale. I am in Valmont's flat – Imperial Flats – you know. Yes, where you went with me the other day. Very well, go to Mr Summertrees, and say to him that Mr Macpherson wants the encyclopaedia for 1893. Do you get that? Yes, encyclopaedia. Oh, he'll understand what it is. Mr Macpherson. No, don't mention my name at all. Just say Mr Macpherson wants the encyclopaedia for the year 1893, and that you are to bring it. Yes, you may tell him that Mr Macpherson is at Imperial Flats, but don't mention my name at all. Exactly. As soon as he gives you the book, get into a cab, and come here as quickly as possible with it. If Summertrees doesn't want to let the book go, then tell him to come with you. If he won't do that, place him under arrest, and bring both him and the book here. All right. Be as quick as you can; we're waiting.'

Macpherson made no protest against Hale's use of the telephone; he merely sat back in his chair, with a resigned expression on his face which, if painted on canvas, might have been entitled 'The Falsely Accused'. When Hale rang off, Macpherson said,

'Of course you know your own business best, but if your man arrests Summertrees, he will make you the laughing-stock of London. There is such a thing as unjustifiable arrest, as well as getting money under false pretences, and Mr Summertrees is not the man to forgive an insult. And then, if you will allow me to say so, the more I think over your absent-minded theory, the more absolutely grotesque it seems, and if the case ever gets into the newspapers, I am sure, Mr Hale, you'll experience an uncomfortable half-hour with your chiefs at Scotland Yard.'

'I'll take the risk of that, thank you,' said Hale stubbornly.

'Am I to consider myself under arrest?' inquired the young man.

'No, sir.'

'Then, if you will pardon me, I shall withdraw. Mr Summertrees will show you everything you wish to see in his books, and can explain his business much more capably than I, because he knows more about it; therefore, gentlemen, I bid you good night.'

'No you don't. Not just yet awhile,' exclaimed Hale, rising to his feet simultaneously with the young man.

'Then I *am* under arrest,' protested Macpherson.

'You're not going to leave this room until Podgers brings that book.'

'Oh very well,' and he sat down again.

And now, as talking is dry work, I set out something to drink, a box of cigars, and a box of cigarettes. Hale mixed his favourite brew, but Macpherson, shunning the wine of his country, contented himself with a glass of plain mineral water, and lit a cigarette. Then he awoke my high regard by saying pleasantly as if nothing had happened,

'While we are waiting, Monsieur Valmont, may I remind you that you owe me five shillings?'

I laughed, took the coin from my pocket, and paid him, whereupon he thanked me.

'Are you connected with Scotland Yard, Monsieur Valmont?' asked Macpherson, with the air of a man trying to make conversation to bridge over a tedious interval; but before I could reply, Hale blurted out,

'Not likely!'

'You have no official standing as a detective, then, Monsieur Valmont?'

'None whatever,' I replied quickly, thus getting in my oar ahead of Hale.

'That is a loss to our country,' pursued this admirable young man, with evident sincerity.

I began to see I could make a good deal of so clever a fellow if he came under my tuition.

'The blunders of our police,' he went on, 'are something deplorable. If they would but take lessons in strategy, say, from France, their unpleasant duties would be so much more acceptably performed, with much less discomfort to their victims.'

'France,' snorted Hale in derision, 'why, they call a man guilty there until he's proven innocent.'

'Yes, Mr Hale, and the same seems to be the case in Imperial Flats. You have quite made up your mind that Mr Summertrees is guilty, and will not be content until he proves his innocence. I venture to predict that you will hear from him before long in a manner that may astonish you.'

Hale grunted and looked at his watch. The minutes passed very slowly as we sat there smoking, and at last even I began to get uneasy. Macpherson, seeing our anxiety, said that when he came in the fog was almost as thick as it had been the week before, and that there might be some difficulty in getting a cab. Just as he was speaking the door was unlocked from the outside, and Podgers entered, bearing a thick volume in his hand. This he gave to his superior, who turned over its pages in amazement, and then looked at the back, crying,

'*Encyclopaedia of Sport, 1893*! What sort of a joke is this, Mr Macpherson?'

There was a pained look on Mr Macpherson's face as he reached forward and took the book. He said with a sigh,

'If you had allowed me to telephone, Mr Hale, I should have made it perfectly plain to Summertrees what was wanted. I might have known this mistake was liable to occur. There is an increasing demand for out-of-date books of sport, and no doubt Mr Summertrees thought this was what I meant. There is nothing for it but to send your man back to Park Lane and tell Mr Summertrees that what we want is the locked volume of accounts for 1893, which we call the encyclopaedia. Allow me to write an order that will bring it. Oh, I'll show you what I have written before your man takes it,' he said, as Hale stood ready to look over his shoulder.

On my notepaper he dashed off a request such as he had outlined, and handed it to Hale, who read it and gave it to Podgers.

'Take that to Summertrees, and get back as quickly as possible. Have you a cab at the door?'

'Yes, sir.'

'Is it foggy outside?'

'Not so much, sir, as it was an hour ago. No difficulty about the traffic now, sir.'

'Very well, get back as soon as you can.'

Podgers saluted, and left with the book under his arm. Again the door was locked, and again we sat smoking in silence until the stillness was broken by the tinkle of the telephone. Hale put the receiver to his ear.

'Yes, this is the Imperial Flats. Yes. Valmont. Oh yes; Macpherson is here. What? Out of what? Can't hear you. Out of print. What, the encyclopaedia's out of print? Who is that speaking? Dr Willoughby; thanks.'

Macpherson rose as if he would go to the telephone, but instead (and he acted so quietly that I did not notice what he was doing until the thing was done), he picked up the sheet which he called his visiting list, and walking quite without haste, held it in the glowing coals of the fireplace until it disappeared in a flash of flame up the chimney. I sprang to my feet indignant, but too late to make even a motion towards saving the sheet. Macpherson regarded us both with that self-deprecatory smile which had several times lighted up his face.

'How dare you burn that sheet?' I demanded.

'Because, Monsieur Valmont, it did not belong to you; because you do not belong to Scotland Yard; because you stole it; because you had no right to it; and because you have no official standing in this country. If it had been in Mr Hale's possession I should not have dared, as you put it, to destroy the sheet, but as this sheet was abstracted from my master's premises by you, an entirely unauthorized person, whom he would have been justified in shooting dead if he had found you housebreaking and you had resisted him on his discovery, I took the liberty of destroying the document. I have always held that these sheets should not have been kept, for as has been the case, if they fell under the scrutiny of so intelligent a person as Eugène Valmont, improper inferences might have been drawn. Mr Summertrees, however, persisted in keeping them, but made this concession, that if I ever telegraphed him or telephoned him the word "Encyclopaedia", he would at once burn these records, and he, on his part, was to telegraph or telephone to me "The *Encyclopaedia* is out of print", whereupon I would know that he had succeeded.

'Now, gentlemen, open this door, which will save me the trouble of forcing it. Either put me formally under arrest, or cease to resist my liberty. I am very much obliged to Mr Hale for telephoning, and I have made no protest to so gallant a host as Monsieur Valmont is, because of the locked door. However, the farce is now terminated. The proceedings I have sat through were entirely illegal, and if you will pardon me, Mr Hale, they have been a little too French to go down here in old England, or to make a report in the newspapers that would be quite satisfactory to your chiefs. I demand either my formal arrest, or the unlocking of that door.'

In silence I pressed a button, and my man threw open the door. Macpherson walked to the threshold, paused, and looked back at Spenser Hale, who sat there silent as a sphinx.

'Good evening, Mr Hale.'

There being no reply, he turned to me with the same ingratiating smile.

'Good evening, Monsieur Eugène Valmont,' he said, 'I shall give myself the pleasure of calling next Wednesday at six for my five shillings.'

6

The Problem of Cell 13

Jacques Futrelle

I

PRACTICALLY all those letters remaining in the alphabet after Augustus S. F. X. Van Dusen was named were afterwards acquired by that gentleman in the course of a brilliant scientific career, and, being honorably acquired, were tacked on to the other end. His name, therefore, taken with all that belonged to it, was a wonderfully imposing structure. He was a Ph.D., an LL.D., an F.R.S., an M.D., and an M.D.S. He was also some other things – just what he himself couldn't say – through recognition of his ability by various foreign educational and scientific institutions.

In appearance he was no less striking than in nomenclature. He was slender with the droop of the student in his thin shoulders and the pallor of a close, sedentary life on his clean-shaven face. His eyes wore a perpetual, forbidding squint – the squint of a man who studies little things – and when they could be seen at all through his thick spectacles, were mere slits of watery blue. But above his eyes was his most striking feature. This was a tall, broad brow, almost abnormal in height and width, crowned by a heavy shock of bushy, yellow hair. All these things conspired to give him a peculiar, almost grotesque, personality.

Professor Van Dusen was remotely German. For generations his ancestors had been noted in the sciences; he was the logical result, the master mind. First and above all he was a logician. At least thirty-five years of the half-century or so of his existence had been devoted exclusively to proving that two and two always equal four, except in unusual cases, where they equal three or five, as the case may be. He stood broadly on the general proposition that all things that start must go somewhere, and was able to bring the concentrated mental force of his forefathers to bear on a given problem. Incidentally it may be remarked that Professor Van Dusen wore a No. 8 hat.

The world at large had heard vaguely of Professor Van Dusen as The Thinking Machine. It was a newspaper catch-phrase applied to him at the time of a remarkable exhibition at chess; he had demonstrated then that a stranger to the game might, by the force of inevitable logic, defeat a champion who had devoted a lifetime to its study. The Thinking Machine! Perhaps that more nearly described him than all his honorary initials, for he spent week after week, month after month, in the seclusion of his small laboratory from which had gone forth thoughts that staggered scientific associates and deeply stirred the world at large.

It was only occasionally that The Thinking Machine had visitors, and these were usually men who, themselves high in the sciences, dropped in to argue a point and perhaps convince themselves. Two of these men, Dr Charles Ransome and Alfred Fielding, called one evening to discuss some theory which is not of consequence here.

'Such a thing is possible,' declared Dr Ransome emphatically, in the course of the conversation.

'Nothing is impossible,' declared The Thinking Machine with equal emphasis. He always spoke petulantly. 'The mind is master of all things. When science fully recognizes that fact a great advance will have been made.'

'How about the airship?' asked Dr Ransome.

'That's not impossible at all,' asserted The Thinking Machine. 'It will be invented some time. I'd do it myself, but I'm busy.'

Dr Ransome laughed tolerantly.

'I've heard you say such things before,' he said. 'But they mean nothing. Mind may be master of matter, but it hasn't yet found a way to apply itself. There are some things that can't be *thought* out of existence, or rather which would not yield to any amount of thinking.'

'What, for instance?' demanded The Thinking Machine.

Dr Ransome was thoughtful for a moment as he smoked.

'Well, say prison walls,' he replied. 'No man can *think* himself out of a cell. If he could, there would be no prisoners.'

'A man can so apply his brain and ingenuity that he can leave a cell, which is the same thing,' snapped The Thinking Machine.

Dr Ransome was slightly amused.

'Let's suppose a case,' he said, after a moment. 'Take a cell where prisoners under sentence of death are confined – men who are desperate and, maddened by fear, would take any chance to escape – suppose you were locked in such a cell. Could you escape?'

'Certainly,' declared The Thinking Machine.

'Of course,' said Mr Fielding, who entered the conversation for the first time, 'you might wreck the cell with an explosive – but inside, a prisoner, you couldn't have that.'

'There would be nothing of that kind,' said The Thinking Machine. 'You might treat me precisely as you treated prisoners under sentence of death, and I would leave the cell.'

'Not unless you entered it with tools prepared to get out,' said Dr Ransome.

The Thinking Machine was visibly annoyed and his blue eyes snapped.

'Lock me in any cell in any prison anywhere at any time, wearing only what is necessary, and I'll escape in a week,' he declared, sharply.

Dr Ransome sat up straight in the chair, interested. Mr Fielding lighted a new cigar.

'You mean you could actually *think* yourself out?' asked Dr Ransome.

'I would get out,' was the response.

'Are you serious?'

'Certainly I am serious.'

Dr Ransome and Mr Fielding were silent for a long time.

'Would you be willing to try it?' asked Mr Fielding, finally.

'Certainly,' said Professor Van Dusen, and there was a trace of irony in his voice. 'I have done more asinine things than that to convince other men of less important truths.'

The tone was offensive and there was an under-current strongly resembling anger on both sides. Of course it was an absurd thing, but Professor Van Dusen reiterated his willingness to undertake the escape and it was decided upon.

'To begin now,' added Dr Ransome.

'I'd prefer that it begin tomorrow,' said The Thinking Machine, 'because –'

'No, now,' said Mr Fielding, flatly. 'You are arrested, figuratively, of course, without any warning locked in a cell with no chance to communicate with friends, and left there with identically the same care and attention that would be given to a man under sentence of death. Are you willing?'

'All right, now, then,' said The Thinking Machine, and he arose.

'Say, the death-cell in Chisholm Prison.'

'The death-cell in Chisholm Prison.'

'And what will you wear?'

'As little as possible,' said The Thinking Machine. 'Shoes, stockings, trousers, and a shirt.'

'You will permit yourself to be searched, of course?'

'I am to be treated precisely as all prisoners are treated,' said The Thinking Machine. 'No more attention and no less.'

There were some preliminaries to be arranged in the matter of obtaining permission for the test, but all three were influential men and everything was done satisfactorily by telephone, albeit the prison commissioners, to whom the experiment was explained on purely scientific grounds, were sadly bewildered. Professor Van Dusen would be the most distinguished prisoner they had ever entertained.

When The Thinking Machine had donned those things which he was to wear during his incarceration he called the little old woman who was his housekeeper, cook, and maid-servant all in one.

'Martha,' he said, 'it is now twenty-seven minutes past nine o'clock. I am going away. One week from tonight, at half past nine, these gentlemen and one, possibly two, others will take supper with me here. Remember Dr Ransome is very fond of artichokes.'

The three men were driven to Chisholm Prison, where the Warden was awaiting them, having been informed of the matter by telephone. He understood merely that the eminent Professor Van Dusen was to be his prisoner, if he could keep him, for one week; that he had committed no crime, but that he was to be treated as all other prisoners were treated.

'Search him,' instructed Dr Ransome.

The Thinking Machine was searched. Nothing was found on him; the pockets of the trousers were empty; the white, stiff-bosomed shirt had no pocket. The shoes and stockings were removed, examined, then replaced. As he watched all these preliminaries – the rigid search and noted the pitiful, childlike physical weakness of the man, the colourless face, and the thin, white hands – Dr Ransome almost regretted his part in the affair.

'Are you sure you want to do this?' he asked.

'Would you be convinced if I did not?' inquired The Thinking Machine in turn.

'No.'

'All right. I'll do it.'

What sympathy Dr Ransome had was dissipated by the

tone. It nettled him, and he resolved to see the experiment to the end; it would be a stinging reproof to egotism.

'It will be impossible for him to communicate with anyone outside?' he asked.

'Absolutely impossible,' replied the warden. 'He will not be permitted writing materials of any sort.'

'And your jailers, would they deliver a message from him?'

'Not one word, directly or indirectly,' said the warden. 'You may rest assured of that. They will report anything he might say or turn over to me anything he might give them.'

'That seems entirely satisfactory,' said Mr Fielding, who was frankly interested in the problem.

'Of course, in the event he fails,' said Dr Ransome, 'and asks for his liberty, you understand you are to set him free?'

'I understand,' replied the warden.

The Thinking Machine stood listening, but had nothing to say until this was all ended, then:

'I should like to make three small requests. You may grant them or not, as you wish.'

'No special favours, now,' warned Mr Fielding.

'I am asking none,' was the stiff response. 'I would like to have some tooth powder – buy it yourself to see that it is tooth powder – and I should like to have one five-dollar and two ten-dollar bills.'

Dr Ransome, Mr Fielding, and the warden exchanged astonished glances. They were not surprised at the request for tooth powder, but were at the request for money.

'Is there any man with whom our friend would come in contact that he could bribe with twenty-five dollars?' asked Dr Ransome of the warden.

'Not for twenty-five hundred dollars,' was the positive reply.

'Well, let him have them,' said Mr Fielding. 'I think they are harmless enough.'

'And what is the third request?' asked Dr Ransome.

'I should like to have my shoes polished.'

Again the astonished glances were exchanged. This last request was the height of absurdity, so they agreed to it. These things all being attended to, The Thinking Machine was led back into the prison from which he had undertaken to escape.

'Here is Cell 13,' said the warden, stopping three doors down the steel corridor. 'This is where we keep condemned murderers. No one can leave it without my permission; and no one in it can communicate with the outside. I'll stake my reputation on that. It's only three doors back of my office and I can readily hear any unusual noise.'

'Will this cell do, gentlemen?' asked The Thinking Machine. There was a touch of irony in his voice.

'Admirably,' was the reply.

The heavy steel door was thrown open, there was a great scurrying and scampering of tiny feet, and The Thinking Machine passed into the gloom of the cell. Then the door was closed and double locked by the warden.

'What is that noise in there?' asked Dr Ransome, through the bars.

'Rats – dozens of them,' replied The Thinking Machine, tersely.

The three men, with final good nights, were turning away when The Thinking Machine called:

'What time is it exactly, warden?'

'Eleven seventeen,' replied the warden.

'Thanks. I will join you gentlemen in your office at half past eight o'clock one week from tonight,' said The Thinking Machine.

'And if you do not?'

'There is no "if" about it.'

2

Chisholm Prison was a great, spreading structure of granite, four storeys in all, which stood in the centre of acres of open space. It was surrounded by a wall of solid masonry eighteen feet high, and so smoothly finished inside and out as to offer no foothold to a climber, no matter how expert. Atop of this fence, as a further precaution, was a five-foot fence of steel rods, each terminating in a keen point. This fence in itself marked an absolute deadline between freedom and imprisonment, for, even if a man escaped from his cell, it would seem impossible for him to pass the wall.

The yard, which on all sides of the prison building was twenty-five feet wide, that being the distance from the building to the wall, was by day an exercise ground for those prisoners to whom was granted the boon of occasional semi-liberty. But that was not for those in Cell 13. At all times of the day there were armed guards in the yard, four of them, one patrolling each side of the prison building.

By night the yard was almost as brilliantly lighted as by day. On each of the four sides was a great arc light which rose above the prison wall and gave to the guards a clear sight. The lights, too, brightly illuminated the spiked top of the wall. The wires which fed the arc lights ran up the side of the prison building on insulators and from the top storey led out to the poles supporting the arc lights.

All these things were seen and comprehended by The Thinking Machine, who was only enabled to see out of his closely barred cell window by standing on his bed. This was on the morning following his incarceration. He gathered, too, that the river lay over there beyond the wall somewhere, because he heard faintly the pulsation of a motor boat and high up in the air saw a river bird. From that same direction came the shouts of boys at play and the occasional crack of a batted ball. He knew then that between the prison wall and the river was an open space, a playground.

Chisholm Prison was regarded as absolutely safe. No man had ever escaped from it. The Thinking Machine, from his perch on the bed, seeing what he saw, could readily understand why. The walls of the cell, though built, he judged, twenty years before, were perfectly solid, and the window bars of new iron had not a shadow of rust on them. The window itself, even with the bars out, would be a difficult mode of egress because it was small.

Yet, seeing these things, The Thinking Machine was not discouraged. Instead, he thoughtfully squinted at the great arc light – there was bright sunlight now – and traced with his eyes the wire which led from it to the building. That electric wire, he reasoned, must come down the side of the building not a great distance from his cell. That might be worth knowing.

Cell 13 was on the same floor with the offices of the prison – that is, not in the basement, nor yet upstairs. There were only four steps up to the office floor, therefore the level of the floor must be only three or four feet above the ground. He couldn't see the ground directly beneath his window, but he could see it farther out towards the wall. It would be an easy drop from the window. Well and good.

Then The Thinking Machine fell to remembering how he had come to the cell. First, there was the outside guard's booth, a part of the wall. There were two heavily barred gates, both of steel. At this gate was one man always on guard. He admitted persons to the prison after much clanking of keys and locks, and let them out when ordered to do so. The warden's office was in the prison building, and in order to reach that official from the prison yard one had to pass a gate of solid steel with only a peep-hole in it. Then coming from that inner office to Cell 13, where he was now, one must pass a heavy wooden door and two steel doors into the corridors of the prison; and always there was the double-locked door of Cell 13 to reckon with.

There were then, The Thinking Machine recalled, seven doors to be overcome before one could pass from Cell 13 into the outer world, a free man. But against this was the fact that he was rarely interrupted. A jailer appeared at his cell door at six in the morning with a breakfast of prison fare; he would come again at noon, and again at six in the afternoon. At nine o'clock at night would come the inspection tour. That would be all.

'It's admirably arranged, this prison system,' was the mental tribute paid by The Thinking Machine. 'I'll have to study it a little when I get out. I had no idea there was such great care exercised in the prisons.'

There was nothing, positively nothing, in his cell, except his iron bed, so firmly put together that no man could tear it to pieces save with sledges or a file. He had neither of these. There was not even a chair, or a small table, or a bit of tin or crockery. Nothing! The jailer stood by when he ate, then took away the wooden spoon and bowl which he had used.

One by one these things sank into the brain of The Thinking Machine. When the last possibility had been considered he began an examination of his cell. From the roof, down the walls on all sides, he examined the stones and the cement between them. He stamped over the floor carefully time after time, but it was cement, perfectly solid. After the examination he sat on the edge of the iron bed and was lost in thought for a long time. For Professor Augustus S. F. X. Van Dusen, The Thinking Machine, had something to think about.

He was disturbed by a rat, which ran across his foot, then scampered away into a dark corner of the cell, frightened at its own daring. After a while The Thinking Machine, squinting steadily into the darkness of the corner where the rat had gone, was able to make out in the gloom many little beady eyes staring at him. He counted six pair, and there were perhaps others; he didn't see very well.

Then The Thinking Machine, from his seat on the bed, noticed for the first time the bottom of his cell door. There was an opening there of two inches between the steel bar and the floor. Still looking steadily at this opening, The Thinking Machine backed suddenly into the corner where he had seen the beady eyes. There was a great scampering of tiny feet, several squeaks of frightened rodents, and then silence.

None of the rats had gone out the door, yet there were none in the cell. Therefore there must be another way out of the cell, however small. The Thinking Machine, on hands and knees, started a search for this spot, feeling in the darkness with his long, slender fingers.

At last his search was rewarded. He came upon a small opening in the floor, level with the cement. It was perfectly round and somewhat larger than a silver dollar. This was the way the rats had gone. He put his fingers deep into the opening; it seemed to be a disused drainage pipe and was dry and dusty.

Having satisfied himself on this point, he sat on the bed again for an hour, then made another inspection of his surroundings through the small cell window. One of the outside guards stood directly opposite, beside the wall, and happened to be looking at the window of Cell 13 when the head of The Thinking Machine appeared. But the scientist didn't notice the guard.

Noon came and the jailer appeared with the prison dinner of repulsively plain food. At home The Thinking Machine merely ate to live; here he took what was offered without comment. Occasionally he spoke to the jailer who stood outside the door watching him.

'Any improvements made here in the last few years?' he asked.

'Nothing particularly,' replied the jailer. 'New wall was built four years ago.'

'Anything done to the prison proper?'

'Painted the woodwork outside, and I believe about seven years ago a new system of plumbing was put in.'

'Ah!' said the prisoner. 'How far is the river over there?'

'About three hundred feet. The boys have a baseball ground between the wall and the river.'

The Thinking Machine had nothing further to say just

then, but when the jailer was ready to go he asked for some water.

'I get very thirsty here,' he explained. 'Would it be possible for you to leave a little water in a bowl for me?'

'I'll ask the warden,' replied the jailer, and he went away. Half an hour later he returned with water in a small earthenware bowl.

'The warden says you may keep this bowl,' he informed the prisoner. 'But you must show it to me when I ask for it. If it is broken, it will be the last.'

'Thank you,' said The Thinking Machine. 'I shan't break it.'

The jailer went on about his duties. For just the fraction of a second it seemed that The Thinking Machine wanted to ask a question, but he didn't.

Two hours later this same jailer, in passing the door of Cell 13, heard a noise inside and stopped. The Thinking Machine was down on his hands and knees in a corner of the cell, and from that same corner came several frightened squeaks. The jailer looked on interestedly.

'Ah, I've got you,' he heard the prisoner say.

'Got what?' he asked, sharply.

'One of these rats,' was the reply. 'See?' And between the scientist's long fingers the jailer saw a small grey rat struggling. The prisoner brought it over to the light and looked at it closely. 'It's a water rat,' he said.

'Ain't you got anything better to do than to catch rats?' asked the jailer.

'It's disgraceful that they should be here at all,' was the irritated reply. 'Take this one away and kill it. There are dozens more where it came from.'

The jailer took the wriggling, squirmy rodent and flung it down on the floor violently. It gave one squeak and lay still. Later he reported the incident to the warden, who only smiled.

Still later that afternoon the outside armed guard on Cell 13 side of the prison looked up again at the window and saw the prisoner looking out. He saw a hand raised to the barred window and then something white fluttered to the ground, directly under the window of Cell 13. It was a little roll of linen, evidently of white shirting material, and tied around it was a five-dollar bill. The guard looked up at the window again, but the face had disappeared.

With a grim smile he took the little linen roll and the five-dollar bill to the warden's office. There together they deciphered something which was written on it with a queer sort of ink, frequently blurred. On the outside was this:

'Finder of this please deliver to Dr Charles Ransome.'

'Ah,' said the warden, with a chuckle. 'Plan of escape number one has gone wrong.' Then, as an afterthought: 'But why did he address it to Dr Ransome?'

'And where did he get the pen and ink to write with?' asked the guard.

The warden looked at the guard and the guard looked at the warden. There was no apparent solution of that mystery. The warden studied the writing carefully, then shook his head.

'Well, let's see what he was going to say to Dr Ransome,' he said at length, still puzzled, and he unrolled the inner piece of linen.

'Well, if that – what – what do you think of that?' he asked, dazed.

The guard took the bit of linen and read this:

'*Epa cseot d'net niiy awe htto n'si sih. "T."*'

3

The warden spent an hour wondering what sort of a cipher it was, and half an hour wondering why his prisoner should attempt to communicate with Dr Ransome, who was the cause of him being there. After this the warden devoted some thought to the question of where the prisoner got writing materials, and what sort of writing materials he had. With the idea of illuminating this point, he examined the linen again. It was a torn part of a white shirt and had ragged edges.

Now it was possible to account for the linen, but what the prisoner had used to write with was another matter. The warden knew it would have been impossible for him to have either pen or pencil, and, besides, neither pen nor pencil had been used in this writing. What, then? The warden decided to personally investigate. The Thinking Machine was his prisoner; he had orders to hold his prisoners; if this one sought to escape by sending cipher messages to persons outside, he would stop it, as he would have stopped it in the case of any other prisoner.

The warden went back to Cell 13 and found The Thinking Machine on his hands and knees on the floor, engaged in nothing more alarming than catching rats. The prisoner heard the warden's step and turned to him quickly.

'It's disgraceful,' he snapped, 'these rats. There are scores of them.'

'Other men have been able to stand them,' said the warden. 'Here is another shirt for you – let me have the one you have on.'

'Why?' demanded The Thinking Machine, quickly. His tone was hardly natural, his manner suggested actual perturbation.

'You have attempted to communicate with Dr Ransome,' said the warden severely. 'As my prisoner, it is my duty to put a stop to it.'

The Thinking Machine was silent for a moment.

'All right,' he said, finally. 'Do your duty.'

The warden smiled grimly. The prisoner arose from the floor and removed the white shirt, putting on instead a striped convict shirt the warden had brought. The warden took the white shirt eagerly, and then and there compared the pieces of linen on which was written the cipher with certain torn places in the shirt. The Thinking Machine looked on curiously.

'The guard brought *you* those, then?' he asked.

'He certainly did,' replied the warden triumphantly. 'And that ends your first attempt to escape.'

The Thinking Machine watched the warden as he, by comparison, established to his own satisfaction that only two pieces of linen had been torn from the white shirt.

'What did you write this with?' demanded the warden.

'I should think it a part of your duty to find out,' said The Thinking Machine, irritably.

The warden started to say some harsh things, then restrained himself and made a minute search of the cell and of the prisoner instead. He found absolutely nothing; not even a match or toothpick which might have been used for a pen. The same mystery surrounded the fluid with which the cipher had been written. Although the warden left Cell 13 visibly annoyed, he took the torn shirt in triumph.

'Well, writing notes on a shirt won't get him out, that's certain,' he told himself with some complacency. He put the linen scraps into his desk to await developments. 'If that man escapes from that cell I'll – hang it – I'll resign.'

On the third day of his incarceration The Thinking Machine openly attempted to bribe his way out. The jailer had brought his dinner and was leaning against the barred door, waiting, when The Thinking Machine began the conversation.

'The drainage pipes of the prison lead to the river, don't they?' he asked.

'Yes,' said the jailer.

'I suppose they are very small?'

'Too small to crawl through, if that's what you're thinking about,' was the grinning response.

There was silence until The Thinking Machine finished his meal. Then:

'You know I'm not a criminal, don't you?'

'Yes.'

'And that I've a perfect right to be freed if I demand it?'

'Yes.'

'Well, I came here believing that I could make my escape,' said the prisoner, and his squint eyes studied the face of the jailer. 'Would you consider a financial reward for aiding me to escape?'

The jailer, who happened to be an honest man, looked at the slender, weak figure of the prisoner, at the large head with its mass of yellow hair, and was almost sorry.

'I guess prisons like these were not built for the likes of you to get out of,' he said, at last.

'But would you consider a proposition to help me get out?' the prisoner insisted, almost beseechingly.

'No,' said the jailer, shortly.

'Five hundred dollars,' urged The Thinking Machine. 'I am not a criminal.'

'No,' said the jailer.

'A thousand?'

'No,' again said the jailer, and he started away hurriedly to escape further temptation. Then he turned back. 'If you should give me ten thousand dollars I couldn't let you out. You'd have to pass through seven doors, and I only have the keys to two.'

Then he told the warden all about it.

'Plan number two fails,' said the warden, smiling grimly. 'First a cipher, then bribery.'

When the jailer was on his way to Cell 13 at six o'clock, again bearing food to The Thinking Machine, he paused, startled by the unmistakable scrape, scrape of steel against steel. It stopped at the sound of his steps, then craftily the jailer, who was beyond the prisoner's range of vision, resumed his tramping, the sound being apparently that of a man going away from Cell 13. As a matter of fact he was in the same spot.

After a moment there came again the steady scrape, scrape, and the jailer crept cautiously on tip-toes to the door and peered between the bars. The Thinking Machine was standing on the iron bed working at the bars of the little window. He was using a file, judging from the backward and forward swing of his arms.

Cautiously the jailer crept back to the office, summoned the warden in person, and they returned to Cell 13 on tip-toes. The steady scrape was still audible. The warden list-ened to satisfy himself and then suddenly appeared at the door.

'Well?' he demanded, and there was a smile on his face.

The Thinking Machine glanced back from his perch on the bed and leaped suddenly to the floor, making frantic efforts to hide something. The warden went in, with hand extended.

'Give it up,' he said.

'No,' said the prisoner, sharply.

'Come, give it up,' urged the warden. 'I don't want to have to search you again.'

'No,' repeated the prisoner.

'What was it, a file?' asked the warden.

The Thinking Machine was silent and stood squinting at the warden with something very nearly approaching dis-appointment on his face – nearly, but not quite. The warden was almost sympathetic.

'Plan number three fails, eh?' he asked, good-naturedly. 'Too bad, isn't it?'

The prisoner didn't say.

'Search him,' instructed the warden.

The jailer searched the prisoner carefully. At last, artfully concealed in the waist band of the trousers, he found a piece of steel about two inches long, with one side curved like a half moon.

'Ah,' said the warden, as he received it from the jailer. 'From your shoe heel,' and he smiled pleasantly.

The jailer continued his search and on the other side of the trousers' waist band found another piece of steel identi-cal with the first. The edges showed where they had been worn against the bars of the window.

'You couldn't saw a way through those bars with these,' said the warden.

'I could have,' said The Thinking Machine firmly.

'In six months, perhaps,' said the warden, good-naturedly.

The warden shook his head slowly as he gazed into the slightly flushed face of his prisoner.

'Ready to give it up?' he asked.

'I haven't started yet,' was the prompt reply.

Then came another exhaustive search of the cell. Carefully the two men went over it, finally turning out the bed and searching that. Nothing. The warden in person climbed upon the bed and examined the bars of the window where the prisoner had been sawing. When he looked he was amused.

'Just made it a little bright by hard rubbing,' he said to the prisoner, who stood looking on with a somewhat crestfallen air. The warden grasped the iron bars in his strong hands and tried to shake them. They were immovable, set firmly in the solid granite. He examined each in turn and found them all satisfactory. Finally he climbed down from the bed.

'Give it up, professor,' he advised.

The Thinking Machine shook his head and the warden and jailer passed on again. As they disappeared down the corridor The Thinking Machine sat on the edge of the bed with his head in his hands.

'He's crazy to try to get out of that cell,' commented the jailer.

'Of course he can't get out,' said the warden. 'But he's clever. I would like to know what he wrote that cipher with.'

*

It was four o'clock next morning when an awful, heart-racking shriek of terror resounded through the great prison. It came from a cell, somewhere about the centre, and its tone told a tale of horror, agony, terrible fear. The warden heard and with three of his men rushed into the long corridor leading to Cell 13.

4

As they ran there came again that awful cry. It died away in a sort of wail. The white faces of prisoners appeared at cell doors upstairs and down, staring out wonderingly, frightened.

'It's that fool in Cell 13,' grumbled the warden.

He stopped and stared in as one of the jailers flashed a lantern. 'That fool in Cell 13' lay comfortably on his cot, flat on his back with his mouth open, snoring. Even as they looked there came again the piercing cry, from somewhere above. The warden's face blanched a little as he started up the stairs. There on the top floor he found a man in Cell 43, directly above Cell 13, but two floors higher, cowering in a corner of his cell.

'What's the matter?' demanded the warden.

'Thank God you've come,' exclaimed the prisoner, and he cast himself against the bars of his cell.

'What is it?' demanded the warden again.

He threw open the door and went in. The prisoner dropped on his knees and clasped the warden about the body. His face was white with terror, his eyes were widely distended, and he was shuddering. His hands, icy cold, clutched at the warden's.

'Take me out of this cell, please take me out,' he pleaded.

'What's the matter with you, anyhow?' insisted the warden impatiently.

'I heard something – something,' said the prisoner, and his eyes roved nervously around the cell.

'What did you hear?'

'I – I can't tell you,' stammered the prisoner. Then, in a sudden burst of terror: 'Take me out of this cell – put me anywhere – but take me out of here.'

The warden and the three jailers exchanged glances.

'Who is this fellow? What's he accused of?' asked the warden.

'Joseph Ballard,' said one of the jailers. 'He's accused of throwing acid in a woman's face. She died from it.'

'But they can't prove it,' gasped the prisoner. 'They can't prove it. Please put me in some other cell.'

He was still clinging to the warden, and that official threw his arms off roughly. Then for a time he stood looking at the cowering wretch, who seemed possessed of all the wild, unreasoning terror of a child.

'Look here, Ballard,' said the warden, finally, 'if you heard anything, I want to know what it was. Now tell me.'

'I can't, I can't,' was the reply. He was sobbing.

'Where did it come from?'

'I don't know. Everywhere – nowhere. I just heard it.'

'What was it – a voice?'

'Please don't make me answer,' pleaded the prisoner.

'You must answer,' said the warden, sharply.

'It was a voice – but – but it wasn't human,' was the sobbing reply.

'Voice, but not human?' repeated the warden, puzzled.

'It sounded muffled and – and far away – and ghostly,' explained the man.

'Did it come from inside or outside the prison?'

'It didn't seem to come from anywhere – it was just here, here, everywhere. I heard it. I heard it.'

For an hour the warden tried to get the story, but Ballard had become suddenly obstinate and would say nothing – only pleaded to be placed in another cell, or to have one of the jailers remain near him until daylight. These requests were gruffly refused.

'And see here,' said the warden, in conclusion, 'if there's any more of this screaming I'll put you in the padded cell.'

Then the warden went his way, a sadly puzzled man. Ballard sat at his cell door until daylight, his face, drawn and white with terror, pressed against the bars, and looking out into the prison with wide, staring eyes.

That day, the fourth since the incarceration of The Thinking Machine, was enlivened considerably by the volunteer prisoner, who spent most of his time at the little window of his cell. He began proceedings by throwing another piece of linen down to the guard, who picked it up dutifully and took it to the warden. On it was written:

'Only three days more.'

The warden was in no way surprised at what he read; he understood that The Thinking Machine meant only three days more of his imprisonment, and he regarded the note as a boast. But how was the thing written? Where had The Thinking Machine found this new piece of linen? Where? How? He carefully examined the linen. It was white, of fine texture, shirting material. He took the shirt which he had taken and carefully fitted the two original pieces of the linen to the torn places. This third piece was entirely superfluous; it didn't fit anywhere, and yet it was unmistakably the same goods.

'And where – where does he get anything to write with?' demanded the warden of the world at large.

Still later on the fourth day The Thinking Machine, through the window of his cell, spoke to the armed guard outside.

'What day of the month is it?' he asked.

'The fifteenth,' was the answer.

The Thinking Machine made a mental astronomical calculation and satisfied himself that the moon would not rise until after nine o'clock that night. Then he asked another question:

'Who attends to those arc lights?'

'Man from the company.'

'You have no electricians in the building?'

'No.'

'I should think you could save money if you had your own man.'

'None of my business,' replied the guard.

The guard noticed The Thinking Machine at the cell

window frequently during that day, but always the face seemed listless and there was a certain wistfulness in the squint eyes behind the glasses. After a while he accepted the presence of the leonine head as a matter of course. He had seen other prisoners do the same thing; it was the longing for the outside world.

That afternoon, just before the day guard was relieved, the head appeared at the window again, and The Thinking Machine's hand held something out between the bars. It fluttered to the ground and the guard picked it up. It was a five-dollar bill.

'That's for you,' called the prisoner.

As usual, the guard took it to the warden. That gentleman looked at it suspiciously; he looked at everything that came from Cell 13 with suspicion.

'He said it was for me,' explained the guard.

'It's a sort of tip, I suppose,' said the warden. 'I see no particular reason why you shouldn't accept –'

Suddenly he stopped. He had remembered that The Thinking Machine had gone into Cell 13 with one five-dollar bill and two ten-dollar bills; twenty-five dollars in all. Now a five-dollar bill had been tied around the first pieces of linen that came from the cell. The warden still had it, and to convince himself he took it out and looked at it. It was five dollars; yet here was another five dollars, and The Thinking Machine had only had ten-dollar bills.

'Perhaps somebody changed one of the bills for him,' he thought at last, with a sigh of relief.

But then and there he made up his mind. He would search Cell 13 as a cell was never before searched in this world. When a man could write at will, and change money, and do other wholly inexplicable things, there was something radically wrong with his prison. He planned to enter the cell at night – three o'clock would be an excellent time. The Thinking Machine must do all the weird things he did sometime. Night seemed the most reasonable.

Thus it happened that the warden stealthily descended

upon Cell 13 that night at three o'clock. He paused at the door and listened. There was no sound save the steady, regular breathing of the prisoner. The keys unfastened the double locks with scarcely a clank, and the warden entered, locking the door behind him. Suddenly he flashed his dark-lantern in the face of the recumbent figure.

If the warden had planned to startle The Thinking Machine he was mistaken, for that individual merely opened his eyes quietly, reached for his glasses, and inquired, in a most matter-of-fact tone:

'Who is it?'

It would be useless to describe the search that the warden made. It was minute. Not one inch of the cell or the bed was overlooked. He found the round hole in the floor, and with a flash of inspiration thrust his thick fingers into it. After a moment of fumbling there he drew up something and looked at it in the light of his lantern.

'Ugh!' he exclaimed.

The thing he had taken out was a rat – a dead rat. His inspiration fled as a mist before the sun. But he continued the search. The Thinking Machine, without a word, arose and kicked the rat out of the cell into the corridor.

The warden climbed on the bed and tried the steel bars on the tiny window. They were perfectly rigid; every bar of the door was the same.

Then the warden searched the prisoner's clothing, beginning at the shoes. Nothing hidden in them! Then the trousers' waist band. Still nothing! Then the pockets of the trousers. From one side he drew out some paper money and examined it.

'Five one-dollar bills,' he gasped.

'That's right,' said the prisoner.

'But the – you had two tens and a five – what the – how do you do it?'

'That's my business,' said The Thinking Machine.

'Did any of my men change this money for you – on your word of honour?'

The Thinking Machine paused just a fraction of a second. 'No,' he said.

'Well, do you make it?' asked the warden. He was prepared to believe anything.

'That's my business,' again said the prisoner.

The warden glared at the eminent scientist fiercely. He felt – he knew – that this man was making a fool of him, yet he didn't know how. If he were a real prisoner he would get the truth – but, then, perhaps, those inexplicable things which had happened would not have been brought before him so sharply. Neither of the men spoke for a long time, then suddenly the warden turned fiercely and left the cell, slamming the door behind him. He didn't dare to speak, then.

He glanced at the clock. It was ten minutes to four. He had hardly settled himself in bed when again came that heart-breaking shriek through the prison. With a few muttered words, which, while not elegant, were highly expressive, he relighted his lantern and rushed through the prison again to the cell on the upper floor.

Again Ballard was crushing himself against the steel door, shrieking, shrieking at the top of his voice. He stopped only when the warden flashed his lamp in the cell.

'Take me out, take me out,' he screamed. 'I did it, I did it, I killed her. Take it away.'

'Take what away?' asked the warden.

'I threw the acid in her face – I did it – I confess. Take me out of here.'

Ballard's condition was pitiable; it was only an act of mercy to let him out into the corridor. There he crouched in a corner, like an animal at bay, and clasped his hands to his ears. It took half an hour to calm him sufficiently for him to speak. Then he told incoherently what had happened. On the night before at four o'clock he had heard a voice – a sepulchral voice, muffled and wailing in tone.

'What did it say?' asked the warden, curiously.

'Acid – acid – acid!' gasped the prisoner. 'It accused me.

Acid! I threw the acid, and the woman died. Oh!' It was a long shuddering wail of terror.

'Acid?' echoed the warden, puzzled. The case was beyond him.

'Acid. That's all I heard – that one word, repeated several times. There were other things, too, but I didn't hear them.'

'That was last night, eh?' asked the warden. 'What happened tonight – what frightened you just now?'

'It was the same thing,' gasped the prisoner. 'Acid – acid – acid!' He covered his face with his hands and sat shivering. 'It was acid I used on her, but I didn't mean to kill her. I just heard the words. It was something accusing me – accusing me.' He mumbled, and was silent.

'Did you hear anything else?'

'Yes – but I couldn't understand – only a little bit – just a word or two.'

'Well, what was it?'

'I heard "acid" three times, then I heard a long, moaning sound, then – then – I heard "No. 8 hat." I heard that twice.'

'No. 8 hat,' repeated the warden. 'What the devil – No. 8 hat? Accusing voices of conscience have never talked about No. 8 hats, so far as I ever heard.'

'He's insane,' said one of the jailers, with an air of finality.

'I believe you,' said the warden. 'He must be. He probably heard something and got frightened. He's trembling now. No. 8 hat! What the –'

5

When the fifth day of The Thinking Machine's imprisonment rolled around the warden was wearing a hunted look. He was anxious for the end of the thing. He could not help but feel that his distinguished prisoner had been amusing himself. And if this were so, The Thinking Machine had lost none of his sense of humour. For on this fifth day he flung down another linen note to the outside guard, bearing the words: 'Only two days more.' Also he flung down half a dollar.

Now the warden knew – he *knew* – that the man in Cell 13 didn't have any half dollars – he *couldn't* have any half dollars, no more than he could have pen and ink and linen, and yet he did have them. It was a condition, not a theory; that is one reason why the warden was wearing a hunted look.

That ghastly, uncanny thing, too, about 'Acid' and 'No. 8 hat' clung to him tenaciously. They didn't mean anything, of course, merely the ravings of an insane murderer who had been driven by fear to confess his crime, still there were so many things that 'didn't mean anything' happening in the prison now since The Thinking Machine was there.

On the sixth day the warden received a postal stating that Dr Ransome and Mr Fielding would be at Chisholm Prison on the following evening, Thursday, and in the event Professor Van Dusen had not yet escaped – and they presumed he had not because they had not heard from him – they would meet him there.

'In the event he had not yet escaped!' The warden smiled grimly. Escaped!

The Thinking Machine enlivened this day for the warden with three notes. They were on the usual linen and bore generally on the appointment at half past eight o'clock Thursday night, which appointment the scientist had made at the time of his imprisonment.

On the afternoon of the seventh day the warden passed Cell 13 and glanced in. The Thinking Machine was lying on the iron bed, apparently sleeping lightly. The cell appeared precisely as it always did from a casual glance. The warden would swear that no man was going to leave it between that hour – it was then four o'clock – and half past eight o'clock that evening.

On his way back past the cell the warden heard the

steady breathing again, and coming close to the door looked in. He wouldn't have done so if The Thinking Machine had been looking, but now – well, it was different.

A ray of light came through the high window and fell on the face of the sleeping man. It occurred to the warden for the first time that his prisoner appeared haggard and weary. Just then The Thinking Machine stirred slightly and the warden hurried on up the corridor guiltily. That evening after six o'clock he saw the jailer.

'Everything all right in Cell 13?' he asked.

'Yes, sir,' replied the jailer. 'He didn't eat much, though.'

It was with a feeling of having done his duty that the warden received Dr Ransome and Mr Fielding shortly after seven o'clock. He intended to show them the linen notes and lay before them the full story of his woes, which was a long one. But before this came to pass the guard from the river side of the prison yard entered the office.

'The arc light on my side of the yard won't light,' he informed the warden.

'Confound it, that man's a hoodoo,' thundered the official. 'Everything has happened since he's been here.'

The guard went back to his post in the darkness, and the warden phoned to the electric light company.

'This is Chisholm Prison,' he said through the phone. 'Send three or four men down here quick, to fix an arc light.'

The reply was evidently satisfactory, for the warden hung up the receiver and passed out into the yard. While Dr Ransome and Mr Fielding sat waiting the guard at the outer gate came in with a special delivery letter. Dr Ransome happened to notice the address, and, when the guard went out, looked at the letter more closely.

'By George!' he exclaimed.

'What is it?' asked Mr Fielding.

Silently the doctor offered the letter. Mr Fielding examined it closely.

'Coincidence,' he said. 'It must be.'

It was nearly eight o'clock when the warden returned to

his office. The electricians had arrived in a wagon, and were now at work. The warden pressed the buzz-button communicating with the man at the outer gate in the wall.

'How many electricians came in?' he asked, over the short phone. 'Four? Three workmen in jumpers and overalls and the manager? Frock coat and silk hat? All right. Be certain that only four go out. That's all.'

He turned to Dr Ransome and Mr Fielding.

'We have to be careful here – particularly,' and there was broad sarcasm in his tone, 'since we have scientists locked up.'

The warden picked up the special delivery letter carelessly, and then began to open it.

'When I have read this I want to tell you gentlemen something about how – Great Caesar!' he ended, suddenly, as he glanced at the letter. He sat with mouth open, motionless, from astonishment.

'What is it?' asked Mr Fielding.

'A special delivery letter from Cell 13,' gasped the warden. 'An invitation to supper.'

'What?' and the two others arose, unanimously.

The warden sat dazed, staring at the letter for a moment, then called sharply to the guard outside in the corridor.

'Run down to Cell 13 and see if that man's in there.'

The guard went as directed, while Dr Ransome and Mr Fielding examined the letter.

'It's Van Dusen's handwriting; there's no question of that,' said Dr Ransome. 'I've seen too much of it.'

Just then the buzz on the telephone from the outer gate sounded, and the warden, in a semi-trance, picked up the receiver.

'Hello! Two reporters, eh? Let 'em come in.' He turned suddenly to the doctor and Mr Fielding. 'Why, the man *can't* be out. He must be in his cell.'

Just at that moment the guard returned.

'He's still in the cell, sir,' he reported. 'I saw him. He's lying down.'

'There, I told you so,' said the warden, and he breathed freely again. 'But how did he mail that letter?'

There was a rap on the steel door which led from the jail yard into the warden's office.

'It's the reporters,' said the warden. 'Let them in,' he instructed the guard; then to the other two gentlemen: 'Don't say anything about this before them, because I'd never hear the last of it.'

The door opened, and the two men from the front gate entered.

'Good evening, gentlemen,' said one. That was Hutchinson Hatch; the warden knew him well.

'Well?' demanded the other, irritably, 'I'm here.'

That was The Thinking Machine.

He squinted belligerently at the warden, who sat with mouth agape. For the moment that official had nothing to say. Dr Ransome and Mr Fielding were amazed, but they didn't know what the warden knew. They were only amazed; he was paralysed. Hutchinson Hatch, the reporter, took in the scene with greedy eyes.

'How – how – how did you do it?' gasped the warden, finally.

'Come back to the cell,' said The Thinking Machine, in the irritated voice which his scientific associates knew so well.

The warden, still in a condition bordering on trance, led the way.

'Flash your light in there,' directed The Thinking Machine.

The warden did so. There was nothing unusual in the appearance of the cell, and there – there on the bed lay the figure of The Thinking Machine. Certainly! There was the yellow hair! Again the warden looked at the man beside him and wondered at the strangeness of his own dreams.

With trembling hands he unlocked the cell door and The Thinking Machine passed inside.

'See here,' he said.

He kicked at the steel bars in the bottom of the cell door and three of them were pushed out of place. A fourth broke off and rolled away in the corridor.

'And here, too,' directed the erstwhile prisoner as he stood on the bed to reach the small window. He swept his hand across the opening and every bar came out.

'What's this in the bed?' demanded the warden, who was slowly recovering.

'A wig,' was the reply. 'Turn down the cover.'

The warden did so. Beneath it lay a large coil of strong rope, thirty feet or more, a dagger, three files, ten feet of electric wire, a thin, powerful pair of steel pliers, a small tack hammer with its handle, and – and a Derringer pistol.

'How did you do it?' demanded the warden.

'You gentlemen have an engagement to supper with me at half past nine o'clock,' said The Thinking Machine. 'Come on, or we shall be late.'

'But how did you do it?' insisted the warden.

'Don't ever think you can hold any man who can use his brain,' said The Thinking Machine. 'Come on; we shall be late.'

6

It was an impatient supper party in the rooms of Professor Van Dusen and a somewhat silent one. The guests were Dr Ransome, Albert Fielding, the warden, and Hutchinson Hatch, reporter. The meal was served to the minute, in accordance with Professor Van Dusen's instructions of one week before; Dr Ransome found the artichokes delicious. At last the supper was finished and The Thinking Machine turned full on Dr Ransome and squinted at him fiercely.

'Do you believe it now?' he demanded.

'I do,' replied Dr Ransome.

'Do you admit that it was a fair test?'

'I do.'

With the others, particularly the warden, he was waiting anxiously for the explanation.

'Suppose you tell us how –' began Mr Fielding.

'Yes, tell us how,' said the warden.

The Thinking Machine readjusted his glasses, took a couple of preparatory squints at his audience, and began the story. He told it from the beginning logically; and no man ever talked to more interested listeners.

'My agreement was,' he began, 'to go into a cell, carrying nothing except what was necessary to wear, and to leave that cell within a week. I had never seen Chisholm Prison. When I went into the cell I asked for tooth powder, two ten- and one five-dollar bills, and also to have my shoes blacked. Even if these requests had been refused it would not have mattered seriously. But you agreed to them.

'I knew there would be nothing in the cell which you thought I might use to advantage. So when the warden locked the door on me I was apparently helpless, unless I could turn three seemingly innocent things to use. They were things which would have been permitted any prisoner under sentence of death, were they not, warden?'

'Tooth powder and polished shoes, but not money,' replied the warden.

'Anything is dangerous in the hands of a man who knows how to use it,' went on The Thinking Machine. 'I did nothing that first night but sleep and chase rats.' He glared at the warden. 'When the matter was broached I knew I could do nothing that night, so suggested next day. You gentlemen thought I wanted time to arrange an escape with outside assistance, but this was not true. I knew I could communicate with whom I pleased, when I pleased.'

The warden stared at him a moment, then went on smoking solemnly.

'I was aroused next morning at six o'clock by the jailer with my breakfast,' continued the scientist. 'He told me dinner was at twelve and supper at six. Between these times, I gathered I would be pretty much to myself. So immediately after breakfast I examined my outside surroundings from my cell window. One look told me it would be useless to try to scale the wall, even should I decide to leave my cell by the window, for my purpose was to leave not only the cell, but the prison. Of course, I could have gone over the wall, but it would have taken me longer to lay my plans that way. Therefore, for the moment, I dismissed all idea of that.

'From this first observation I knew the river was on that side of the prison, and that there was also a playground there. Subsequently these surmises were verified by a keeper. I knew then one important thing – that anyone might approach the prison wall from that side if necessary without attracting any particular attention. That was well to remember. I remembered it.

'But the outside thing which most attracted my attention was the feed wire to the arc light which ran within a few feet – probably three or four – of my cell window. I knew that would be valuable in the event I found it necessary to cut off that arc light.'

'Oh, you shut it off tonight, then?' asked the warden.

'Having learned all I could from that window,' resumed The Thinking Machine, without heeding the interruption, 'I considered the idea of escaping through the prison proper. I recalled just how I had come into the cell, which I knew would be the only way. Seven doors lay between me and the outside. So, also for the time being, I gave up the idea of escaping that way. And I couldn't go through the solid granite walls of the cell.'

The Thinking Machine paused for a moment and Dr Ransome lighted a new cigar. For several minutes there was silence, then the scientific jail-breaker went on:

'While I was thinking about these things a rat ran across my foot. It suggested a new line of thought. There were at least half a dozen rats in the cell – I could see their beady eyes. Yet I had noticed none come under the cell door. I frightened them purposely and watched the cell door to see if they went out that way. They did not, but they were gone. Obviously they went another way. Another way meant another opening.

'I searched for this opening and found it. It was an old drain pipe, long unused and partly choked with dirt and dust. But this was the way the rats had come. They came from somewhere. Where? Drain pipes usually lead outside prison grounds. This one probably led to the river, or near it. The rats must therefore come from that direction. If they came a part of the way, I reasoned that they came all the way, because it was extremely unlikely that a solid iron or lead pipe would have any hole in it except at the exit.

'When the jailer came with my luncheon he told me two important things, although he didn't know it. One was that a new system of plumbing had been put in the prison seven years before; another that the river was only three hundred feet away. Then I knew positively that the pipe was a part of an old system; I knew, too, that it slanted generally towards the river. But did the pipe end in the water or on land?

'This was the next question to be decided. I decided it by catching several of the rats in the cell. My jailer was surprised to see me engaged in this work. I examined at least a dozen of them. They were perfectly dry; they had come through the pipe, and, most important of all, they were *not house rats, but field rats*. The other end of the pipe was on land, then, outside the prison walls. So far, so good.

'Then, I knew that if I worked freely from this point I must attract the warden's attention in another direction. You see, by telling the warden that I had come there to escape you made the test more severe, because I had to trick him by false scents.'

The warden looked up with a sad expression in his eyes.

'The first thing was to make him think I was trying to communicate with you, Dr Ransome. So I wrote a note on a piece of linen I tore from my shirt, addressed it to Dr Ransome, tied a five-dollar bill around it and threw it out of the window. I knew the guard would take it to the warden but I rather hoped the warden would send it as addressed. Have you that first linen note, warden?'

The warden produced the cipher.

'What the deuce does it mean, anyhow?' he asked.

'Read it backwards, beginning with the "T" signature and disregard the division into words,' instructed The Thinking Machine.

The warden did so.

'T–h–i–s, this,' he spelled, studied it a moment, then read it off, grinning:

'This is not the way I intend to escape.'

'Well, now what do you think o' that?' he demanded, still grinning.

'I knew that would attract your attention, just as it did,' said The Thinking Machine, 'and if you really found out what it was it would be a sort of gentle rebuke.'

'What did you write it with?' asked Dr Ransome, after he had examined the linen and passed it to Mr Fielding.

'This,' said the erstwhile prisoner, and he extended his foot. On it was the shoe he had worn in prison, though the polish was gone – scraped off clean. 'The shoe blacking, moistened with water, was my ink; the metal tip of the shoe lace made a fairly good pen.'

The warden looked up and suddenly burst into a laugh, half of relief, half of amusement.

'You're a wonder,' he said, admiringly. 'Go on.'

'That precipitated a search of my cell by the warden, as I had intended,' continued The Thinking Machine. 'I was anxious to get the warden into the habit of searching my cell, so that finally, constantly finding nothing, he would get disgusted and quit. This at last happened, practically.'

The warden blushed.

'He then took my white shirt away and gave me a prison shirt. He was satisfied that these two pieces of the shirt were all that was missing. But while he was searching my cell I had another piece of that same shirt, about nine inches square, rolled up into a small ball in my mouth.'

'Nine inches of that shirt?' demanded the warden. 'Where did it come from?'

'The bosoms of all stiff white shirts are of triple thickness,' was the explanation. 'I tore out the inside thickness, leaving the bosom only two thicknesses. I knew you wouldn't see it. So much for that.'

There was a little pause, and the warden looked from one to another of the men with sheepish grin.

'Having disposed of the warden for the time being by giving him something else to think about, I took my first serious step towards freedom,' said Professor Van Dusen. 'I knew, within reason, that the pipe led somewhere to the playground outside; I knew a great many boys played there; I knew that rats came into my cell from out there. Could I communicate with someone outside with these things at hand?

'First was necessary, I saw, a long and fairly reliable thread, so – but here,' he pulled up his trouser legs and showed that the tops of both stockings, of fine, strong lisle, were gone. 'I unravelled those – after I got them started it wasn't difficult – and I had easily a quarter of a mile of thread I could depend on.

'Then on half of my remaining linen I wrote, laboriously enough I assure you, a letter explaining my situation to this gentleman here,' and he indicated Hutchinson Hatch. 'I knew he would assist me – for the value of the newspaper story. I tied firmly to this linen letter a ten-dollar bill – there is no surer way of attracting the eye of anyone – and wrote on the linen: "Finder of this deliver to Hutchinson Hatch, *Daily American*, who will give another ten dollars for the information."

'The next thing was to get this note outside on that playground where a boy might find it. There were two ways, but I chose the best. I took one of the rats – I became adept in catching them – tied the linen and money firmly to one leg, fastened my lisle thread to another, and turned him loose in the drain pipe. I reasoned that the natural fright of the rodent would make him run until he was outside the pipe and then out on earth he would probably stop to gnaw off the linen and money.

'From the moment the rat disappeared into that dusty pipe I became anxious. I was taking so many chances. The rat might gnaw the string, of which I held one end; other rats might gnaw it; the rat might run out of the pipe and leave the linen and money where they would never be found; a thousand other things might have happened. So began some nervous hours, but the fact that the rat ran on until only a few feet of the string remained in my cell made me think he was outside the pipe. I had carefully instructed Mr Hatch what to do in case the note reached him. The question was: would it reach him?

'This done, I could only wait and make other plans in case this one failed. I openly attempted to bribe my jailer, and learned from him that he held the keys to only two of seven doors between me and freedom. Then I did something else to make the warden nervous. I took the steel supports out of the heels of my shoes and made a pretence of sawing the bars of my cell window. The warden raised a pretty row about that. He developed, too, the habit of shaking the bars of my cell window to see if they were solid. They were – then.'

Again the warden grinned. He had ceased being astonished.

'With this one plan I had done all I could and could only wait to see what happened,' the scientist went on. 'I couldn't know whether my note had been delivered or even found, or whether the rat had gnawed it up. And I didn't dare to draw back through the pipe that one slender thread which connected me with the outside.

'When I went to bed that night I didn't sleep, for fear there would come the slight signal twitch at the thread which was to tell me that Mr Hatch had received the note.

At half past three o'clock, I judge, I felt this twitch, and no prisoner actually under sentence of death ever welcomed a thing more heartily.'

The Thinking Machine stopped and turned to the reporter.

'You'd better explain just what you did,' he said.

'The linen note was brought to me by a small boy who had been playing baseball,' said Mr Hatch. 'I immediately saw a big story in it, so I gave the boy another ten dollars, and got several spools of silk, some twine, and a roll of light, pliable wire. The professor's note suggested that I have the finder of the note show me just where it was picked up, and told me to make my search from there, beginning at two o'clock in the morning. If I found the other end of the thread I was to twitch it gently three times, then a fourth.

'I began the search with a small bulb electric light. It was an hour and twenty minutes before I found the end of the drain pipe, half hidden in weeds. The pipe was very large there, say twelve inches across. Then I found the end of the lisle thread, twitched it as directed and immediately I got an answering twitch.

'Then I fastened the silk to this and Professor Van Dusen began to pull it into his cell. I nearly had heart disease for fear the string would break. To the end of the silk I fastened the twine, and when that had been pulled in I tied on the wire. Then that was drawn into the pipe and we had a substantial line, which rats couldn't gnaw, from the mouth of the drain into the cell.'

The Thinking Machine raised his hand and Hatch stopped.

'All this was done in absolute silence,' said the scientist. 'But when the wire reached my hand I could have shouted. Then we tried another experiment, which Mr Hatch was prepared for. I tested the pipe as a speaking tube. Neither of us could hear very clearly, but I dared not speak loud for fear of attracting attention in the prison. At last I made him understand what I wanted immediately. He seemed to

have great difficulty in understanding when I asked for
nitric acid, and I repeated the word "acid" several times.

'Then I heard a shriek from a cell above me. I knew
instantly that someone had overheard, and when I heard
you coming, Mr Warden, I feigned sleep. If you had entered my cell at that moment the whole plan of escape
would have ended there. But you passed on. That was the
nearest I ever came to being caught.

'Having established this improvised trolley it is easy to
see how I got things in the cell and made them disappear at
will. I merely dropped them back into the pipe. You, Mr
Warden, could not have reached the connecting wire with
your fingers; they are too large. My fingers, you see, are
longer and more slender. In addition I guarded the top of
that pipe with a rat – you remember how.'

'I remember,' said the warden, with a grimace.

'I thought that if anyone were tempted to investigate
that hole the rat would dampen his ardour. Mr Hatch
could not send me anything useful through the pipe until
next night, although he did send me change for ten dollars
as a test, so I proceeded with other parts of my plan. Then I
evolved the method of escape, which I finally employed.

'In order to carry this out successfully it was necessary for
the guard in the yard to get accustomed to seeing me at the
cell window. I arranged this by dropping linen notes to him,
boastful in tone, to make the warden believe, if possible,
one of his assistants was communicating with the outside
for me. I would stand at my window for hours gazing out, so
the guard could see, and occasionally I spoke to him. In
that way I learned that the prison had no electricians of its
own, but was dependent upon the lighting company if anything should go wrong.

'That cleared the way to freedom perfectly. Early in the
evening of the last day of my imprisonment, when it was
dark, I planned to cut the feed wire which was only a few
feet from my window, reaching it with an acid-tipped wire I
had. That would make that side of the prison perfectly dark

while the electricians were searching for the break. That would also bring Mr Hatch into the prison yard.

'There was only one more thing to do before I actually began the work of setting myself free. This was to arrange final details with Mr Hatch through our speaking tube. I did this within half an hour after the warden left my cell on the fourth night of my imprisonment. Mr Hatch again had serious difficulty in understanding me, and I repeated the word "acid" to him several times, and later the words: "Number eight hat" – that's my size – and these were the things which made a prisoner upstairs confess to murder, so one of the jailers told me next day. This prisoner heard our voices, confused of course, through the pipe, which also went to his cell. The cell directly over me was not occupied, hence no one else heard.

'Of course the actual work of cutting the steel bars out of the window and door was comparatively easy with nitric acid, which I got through the pipe in thin bottles, but it took time. Hour after hour on the fifth and sixth and seventh days the guard below was looking at me as I worked on the bars of the window with the acid on a piece of wire. I used the tooth powder to prevent the acid spreading. I looked away abstractedly as I worked and each minute the acid cut deeper into the metal. I noticed that the jailers always tried the door by shaking the upper part, never the lower bars, therefore I cut the lower bars, leaving them hanging in place by thin strips of metal. But that was a bit of dare-devilry. I could not have gone that way so easily.'

The Thinking Machine sat silently for several minutes.

'I think that makes everything clear,' he went on. 'Whatever points I have not explained were merely to confuse the warden and jailers. These things in my bed I brought in to please Mr Hatch, who wanted to improve the story. Of course, the wig was necessary in my plan. The special delivery letter I wrote and directed in my cell with Mr Hatch's fountain pen, then sent it out to him and he mailed it. That's all, I think.'

'But your actually leaving the prison grounds and then coming in through the outer gate to my office?' asked the warden.

'Perfectly simple,' said the scientist. 'I cut the electric light wire with acid, as I said, when the current was off. Therefore when the current was turned on the arc didn't light. I knew it would take some time to find out what was the matter and make repairs. When the guard went to report to you the yard was dark, I crept out of the window – it was a tight fit, too – replaced the bars by standing on a narrow ledge and remained in a shadow until the force of electricians arrived. Mr Hatch was one of them.

'When I saw him I spoke and he handed me a cap, a jumper and overalls, which I put on within ten feet of you, Mr Warden, while you were in the yard. Later Mr Hatch called me, presumably as a workman, and together we went out the gate to get something out of the wagon. The gate guard let us pass out readily as two workmen who had just passed in. We changed our clothing and reappeared, asking to see you. We saw you. That's all.'

There was silence for several minutes. Dr Ransome was first to speak.

'Wonderful!' he exclaimed. 'Perfectly amazing.'

'How did Mr Hatch happen to come with the electricians?' asked Mr Fielding.

'His father is manager of the company,' replied The Thinking Machine.

'But what if there had been no Mr Hatch outside to help?'

'Every prisoner has one friend outside who would help him escape if he could.'

'Suppose – just suppose – there had been no old plumbing system there?' asked the warden, curiously.

'There were two other ways out,' said The Thinking Machine, enigmatically.

Ten minutes later the telephone bell rang. It was a request for the warden.

'Light all right, eh?' the warden asked, through the phone. 'Good. Wire cut beside Cell 13? Yes, I know. One electrician too many? What's that? Two came out?'

The warden turned to the others with a puzzled expression.

'He only let in four electricians, he has let out two and says there are three left.'

'I was the odd one,' said The Thinking Machine.

'Oh,' said the warden. 'I see.' Then through the phone: 'Let the fifth man go. He's all right.'

7

Arsène Lupin in Prison

Maurice Leblanc

EVERY tripper by the banks of the Seine must have noticed, between the ruins of Jumièges and those of Saint-Wandrille, the curious little feudal castle of the Malaquis, proudly seated on its rock in mid-stream. A bridge connects it with the road. The base of its turrets seems to make one with the granite that supports it, a huge block detached from a mountain-top and flung where it stands by some formidable convulsion of nature. All around, the calm water of the broad river ripples among the reeds, while wagtails perch timidly on the top of the moist pebbles.

The history of the Malaquis is as rough as its name, as harsh as its outlines, and consists of endless fights, sieges, assaults, sacks, and massacres. Stories are told in the Caux country, late at night, with a shiver, of the crimes committed there. Mysterious legends are conjured up. There is talk of a famous underground passage that led to the Abbey of Jumièges and to the manor-house of Agnes Sorel, the favourite of Charles VII.

This erstwhile haunt of heroes and robbers is now occupied by Baron Nathan Cahorn, or Baron Satan as he used to be called on the Bourse, where he made his fortune a little too suddenly. The ruined owners of the Malaquis were compelled to sell the abode of their ancestors to him for a song. Here he installed his wonderful collections of pictures and furniture, of pottery and carvings. He lives here alone, with three old servants. No one ever enters the doors. No one has ever beheld, in the setting of those ancient halls, his three Rubens, his two Watteaus, his pulpit carved by Jean Goujon, and all the other marvels snatched by force of money from before the eyes of the wealthiest frequenters of the public sale-rooms.

Baron Satan leads a life of fear. He is afraid not for himself, but for the treasures which he has accumulated with so tenacious a passion and with the perspicacity of a collector whom not the most cunning of dealers can boast of having ever taken in. He loves his curiosities with all the greed of a miser, with all the jealousy of a lover.

Daily, at sunset, the four iron-barred doors that command both ends of the bridge and the entrance to the principal court are locked and bolted. At the least touch, electric bells would ring through the surrounding silence. There is nothing to be feared on the side of the Seine, where the rock rises sheer from the water.

One Friday in September, the postman appeared as usual at the bridge-head. And, in accordance with his daily rule, the baron himself opened the heavy door.

He examined the man as closely as if he had not for years known that good jolly face and those crafty peasant eyes. And the man said, with a laugh:

'It's me all right, monsieur le baron. It's not another chap in my cap and blouse!'

'One never knows!' muttered Cahorn.

The postman handed him a bundle of newspapers. Then he added:

'And now, monsieur le baron, I have something special for you.'

'Something special? What do you mean?'

'A letter ... and a registered letter at that!'

Living cut off from everybody, with no friends nor any one that took an interest in him, the baron never received letters; and this suddenly struck him as an ill-omened event which gave him good cause for nervousness. Who was the mysterious correspondent that came to worry him in his retreat?

'I shall want your signature, monsieur le baron.'

He signed the receipt, cursing as he did so. Then he took the letter, waited until the postman had disappeared round the turn of the road and, after taking a few steps to and fro, leaned against the parapet of the bridge and opened the envelope. It contained a sheet of ruled paper, headed, in writing:

Prison de la Santé, Paris.

He looked at the signature:

Arsène Lupin.

Utterly dumbfounded, he read:

Monsieur le Baron,

In the gallery that connects your two drawing-rooms there is a picture by Philippe de Champaigne, an excellent piece of work, which I admire greatly. I also like your Rubens pictures and the smaller of your two Watteaus. In the drawing-room on the right, I note the Louis XIII credence-table, the Beauvais tapestries, the Empire stand, signed by Jacob, and the Renascence chest. In the room on the left, the whole of the case of trinkets and miniatures.

This time, I will be satisfied with these objects, which, I think, can be easily turned into cash. I will therefore ask you to have them properly packed and to send them to my name, carriage paid, to the Gare de Batignolles, on or before this day week, failing which I will myself see to their removal on the night of Wednesday the 27th instant. In the latter case, as is only fair, I shall not be content with the above-mentioned objects.

Pray excuse the trouble which I am giving you, and believe me to be

Yours very truly,
Arsène Lupin

P.S. Be sure not to send me the larger of the two Watteaus. Although you paid thirty thousand francs for it at the sale-rooms, it is only a copy, the original having been burnt under the Directory, by Barras, in one of his orgies. See Garat's unpublished Memoirs.

I do not care either to have the Louis XVI chatelaine, the authenticity of which appears to me to be exceedingly doubtful.

This letter thoroughly upset Baron Cahorn. It would have alarmed him considerably had it been signed by any other hand. But signed by Arsène Lupin! ...

He was a regular reader of the newspapers, knew of everything that went on in the way of theft and crime and had heard all about the exploits of the infernal housebreaker. He was quite aware that Lupin had been arrested in America by his enemy, Ganimard; that he was safely under lock and key; and that the preliminaries of his trial were now being conducted ... with great difficulty, no doubt! But he also knew that one could always expect anything of Arsène Lupin. Besides, this precise knowledge of the castle, of the arrangement of the pictures and furniture, was a very formidable sign. Who had informed Lupin of things which nobody had ever seen?

The baron raised his eyes and gazed at the frowning outline of the Malaquis, its abrupt pedestal, the deep water that surrounds it. He shrugged his shoulders. No, there was no possible danger. No one in the world could penetrate to the inviolable sanctuary that contained his collections.

No one in the world, perhaps; but Arsène Lupin? Did doors, draw-bridges, walls so much as exist for Arsène Lupin? Of what use were the most ingeniously contrived obstacles, the most skilful precautions, once that Arsène Lupin had decided to attain a given object? ...

That same evening, he wrote to the public prosecutor at Rouen. He enclosed the threatening letter and demanded police protection.

The reply came without delay: the said Arsène Lupin was at that moment a prisoner at the Santé, where he was kept under strict observation and not allowed to write. The letter, therefore, could only be the work of a hoaxer. Every-thing went to prove this: logic, common sense, and the actual facts. However, to make quite sure, the letter had been submitted to a handwriting expert, who declared that, notwithstanding certain points of resemblance, it was not in the prisoner's writing.

'Notwithstanding certain points of resemblance.' The baron saw only these five bewildering words, which he re-garded as the confession of a doubt which alone should have been enough to justify intervention of the police. His fears increased. He read the letter over and over again. 'I will myself see to their removal.' And that fixed date, the night of Wednesday, the 27th of September!

Of a naturally suspicious and silent disposition, he dared not unburden himself to his servants, whose devotion he did not consider proof against all tests. And yet, for the first time for many years, he felt a need to speak, to take advice. Abandoned by the police of his country, he had no hope of protecting himself by his own resources and thought of go-ing to Paris to beg for the assistance of some retired detec-tive or other.

Two days elapsed. On the third day, as he sat reading his newspapers, he gave a start of delight. The *Réveil de Caudebec* contained the following paragraph:

We have had the pleasure of numbering among our visitors, for nearly three weeks, Chief-Inspector Ganimard, one of the veterans of the detective service. M. Ganimard, for whom his last feat, the arrest of Arsène Lupin, has won a European reputation, is enjoying a rest from his arduous labours and spending a short holiday fishing for bleak and gudgeon in the Seine.

Ganimard! The very man that Baron Cahorn wanted – Who could baffle Lupin's plans better than the cunning and patient Ganimard?

The baron lost no time. It is a four-mile walk from the castle to the little town of Caudebec. He did the distance with a quick and joyous step, stimulated by the hope of safety.

After many fruitless endeavours to discover the chief-inspector's address, he went to the office of the *Réveil*, which is on the quay. He found the writer of the paragraph, who, going to the window, said:

'Ganimard! Why, you're sure to meet him, rod in hand, on the quay. That's where I picked up with him and read his name, by accident, on his fishing-rod. Look, there he is, the little old man in the frock-coat and a straw hat, under the trees.'

'A frock-coat and a straw hat?'

'Yes. He's a queer specimen, close-tongued and a trifle testy.'

Five minutes later, the baron accosted the famous Ganimard, introduced himself and made an attempt to enter into conversation. Failing in this, he broached the question quite frankly and laid his case before him.

The other listened, without moving a muscle or taking his eyes from the water. Then he turned his head to the Baron, eyed him from head to foot with a look of profound compassion and said:

'Sir, it is not usual for criminals to warn the people whom they mean to rob. Arsène Lupin, in particular, never indulges in that sort of bounce.'

'Still . . .'

'Sir, if I had the smallest doubt, believe me, the pleasure of once more locking up that dear Lupin would outweigh every consideration. Unfortunately, the youth is already in prison.'

'Suppose he escapes?'

'People don't escape from the Santé.'

'But Lupin . . .'

'Lupin no more than another.'

'Still . . .'

'Very well, if he does escape, so much the better; I'll nab him again. Meanwhile, you can sleep soundly and stop frightening my fish.'

The conversation was ended. The baron returned home

feeling more or less reassured by Ganimard's indifference. He saw to his bolts, kept a watch upon his servants, and another forty-eight hours passed, during which he almost succeeded in persuading himself that, after all, his fears were groundless. There was no doubt about it: as Ganimard had said, criminals don't warn the people whom they mean to rob.

The date was drawing near. On the morning of Tuesday the twenty-sixth, nothing particular happened. But, at three o'clock in the afternoon, a boy rang and handed in this telegram:

No goods Batignolles. Get everything ready for tomorrow night – *Arsène*.

Once again, Cahorn lost his head, so much so that he asked himself whether he would not do better to yield to Arsène Lupin's demands.

He hurried off to Caudebec. Ganimard was seated on a camp-stool, fishing, in the same spot as before. The baron handed him the telegram without a word.

'Well?' said the detective.

'Well what? It's fixed for tomorrow!'

'What is?'

'The burglary! The theft of my collections!'

Ganimard turned to him, and, folding his arms across his chest, cried, in a tone of impatience:

'Why, you don't really mean to say that you think I'm going to trouble myself about this stupid business?'

'What fee will you take to spend Wednesday night at the castle?'

'Not a penny. Don't bother me!'

'Name your own price. I'm a rich man, a very rich man.'

The brutality of the offer took Ganimard aback. He replied, more calmly.

'I am here on leave and I have no right to . . .'

'No one shall know. I undertake to be silent, whatever happens!'

'Oh, nothing will happen!'

'Well, look here; is three thousand francs enough?'

The inspector took a pinch of snuff, reflected and said:

'Very well. But it's only fair to tell you that you are throwing your money away.'

'I don't mind.'

'In that case ... And besides, after all, one can never tell, with that devil of a Lupin! He must have a whole gang at his orders ... Are you sure of your servants?'

'Well, I ...'

'Then we must not rely upon them. I'll wire to two of my own men; that will make us feel safer ... And, now, leave me; we must not be seen together. Tomorrow evening, at nine o'clock.'

On the morning of the next day, the date fixed by Arsène Lupin, Baron Cahorn took down his trophy of arms, polished up his pistols and made a thorough inspection of the Malaquis, without discovering anything suspicious.

At half past eight in the evening, he dismissed his servants for the night. They slept in a wing facing the road, but set a little way back and right at the end of the castle. As soon as he was alone, he softly opened the four doors. In a little while, he heard footsteps approaching.

Ganimard introduced his assistants, two powerfully-built fellows, with bull necks and huge, strong hands, and asked for certain explanations. After ascertaining the disposition of the place, he carefully closed and barricaded every issue by which the threatened rooms could be entered. He examined the walls, lifted up the tapestries, and finally installed his detectives in the central gallery. 'No nonsense, do you understand? You're not here to sleep. At the least sound, open the windows on the court and call me. Keep a look-out also on the water side. Thirty feet of steep cliff doesn't frighten scoundrels of that stamp.'

He locked them in, took away the keys and said to the baron:

'And now to our post.'

He had selected, as the best place in which to spend the night, a small room contrived in the thickness of the outer walls, between the two main doors. It had at one time been the watchman's lodge. A spy-hole opened upon the bridge, another upon the court. In one corner was what looked like the mouth of a well.

'You told me, did you not, monsieur le baron, that this well is the only entrance to the underground passage and that it has been stopped up since the memory of man?'

'Yes.'

'Therefore, unless there should happen to be another outlet, unknown to any but Arsène Lupin, which seems pretty unlikely, we can be easy in our minds.'

He placed the three chairs in a row, settled himself comfortably at full length, lit his pipe, and sighed:

'Upon my word, monsieur le baron, I must be very eager to build an additional storey to the little house in which I mean to end my days, to accept so elementary a job as this. I shall tell the story to our friend Lupin; he'll split his sides with laughter.'

The baron did not laugh. With ears pricked up, he questioned the silence with ever-growing restlessness. From time to time, he leaned over the well and plunged an anxious eye into the yawning cavity.

The clock struck eleven; midnight; one o'clock.

Suddenly, he seized the arm of Ganimard, who woke with a start:

'Do you hear that?'

'Yes.'

'What is it?'

'It's myself, snoring!'

'No, no, listen . . .'

'Oh yes, it's a motor-horn.'

'Well?'

'Well, it's as unlikely that Lupin should come by motor-car as that he should use a battering-ram to demolish your castle. So I should go to sleep, if I were you, monsieur le baron ... as I shall have the honour of doing once more. Good night!'

This was the only alarm. Ganimard resumed his interrupted slumbers; and the baron heard nothing save his loud and regular snoring.

At break of day, they left their cell. A great calm peace, the peace of the morning by the cool waterside, reigned over the castle. Cahorn, beaming with joy, and Ganimard, placid as ever, climbed the staircase. Not a sound. Nothing suspicious.

'What did I tell you, monsieur le baron? I really ought not to have accepted ... I feel ashamed of myself ...'

He took the keys and entered the gallery.

On two chairs, with bent bodies and hanging arms, sat the two detectives, fast asleep.

'What, in the name of all the ...' growled the inspector.

At the same moment, the baron uttered a cry:

'The pictures! ... The credence-table!'

He stammered and spluttered, with his hand outstretched towards the dismantled walls, with their bare nails and slack cords. The Watteau and the two Rubens had disappeared! The tapestries had been removed, the glass cases emptied of their trinkets!

'And my Louis XVI sconces! ... And the Regency chandelier! ... And my twelfth-century Virgin! ...'

He ran from place to place, maddened, in despair. Distraught with rage and grief, he quoted the purchase-prices, added up his losses, piled up figures, all promiscuously, in indistinct words and incomplete phrases. He stamped his feet, flung himself about and, in short, behaved like a ruined man who had nothing before him but suicide.

If anything could have consoled him, it would have been the sight of Ganimard's stupefaction. Contrary to the baron, the inspector did not move. He seemed petrified, and with a dazed eye, examined things. The windows? They were fastened. The locks of the doors? Untouched. There was not a crack in the ceiling, not a hole in the floor. Everything was in perfect order. The whole thing must have been carried out methodically, after an inexorable and logical plan.

'Arsène Lupin ... Arsène Lupin,' he muttered, giving way.

Suddenly, he leapt upon the two detectives, as though at last overcome with rage, and shook them and swore at them furiously. They did not wake up!

'The deuce!' he said. 'Can they have been ...?'

He bent over them and scrutinized them closely, one after the other: they were both asleep, but their sleep was not natural. He said to the baron:

'They have been drugged.'

'But by whom?'

'By him, of course ... or by his gang, acting under his instructions. It's a trick in his own manner. I recognize his touch.'

'In that case, I am undone: the thing is hopeless.'

'Hopeless.'

'But this is abominable; it's monstrous.'

'Lodge an information.'

'What's the good?'

'Well, you may as well try ... the law has its resources ...'

'The law! But you can see for yourself ... Why, at this very moment, when you might be looking for a clue, discovering something, you're not even stirring.'

'Discover something, with Arsène Lupin! But, my dear sir, Arsène Lupin never leaves anything behind him! There's no chance with Arsène Lupin! I am beginning to wonder whether he got himself arrested by me of his own free will, in America!'

'Then I must give up the hope of recovering my pictures or anything! But he has stolen the pearls of my collection. I would give a fortune to get them back. If there's nothing to be done against him, let him name his price.'

Ganimard looked at him steadily:

'That's a sound notion. Do you stick to it?'

'Yes, yes, yes! But why do you ask?'

'I have an idea.'

'What idea?'

'We'll talk of it if nothing comes of the inquiry ... Only, not a word about me, to a soul, if you wish me to succeed.'

And he added, between his teeth:

'Besides, I have nothing to be proud of.'

The two men gradually recovered consciousness, with the stupefied look of men awakening from an hypnotic sleep. They opened astounded eyes, tried to make out what had happened. Ganimard questioned them. They remembered nothing.

'Still you must have seen somebody?'

'No, nobody.'

'Try and think?'

'No, nobody.'

'Did you have a drink?'

They reflected and one of them replied:

'Yes, I had some water.'

'Out of that bottle there?'

'Yes.'

'I had some too,' said the other.

Ganimard smelt the water, tasted it. It had no particular scent or flavour.

'Come,' he said, 'we are wasting our time. Problems set by Arsène Lupin can't be solved in five minutes. But, by Jingo, I swear I'll catch him! He's won the second bout. The rubber game to me!'

That day, a charge of aggravated larceny was brought by Baron Cahorn against Arséne Lupin, a prisoner awaiting trial at the Santé.

The baron often regretted having laid his information when he saw the Malaquis made over to the gendarmes, the public prosecutor, the examining magistrate, the newspaper-reporters, and all the inquisitive who worm themselves in wherever they have no business to be.

Already the case was filling the public mind. It had taken place under such peculiar conditions and the name of Arsène Lupin excited men's imaginations to such a pitch that the most fantastic stories crowded the columns of the press and found acceptance with the public.

But the original letter of Arsène Lupin, which was published in the *Echo de France* – and no one ever knew who had supplied the text – the letter in which Baron Cahorn was insolently warned of what threatened him, caused the greatest excitement. Fabulous explanations were offered forthwith. The old legends were revived. The newspapers reminded their readers of the existence of the famous subterranean passages. And the public prosecutor, influenced by these statements, pursued his search in that direction.

The castle was ransacked from top to bottom. Every stone was examined; the wainscotings and chimneys, the frames of the mirrors and the rafters of the ceilings were carefully inspected. By the light of torches, the searchers investigated the immense cellars in which the lords of the Malaquis had been used to pile up their provisions and munitions of war. They sounded the very bowels of the rock. All to no purpose. They discovered not the slightest trace of a tunnel. No secret passage existed.

Very well, was the answer on every side; but pictures and furniture don't vanish like ghosts. They go out through doors and windows; and the people that take them also go in and out through doors and windows. Who are these people? How did they get in? And how did they get out?

The public prosecutor of Rouen, persuaded of his own incompetence, asked for the assistance of the Paris police. M. Dudouis, the chief of the detective-service, sent the most efficient bloodhounds in his employ. He himself paid a forty-eight hours' visit to the Malaquis, but met with no greater success.

It was after his return that he sent for Chief-Inspector

Ganimard, whose services he had so often had occasion to value.

Ganimard listened in silence to the instructions of his superior and then, tossing his head, said:

'I think we shall be on a false scent so long as we continue to search the castle. The solution lies elsewhere.'

'With Arsène Lupin? If you think that, then you believe that he took part in the burglary.'

'I do think so. I go further, I consider it certain.'

'Come, Ganimard, this is absurd. Arsène Lupin is in prison.'

'Arsène Lupin is in prison, I agree. He is being watched, I grant you. But, if he had his legs in irons, his hands bound and his mouth gagged, I should still be of the same opinion.'

'But why this persistency?'

'Because no one else is capable of contriving a plan on so large a scale and of contriving it in such a way that it succeeds . . . as this has succeeded.'

'Words, Ganimard!'

'They are true words, for all that. Only, it's no use looking for underground passages, for stones that turn on a pivot, and stuff and nonsense of that kind. Our friend does not employ such antiquated measures. He is a man of to-day, or rather of tomorrow.'

'And what do you conclude?'

'I conclude by asking you straight to let me spend an hour with Lupin.'

'In his cell?'

'Yes. We were on excellent terms during the crossing from America and I venture to think that he is not without friendly feeling for the man who arrested him. If he can tell me what I want to know, without compromising himself, he will be quite willing to spare me an unnecessary journey.'

It was just after mid-day when Ganimard was shown into Arsène Lupin's cell. Lupin, who was lying on his bed, raised his head and uttered an exclamation of delight:

'Well, this is a surprise! Dear old Ganimard here!'

'Himself.'

'I have hoped for many things in this retreat of my own choosing, but for none more eagerly than the pleasure of welcoming you here.'

'You are too good.'

'Not at all, not at all. I have the liveliest regard for you.'

'I am proud to hear it.'

'I have said it a thousand times: Ganimard is our greatest detective. He's *almost* – see how frank I am – *almost* as clever as Holmlock Shears. But, really, I'm awfully sorry to have nothing better than this stool to offer you. And not a drink of any kind! Not so much as a glass of beer! Do forgive me: I am only just passing through town, you see!'

Ganimard smiled and sat down on the stool; and the prisoner, glad of the opportunity of speaking, continued:

'By Jove, what a treat to see a decent man's face! I am sick of the looks of all these spies who go through my cell and my pockets ten times a day to make sure that I am not planning an escape. Gad, how fond the government must be of me!'

'They show their judgement.'

'No, no! I should be so happy if they would let me lead my own quiet life.'

'On other people's money.'

'Just so. It would be so simple. But I'm letting my tongue run on, I'm talking nonsense and I daresay you're in a hurry. Come, Ganimard, tell me to what I owe the honour of this visit.'

'The Cahorn case,' said Ganimard, abruptly.

'Stop! Wait a bit ... You see, I have so many on hand! First, let me search my brain for the Cahorn pigeonhole ... Ah, I have it! Cahorn, Château de Malaquis, Seine-Inférieure ... Two Rubens, a Watteau, and a few minor trifles.'

'Trifles!'

'Oh yes, all this is of small importance. I have bigger things on hand. However, you're interested in the case and that's enough for me ... Go ahead, Ganimard.'

'I need not tell you, need I, how far we have got with the investigation?'

'No, not at all. I have seen the morning papers. And I will even take the liberty of saying that you are not making much progress.'

'That's just why I have come to throw myself upon your kindness.'

'I am entirely at your service.'

'First of all, the thing was done by you, was it not?'

'From start to finish.'

'The registered letter? The telegram?'

'Were sent by yours truly. In fact, I ought to have the receipts somewhere.'

Arsène opened the drawer of a little deal table which, with the bed and the stool, composed all the furniture of his cell, took out two scraps of paper and handed them to Ganimard.

'Hullo!' cried the latter. 'Why, I thought you were being kept under constant observation and searched on the slightest pretext. And it appears that you read the papers and collect post-office receipts ...'

'Bah! Those men are such fools. They rip up the lining of my waistcoat, explore the soles of my boots, listen at the walls of my cell; but not one of them would believe that Arsène Lupin could be such a fool as to choose so obvious a hiding-place. That's just what I reckoned on.'

Ganimard exclaimed, in amusement:

'What a funny chap you are! You're beyond me. Come, tell me the story.'

'Oh, I say! Not so fast! Initiate you into all my secrets ... reveal my little tricks to you? That's a serious matter.'

'Was I wrong in thinking that I could rely on you to oblige me?'

'No, Ganimard, and, as you insist upon it . . .'

Arsène Lupin took two or three strides across his cell. Then, stopping:

'What do you think of my letter to the baron?' he asked.

'I think you wanted to have some fun, to tickle the gallery a bit.'

'Ah, there you go! Tickle the gallery, indeed! Upon my word, Ganimard, I gave you credit for more sense! Do you really imagine that I, Arsène Lupin, waste my time with such childish pranks as that? Is it likely that I should have written the letter, if I could have rifled the baron without it? Do try and understand that the letter was the indispensable starting-point, the main-spring that set the whole machine in motion. Look here, let us proceed in order and, if you like, prepare the Malaquis burglary together.'

'Very well.'

'Now follow me. I have to do with an impregnable and closely-guarded castle . . . Am I to throw up the game and forgo the treasures which I covet, because the castle that contains them happens to be inaccessible?'

'Clearly not.'

'Am I to try to carry it by assault as in the old days, at the head of a band of adventurers?'

'That would be childish.'

'Am I to enter it by stealth?'

'Impossible.'

'There remains only one way, which is to get myself invited by the owner of the foresaid castle.'

'It's an original idea.'

'And so easy! Suppose that, one day, the said owner receives a letter warning him of a plot hatched against him by one Arsène Lupin, a notorious housebreaker. What is he sure to do?'

'Send the letter to the public prosecutor.'

'Who will laugh at him, *because the said Lupin is actually under lock and key.* The natural consequence is the utter bewilderment of the worthy man, who is ready and anxious to ask for the assistance of the first-comer. Am I right?'

'Quite so.'

'And, if he happens to read in the local rag that a famous detective is staying in the neighbourhood ...?'

'He will go and apply to that detective.'

'Exactly. But, on the other hand, let us assume that, foreseeing this inevitable step, Arsène Lupin has asked one of his ablest friends to take up his quarters at Caudebec, to pick up acquaintance with a contributor to the *Réveil*, a paper, mark you, to which the baron subscribes, and to drop a hint that he is so-and-so, the famous detective. What will happen next?'

'The contributor will send a paragraph to the *Réveil* stating that the detective is staying at Caudebec.'

'Exactly; and one of two things follows; either the fish – I mean Cahorn – does not rise to the bait, in which case nothing happens. Or else – and this is the more likely presumption – he nibbles, in which case you have our dear Cahorn imploring the assistance of one of my own friends against me!'

'This is becoming more and more original.'

'Of course, the sham detective begins by refusing. Thereupon, a telegram from Arsène Lupin. Dismay of the baron, who renews his entreaties with my friend and offers him so much to watch over his safety. The friend aforesaid accepts and brings with him two chaps of our gang, who, during the night, while Cahorn is kept in sight by his protector, remove a certain number of things through the window and lower them with ropes into a barge freighted for the purpose. It's as simple as ... Lupin.'

'And it's just wonderful,' cried Ganimard, 'and I have no words in which to praise the boldness of the idea and the ingenuity of the details. But I can hardly imagine a detective so illustrious that his name should have attracted and impressed the baron to that extent.'

'There is one and one only.'

'Who?'

'The most illustrious of them all, the arch-enemy of Arsène Lupin, in short, Inspector Ganimard.'

'What, myself?'

'Yourself, Ganimard. And that's the delightful part of it: if you go down and persuade the baron to talk, he will end by discovering that it is your duty to arrest yourself, just as you arrested me in America. A humorous revenge, what? I shall have Ganimard arrested by Ganimard!'

Arsène Lupin laughed loud and long, while the inspector bit his lips with vexation. The joke did not appear to him worthy of so much merriment.

The entrance of a warder gave him time to recover. The man brought the meal which Arsène Lupin, by special favour, was allowed to have sent in from the neighbouring restaurant. After placing the tray on the table, he went away. Arsène sat down, broke his bread, ate a mouthful or two, and continued:

'But be easy, my dear Ganimard, you won't have to go. I have something to tell you that will strike you dumb. The Cahorn case is about to be withdrawn.'

'What!'

'About to be withdrawn, I said.'

'Nonsense! I have just left the chief.'

'And then? Does Monsieur Dudouis know more than I do about my concerns? You must learn that Ganimard – excuse me – that the sham Ganimard remained on very good terms with Baron Cahorn. The baron – and this is his main reason for keeping the thing quiet – charged him with the very delicate mission of negotiating a deal with me; and the chances are that by this time, on payment of a certain sum, the baron is once more in possession of his pet knick-knacks. In return for which he will withdraw the charge. Wherefore there is no question of theft. Wherefore the public prosecutor will have to abandon...'

Ganimard gazed at the prisoner with an air of stupefaction:

'But how do you know all this?'

'I have just received the telegram I was expecting.'

'You have just received a telegram?'

'This very moment, my friend. I was too polite to read it in your presence. But, if you will allow me . . .'

'You're poking fun at me, Lupin.'

'Have the kindness, my friend, to cut off the top of that egg, gently. You will see for yourself that I am not poking fun at you.'

Ganimard obeyed mechanically and broke the egg with the blade of a knife. A cry of surprise escaped him. The shell was empty but for a sheet of blue paper. At Arsène's request, he unfolded it. It was a telegram, or rather a portion of a telegram from which the postal indications had been removed. He read,

Arrangement settled. Hundred thousand paid over, delivered. All well.

'Hundred thousand paid over?' he uttered.

'Yes, a hundred thousand francs. It's not much, but these are hard times . . . And my general expenses are so heavy! If you knew the amount of my budget . . . it's like the budget of a big town!'

Ganimard rose to go. His ill-humour had left him. He thought for a few moments and cast a mental glance over the whole business, trying to discover a weak point. Then, in a voice that frankly revealed his admiration as an expert, he said:

'It's a good thing that there are not dozens like you, or there would be nothing for us but to shut up shop.'

Arsène Lupin assumed a modest simper and replied:

'Oh, I had to do something to amuse myself, to occupy my spare time . . . especially as the scoop could only succeed while I was in prison.'

'What do you mean?' exclaimed Ganimard. 'Your trial your defence, your examination: isn't that enough for you to amuse yourself with?'

'No, because I have decided not to attend my trial.'

'Oh, I say!'

Arsène Lupin repeated deliberately:

'I shall not attend my trial.'

'Really!'

'Why, my dear fellow, you surely don't think I mean to rot in gaol? The mere suggestion is an insult. Let me tell you that Arsène Lupin remains in prison as long as he thinks fit and not a moment longer.'

'It might have been more prudent to begin by not entering it,' said the inspector, ironically.

'Ah, so you're chaffing me, sirrah? Do you remember that you had the honour to effect my arrest? Well, learn from me, my respectable friend, that no one, neither you nor another, could have laid a hand upon me, if a much more important interest had not occupied my attention at that critical moment.'

'You surprise me.'

'A woman had cast her eyes upon me, Ganimard, and I loved her. Do you realize all that the fact implies when a woman whom one loves casts her eyes upon one? I cared about little else, I assure you. And that is why I'm here.'

'You've been here a long time, allow me to observe.'

'I was anxious to forget. Don't laugh, it was a charming adventure and I still have a tender recollection of it ... And then I have had a slight nervous breakdown. We lead such a feverish existence nowadays! It's a good thing to take a rest-cure from time to time. And there's no place for it like this. They carry out the cure in all its strictness at the Santé.'

'Arsène Lupin,' said Ganimard, 'you're pulling my leg.'

'Ganimard,' replied Lupin, 'this is Friday. On Wednesday next, I'll come and smoke a cigar with you, in the Rue Pergolese, at four o'clock in the afternoon.'

'Arsène Lupin, I shall expect you.'

They shook hands like two friends who have a proper

sense of each other's value and the old detective turned towards the door.

'Ganimard!'

Ganimard looked round:

'What is it?'

'Ganimard, you've forgotten your watch.'

'My watch?'

'Yes, I've just found it in my pocket.'

He returned it, with apologies:

'Forgive me ... it's a bad habit ... They've taken mine, but that's no reason why I should rob you of yours. Especially as I have a chronometer here which keeps perfect time and satisfies all my requirements.'

He took out of the drawer a large, thick, comfortable-looking gold watch, hanging to a heavy chain.

'And out of whose pocket does this come?' asked Ganimard.

Arsène Lupin carelessly inspected the initials:

'J.B. ... What on earth does that stand for? ... Oh yes, I remember: Jules Bouvier, my examining magistrate, a charming fellow...'

8

The Superfluous Finger

Jacques Futrelle

S H E drew off her left glove, a delicate, crinkled suede affair, and offered her bare hand to the surgeon. An artist would have called it beautiful, perfect, even; the surgeon, professionally enough, set it down as an excellent structural specimen. From the polished pink nails of the tapering fingers to the firm, well-moulded wrist, it was distinctly the hand of a woman of ease – one that had never known labour, a pampered hand Dr Prescott told himself.

'The fore-finger,' she explained calmly. 'I should like to have it amputated at the first joint, please.'

'Amputated?' gasped Dr Prescott. He stared into the pretty face of his caller. It was flushed softly, and the red lips were parted in a slight smile. It seemed quite an ordinary affair to her. The surgeon bent over her hand with quick interest. 'Amputated!' he repeated.

'I came to you,' she went on with a nod, 'because I have been informed that you are one of the most skilful men of your profession, and the cost of the operation is quite immaterial.'

Dr Prescott pressed the pink nail of the fore-finger, then permitted the blood to rush back into it. Several times he did this, then he turned the hand over and scrutinized it closely inside from the delicately lined palm to the tips of the fingers. When he looked up at last there was an expression of frank bewilderment on his face.

'What's the matter with it?' he asked.

'Nothing,' the woman replied pleasantly. 'I merely want it off from the first joint.'

The surgeon leaned back in his chair with a frown of perplexity on his brow, and his visitor was subjected to a sharp, professional stare. She bore it unflinchingly and even smiled a little at his obvious perturbation.

'Why do you want it off?' he demanded.

The woman shrugged her shoulders a little impatiently.

'I can't tell you that,' she replied. 'It really is not necessary that you should know. You are a surgeon, I want an operation performed. That is all.'

There was a long pause; the mutual stare didn't waver.

'You must understand, Miss – Miss – er –' began Dr Prescott at last. 'By the way, you have not introduced yourself?' She was silent. 'May I ask your name?'

'My name is of no consequence,' she replied calmly. 'I might, of course, give you a name, but it would not be mine, therefore any name would be superfluous.'

Again the surgeon stared.

'When do you want the operation performed?' he inquired.

'Now,' she replied. 'I am ready.'

'You must understand,' he said severely, 'that surgery is a profession for the relief of human suffering, not for mutilation – wilful mutilation I might say.'

'I understand that perfectly,' she said. 'But where a person submits of her own desire to – to mutilation as you call it, I can see no valid objection on your part.'

'It would be criminal to remove a finger where there is no necessity for it,' continued the surgeon bluntly. 'No good end could be served.'

A trace of disappointment showed in the young woman's face, and again she shrugged her shoulders.

'The question after all,' she said finally, 'is not one of

ethics but is simply whether or not you will perform the operation. Would you do it for, say, a thousand dollars?'

'Not for five thousand dollars,' blurted the surgeon.

'Well, for ten thousand then?' she asked, quite casually.

All sorts of questions were pounding in Dr Prescott's mind. Why did a young and beautiful woman desire – why was she anxious even – to sacrifice a perfectly healthy finger? What possible purpose would it serve to mar a hand which was as nearly perfect as any he had ever seen? Was it some insane caprice? Staring deeply into her steady, quiet eyes he could only be convinced of her sanity. Then what?

'No, madam,' he said at last, vehemently, 'I would not perform the operation for any sum you might mention, unless I was first convinced that the removal of that finger was absolutely necessary. That, I think, is all.'

He arose as if to end the consultation. The woman remained seated and continued thoughtful for a minute.

'As I understand it,' she said, 'you *would* perform the operation if I could convince you that it was absolutely necessary?'

'Certainly,' he replied promptly, almost eagerly. His curiosity was aroused. 'Then it would come within the range of my professional duties.'

'Won't you take my word that it is necessary, and that it is impossible for me to explain why?'

'No. I must know why.'

The woman arose and stood facing him. The disappointment had gone from her face now.

'Very well,' she remarked steadily. 'You *will* perform the operation if it is necessary, therefore if I should shoot the finger off, perhaps –?'

'Shoot it off?' exclaimed Dr Prescott in amazement. 'Shoot it off?'

'That is what I said,' she replied calmly. 'If I should shoot the finger off you would consent to dress the wound? You would make any necessary amputation?'

She held up the finger under discussion and looked at it

curiously. Dr Prescott himself stared at it with a sudden new interest.

'Shoot it off?' he repeated. 'Why you must be mad to contemplate such a thing,' he exploded, and his face flushed in sheer anger. 'I – I will have nothing whatever to do with the affair, madam. Good day.'

'I should have to be very careful of course,' she mused, 'but I think perhaps one shot would be sufficient, then I should come to you and demand that you dress it?'

There was a question in the tone. Dr Prescott stared at her for a full minute then walked over and opened the door.

'In my profession, madam,' he said coldly, 'there is too much possibility of doing good and relieving actual suffering for me to consider this matter or discuss it further with you. There are three persons now waiting in the ante-room who *need* my services. I shall be compelled to ask you to excuse me.'

'But you will dress the wound?' the woman insisted, undaunted by his forbidding tone and manner.

'I shall have nothing whatever to do with it,' declared the surgeon, positively, finally. 'If you need the services of any medical man permit me to suggest that it is an alienist and not a surgeon.'

The woman didn't appear to take offence.

'Someone would have to dress it,' she continued insistently. 'I should much prefer that it be a man of undisputed skill – you, I mean, therefore I shall call again. Good day.'

There was a rustle of silken skirts and she was gone. Dr Prescott stood for an instant gazing after her in frank wonder and annoyance in his eyes, his attitude, then he went back and sat down at the desk. The crinkled suede glove still lay where she had left it. He examined it gingerly then with a final shake of his head dismissed the affair and turned to other things.

Early next afternoon Dr Prescott was sitting in his office writing when the door from the ante-room where patients awaited his leisure was thrown open and the young man in attendance rushed in.

'A lady has fainted, sir,' he said hurriedly. 'She seems to be hurt.'

Dr Prescott arose quickly and strode out. There, lying helplessly back in her chair with white face and closed eyes, was his visitor of the day before. He stepped towards her quickly then hesitated as he recalled their conversation. Finally, however, professional instinct, the desire to relieve suffering, and perhaps curiosity too, caused him to go to her. The left hand was wrapped in an improvised bandage through which there was a trickle of blood. He glared at it with incredulous eyes.

'Hanged if she didn't do it,' he blurted out, angrily.

The fainting spell, Dr Prescott saw, was due only to loss of blood and physical pain, and he busied himself trying to restore her to consciousness. Meanwhile he gave some hurried instructions to the young man who was in attendance in the ante-room.

'Call up Professor Van Dusen on the phone,' he directed, 'and ask him if he can assist me in a minor operation. Tell him it's rather a curious case and I am sure it will interest him.'

It was in this manner that the problem of the superfluous finger first came to the attention of The Thinking Machine. He arrived just as the mysterious woman was opening her eyes to consciousness from the fainting spell. She stared at him glassily, unrecognizingly; then her glance wandered to Dr Prescott. She smiled.

'I knew you'd have to do it,' she murmured weakly.

After the ether had been administered for the operation, a simple and an easy one, Dr Prescott stated the circumstances of the case to The Thinking Machine. The scientist stood with his long, slender fingers resting lightly on the young woman's pulse, listening in silence.

'What do you make of it?' demanded the surgeon.

The Thinking Machine didn't say. At the moment he

was leaning over the unconscious woman squinting at her forehead. With his disengaged hand he stroked the delicately pencilled eyebrows several times the wrong way, and again at close range squinted at them. Dr Prescott saw and seeing, understood.

'No, it isn't that,' he said and he shuddered a little. 'I thought of it myself. Her bodily condition is excellent, splendid.'

It was some time later when the young woman was sleeping lightly, placidly under the influence of a soothing potion, that The Thinking Machine spoke of the peculiar events which had preceded the operation. Then he was sitting in Dr Prescott's private office. He had picked up a woman's glove from the desk.

'This is the glove she left when she first called, isn't it?' he inquired.

'Yes.'

'Did you happen to see her remove it?'

'Yes.'

The Thinking Machine curiously examined the dainty, perfumed trifle, then, arising suddenly, went into the adjoining room where the woman lay asleep. He stood for an instant gazing down admiringly at the exquisite, slender figure; then, bending over, he looked closely at her left hand. When at last he straightened up it seemed that some unspoken question in his mind had been answered. He rejoined Dr Prescott.

'It's difficult to say what motive is back of her desire to have the finger amputated,' he said musingly. 'I could perhaps venture a conjecture but if the matter is of no importance to you beyond mere curiosity I should not like to do so. Within a few months from now, I daresay, important developments will result and I should like to find out something more about her. That I can do when she returns to wherever she is stopping in the city. I'll phone to Mr Hatch and have him ascertain for me where she goes, her name and other things which may throw a light on the matter.'

'He will follow her?'

'Yes, precisely. Now we only seem to know two facts in connection with her. First, she is English.'

'Yes,' Dr Prescott agreed. 'Her accent, her appearance, everything about her suggests that.'

'And the second fact is of no consequence at the moment,' resumed The Thinking Machine. 'Let me use your phone please.'

Hutchinson Hatch, reporter, was talking.

'When the young woman left Dr Prescott's she took the cab which had been ordered for her and told the driver to go ahead until she stopped him. I got a good look at her, by the way. I managed to pass just as she entered the cab and walking on down got into another cab which was waiting for me. Her cab drove for three or four blocks aimlessly, and finally stopped. The driver stooped down as if to listen to someone inside, and my cab passed. Then the other cab turned across a side street and after going eight or ten blocks pulled up in front of an apartment house. The young woman got out and went inside. Her cab went away. Inside I found out that she was Mrs Frederick Chevedon Morey. She came there last Tuesday – this is Friday – with her husband, and they engaged –'

'Yes, I knew she had a husband,' interrupted The Thinking Machine.

'– engaged apartments for three months. When I had learned this much I remembered your instructions as to steamers from Europe landing on the day they took apartments or possibly a day or so before. I was just going out when Mrs Morey stepped out of the elevator and preceded me to the door. She had changed her clothing and wore a different hat.

'It didn't seem to be necessary then to find out where she was going for I knew I could find her when I wanted to, so I went down and made inquiries at the steamship offices. I found, after a great deal of work, that no one of the three steamers which arrived the day they took apartments brought a Mr and Mrs Morey, but one steamer on the day before brought a Mr and Mrs David Girardeau from Liverpool. Mrs Girardeau answered Mrs Morey's description to the minutest detail even to the gown she wore when she left the steamer – that is the same she wore when she left Dr Prescott's after the operation.'

That was all. The Thinking Machine sat with his enormous yellow head pillowed against a high-backed chair and his long slender fingers pressed tip to tip. He asked no questions and made no comment for a long time, then :

'About how many minutes was it from the time she entered the house until she came out again?'

'Not more than ten or fifteen,' was the reply. 'I was still talking casually to the people downstairs trying to find out something about them.'

'What do they pay for their apartment?' asked the scientist, irrelevantly.

'Three hundred dollars a month.'

The Thinking Machine's squint eyes were fixed immovably on a small discoloured spot on the ceiling of his laboratory.

'Whatever else may develop in this matter, Mr Hatch,' he said after a time, 'we must admit that we have met a woman with extraordinary courage – nerve, I daresay you'd call it. When Mrs Morey left Dr Prescott's operating room she was so ill and weak from the shock that she could hardly stand, and now you tell me she changed her dress and went out immediately after she returned home.'

'Well, of course –' Hatch said, apologetically.

'In that event,' resumed the scientist, 'we must assume also that the matter is one of the utmost importance to her, and yet the nature of the case had led me to believe that it might be months, perhaps, before there would be any particular development in it.'

'What? How?' asked the reporter.

'The final development doesn't seem, from what I know,

to belong on this side of the ocean at all,' explained The Thinking Machine. 'I imagine it is a case for Scotland Yard. The problem of course is: What made it necessary for her to get rid of that finger. If we admit her sanity we can count the possible answers to this question on one hand, and at least three of these answers take the case back to England.' He paused. 'By the way, was Mrs Morey's hand bound up in the same way when you saw her the second time?'

'Her left hand was in a muff,' explained the reporter. 'I couldn't see but it seems to me that she wouldn't have had time to change the manner of its dressing.'

'It's extraordinary,' commented the scientist. He arose and paced back and forth across the room. 'Extraordinary,' he repeated. 'One can't help but admire the fortitude of women under certain circumstances, Mr Hatch. I think perhaps this particular case had better be called to the attention of Scotland Yard, but first I think it would be best for you to call on the Moreys tomorrow – you can find some pretext – and see what you can learn about them. You are an ingenious young man – I'll leave it all to you.'

Hatch did call at the Morey apartments on the morrow but under circumstances which were not at all what he expected. He went there in a cab at full speed because the manager of the apartment house had phoned that Mrs Frederick Chevedon Morey had been found murdered in her apartments. The detective ran up two flights of stairs and blundered, heavy-footed into the rooms, and there he paused in the presence of death.

The body of the woman lay on the floor and some one had mercifully covered it with a cloth from the bed. Detective Mallory drew the covering down from over the face and Hatch stared with a feeling of awe at the beautiful countenance which had, on the day before, been so radiant with life. Now it was distorted into an expression of awful agony and the limbs were drawn up convulsively. The mark of the murderer was at the white, exquisitely rounded throat – great black bruises, where powerful merciless fingers had sunk deeply into the soft flesh.

A physician in the house had preceded the police. After one glance at the woman and a swift, comprehensive look about the room, Detective Mallory turned to him inquiringly.

'She has been dead for several hours,' the doctor volunteered, 'possibly since early last night. It appears that some virulent, burning poison was administered and then she was choked. I gather this from an examination of her mouth.'

These things were readily to be seen; also it was plainly evident for many reasons that the finger marks at the throat were those of a man, but each step beyond these obvious facts only served to further bewilder the investigators. First was the statement of the night elevator boy.

'Mr and Mrs Morey left here last night about eleven o'clock,' he said. 'I know because I telephoned for a cab, and later brought them down from the third floor. They went into the manager's office leaving two suitcases in the hall. When they came out I took the suitcases to a cab that was waiting. They got in it and drove away.'

'When did they return?' inquired the detective.

'They didn't return, sir,' responded the boy. 'I was on duty until six o'clock this morning. It just happened that no one came in after they went out until I was off duty at six.'

The detective turned to the physician again.

'Then she couldn't have been dead since early last night,' he said.

'She has been dead for several hours – at least twelve, possibly longer,' said the physician firmly. 'There's no possible argument about that.'

The detective stared at him scornfully for an instant, then looked at the manager of the house.

'What was said when Mr and Mrs Morey entered your office last night?' he asked. 'Were you there?'

'I was there, yes,' was the reply. 'Mr Morey explained that

they had been called away for a few days unexpectedly, and left the keys of the apartment with me. That was all that was said; I saw the elevator boy take the suitcases out for them as they went to the cab.'

'How did it come, then, if you knew they were away, that someone entered here this morning, and so found the body?'

'I discovered the body myself,' replied the manager. 'There was some electric wiring to be done in here and I thought their absence would be a good time for it. I came up to see about it and saw – that.'

He glanced at the covered body with a little shiver and a grimace. Detective Mallory was deeply thoughtful for several minutes.

'The woman is here and she's dead,' he said finally. 'If she is here she came back here, dead or alive last night between the time she went out with her husband and the time her body was found this morning. Now that's an absolute fact. But *how* did she come here?'

Of the three employees of the apartment house only the elevator boy on duty had not spoken. Now he spoke because the detective glared at him fiercely.

'I didn't see either Mr or Mrs Morey come in this morning,' he explained hastily. 'Nobody had come in at all except the postman and some delivery wagon drivers up to the time the body was found.'

Again Detective Mallory turned on the manager.

'Does any window of this apartment open on a fire escape?' he demanded.

'Yes – this way.'

They passed through the short hallway to the back. Both the windows were locked on the inside, so instantly it appeared that even if the woman had been brought into the room that way the windows would not have been fastened unless her murderer went out of the house the front way. When Detective Mallory reached this stage of the investigation he sat down and stared from one to the other of the silent little party as if he considered the entire matter some affair which they had perpetrated to annoy him.

Hutchinson Hatch started to say something, then thought better of it, and turning, went to the telephone below. Within a few minutes The Thinking Machine stepped out of a cab in front and paused in the lower hall long enough to listen to the facts developed. There was a perfect network of wrinkles in the dome-like brow when the reporter concluded.

'It's merely a transfer of the final development in the affair from England to this country,' he said enigmatically. 'Please phone for Dr Prescott to come here immediately.'

He went on to the Morey apartments. With only a curt nod for Detective Mallory, the only one of the small party who knew him, he proceeded to the body of the dead woman and squinted down without a trace of emotion into the white, pallid face. After a moment he dropped on his knees beside the inert body and examined the mouth and the finger-marks about the white throat.

'Carbolic acid and strangulation,' he remarked tersely to Detective Mallory who was leaning over watching him with something of hopeful eagerness in his stolid face. The Thinking Machine glanced past him to the manager of the house. 'Mr Morey is a powerful, athletic man in appearance?' he asked.

'Oh no,' was the reply. 'He's short and slight, only a little larger than you are.'

The scientist squinted aggressively at the manager as if the description were not quite what he expected. Then the slightly puzzled expression passed.

'Oh, I see,' he remarked. 'Played the piano.' This was not a question; it was a statement.

'Yes, a great deal,' was the reply, 'so much so in fact that twice we had complaints from other persons in the house despite the fact that they had been here only a few days.'

'Of course,' mused the scientist abstractedly. 'Of course. Perhaps Mrs Morey did not play at all?'

'I believe she told me she did not.'

The Thinking Machine drew down the thin cloth which had been thrown over the body and glanced at the left hand.

'Dear me! Dear me!' he exclaimed suddenly, and he arose. 'Dear me!' he repeated. 'That's the –' He turned to the manager and the two elevator boys. 'This is Mrs Morey beyond any question?'

The answer was a chorus of affirmation accompanied by some startling facial expressions.

'Did Mr and Mrs Morey employ any servants?'

'No,' was the reply. 'They had their meals in the café below most of the time. There is no housekeeping in these apartments at all.'

'How many persons live in the building?'

'A hundred I should say.'

'There is a great deal of passing to and fro, then?'

'Certainly. It was rather unusual that so few persons passed in and out last night and this morning, and certainly Mrs Morey and her husband were not among them if that's what you're trying to find out.'

The Thinking Machine glanced at the physician who was standing by silently.

'How long do you make it that she's been dead?' he asked.

'At least twelve hours,' replied the physician. 'Possibly longer.'

'Yes, nearer fourteen, I imagine.'

Abruptly he left the group and walked through the apartment and back again slowly. As he re-entered the room where the body lay, the door from the hall opened and Dr Prescott entered, followed by Hutchinson Hatch. The Thinking Machine led the surgeon straight to the body and drew the cloth back down from the face. Dr Prescott started back with an exclamation of astonishment, recognition.

'There's no doubt about it at all in your mind?' inquired the scientist.

'Not the slightest,' replied Dr Prescott positively. 'It's the same woman.'

'Yet look here!'

With a quick movement The Thinking Machine drew down the cloth still more. Dr Prescott, together with those who had no idea of what to expect, peered down at the body. After one glance the surgeon dropped on his knees and examined closely the dead left hand. The forefinger was off at the first joint. Dr Prescott stared, stared incredulously. After a moment his eyes left the maimed hand and settled again on her face.

'I have never seen – never dreamed – of such a startling –' he began.

'That settles it all, of course,' interrupted The Thinking Machine. 'It solves and proves the problem at once. Now, Mr Mallory, if we can go to your office or some place where we will be undisturbed I will –'

'But who killed her?' demanded the detective abruptly.

'I have the photograph of her murderer in my pocket,' returned The Thinking Machine. 'Also a photograph of an accomplice.'

*

Detective Mallory, Dr Prescott, The Thinking Machine, Hutchinson Hatch, and the apartment house physician were seated in the front room of the Morey apartments with all doors closed against prying, inquisitive eyes. At the scientist's request Dr Prescott repeated the circumstances leading up to the removal of the woman's left forefinger, and there The Thinking Machine took up the story.

'Suppose, Mr Mallory,' and the scientist turned to the detective, 'a woman should walk into *your* office and say she must have a finger cut off, what would you think?'

'I'd think she was crazy,' was the prompt reply.

'Naturally, in your position,' The Thinking Machine went on, 'you are acquainted with many strange happenings. Wouldn't this one instantly suggest something to you? Something that was to happen months off?'

Detective Mallory considered it wisely, but was silent.

'Well,' declared The Thinking Machine. 'A woman whom we now know to be Mrs Morey wanted her finger cut off. It instantly suggested three, four, five, a dozen possibilities. Of course only one, or possibly two in combination, could be true. Therefore, which one? A little logic now to prove that two and two always make four – not *some* times but *all* the time.

'Naturally the first supposition was insanity. We pass that as absurd on its faces. Then disease – a taint of leprosy perhaps which had been visible on the left forefinger. I tested for that, and that was eliminated. Three strong reasons for desiring the finger off, either of which is strongly probable, remained. The fact that the woman was English unmistakably was obvious. From the mark of a wedding ring on her glove and a corresponding mark on her finger – she wore no such ring – we could safely surmise that she was married. These were the two first facts I learned. Substantive evidence that she was married and not a widow came partly from her extreme youth and the lack of mourning in her attire.

'Then Mr Hatch followed her, learned her name, where she lived, and later the fact that she had arrived with her husband on a steamer a day or so before they took apartments here. This was proof that she was English, and proof that she had a husband. They came over on the steamer as Mr and Mrs David Girardeau – here they were Mr and Mrs Frederick Chevedon Morey. Why this difference in name? The circumstance in itself pointed to irregularity – crime committed or contemplated. Other things made me think it was merely contemplated and that it could be prevented; for then absence of every fact gave me no intimation that there would be murder. Then came the murder presumably of – Mrs Morey?'

'Isn't it Mrs Morey?' demanded the detective.

'Mr Hatch recognized the woman as the one he had followed, I recognized her as the one on which there had been

an operation. Dr Prescott also recognized her,' continued
The Thinking Machine. 'To convince myself, after I had
found the manner of death, that it was the woman, I looked
at her left hand. I found that the forefinger was gone – it
had been removed by a skilled surgeon at the first joint.
And this fact instantly showed me that the dead woman was
not Mrs Morey at all, but somebody else; and incidentally
cleared up the entire affair.'

'How?' demanded the detective. 'I thought you just said
that you had helped cut off her forefinger?'

'Dr Prescott and I cut off that finger yesterday,' replied
The Thinking Machine calmly. 'The finger of the dead
woman had been cut off months, perhaps years, ago.'

There was blank amazement on Detective Mallory's face,
and Hatch was staring straight into the squint eyes of the
scientist. Vaguely, as through a mist, he was beginning to
account for many things which had been hitherto inexplicable.

'The perfectly healed wound on the hand eliminated
every possibility but one,' The Thinking Machine resumed.
'Previously I had been informed that Mrs Morey did not –
or said she did not – play the piano. I had seen the bare
possibility of an immense insurance on her hands, and some
trick to defraud the insurance company by marring one. Of
course against this was the fact that she had offered to pay
a large sum for the operation; that their expenses here must
have been enormous, so I was beginning to doubt the ten-
ability of this supposition. The fact that the dead woman's
finger was off removed that possibility completely, as it also
removed the possibility of a crime of some sort in which
there might have been left behind a tell-tale print of that
forefinger. If there had been a serious crime with the trace
of the finger as evidence, its removal would have been
necessary to her.

'Then the one thing remained – that is that Mrs Morey
or whatever her name is – was in a conspiracy with her
husband to get possession of certain properties, perhaps a

title – remember she is English – by sacrificing that finger so that identification might be in accordance with the description of an heir whom she was to impersonate. We may well believe that she was provided with the necessary documentary evidence, and we know conclusively – we don't conjecture but we *know* – that the dead woman in there is the woman whose rights were to have been stolen by the so-called Mrs Morey.'

'But that is Mrs Morey, isn't it?' demanded the detective again.

'No,' was the sharp retort. 'The perfect resemblance to Mrs Morey and the finger removed long ago makes that clear. There is, I imagine, a relationship between them – perhaps they are cousins. I can hardly believe they are twins because the necessity, then, of one impersonating the other to obtain either money or a title, would not have existed so palpably although it is possible that Mrs Morey, if disinherited or disowned, would have resorted to such a course. This dead woman is Miss – Miss –' and he glanced at the back of a photograph, 'Miss Evelyn Rossmore, and she has evidently been living in this city for some time. This is her picture, and it was made at least a year ago by Hutchinson here. Perhaps he can give you her address as well.'

There was silence for several minutes. Each member of the little group was turning over the stated facts mentally, and Detective Mallory was staring at the photograph, studying the handwriting on the back.

'But how did she come here – like this?' Hatch inquired.

'You remember, Mr Hatch, when you followed Mrs Morey here you told me she dressed again and went out?' asked the scientist in turn. 'It was not Mrs Morey you saw then – she was ill and I knew it from the operation – it was Miss Rossmore. The manager says a hundred persons live in this house – that there is a great deal of passing in and out. Can't you see that when there is such a startling resemblance Miss Rossmore could pass in and out at will and always be mistaken for Mrs Morey? That no one would ever notice the difference?'

'But who killed her?' asked Detective Mallory, curiously. 'How? Why?'

'Morey killed her,' said The Thinking Machine flatly, and he produced two other photographs from his pocket. 'There's his picture and his wife's picture for identification purposes. How did he kill her? We can fairly presume that first he tricked her into drinking the acid, then perhaps she was screaming with the pain of it, and he choked her to death. I imagined first he was a large, powerful man because his grip on her throat was so powerful that he ruptured the jugular inside; but instead of that he plays the piano a great deal, which would give him the hand-power to choke her. And why? We can suppose only that it was because she had in some way learned of their purpose. That would have established the motive. The crowning delicacy of the affair was Morey's act in leaving his keys with the manager here. He did not anticipate that the apartments would be entered for several days – after they were safely away – while there was a chance that if neither of them had been seen here and their disappearance was unexplained the rooms would have been opened to ascertain why. That is all, I think.'

'Except to catch Morey and his wife,' said the detective grimly.

'Easily done with those photographs,' said The Thinking Machine. 'I imagine, if this murder is kept out of the newspapers for a couple of hours you can find them about to sail for Europe. Suppose you try the line they came over on?'

It was just three hours later that the accused man and wife were taken prisoner. They had just engaged passage on the steamer which sailed at half past four o'clock. Their trial was a famous one and resulted in conviction after an astonishing story of an attempt to seize an estate and title belonging rightfully to Miss Evelyn Rossmore who had mysteriously disappeared years before.

9

A Sensible
Course of Action

Palle Rosenkrantz

TRANSLATED FROM THE DANISH BY
MICHAEL MEYER

SHE was very pretty; indeed, she was beautiful. Twenty-six at most, slim, very smart in a foreign style; unpretentious, but the real thing. She turned to Holst as he entered, and her grey dress rustled with the light whisper of silk. It sat as though moulded to her fine body, almost as though cast and not yet set. Her cheeks flushed, a little too redly, and her eyes flickered nervously.

Holst bowed to the Inspector. His eyes rested on her for no more than a second; but he saw much in a glance.

The Inspector asked him to sit. He sounded somewhat embarrassed. He sat at his desk facing the lady, restless as always, toying with a paper-knife, which he put down to scratch his sparse reddish hair.

Holst seated himself and looked at the lady.

'Lieutenant Holst, my assistant,' explained the Inspector in French. Holst bowed slightly.

The Inspector broke into Danish. He was not very fluent in French.

'A ridiculous business, Holst,' he said. 'I'm damned if I know what course of action we should take. This lady says her name is Countess Wolkonski, and that she is from Russia. Her papers are in order.'

He tapped the desk with some documents which had been lying in front of him.

'Countess Wolkonski from Volhynien, to be precise from Shitomir in the district of Kiev. She is a widow. Her husband died in a Russian prison. He was a naval officer who was implicated in the Odessa mutiny – she says. Her only son died too, not long after his father – she says. She is passing through Copenhagen and is staying at the Hotel Phoenix. She arrived the day before yesterday. But, and this is the point, she asserts that her husband's brother, who is also named Count Wolkonski, is trailing her and intends to murder her, because he believes she betrayed her husband to the Russian authorities. She went into a long rigmarole about it, all straight out of a novelette. To cut a long story short, she wants me to protect her. A charming person, as you can see, but I'm damned if I know what to do about her.'

'I am handing this case over to Mr Holst,' he added in French to the lady.

She inclined her head and looked at Holst, as though seeking his help. Her eyes were at the same time searching and pleading. She was very beautiful.

'I have checked,' continued the Inspector, 'that there is a Count Wolkonski staying at the Phoenix. He arrived a few hours ago from Malmö, and asked to see the Countess. When the porter sent up to her she was out, but as soon as she returned and learned that the Count was there she came along here like a scalded cat. I've tried to explain to her that there's really nothing I can do. She practically fell around my neck, which would have been delightful, but how can I possibly help her? We can't arrest the man, for we've nothing against him, we can't take her into custody, and she genuinely seems too terrified to go back to her cab. I've promised her I'll send a man down to the hotel. You must have a word with this Russian fellow and find what it's all about. Of course we could send her papers along to the Embassy, but I can't keep her here. You take her along and do what you can. I know I can rely on you to take a sensible course of action.'

Holst said nothing, but rose and bowed.

'Please go with this gentleman,' explained the Inspector, thinking how much more charming the words sounded in French: 'voulez-vous aller avec ce monsieur?'

The lady protested. She would not go.

'Madame,' said Holst. 'You need have no fear. No harm can befall you if you come with me.' He looked impressively heroic as he said it. He was much better-looking than the Inspector, and spoke much better French. His appearance radiated reliability. He was a handsome man.

She accepted his hand a little timidly and looked at him with two deep black eyes in a way that would have bothered Holst's wife Ulla if she could have seen it. He noticed a small movement at the corners of her mouth, a faint tremor of emotion. She looked very unhappy.

The Inspector seemed impatient.

Eventually the lady agreed to go with Holst; and as they walked through the offices, all the station clerks almost audibly craned their necks.

The Inspector muttered something to himself and, most uncharacteristically, bit one of his nails.

*

Holst drove with the lady towards Vimmelskaftet. As soon as she realized where they were going, she became very nervous.

'Monsieur Olst,' she said. 'You must not take me to the hotel. He will kill me. He has sworn to kill me, and he will do it, at whatever cost. I am innocent, but he is a traitor, a very great traitor. He has killed my little Ivan – do you hear, they murdered my little Ivan!' She was totally distraught, and began a long story which lasted until they reached the corner of Pilestraede. It was a strange story, involving Dimitri Ivanovitch and Nicolai and the police and an Admiral Skrydlov and a Lieutenant Schmidt and others besides.

But she would not return to the Hotel Phoenix, and at the corner of Ny Olstergade she tried to get out of the cab. Is she mad, wondered Holst. But she looked, no, sensible. Hysterical, yes, afraid certainly; this Dimitri Ivanovitch wanted to shoot her, of that she was sure.

Holst did not get many words in. He leaned out of the cab and told the man to drive down St Kongensgade to Marmorpladsen. At least that would provide a temporary respite. Then he explained to her what he had in mind, and that calmed her somewhat. She continued her narrative about Odessa, Lieutenant Schmidt, and several Admirals.

Her voice was deep and rich. When she was calm, her face revealed a certain strength. But she was plainly very frightened, and it seemed unlikely to Holst that these fears could be wholly without foundation. Unless of course, she was mad.

The cab stopped at Holst's house, and he led the lady up the stairs and rang the bell. His wife was at home. It was lunchtime, and he introduced the Russian lady with a brief explanation of her presence. 'Either she is mad,' he said, 'in which case I must get a doctor to her, or she is in genuine trouble, in which case we must try to help her. Talk French to her and see if you can make anything of her. I'll be back in half an hour.'

So Ulla Holst found herself alone with the lady. It was the first time her husband had asked her to do anything like this. However, it seemed to her that if one member of the family had to have a tête-à-tête with so extraordinarily beautiful a woman, it was just as well that it should be she.

The lady accepted a cup of coffee, sat down, and began to talk in a more ordered and logical manner. Gradually but visibly, she regained her self-composure. Ulla Holst sat and listened, blonde and calm, and found the Russian lady's story by no means incredible. As she listened to its ramifications, Holst drove to the Hotel Phoenix and asked to see Count Dimitri Ivanovitch Wolkonski.

He was in his room, and the porter took Holst up.

The Count was a tall man, of military appearance, rather short-sighted, very swarthy, and far from attractive. A real Tartar, thought Holst. But he was courteous, and spoke exquisite French.

'Count Wolkonski?' asked Holst. The man nodded.

'I am from the city police,' continued Holst. 'A lady residing in this hotel has come to us and asked for protection against you, on the grounds that you have designs upon her life.'

Holst smiled politely and shrugged his shoulders. 'The lady was in a very excited frame of mind –'

'Where is she?' interrupted the Russian, looking sharply at Holst.

Holst didn't like his eyes.

'She struck us as mentally confused,' replied Holst. 'So we are keeping her under observation. Her story was so involved and improbable that we felt unable to regard it as anything but a – a hallucination.'

The Russian said nothing.

Holst went on: 'I should appreciate it if you could tell me the truth of the matter. We naturally thought of approaching your Embassy –'

'There is no need for that,' interrupted the Russian quickly. 'No need whatever. My sister-in-law is – not mentally ill – certainly not insane. But my brother's unhappy fate upset her balance. Then her only child died. In my house, unfortunately, and she is convinced that I was to blame. That is the situation – as you have seen. I followed her here. She sold her estates in Russia; she had a fortune – she is very wealthy and spoiled. I traced her in Stockholm. She has made insane dispositions of her property, involving considerable sums that concern me. *Enfin.* I must speak to her, to try to bring her to her senses. Where is she?'

Holst looked closely at the Russian. He thought the fellow was talking jerkily and a little hectically. But he might be telling the truth, and the lady's behaviour had certainly been curious.

'If you could accompany me to the Embassy it is possible that by discussing the matter with His Excellency and the Embassy doctor we might be able to arrange matters to your satisfaction. We cannot possibly take any action in this affair except through the authorities.'

The Russian nibbled his lip.

'You realize, officer, that our position in Russia is not easy. My brother was deeply compromised in a naval mutiny. He died in prison. I myself – God knows, I have been guilty of no crime, but I neither can nor will deal with the representative in your country of a ruler whom I regard as a tyrant. I hope you understand. Yours is a free country. Such political differences of opinion as may exist between the Tsarist régime and myself are no concern of yours, as I think you will agree. But I do not wish to have any intercourse with the Ambassador, or anything whatever to do with our Embassy.'

Holst reflected.

'It is unfortunate,' he said. 'But I appreciate your point of view. I have no official cause to take action against you. We do not perform political errands for foreign governments. I have received no orders in this affair and have no desire to take any step on my own initiative. Your sister-in-law asserts that you have designs on her life, but we cannot act on so vague a charge. But I must warn you that we shall be compelled to contact the Embassy, and it is possible that their reaction may alter the position.'

'Will you arrest me?' asked the Russian sharply.

'Certainly not,' replied Holst. 'I have not the slightest ground or justification for that. But if you feel that any unpleasantness may result for you, my advice is that you should leave immediately. We shall have to speak to the Embassy and – well, I don't know, but it is always possible

that – By leaving you will avoid any disagreeable consequences.'

'I shall not leave without my sister-in-law,' replied the
Count.

Holst was silent.

'Where is she?'

'At the police station,' said Holst. 'If you care to go there,
you can see her there.'

'And meanwhile you will contact the Embassy?'

'My superior has probably already done so,' replied Holst.
The Russian's face pleased him less and less.

'Very well. Then I shall come at once with you to the
police station. When my sister-in-law has seen me and
spoken with me, I hope she may come to her senses, unless –'

He shrugged his shoulders.

Holst felt unhappy. Now the Inspector would have another Russian on his hands. But what could be done? If this
sinister character was really at odds with the Tsar, his position was hardly of the kind that could justify any action
against him in Denmark. The newspapers had their eyes
open, and the government would hardly be anxious to
stretch itself to assist the present Russian régime. The main
danger was for the Countess, if her brother-in-law really –
but that was unthinkable. He scarcely suggested a mad
Nihilist with a revolver in his pocket; indeed, she seemed
rather the less balanced of the two. Besides, he was under
the eye of the police, and if the worst came to the worst
Holst could help her to get out of the country while the
Count discussed the matter with the Chief of Police, who
would have to be brought in where such international issues
were involved. Then the two could work out their problems
in Malmö or Berlin, which were not in Holst's district.

To gain time, however, he prepared a long report giving
the Count's explanation of why he was trailing his sister-in-
law. It read very plausibly. She had fled after somewhat
precipitately disposing of her estates, to which he appar-

ently had some legal claim; she was in a highly nervous and distraught state. His political opinions made it impossible for him to seek the assistance of the Russian Embassy; he therefore appealed to the police for assistance and, if necessary, medical aid, and undertook to present himself before the Chief of Police that day.

Holst pocketed this paper and returned to his apartment.

*

Ulla Holst had become quite friendly with the Countess. She had a kind heart, and the Countess's story was of the kind to bring two sensitive ladies close together. Countess Helena Wolkonski was the daughter of a Lithuanian landowner; at an early age she had married a naval officer, Count Nicolai Wolkonski, with whom she had spent six happy years. Then her husband, who was attached to the marine depot at Odessa, had become addicted to drink and cards. Marital infidelity had followed, and their home had broken up. The Count had allied himself to the forces of political discontent, thereby threatening the safety of his wife and child. In her despair the young wife had gone to his commanding officer and – she did not deny it – had betrayed him and his brother, who were hostile to the existing régime and were deeply implicated in the revolutionary movement. Count Wolkonski, by now in a state of physical degeneration, had been arrested and shortly afterwards had died in prison. His brother had saved himself by flight, taking with him her son, a boy of seven. Before long he had written to her demanding that she visit him in Vienna, whither he had betaken himself. She had no other relatives to turn to, and had therefore sold her estates. These realized a considerable sum. In Vienna she learned that her son was dead and – she declared – an old woman who had accompanied her brother-in-law on his flight had warned her that he was planning revenge. She said he had sworn to kill her to repay her for her treachery.

Such was her story.

She had fled, and he had followed her. She dared not return to Russia, for fear of the revolutionaries, so had gone to Stockholm, where he had traced her. Now she was fleeing southwards.

Ulla Holst believed her story, and Holst had no evidence to contradict it. He briefly summarized his meeting with the Count and advised the Countess to leave the country with all speed, since she could produce no evidence for her charges against her brother-in-law. Her son's death had been caused by pneumonia, and although it was not impossible that the Count was responsible there could be no means of proving this, or of taking any action against him.

Ulla deplored the masculine indifference of the police, but Holst had to explain that there was nothing they could do in this case.

'And if he murders her?' she asked.

'Well, then we must arrest him,' said Holst. 'But let us hope he won't.'

'And you call that police work?'

Holst shrugged his shoulders. 'We can't put people in custody for things they might do.'

Ulla could not understand that; but women do not understand everything, least of all matters relating to the police. Countess Wolkonski despaired; however, her despair did not express itself in any violent outbursts. Holst explained to her that the police could not take her into custody, since she had not committed any unlawful act, nor could they act against her brother-in-law, for the same reason. But he was willing to help her to leave the country.

'To be hunted to death like a wild beast?' was all she replied.

She calmed down, however. It was almost as though she had conceived some plan. She thanked Ulla warmly for all her kindness, kissed Holst's son, and wept as she patted his curls. Holst got her cab. She refused his offer to accompany her, and drove away.

Ulla was very angry, and Holst not altogether at ease. He

hurried back to the police station to keep an eye on the Russian.

*

At three o'clock the police station in Antoniestraede received a report that an elegantly dressed foreign lady had been arrested in a jeweller's shop on Købmagergade while attempting to steal a diamond ring. Holst was in his office: the Russian had not yet arrived. Holst had told him that the Chief of Police was unlikely to be available before three-thirty, since there was a parade at three.

A police van arrived, and Holst stood at the window as it rolled into the gloomy yard. A plain-clothes policeman stepped out, followed by a lady in grey.

It was Countess Wolkonski, arrested for attempted theft. Holst was slowly beginning to believe her story.

When she was brought into the station he went to meet her. She greeted him with a melancholy smile. 'Now you will have to take care of me,' she said.

Holst bowed.

As he did so, he noticed through the window the figure of the Russian standing in the gateway of the yard. At once, with a quick word to the astonished desk sergeant, he ordered the Countess to be taken to the Inspector's office.

A few moments later Count Wolkonski entered and asked in German for the Chief of Police.

He was asked to take a seat.

Holst withdrew into his office to formulate a plan. If Countess Wolkonski had resorted to so desperate a measure as shoplifting to get taken into custody, her fears could not lightly be dismissed. In any case, it would be unpardonable under the circumstances to leave her to her own devices. There was no knowing what she might not do next. Besides, now she was under arrest she could be placed under observation; the magistrate would certainly order this, and in the meantime one might, through official channels, obtain at any rate some information which might throw light on this complicated affair. And the Count was sitting outside. He would certainly demand to be allowed to see her.

A cold shiver ran down Holst's spine. It was a momentary thought, a stupid, crazy, insane notion, but if – if that Russian was a fanatical revolutionary, an avenger – God knows, the whole business might have come out of a Russian novel, but in Russia, as one knew from the newspapers, anything was possible. Certainly a Copenhagen police officer had no right to believe all that is in the newspapers; he has no right to believe that novels can come to life; he must act soberly and professionally. But – Russia is, when all is said and done, Russia, and it cannot all be lies. Suppose that Count Wolkonski before the very eyes of the Chief of Police were to draw a pistol from his pocket and shoot his sister-in-law, or – suppose he took out a bomb, a bomb, that might blow the whole police station with its lord and master into the air?

Of course it was totally impossible, idiotic, crazy, insane. This was Copenhagen, A.D. 1905. But the notion had got inside Holst's head, and was beating away with impish hammers in a way to drive any man from his wits.

He could not possibly say all this to anyone. The Inspector would think he had lost his reason. And so he had; it was an obsession, a foolish obsession from which he could not free himself. In ten minutes the parade would be over, and the case would be on the carpet. The Countess, now a shoplifter caught red-handed, would be confronted with the Count. A flash, an explosion, and the Chief of Police himself might be flying skywards.

Then Lieutenant Eigil Holst, of the Copenhagen police force, on his own responsibility, and at his own risk took a decision which branded him not as a sober, reliable, and trained officer but as a man of dangerous fantasy.

He summoned one of the youngest and most slavishly obedient of the station's constables, went to the window where Count Wolkonski was seated correctly on a bench, formally charged him with being implicated in an attempted robbery committed at a shop in Købmagergade by a woman calling herself his sister-in-law, had the amazed Count marched into an adjacent room, had him, despite some considerable resistance, searched, and found in his right trouser pocket a small American revolver containing six sharp bullets.

Holst drafted a stylish report to his Chief of Police, with the result that the sun set that evening over a cell at Nytorv in which Count Dimitri Ivanovitch Wolkonski sat sadly with sunken head, following a highly suspicious interrogation. And, it must be added, when the sun rose over the same cell, Count Dimitri Ivanovitch Wolkonski was found hanging by his braces dead on a gas bracket.

It is well known that it is easier to enter the clutches of the law than escape from them. Countess Wolkonski had found great difficulty in persuading the police to put her under their protection. She had resorted to a radical method. She had succeeded; but she remained in custody. The Chief of Police dared not set her at liberty. Her theft had been barefaced and her explanation, however truthful it might seem, buttressed by Holst's evidence and a quantity of bonds and jewels in her possession valued at a considerable fortune, at the least required a closer investigation.

She was arrested, to Holst's distress, and Ulla Holst was less than respectful in her comments upon her husband's superior. The Countess spent the night in a cell, not far from the place where her enemy had met his death. The next day she was freed, Count Wolkonski's suicide having weighed powerfully in her favour.

Not everything that was written in the newspapers about this affair was untrue, but the full facts of what happened have not previously been revealed. The Embassy bestirred itself and obtained further details concerning the background of the case. Countess Wolkonski had in fact betrayed her husband. She was not a heroine, and could never be one.

But she was certainly beautiful, and now she had found peace of mind. Count Dimitri Wolkonski was a revolutionary, and as such was entitled to his due share of sympathy from all good and peace-loving Danish citizens who cannot bear to think of a butcher slaughtering a calf but support with all their hearts the bomb-throwing barricade heroes of darkest Russia. In truth, this Dimitri Wolkonski was one of the blackest villains upon whom the sun of Russia has ever shone. His conscience was so heavy with evil deeds that it is a wonder that the gas bracket in the cell at Nytorv did not break beneath his weight.

This must serve as some excuse for the pretty Countess, and may explain why her brother-in-law, once he found himself in the hands of justice, settled his account with his Maker, whether the bill was right or no.

Yet Holst had a lingering suspicion that the Countess's life had never in fact been in danger, nor that of the Chief of Police; and that the Count had been carrying the pistol only in case his own life was threatened by his enemies. And he shared the doubts later drily expressed by the coroner as to whether his arrest and search of the Count had been justified.

Countess Helena stayed for some time in Copenhagen and was a frequent visitor at Ulla Holst's. Ulla enjoyed her company, and refused to believe that she had behaved wrongly in any way regarding those revolutionaries. Ulla was, after all, a policeman's wife, and was therefore opposed to any movement whose activities threatened the lives of policemen anywhere. When the Countess finally left Denmark, accompanied by Ulla's best wishes, the latter expressed her opinion of the affair to her husband. 'It may well be, Eigil,' she said, 'that you had no right to search that Russian, and that as you say it was a stupid idea you got into your head that afternoon in the station. But if you want my opinion, I think you took a very sensible course of action.'

10
Anonymous Letters

Balduin Groller

TRANSLATED FROM THE GERMAN BY
CHRISTOPHER DILKE

FOR some time past Andreas Grumbach had been pestered
by a spate of anonymous letters. Admittedly, this did not
cause him much inconvenience. His enormous wealth, his
social position and his industrial power make Grumbach
into one of the great ones of the Earth. He owns a jute mill
and presides over the A.B.B., one of the biggest Banks in
Austria. He is also for the time being Chairman of the
Industrialists' Club. So a few letters are hardly likely to
intimidate him. A person who gets more than a hundred
letters a day, and reads through them at breakneck speed,
gradually finds his sensibilities getting blunted. So much so
that the writers of the letters would be very much disillu-
sioned to discover how little moral effect their compositions
have. Grumbach does not retain any trace of the naïve enthusiasm which someone who only receives a letter once in
a while feels at the sight of the postman.

He soon got to know the look of the anonymous letters.
They were always written on a particular kind of paper and
were always in the same pointed handwriting. Nowadays he
invariably threw them into the waste-paper basket unopened. And that might well have been the end of the
matter. There was, however, a complicating factor. Andreas

Grumbach's wife was also subjected to a spate of these letters and she was far from encountering them with the same
philosophic detachment as her husband. Normally she was
an uncommonly attractive woman: on the small side and a
little plumper than in former days, with blonde hair, grey
eyes, a pert little snub nose, and a charmingly childlike expression on her round face. But now she was unhappy, cried
a lot, suffered from nerves, and found it difficult to be with
other people. Any amount of trying to talk her out of it had
no effect. She remained deeply sunk in her depression and
had ceased to find any real enjoyment in life.

Like her husband, Frau Grumbach was used to taking a
leading part in society but she was more anxious about it
than she had any reason to be. It would never have occurred to anyone to challenge her position, let alone try and
undermine it, but she nevertheless had a deep feeling of
insecurity. When Grumbach married her she had been the
little-known actress Violet Moorlank and it was from this
that the insecurity stemmed. Nobody had ever dared to
attack her reputation, but she was still unable to get over
the fear that society would refuse to accept her as she was.
Such anxiety, it should be said again, was entirely superfluous. Her husband's prestige was so strong and indeed un-
assailable as to put her own position above all criticism. But
the insecurity existed and could not easily be exorcized.
Obviously it was immensely boosted by these anonymous
letters with their insidious, malign, and unspeakably nasty
contents.

This was why Andreas Grumbach made up his mind to
do everything possible to bring the whole affair to a head.
He had at his disposal his friend Dagobert Trostler, an experienced man of the world, extremely well-off, whose joy it
was to spend his hours of leisure acting as an amateur detective. In a number of difficult and delicate cases this
man's ingenuity and chess-player's skill had sometimes
rendered important services. Surely, in the present situation,
he would be able to give good advice at least.

Dagobert was a frequent visitor at the house and, the next time they were sitting together over a meal, Andreas Grumbach told him about the anonymous letters which he had been getting.

Immediately Dagobert turned towards the lady of the house and said: 'So that's what it's all about! You know, Frau Violet, I'm really upset with you. There you were with your secret sorrow and you kept it hidden away from me. Not the merest whisper was I allowed to hear. I really don't think that's a proper way to behave.'

'Who's talking about me?'

'We're all talking about you. Your husband is a man, and a man knows how to deal with any amount of men's non-sense. But I must say I'd find it hard to understand the psychology of an anonymous letter-writer who just tormented the husband, when he had such a marvellous op-portunity of extending his attentions to the wife. Torturing the wife is not only the safer, but much more rewarding.'

'Dagobert,' said Frau Violet, 'it's impossible to hide any-thing from you. All right, I admit that I've been victimized by these dreadful letters and they're quite capable of driv-ing me to distraction.'

'After what your husband told me, it wasn't difficult to account for your state of mind. It's long been obvious to me that you were unhappy, but as you chose to say nothing it wouldn't have been right for me to ask awkward questions. Would you like to show me the letters?'

'Not for anything in the world!'

'I understand. They're too obscene. But it's really neces-sary to study the letters, if we're going to try and find the man – or the woman – who wrote them.'

'The woman? Is any woman capable of writing letters like that?'

'We must try and avoid being prejudiced. You know my views, Frau Violet. In everything which is good and great I put woman higher than man. In everything which is evil or malicious I put woman lower. In any case, please let me have all the letters which you have in your possession. Your husband has thrown his away. That was very hasty of him and it's a great pity. The more material I have, the more likely I am to discover a clue.'

Frau Violet brought him a whole pile of letters, some sixty or eighty in number.

'But you mustn't read them in my presence,' she told him, 'or I'd be so ashamed that I'd sink into the ground.'

Dagobert set her mind at rest: 'I'll wait and study them at home. Here and now, let's just look at their outward appearance. For one thing they're all exactly the same. The paper is mignonette green and evidently intended to look elegant, but it's still a cheap and unconvincing imitation of the solid Dutch hand-made paper, unfortunately.'

'Why do you say "unfortunately", Dagobert?'

'Well, because in the depths of my soul I was hoping for something better. You see, I once had another case of anonymous letters, but that was easy to solve. This one gives every sign of being far more difficult.'

'What sort of a case did you have, Dagobert?' the lady asked. 'I insist on your telling me.'

'With pleasure, dear lady, but just for the moment I'd rather stick to the subject in hand. Everything indicates that the writer of these present letters goes about his or her task with the greatest circumspection. For instance, the handwriting does not reveal any sign of the person's sex. I'm entitled to say that with some certainty, because I've studied graphology as closely as it's possible to study it.'

Dagobert looked at the addresses through his pocket magnifying-glass and then gave himself up to a few seconds of intensive thought. At the same time he twisted the tuft of hair on his forehead until it stuck up in the air and gave him the look of a clown in a circus.

'There's such a mixture of male and female characteristics,' he said reflectively, 'that it's enough to drive one crazy. Either it's a very mannish woman or it's an effeminate man. Isn't there anybody whom you suspect, Frau Violet?'

'I haven't the faintest idea.'

'There's nothing to be hoped for from graphology. It's bound to fail in cases where the handwriting is disguised, and here it's been disguised most methodically. We can only assume that the writer's normal handwriting is a sloping one. That's all. This pointed, upright style has of course completely altered its nature. It's very doubtful whether the letters will produce enough evidence to enable me to reconstruct the original character.'

'So you don't think there's a chance of discovering the criminal?'

'I find the case interesting and I'm prepared to go to a lot of trouble. The first thing is to study the letters really carefully. I may be able to find some clues in the content, the literary style, particular phrases, and the spelling and punctuation. It's impossible to promise anything in advance. You can tell from the postmarks how methodically everything has been planned. Look! Almost every letter has a different stamp. This one comes from post-office 66, this one from 125, and these from 13, 47, 59 ... They were obviously posted in the course of circuitous walks or carriage-rides. So it's no good setting a watch on any particular post-office or post-box.'

'Does that mean we really have no hope?'

'I told you I was prepared to take trouble, so I do have hope.'

'You sound quite confident, I must say.'

'Well, one has to believe in oneself.'

'You said you'd once known another case, Dagobert. What was that?' asked Frau Violet, who felt an understandable curiosity to know all the details.

'As I mentioned, it was a very simple matter,' Dagobert told her, 'but it still gave me a good deal of pleasure. One day the Archduke Othmar's Adjutant called on me and summoned me to the Palace. I went with him immediately and the Archduke, in a private audience, was kind enough to say that he had been specially interested in my achieve-

ments as an amateur detective. He told me he had a proposition, or rather a request, to make of me. Of course I at
once signified my readiness. I said in fact that His Imperial
Highness had only to command and I would obey.

'The case was similar to the present one. Anonymous letters had been sent not only to him as the head of the
household but to his lady wife. The Archduke told me that
he attached great importance to discovering the writer's
identity, but that he was disinclined to call in the police. On
the basis of what he had heard, he had more confidence in
my own ability to solve the case.

'Very well. I asked for the letters to be handed over. To
my amazement there were hundreds of them. I took them
away with me.'

Frau Violet, in her excitement, asked: 'Were they as vul-
gar and horrible as mine?'

'Oh, my dear lady, whatever has been written to you
could not possibly equal, let alone surpass, the filth and
obscenity in that pile of letters.'

'And did you solve the mystery?'

'I was lucky. The case was over and done with in 24 hours.'

'Tell me the story, Dagobert.'

'When I received the letters, my first question to Their
Highnesses was whether they had any suspicion or clue
about the writer. The answer was in the negative. So I took
the letters home, read them through carefully, and then
gave myself up to silent meditation for more than two
hours. However, I wasn't able to reach a single important
conclusion. The first half-day went by without any sensible
idea coming into my head. Only at night, when I was actually asleep, did enlightenment emerge. I had gone to bed,
tired out by my fruitless exertions, and had fallen into the
first light slumber. A moment later I sat up as if a shock
had passed through my body. Suddenly I had an idea upon
which an investigation could be based. The letters were
lying on my bedside table. A waft of Chypre had been ex-
haled from them and had reached my nostrils. Chypre is a

scent used by the most distinguished people. I fetched some lights, as many as I could find, and resumed my study of the letters. At once it became clear to me that I had been wasting my time on the handwriting and the contents. I needed to concentrate on outward appearances and use these as my starting-point. Whatever the turpitude of the contents, an air of great distinction surrounded their outward form. Admittedly, an intention to mislead the reader might have played a part in this. All the same, one had the sense of a distinguished house, if not an entirely distinguished origin. A sly footman or a disgruntled lady's maid might be involved. People of this sort might have purloined their employers' writing-paper. From the scent I did not expect any enlightenment, but ... the paper! I know something about different kinds of writing-paper. It was the most exquisite and also the most expensive one that had ever come into my hands. So it was a fairly costly luxury to send out these letters in any quantity. If the sender had not stolen the paper, he must be in a way of life in which he could afford the luxury.

'Early the following morning I dressed in a nondescript style and drove to the shops of some of the better stationers of Vienna. I laid down a torn-off scrap of blank paper on the counter and asked for the same kind, the answer which I was given was the one which I expected. The stationer did not stock this paper. It was too dear and there would be a dearth of customers. This information pleased me greatly, because it narrowed down the scope of my investigation.

'Now I entered in some excitement the shop in the Graben of "L. Wiegand, Purveyor to the Imperial and Royal Court". I was well aware that this establishment possessed unquestionably the most distinguished clientele in the city. I showed the pattern and the proprietor came to serve me personally. He immediately laid an elegant box of 100 sheets of the right paper, with the corresponding number of envelopes, before me. "60 crowns". I made the purchase and thereupon asked for a private interview.

'The proprietor led the way into his little office behind the shop.

' "I should like to know, Herr Wiegand," I began, "whether this paper is stocked by any other shop in Vienna."

' "Certainly not," he answered confidently. "The source from which I get it is a trade secret."

' "It's manufactured in England," I put in, wanting to show off my expertise a little.

' "Yes, indeed, but there's only one factory capable of making it. Other shops," he added contemptuously, "wouldn't have any use for it. It would stay on their shelves."

' "Do you sell much of it?"

' "Oh, a great deal. I've got no complaints."

'I saw that I had gone about things in the wrong way. If I allowed him to go on singing his own praises I'd find myself farther and farther away from my objective. Therefore, with the idea of presenting my credentials, I took a dozen of the anonymous letters out of my pocket and showed him the address on the envelopes. The effect was highly gratifying. His face at once took on an expression of marked respect.

' "Herr Wiegand," I said, "You're a Court purveyor and so I'm sure you'd appreciate the chance of obliging the Court."

'He bowed very devotedly and laid his hand on his heart. The implication was that he was even willing to give his life, if it was for the Imperial Court!

' "Well, Herr Wiegand," I went on, "you'll be earning the thanks of the highest people in the land if you'll just answer a few questions. Do you really sell much of this paper?"

' "It's my business, sir. I handle it along with the rest of my stationery. But naturally I couldn't make my living out of this kind alone."

' "So I imagine. Would you be willing to tell me the names of the principal customers of this writing-paper?

Please understand, Herr Wiegand, that an accurate answer to this question is specially important to Their Highnesses."

'The man was all deference and anxiety to assist. He bowed double whenever I mentioned my distinguished connections. After a little thought he confessed that he only had three customers for the paper. He supplied it to the Serbian Court. Lady Primrose also bought some for the British Embassy. But far the biggest custom came from Countess Tildi Leys, who visited the shop at least once a month to get another box.

' "Thank you, Herr Wiegand. I won't fail to mention your kind assistance in the highest places."

'With this I took my leave. I was satisfied, because now the scope of my inquiry had become very narrow indeed. There were just three possibilities and all of them were of equal interest to me. I needed to appraise them one by one, for it has always been a principle of mine that nothing should be regarded as improbable unless there are excellent reasons for such a belief.

'Unquestionably Countess Leys was the right person to start with. Not only was the investigation easiest in her case. There was also a definite and promising clue. Her heavy consumption of the writing-paper was significant, to say the least.

'I looked at my watch and saw that it was ten o'clock. Now, I had discovered from the postmarks on the letters that although they were posted in different places the time of posting was almost invariably the same: getting on towards mid-day.

'I gave my coachman the address of the Reisnerstrasse and stopped him opposite the Leys Palace. There I remained, leaning back in my seat and keeping watch. In my business it's necessary to have a lot of patience. I didn't allow the long wait to upset me and kept a sharp eye on anybody coming out of the Palace. But the servants didn't engage my interest. Two things had become clear to me.

First, the letters hadn't originated in the servants' quarters. If the Countess only used about one box of writing-paper a month – which in normal conditions was admittedly a great deal – it would have been impossible for the paper for all those letters to be stolen without the deficiency being noticed. And, secondly, someone who writes that sort of letter doesn't entrust its delivery to servants. Instead, the posting becomes a highly personal matter.

'I had been waiting for about an hour when a magnificent-looking porter emerged from the Palace gates and waved a carriage out into the street. I gave a sign to my coachman and we followed the other vehicle.

'As long as we kept moving I remained seated peacefully in the assurance that nothing could happen. But when a halt was made after a roundabout drive lasting half an hour, I quickly jumped out of my carriage. We were in the Schottenring in glorious Spring sunshine.

'In the course of a quick scrutiny I saw that there was a letter-box nearby. Meanwhile an elegant young lady of quite extraordinary beauty, a real fair-haired Madonna, descended from the carriage in front with the assistance of a flunkey. She walked towards the letter-box, but I was there first and opened the metal flap as if I wanted to give way to her or make her task easier. She thanked me with a slight nod of her head and an obliging smile. Then as she tried to slip her letter into the box, I snatched it out of her fingers with a quick movement and put it safely away in my pocket.

'She looked up at me as if paralysed by the shock. For the moment she said nothing and seemed close to fainting.

' "You must excuse me, Countess," I said. "It had to be done."

'Now she was able to find words again.

' "Who are you? What do you want? It's infamous, what you've done. Give me my letter back or I'll call the police."

' "That's the best thing you can possibly do, Countess.

231

You may be interested to know that there's a police station just here. So, if it's convenient ... I've got one or two other letters here, which we can compare with the new one."

'I took a wad of the letters out of my pocket and showed it to her. She went very pale and almost completely lost her self-possession. The flunkey, who appeared to have just noticed that there was something amiss, came up as if to protect her.

' "Before we go any further, Countess, please get rid of this fellow. It's best if he doesn't hear what we're talking about."

'One flash from her eyes sent the timid soul about his business.

' "And now, Countess, let me introduce myself. My name is Dagobert Trostler. You may be glad to know that I don't hold any official position, but I've been asked by Their Highnesses to put an end to an ugly persecution. This is the last letter of its kind that you'll ever write."

'She nodded dumbly and as she seemed at the end of her resources I began to feel sorry for her. What do you expect? All of us have our weaknesses and I've never been able to resist feminine beauty. Yes, she was guilty all right, but she was charming.

' "We can't stand about all day," I continued. "Would you like me to get into your carriage or would you prefer to come for a walk with me and let our vehicles follow?"

'She preferred the second alternative and so we walked along confidentially side by side.

' "What are you going to do now, Herr Trostler?" she asked.

' "What I'm compelled to do, Countess. I shall report back to my distinguished clients."

' "Will you give them my name?"

' "I'm afraid I must."

' "It would be a sentence of death for me."

' "Of social death perhaps, but the sentence would be deserved."

' "Not only social death. If you do that, I swear this will be my last day of life."

'I looked at her. What she had said was not just an empty phrase. A flicker in her eyes told me that her will was inflexible. Well, you know, Frau Violet, when all's said and done one isn't a monster. Of course she had committed a nasty and hateful crime. This paragon of maidenly beauty had written down words on paper, day after day, which would have brought a blush to the cheeks of a sergeant of Dragoons. But as for suicide, I didn't want that on my conscience!'

'You didn't let her go free, Dagobert?' asked Frau Violet with a dismay which she could scarcely hide.

'No, indeed. Punishment was certainly required. I was wavering only because I wondered if it had to be the death penalty. One or two facts about the Leys family were stored up in my memory. The father, an alcoholic, had died in delirium. A brother was an epileptic. Unquestionably there was some congenital taint, which explained the perverse habit of this young lady of writing down disgraceful things on paper.'

'Congenital taint!' repeated Frau Violet with obvious displeasure. 'That's the usual excuse. Let's be honest, Dagobert, and admit that you were looking for some mitigation of the offence.'

'Not so much mitigation, but a psychological reason for an act that would otherwise seem inexplicable. After a long argument I still refused to make any promise, but I agreed to try and shield the Countess's name if it was at all possible. At that stage she took a small golden box out of her handbag, opened it and showed me what was inside. There were some sizeable lumps of cyanide. I'm familiar with that particular poison, and the quantity was enough to destroy a whole generation root and branch. Without any play-acting, but convincingly, she repeated that she would take her life that same day if I revealed her name.

'I took the little box out of her hand, so as to be able to

233

admire the wonderfully delicate workmanship. It was a miniature masterpiece in the baroque style. Of course I refused to give it back. I made a pact with her. I promisd to pay her a visit later that same day and return the box with its contents. She in her turn promised not to do anything rash or indiscreet and definitely to abandon any intention of suicide if I was successful in bringing the whole affair to a conclusion without betraying her identity.'

'Didn't you offer her any reward for her splendid performance?' asked Frau Violet with a good deal of ill-humour.

'On the contrary, I prescribed a punishment for her. Our pact was absolutely clear. I'm in favour of clarity in all such agreements. If I failed to shield her by keeping her name secret, then *vogue la galère*, she was free to do whatever she thought right. But if I succeeded in my efforts on her behalf she had to perform a penance.'

'What penance?' Frau Violet wanted to know.

'I think I was sufficiently severe. The solemn promise that she wouldn't do anything of the kind again didn't count as a penance, of course. That went without saying. No, I insisted on either two years in a convent or five years' exile from Vienna, which should begin immediately. Failing one or other of these alternatives ... But she rapidly decided in favour of the exile, whereupon we parted with a friendly handshake.

'I drove straight to the Archducal Palace and was admitted without question, although Their Highnesses were at luncheon and I was most improperly dressed for such an occasion. The Imperial couple were eating by themselves. At a single gesture from the hostess a place was laid for me and I set to with a will, for my expedition had given me a good appetite.

'As long as the servants were still waiting at table not a word was said about the matter which had brought me there. But when the crumbs had been swept away and the air was at last clear, His Imperial Highness turned to our private business.

'"Well now, my dear Herr Dagobert," he began with a smile. Please note, dear lady, that he called me Dagobert, no doubt because he'd heard it was the way I was always addressed among friends. So he wanted to show me some special sign of favour. "No doubt," he went on, "you've come to ask for some further information, but unfortunately we're not able to help you."

'"I've really come," I replied, "as a messenger-boy": and I took the letter, which I had rescued from the pillar-box, out of my pocket and handed it respectfully to the Archduchess, to whom it was addressed.

'As you can imagine, she was not exactly enraptured. She had already suffered enough from such letters.

'"I'd like to draw Your Imperial Highness's attention," I went on, "to one particular circumstance. This letter hasn't got a postmark."

'It was the Archduke who first saw the significance of my remark.

'"Yes, but in that case, Herr Dagobert, you must have found the criminal. You've succeeded again. What other explanation can there be?"

'"The explanation, Your Highness, is that I've discovered the source of all your affliction and stopped it up for good. That was the last of these letters. There won't be any more. Even in this case I was able to do without the services of the Post Office. I guarantee that no repetition will occur."

'"Many, many thanks, Herr Dagobert."

'The Archduchess thanked me in her turn with great warmth and asked: "So who sent the letters?"

'"A lady."

'"A lady? I can't believe it."

'"It's true, Your Highness. A society lady."

'The Imperial couple had to make an effort before they could bring themselves to believe what I'd just told them.

Then, of course, they were all agog to discover the letter-writer's name.

'I first of all gave the details of my investigation as far as these seemed communicable and I was interrupted again and again by their complimentary remarks. No doubt I'm guilty of vanity, but I was never the sort of person to hide his light under a bushel.

'At the end of my report, when I came to the matter of the name, I said that I'd leave the decision whether I should reveal it or not to Their Highnesses' wisdom and sense of charity. I gave a true account of the situation and did not hide my opinion that any disclosure of the name would probably lead to a catastrophe.

'The Archduke wrinkled his brow and observed that this was hardly an occasion for the exercise of any special degree of mercy.'

'That's exactly my opinion,' Frau Violet interrupted. With some justification, she held strong views about people who wrote anonymous letters.

'Nevertheless I asked for clemency,' Dagobert continued, 'and gave my reasons for doing so. I was convinced that the threat of suicide had not been an empty turn of phrase. As a proof of my contention I mentioned the golden box with the lumps of cyanide and added that I had promised to return it on that same day.

' "You can't do that, Herr Dagobert," said the Archduke impulsively.

' "I've given my promise, Your Highness. And also, when someone has made a resolution of that kind, they'll find a way of carrying it out even without a box of cyanide. I'm prepared to give the lady's name if Your Highnesses insist on it, but I'd like to mention one practical ground for clemency. Your Highnesses are anxious to have everything settled quietly and without fuss. If there's a suicide it's impossible to ensure that some letter isn't left behind, which could lead to sensational and unwelcome consequences.

And also I've thought fit to impose, I hope with your approval, a punishment of five years' exile from Vienna."

'The Archduke was quick to agree with my view and this change of attitude on his part rather astonished me.

' "Incidentally," I said with a glance towards his lady, "I think we ought to hear the Archduchess's verdict."

'The Archduchess had been contemplating the deadly poison in the box, which she had taken in her hand. Now she looked up and replied: "It's not for me to pronounce a death sentence."

'She gave the box back to me, thanked me cordially once more and gave me her hand to kiss. As she withdrew from the room, the Archduke touched me lightly on the shoulder. I took this as a sign that I should stay behind for a confidential word with him, and I was not mistaken.

' "Just one second, Herr Dagobert," he said when the lady had gone. "There's something I'd like to tell you. I know now who the letter-writer is. You see, I noticed at a glance what you and my wife both overlooked. In the middle of all the ornamentation on the lid of that box, engraved very small and almost concealed, there's a coat-of-arms which I recognized."

'I took out the box again and confirmed the truth of what he said, not without some shame. I had indeed overlooked the tiny shield.

' "All the same, you were a lot cleverer than I was, Herr Dagobert. It's really a very sad story. I was in love with this lady and I think I can say that she cared for me. It's quite possible that her love turned into a distorted image of itself and became hatred. It's no bad thing if the lady is granted a few years of leisure at one of her castles, or in London or Paris for that matter, to reflect on the error of her ways . . ."

'And that, Frau Violet, is the story of my first case with anonymous letters.'

'But you saw the Countess again, Dagobert?'

'Of course. I saw her that same day, as I had promised.'

'Well?'

'She was composed and ready for any eventuality. She was sorry for what she had done and accepted her punishment.'

'That was a lovely punishment, living in castles or going to Paris.'

'But still a punishment, Frau Violet, which opened up the possibility of self-examination and even complete reform, whereas –'

'You wouldn't ooze quite so much loving-kindness, my dear, if the girl hadn't been pretty.'

'Possibly. I won't protest too much,' Dagobert replied, tugging again at his tuft of hair. 'At any rate I was and am quite content with my part in the affair. The Countess asked me to keep the little box as a memento and a pledge of her change of heart. She said I should have something to remember her by, as she would always think of me with gratitude. I accepted and added the trinket to my collection.'

'The only thing that occurs to me, Dagobert, is that I've never in my life heard of a noble family called Leys.'

'And did you imagine, dear lady, that I'd give the name of a real living person. The name I gave you was naturally invented.'

'But the real person is alive?'

'She's alive and so far she's kept her promise. There's very little likelihood that she'll come back to Vienna in the near future, or indeed ever. She married a foreign peer and keeps up quite a state, I believe.'

'What mainly interests me,' put in Andreas Grumbach, who had hitherto been listening in silence, 'is how a well-brought-up girl of good family can possibly take such a dreadful and dishonourable step.'

'You've brought us back to our starting-point,' Dagobert countered. 'I only told you my story to establish the principle that prejudices ought to be avoided. "No woman is capable of writing letters like that" was what Frau Violet told us in the most positive and categorical manner. I've just established that a woman, indeed a tender young girl, can write like that and worse. I don't mean to convey that these letters of yours are necessarily a woman's work. I simply ask for a little caution and avoidance of over-hasty conclusions.'

'Now at last I understand,' said Frau Violet, 'why you were so upset about the cheap pretentiousness of our correspondent's stationery, Dagobert.'

'Absolutely right, dear lady. Yes, it isn't always quite so easy. At least 20,000 or 30,000 people in Vienna write on this kind of paper. It wouldn't be worth my while making the round of the stationers.'

'But you'll go to some trouble, Dagobert?'

'Certainly, I'll go to a lot of trouble, dear lady.'

'You promise?'

'I promise.'

Dagobert packed up the letters and made a definite point with Grumbach that any ones which arrived in future, which they were bound to do, should be spared from the waste-paper basket. They could remain unread, as in the past, and in the case of Frau Violet it was actually preferable that they should be unread, but they had to be handed over to him. The more he had to work on, the better. This case was definitely more difficult than the earlier one and a careful search for clues was required. This involved the study of each individual letter, without exception.

Frau Violet was very impatient. If at all possible, she would have liked the mystery to be solved the next day. But Dagobert warned her that it would take time. He could not even promise that he would be successful in lifting the veil and weeks, if not months, were likely to elapse before he could report progress. Finally, so as to have some peace, he forbade Frau Violet to mention the affair at all. He himself would bring up the subject if he had anything to report. Until then, all the talk in the world would serve no purpose.

Frau Violet listened and obeyed. She asked no more questions although the strain on her nerves was terrible. It was torture for her to contain her curiosity. After dinner, when the three of them were sitting together and chattering in the smoking-room – she in her favourite seat by the marble chimney-piece, Dagobert opposite and Andreas Grumbach in his comfortable leather chair drawn back into the room – she often cast an imploring look at Dagobert.

She had held out bravely for several days when Dagobert allowed himself to be melted by her inquiring glances.

'It's coming along, Frau Violet,' he volunteered. 'Progress is definitely being made. We already have one or two small clues.'

'Have you really discovered something, Dagobert?' she asked in great excitement.

'Very little, but at any rate it's something to go on. Perhaps it's even the famous point of Archimedes.'

'What sort of point is that?'

'It's the pivotal point for lifting the world. As you're well aware, Archimedes –'

'Yes, I know, but don't let's bring mythology into this, Dagobert.'

'With respect, my dear, Archimedes isn't a mythical figure –'

'As far as I'm concerned he is. Anyway, let's leave all these Archimandrites, or whatever they're called, in peace. I'm prepared to accept whatever you say about them, but now tell me what you've discovered.'

'Just a few small details. Well then, the writer – I'm pretty sure it's a man and not a woman, by the way – is almost certainly clean-shaven and a cigarette-smoker. Am I right in thinking you're disappointed? I know it isn't very much, but it ought to be possible to build up some more information from these deductions.'

'But you can't possibly go through all the clean-shaven cigarette-smokers in existence, Dagobert.'

'Yes, it would be a laborious process, but not quite as laborious as you suppose, Frau Violet. The letter-writer, as I've been able to prove, knows you extremely well. So you see we're dealing with a very limited circle of people. In fact it wouldn't be particularly laborious to go through the list, but the method isn't sure enough for my taste.'

'How do you know he's clean-shaven?'

'That's only a guess and not yet a certainty. I wouldn't like to say anything more about it at present. I'm asking for a few more days' grace, say a week. At that stage I'll be able to reveal more, perhaps even everything.'

'And why a cigarette-smoker?'

'I'm prepared to talk about that. Just to find out that he's a cigarette-smoker wouldn't be enough of a clue for me. I'm able to go a bit further than that. He's someone who's in the habit of rolling his own cigarettes. I know that still doesn't take us very far, but every circumstance which tends to narrow the circle of suspects is of some value.'

'How did you reach your conclusion, Dagobert?'

'In my business, it's necessary to study details. In two letters out of that great pile I found tiny shreds of tobacco, scarcely larger than a pin's head, in fact just the quantity that would adhere to a pen-stroke as the ink was drying. As you know, I'm a connoisseur of tobacco. I only needed my magnifying-glass to confirm what I had already noticed with the naked eye, because I have good eyes. The shreds of tobacco were a variety known as Sultan Flor.'

'And equipped with all this knowledge, Dagobert, are you going to look for your man?'

'Sultan Flor is a light-yellow Turkish tobacco, which is cut rather long and fine. It's only used in self-made cigarettes, or conceivably in a long-stemmed Turkish pipe. That's why I have to reserve judgement on my original view that we're concerned with cigarettes. Our man could also be a pipe-smoker, but people who smoke that special sort of pipe are not nearly as numerous as cigarette-smokers. Sultan Flor is quite a good tobacco and made to measure for those who want to smoke something half-way decent at not too great a cost. You get something pretty solid for your money.'

'It's very comforting, what you say,' Frau Violet commented, leaving it to be inferred that she was slightly irritated at the scarcity of the information that had been disclosed. But on that particular day Dagobert refused to say another word and there was nothing she could do about it.

Fortunately for her, Frau Violet had no cause to concern herself during the next week with the disagreeable business of the letters. Her head was full of other matters and she had plenty to do. There were to be two big evening parties at the Grumbachs' in one week. Dagobert was responsible for them, but he kept himself hidden behind the figure of Andreas Grumbach. Frau Violet was to remain in the dark about his intentions. He wanted a chance to observe the whole Grumbach circle at close range in comfort. There would have been too many people to fit into one evening, so two entertainments had to be arranged. The guests were divided up. The first evening was for Andreas' friends and the second for Frau Violet's. Preparing for two such occasions and then presiding over them was no light matter. It was no wonder that Dagobert enjoyed a respite from Frau Violet's questions during this time.

When at last the whole rumpus was over, the three of them were able to settle down in the smoking-room again for one of their sessions. Dagobert began by complimenting his hostess on her two parties.

'The whole town's talking about them,' he said, 'and everyone's full of admiration for your housewifely virtues, Frau Violet.'

'And were you pleased with me too, Dagobert?'

'I was simply delighted.'

'That's good, because I know you're an exacting critic, Dagobert. But I can't get rid of a certain suspicion. Looking back, I have the feeling that I was really giving these parties for you.'

'For me?'

'Yes, to help your investigations. I think you wanted all these people to come because of your interest in the business of the letters.'

'I bow my head in submission, dear lady. You've seen right through me.'

'Well, has it at least helped you at all?'

'Yes, I believe we're a step further forward. It seemed clear from the letters that their writer belonged to your circle, perhaps even the most intimate circle. I'd have regarded it as some sort of success if the outcome of these parties had been a purely negative one and if I'd become convinced that the writer didn't in fact belong to the circle of your close friends.'

'It would be a great relief to me, Dagobert, if you'd come to such a view. I wouldn't have minded all my trouble over the parties going for nothing.'

'But I'd have a bad conscience over causing you the trouble.'

'Did you find anything out, Dagobert?'

'I was able to strengthen an opinion I'd formed, and that's of some value. I'm following up a line of inquiry which I believe is the right one.'

'It would be marvellous, Dagobert, if you were able to solve the problem for us. Tell us whom you suspect.'

'That would be premature, dear lady. Guesses aren't very helpful. We need to have proofs.'

'Don't torture me so, Dagobert. You know something, so say what it is.'

'It wouldn't be right to talk so soon. I'm taking it for granted, dear lady, that you yourself haven't spoken about this ugly business to anybody.'

'Of course not. At least, I admit that I've poured out my heart to one person, but that's the same as if I'd told nobody. Walter Frankenburg –'

'Walter Frankenburg, you say?'

'Yes, he's my oldest friend from the time when I was on

the stage. He's always been like a father to me. He was my witness at the altar, when Andreas and I were married. I can tell everything to somebody like that.'

'I was watching you, dear lady, while you were talking to him at the party. I wouldn't have made my remark if I hadn't guessed that you'd taken him into your confidence.'

'You can't hold it against me, Dagobert. He's absolutely reliable.'

'I'd have preferred you not to say anything whatever. Did you tell him in the course of your talk that you'd put the investigations in my hands?'

'You weren't mentioned, Dagobert. And I repeat that I'd go to the stake for Walter Frankenburg. He's a truly good and honourable person. But never mind that and go on about what you observed.'

'We had the two groups of guests, Andreas's friends and your friends. From the start I had no great hopes of the first lot. All these big industrialists and financial Barons have their own troubles without sitting down day after day and scrawling anonymous letters. They don't even have the time for it, or at least they don't easily give up that amount of time. No, the second lot, the artistic population, offered a more promising prospect.'

'On behalf of the artists, thank you for the compliment.'

'I have no wish to hurt your feelings, Frau Violet. If you insist upon it, I'm prepared to state publicly that envy, hatred, and malice are failings which are never found in the world of the theatre. You see how understanding I am!'

'I don't insist upon it.'

'Good. Now, I mentioned to you the other day that the letters had probably been written by a clean-shaven man. I didn't want to imply that I could discover that simply from the handwriting. The truth is that I went through the letters very carefully with an eye to the style of expression of the writer. I was struck by certain turns of phrase which constantly recurred. To give a few examples, "It's a howl", "I was tickled pink", "a gem of a part", "untalented beast", "drum up publicity" ... I could add any number to the list. Well, Frau Violet, don't you see a pointer in all that?'

'Indeed I do, now that you draw my attention to it.'

'I reached the conclusion that our author was somewhat effeminate and therefore likely to be one of those clean-shaven gentlemen.'

'Why must he be a gentleman and not a lady?'

'Let me remind you of the Sultan Flor!'

'There are ladies who smoke.'

'Yes, but they don't smoke pipes and they don't roll their own cigarettes. So I took a good look at your little friends at the party and when it broke up I left in the company of some people who seemed to me promising.'

'I was watching you, Dagobert. Walter Frankenburg was one of the group.'

'Yes, he came with us. And I'm happy to confirm that in those circles he's highly thought of. Outside the theatre, even, he plays the part of a noble-hearted father. We went from your party to a coffee-house in the usual way. Obviously the evening's entertainment was reviewed in a thoroughgoing style.'

'Was I pulled to pieces?'

'Not in the least, I assure you. On the contrary. As a matter of fact, at one moment I felt tempted to start tearing you asunder myself, so as to encourage the others to do likewise.'

'A fine friend, you are!'

'I didn't do it, although I was sure it would achieve a useful purpose. This letter-writer of ours must have developed a thick sediment of malice in his nature and in company, in an unguarded moment, the malice would be liable to appear. You needn't worry, Frau Violet. As I say, I didn't do it. One has one's principles, and even in the greatest extremity I personally am not prepared to act as an agent provocateur.'

'With so much to gain you ought to have tried it, Dagobert.'

'Not for anything. But to continue, we got on very well, of course, since we were all still feeling the after-effects of your admirable hock and your Heidsieck. I offered my best Havana cigars round the circle and asked for a cigarette in exchange. At once a dozen cases were reached towards me. I refused. I said I had a fancy for a home-made cigarette to go with my black coffee. Only one person in the group was able to oblige. I took his box in my hand. The tobacco was Sultan Flor.'

'Ah!'

'We got into conversation together. The man who had helped me out told a funny story and he began it with the words "You'll howl at this one". The story itself was pretty tasteless, but the introduction had caught my attention. Then he began to talk about you and he said that "Violet had given a gem of a party".'

'Who was the man, Dagobert?'

'If you don't mind, I'd rather go on being cautious, Frau Violet.'

'But you really do seem to be on the edge of a discovery.'

'Perhaps I've got further even than you imagine, dear lady. I propose to visit you tomorrow morning at the unusual hour of ten o'clock. If we don't succeed tomorrow, then I shall come at the same time on the following day. I'd be obliged if you too, Grumbach, would stay at home until I come. Your office won't run away in the meantime.'

'Don't you intend to tell us any more, Dagobert?'

'I can't. Only one thing. If one of these letters should come before my arrival, please hold up the envelope so that the light falls on it aslant. I hope you'll notice a new feature. My guess is that the ink will have a metallic sheen.'

When Dagobert arrived the next morning he found the Grumbachs eagerly employed in holding up to the light a letter which had just been delivered, and tilting it all over the place. Unmistakably it could be seen that the ink had a metallic, greenish-gold lustre. Frau Violet was in a state of great excitement.

'Dagobert,' she called, 'you're a sorcerer. How could you possibly know?'

'Please excuse my unpunctuality, dear lady. I intended to be present in person when the postman came. I was well aware what time these precious letters usually arrive, but you know how apt I am to oversleep. Still, it makes no odds. Let me have a look. That's right. The most exquisite metallic sheen, isn't it? And now, if you'll forgive me, I'll make my adieux –'

'What's this, Dagobert, you can't be thinking of running away. First you must explain.'

'I can't spare a moment if I'm to spring the trap on our villain, Frau Violet. There's still a lot to do. But I'd like to invite myself to dinner and at that stage I'll give you as full an account as you want.'

He hurried away, but returned punctually for the meal at five o'clock as he had promised. He ate with relish, while Frau Violet in her excitement left the most exquisite dishes practically untouched. She could hardly contain herself until the time came for his report, but she knew that he would not say a word as long as they were at table and the presence of the servants inclined her to accept his silence.

But after the meal, when she was back in her favourite place in the chimney-corner of the smoking-room and the others had made themselves comfortable, she at once asked Dagobert to tell his story.

'My work is finished, Frau Violet,' he began. 'My mission is complete. You'll never be pestered with those wretched letters again. And even you, Grumbach, will be relieved of a disagreeable experience, I suppose.'

'As far as I'm concerned,' the industrialist replied, 'my way of life wouldn't be greatly disturbed if the letters kept on coming. But I'm still deeply indebted to you once again, Dagobert.'

'Tell us!' Frau Violet insisted.

'I only wonder, dear lady, whether it wouldn't be preferable for you to just be freed from your torment without going into all the details.'

'Oh no, Dagobert, I want to know everything.'

'Good. Well then, we've got our man.'

'Who is it?'

'As I mentioned before, he's a smoker and he's clean-shaven. You already know how I arrived at those deductions. I was telling you, wasn't I, that a friend of yours offered me some of his good, wholesome, Sultan Flor tobacco?'

'What friend?'

'The next day I visited this same man at an hour when I was well aware that he wouldn't be at home. I knew because I had made inquiries. At that time he was engaged in a rehearsal at the theatre. My visit was both necessary and useful, because I was able to take certain precautions. When I left you this morning I went straight to Dr Weinlich, the Commissioner of Police, who's the only really capable man in our crime department. We're good friends and we often exchange news and gossip. I can even say without conceit that we stimulate each other and often learn quite a lot from one another. I told him about the case and asked if he was willing to help protect the good name and the peace of mind of a distinguished household. I didn't ask for official action and indeed I said this could be ruled out in advance. All I required was an expert and observant witness of the proceedings which I had in mind. He at once agreed to join me and we drove to the house of your friend, whom we found at home on this occasion as I expected. Really, Frau Violet, your coffee today is quite excellent again and as for the brandy, I've long been meaning to ask –'

'Oh, Dagobert, never mind about the brandy! Go on with your story.'

'No, really, I happen to know quite a lot about brandy.'

'Dagobert!'

'All right, then, we called on this man at his house.'

'For Heaven's sake, can't you tell us who the man is?'

'He received us in style. At home, in his own house, he was still the noble-hearted father.'

'Dagobert. You're not telling me it's –'

'That's just what I am telling you.'

'Not Walter –'

'Walter Frankenburg, the celebrated actor and the most fatherly character in your circle.'

'But this is terrible!'

'As I say, he received us in style. He was actually on the point of embracing me, but I gave a sign to him to desist. I made it short and to the point. I introduced the Imperial and Royal Commissioner of Police, Dr Weinlich, whom I had brought with me because we were on the track of a really ugly business. Then I took two letters out of my pocket, the one from the day before yesterday and today's one, both of them unopened.

' "Do you recognize these letters, Herr Frankenburg?"

' "Certainly not. Nobody's going to believe –"

' "What aren't they going to believe?"

' "That I wrote them."

' "But why shouldn't you have written them? What's inside them could be perfectly respectable, couldn't it?"

'He saw that he had fallen into a trap and turned pale, but still looked every inch the heroic father. This was his house and he was going to show us it was his castle too. He told us he wasn't going to allow himself to be cross-examined on his own premises because of some scandalous and utterly unfounded suspicion.

' "I just thought," I countered, "that you might prefer an examination here to one in the court-room."

' "You're the one, sir, who'll have to answer for your conduct in the court-room."

' "I'm afraid you won't be able to give me that pleasure. The fact is that you're lying. That's your own affair. Unfortunately you seem to be unaware that I can produce proofs of my case and that I've got you in a steel vice. You can twist and turn as much as you like, but you won't get away."

' "What are these proofs?"

' "I'm coming to them. Yesterday I did myself the honour of calling on you. I expect you found my card."

' "Yes."

' "Have you still got it?"

' "Yes, here it is."

' "That's a pity from your point of view. You should have destroyed it, because it's about the strongest link in the chain of evidence against you."

' "What can a visiting-card possibly prove? You've written a note on it, inviting me to give a lecture at the Industrialists' Club. So far I haven't either accepted or refused. So what have I done to incriminate myself?"

' "You still don't want to admit anything, so let's go into the whole business in a methodical way. First of all, I could prove that the writing-paper, which was used for all this anonymous filth, is kept in one of the drawers of your bureau."

' "How can you say that?"

' "Because I didn't waste the five minutes during which I was sitting at your desk, even though your housekeeper was keeping a careful eye on me." Here I turned to the Commissioner and asked: "What kind of scent would you say this is, on the letters?"

'Dr Weinlich held them under his nose for a moment and replied: "I should say it's a faint scent of violets."

' "Whatever it is," I explained, "it's a cheap scent. I'm something of an expert on scent, incidentally. But the important thing, Commissioner, is that you should sniff at this upper drawer on the right-hand side of the bureau. What can you smell?"

' "It's exactly the same scent, I can testify."

' "That's the main thing. I can see you're going to refuse to open the drawer, Herr Frankenburg. I shan't oblige you to do so, although I'm sure we'd find one of our proofs

250

inside. But it wouldn't be a conclusive one, I admit. And I can reassure you by confessing that we haven't brought a search-warrant with us, so we're not in a position to bring legal pressure to bear. Actually we could easily obtain a warrant, but we don't need one. I've got something better. While I was enjoying the honour of sitting at your desk, I took the opportunity of trickling three drops of a bronze colour dissolved in a solution of water into your ink-well. I have the colour hidden in this ring that I'm wearing on my finger. You weren't able to notice my little trick, Herr Frankenburg, but it's caught you out completely. The note which I wrote on the visiting-card was the last document written at this desk with untreated ink. Whatever was written later would develop a treacherous and undeniable metallic sheen as soon as the ink dried. Commissioner, perhaps you'll be so kind as to compare these two letters. As the postmarks demonstrate, one of them was written before and one after my visit."

' "Yes, it's unmistakable," Dr Weinlich confirmed.

' "The fact is that you could carry out a judicial search of all the writing-desks in Vienna and in none of the others would you find this remarkable kind of ink. Do you admit now, Herr Walter Frankenburg, that I've caught you out?" '

'Well, did he confess?' Frau Violet asked in a high state of excitement.

'He was a broken man. He abandoned all resistance and admitted everything. So now, Frau Violet, you must get ready for the hearing in the law-courts.'

'What are you thinking of, Dagobert? Am I supposed to appear as a witness and get myself dragged into sensational reports in all the papers?'

'Yes, I see your point, but what else can I do with the man?'

'Get him out of Vienna. Give him some penance, whatever you like. Only leave me out of it!'

'It's amazing, how mistaken one can be! I thought,

since you considered the Countess's punishment much too lenient –'

'Oh, that was something quite different.'

'I don't know how different it was, but in any case I've already banished your Walter Frankenburg. He'll never appear on a stage in Vienna again and he'll let you have a contribution for your favourite charity, dear lady. He'll be able to read the announcement in the newspaper. The headline will be "From a scoundrel who was found out" and he won't have the slightest difficulty in recognizing himself.'

I I

The Red Silk Scarf

Maurice Leblanc

ON leaving his house one morning, at his usual early hour for going to the Law Courts, Chief-Inspector Ganimard noticed the curious behaviour of an individual who was walking along the Rue Pergolèse in front of him. Shabbily dressed and wearing a straw hat, though the day was the 1st of December, the man stooped at every thirty or forty yards to fasten his boot-lace, or pick up his stick or for some other reason. And, each time, he took a little piece of orange-peel from his pocket and laid it stealthily on the kerb of the pavement. It was probably a mere display of eccentricity, a childish amusement to which no one else would have paid attention; but Ganimard was one of those shrewd observers who are indifferent to nothing that strikes their eyes and who are never satisfied until they know the secret cause of things. He therefore began to follow the man.

Now, at the moment when the fellow was turning to the right, into the Avenue de la Grand-Armée, the inspector caught him exchanging signals with a boy of twelve or thirteen, who was walking along the houses on the left-hand side. Twenty yards farther, the man stooped and turned up the bottom of his trouser-legs. A bit of orange-peel marked the place. At the same moment, the boy stopped and, with a piece of chalk, drew a white cross, surrounded by a circle, on the wall of the house next to him.

The two continued on their way. A minute later, a fresh halt. The strange individual picked up a pin and dropped a piece of orange-peel; and the boy at once made a second cross on the wall and again drew a white circle round it.

'By Jove!' thought the chief-inspector, with a grunt of satisfaction. 'This is rather promising ... What on earth can those two merchants be plotting?'

The two 'merchants' went down the Avenue Friedland and the rue du Faubourg-Saint-Honoré, but nothing occurred that was worthy of special mention. The double performance was repeated at almost regular intervals and, so to speak, mechanically. Nevertheless, it was obvious, on the one hand, that the man with the orange-peel did not do his part of the business until after he had picked out with a glance the house that was to be marked, and on the other hand, that the boy did not mark that particular house until after he had observed his companion's signal. It was certain, therefore, that there was an agreement between the two; and the proceedings presented no small interest in the chief-inspector's eyes.

At the Place Beauveau, the man hesitated. Then, apparently making up his mind, he twice turned up and twice turned down the bottom of his trouser-legs. Hereupon, the boy sat down on the kerb, opposite the sentry who was mounting guard outside the Ministry of the Interior, and marked the flagstone with two little crosses contained within two circles. The same ceremony was gone through a little further on, when they reached the Elysée. Only, on the pavement where the President's sentry was marching up and down, there were three signs instead of two.

'Hang it all!' muttered Ganimard, pale with excitement and thinking, in spite of himself, of his inveterate enemy, Lupin, whose name came to his mind whenever a mysterious circumstance presented itself. 'Hang it all, what does it mean?'

He was nearly collaring and questioning the two 'merchants'. But he was too clever to commit so gross a blunder. The man with the orange-peel had now lit a cigarette; and the boy, also placing a cigarette-end between his lips, had gone up to him, apparently with the object of asking for a light.

They exchanged a few words. Quick as thought, the boy handed his companion an object which looked – at least, so the inspector believed – like a revolver. They both bent over this object; and the man, standing with his face to the wall, put his hand six times in his pocket and made a movement as though he were loading a weapon.

As soon as this was done, they walked briskly to the rue de Surène; and the inspector, who followed them as closely as he was able to do without attracting their attention, saw them enter the gateway of an old house of which all the shutters were closed, with the exception of those on the third or top floor.

He hurried in after them. At the end of the carriage-entrance, he saw a large courtyard, with a house-painter's sign at the back and a staircase on the left.

He went up the stairs and, as soon as he reached the first floor, ran still faster, because he heard, right up at the top, a din as of a free-fight.

When he came to the last landing, he found the door open. He entered, listened for a second, caught the sound of a struggle, rushed to the room from which the sound appeared to proceed, and remained standing on the threshold, very much out of breath and greatly surprised to see the man of the orange-peel and the boy banging the floor with chairs.

At that moment, a third person walked out of an adjoining room. It was a young man of twenty-eight or thirty, wearing a pair of short whiskers in addition to his moustache, spectacles and a smoking-jacket with an astrakhan collar and looking like a foreigner, a Russian.

'Good morning, Ganimard,' he said. And turning to the two companions, 'Thank you, my friends, and all my congratulations on the successful result. Here's the reward I promised you.'

He gave them a hundred-franc note, pushed them outside, and shut both doors.

'I am sorry, old chap,' he said to Ganimard. 'I wanted to talk to you ... wanted to talk to you badly.'

He offered him his hand and, seeing that the inspector remained flabbergasted and that his face was still distorted with anger, he exclaimed:

'Why, you don't seem to understand! ... And yet it's clear enough ... I wanted to see you particularly ... So what could I do?' And, pretending to reply to an objection, 'No, no, old chap,' he continued. 'You're quite wrong. If I had written or telephoned, you would not have come ... or else you would have come with a regiment. Now I wanted to see you all alone; and I thought the best thing was to send those two decent fellows to meet you, with orders to scatter bits of orange-peel and draw crosses and circles, in short, to mark out your road to this place ... Why, you look quite bewildered! What is it? Perhaps you don't recognize me? Lupin ... Arsène Lupin ... Ransack your memory ... Doesn't the name remind you of anything?'

'You dirty scoundrel!' Ganimard snarled between his teeth.

Lupin seemed greatly distressed, and in an affectionate voice:

'Are you vexed? Yes, I can see it in your eyes ... The Dugrival business, I suppose? I ought to have waited for you to come and take me in charge? ... There now, the thought never occurred to me! I promise you, next time...'

'You scum of the earth!' growled Ganimard.

'And I thinking I was giving you a treat! Upon my word, I did. I said to myself, "That dear old Ganimard! We haven't met for an age. He'll simply rush at me when he sees me!"'

Ganimard, who had not yet stirred a limb, seemed to be waking from his stupor. He looked around him, looked at Lupin, visibly asked himself whether he would not do well to rush at him in reality, and then, controlling himself, took hold of a chair and settled himself in it, as though he had suddenly made up his mind to listen to his enemy.

'Speak,' he said. 'And don't waste my time with any nonsense. I'm in a hurry.'

'That's it,' said Lupin, 'let's talk. You can't imagine a quieter place than this. It's an old manor-house, which once stood in the open country, and it belongs to the Duc de Rochelaure. The Duke, who has never lived in it, lets this floor to me and the outhouses to a painter and decorator. I always keep up a few establishments of this kind: it's a sound, practical plan. Here, in spite of my looking like a Russian nobleman, I am M. Daubreuil, an ex-cabinet-minister ... You understand, I had to select a rather over-stocked profession, so as not to attract attention...'

'Do you think I care a hang about all this?' said Ganimard, interrupting him.

'Quite right, I'm wasting words and you're in a hurry. Forgive me. I shan't be long now ... Five minutes that's all ... I'll start at once ... Have a cigar? No? Very well, no more will I.'

He sat down also, drummed his fingers on the table, while thinking, and began in this fashion:

'On the 17th of October, 1599, on a warm and sunny autumn day ... Do you follow me? ... But, now that I come to think of it, is it really necessary to go back to the reign of Henry IV and tell you all about the building of the Pont-Neuf? No, I don't suppose you are very well up in French history; and I should only end by muddling you. Suffice it, then, for you to know that, last night, at one o'clock in the morning, a boatman passing under the last arch of the Pont-Neuf aforesaid, along the left bank of the river, heard something drop into the front part of his barge. The thing had been flung from the bridge and its evident destination was the bottom of the Seine. The bargee's dog rushed forward, barking, and, when the man reached the end of his craft, he saw the animal worrying a piece of newspaper that had served to wrap up a number of objects. He took from the dog such of the contents as had not fallen into the water, went to his cabin and examined them carefully. The result struck him as interesting; and, as the man is connected with one of my friends, he sent to let me know. This morning, I was woken up and placed in possession of the facts and of the objects which the man had collected. Here they are.'

He pointed to them, spread out on a table. There were, first of all, the torn pieces of a newspaper. Next came a large cut-glass inkstand, with a long piece of string fastened to the lid. There was a bit of broken glass and a sort of flexible cardboard, reduced to shreds. Lastly, there was a piece of bright scarlet silk, ending in a tassel of the same material and colour.

'You see our exhibits, friend of my youth,' said Lupin. 'No doubt, the problem would be more easily solved if we had the other objects which went overboard owing to the stupidity of the dog. But it seems to me, all the same, that we ought to be able to manage, with a little reflection and intelligence. And those are just your great qualities. How does the business strike you?'

Ganimard did not move a muscle. He was willing to stand Lupin's chaff, but his dignity commanded him not to speak a single word in answer nor even to give a nod or shake of the head that might have been taken to express approval or criticism.

'I see that we are entirely of one mind,' continued Lupin, without appearing to remark the chief-inspector's silence. 'And I can sum up the matter briefly, as told us by these exhibits. Yesterday evening, between nine and twelve o'clock, a showily-dressed young woman was wounded with a knife and then caught round the throat and choked to death by a well-dressed gentleman, wearing a single eyeglass and interested in racing, with whom the aforesaid showily-dressed young lady had been eating three meringues and a coffee éclair.'

Lupin lit a cigarette and, taking Ganimard by the sleeve:

'Aha, that's up against you, chief-inspector! You thought that, in the domain of police deductions, such feats as those were prohibited to outsiders! Wrong, sir! Lupin juggles with inferences and deductions for all the world like a detective in a novel. My proofs are dazzling and absolutely simple.'

And, pointing to the objects one by one, as he demonstrated his statement, he resumed:

'I said, after nine o'clock yesterday evening. This scrap of newspaper bears yesterday's date, with the words, "Evening edition". Also, you will see here, pasted to the paper, a bit of one of those yellow wrappers in which the subscribers' copies are sent out. These copies are always delivered by the nine o'clock post. Therefore, it was after nine o'clock. I said, a well-dressed man. Please observe that this tiny piece of glass has the round hole of a single eyeglass at one of the edges and that the single eyeglass is an essentially aristocratic article of wear. This well-dressed man walked into a pastry-cook's shop. Here is the very thin cardboard, shaped like a box and still showing a little of the cream of the meringues and éclairs which were packed in it in the usual way. Having got his parcel, the gentleman with the eyeglass joined a young person whose eccentricity in the matter of dress is pretty clearly indicated by this bright-red silk scarf. Having joined her, for some reason as yet unknown, he first stabbed her with a knife and then strangled her with the help of this same scarf. Take your magnifying glass, chief-inspector, and you will see, on the silk, stains of a darker red which are, here, the marks of a knife wiped on the scarf and there, the marks of a hand, covered with blood, clutching the material. Having committed the murder, his next business is to leave no trace behind him. So he takes from his pocket, first, the newspaper to which he subscribes – a racing-paper, as you will see by glancing at the contents of this scrap; and you will have no difficulty in discovering the title – and, secondly, a cord, which, on inspection, turns out to be a length of whip-cord. These two details prove – do they not? – that our man is interested in racing and that he himself rides. Next, he picks up the fragments of his eyeglass, the cord of which has been broken in the struggle. He takes a pair of scissors – observe the hacking of the scissors – and cuts off the stained part of the scarf, leaving the other end, no doubt, in his victim's clenched hands. He makes a ball of the confectioner's cardboard box. He also puts in certain things that would have betrayed him, such as the knife, which must have slipped into the Seine. He wraps everything in the newspaper, ties it with the cord and fastens this cut-glass inkstand to it, as a make-weight. Then he makes himself scarce. A little later, the parcel falls into the waterman's barge. And there you are. Oof, it's hot work! . . . What do you say to the story?'

He looked at Ganimard to see what impression his speech had produced on the inspector. Ganimard did not depart from his attitude of silence.

Lupin began to laugh:

'As a matter of fact, you're annoyed and surprised. But you're suspicious as well: "Why should that confounded Lupin hand the business over to me," say you, "instead of keeping it for himself, hunting down the murderer and rifling his pockets, if there was a robbery?" The question is quite logical, of course. But – there is a "but" – I have no time, you see. I am full up with work at the present moment: a burglary in London, another at Lausanne, an exchange of children at Marseilles, to say nothing of having to save a young girl who is at this moment shadowed by death. That's always the way: it never rains but it pours. So I said to myself, "Suppose I handed the business over to my dear old Ganimard? Now that it is half-solved for him, he is quite capable of succeeding. And what a service I shall be doing him! How magnificently he will be able to distinguish himself! No sooner said than done. At eight o'clock in the morning, I sent the joker with the orange-peel to meet you. You swallowed the bait; and you were here by nine, all on edge and eager for the fray.'

Lupin rose from his chair. He bent over to the inspector and, with his eyes on Ganimard's, said:

'That's all. You now know the whole story. Presently, you will know the victim: some ballet-dancer, probably, some singer at a music-hall. On the other hand, the chances are that the criminal lives near the Pont-Neuf, most likely on the left bank. Lastly, here are all the exhibits. I make you a present of them. Set to work. I shall only keep this end of the scarf. If ever you want to piece the scarf together, bring me the other end, the one which the police will find round the victim's neck. Bring it me in four weeks from now to the day, that is to say, on the 29th of December, at ten o'clock in the morning. You can be sure of finding me here. And don't be afraid: this is all perfectly serious, friend of my youth; I swear it is. No humbug, honour bright. You can go straight ahead. Oh, by the way, when you arrest the fellow with the eyeglass, be a bit careful: he is left-handed! Good-bye, old dear, and good luck to you!'

Lupin spun round on his heel, went to the door, opened it and disappeared before Ganimard had even thought of taking a decision. The inspector rushed after him, but at once found that the handle of the door, by some trick of mechanism which he did not know, refused to turn. It took him ten minutes to unscrew the lock and ten minutes more to unscrew the lock of the hall-door. By the time that he had scrambled down the three flights of stairs, Ganimard had given up all hope of catching Arsène Lupin.

Besides, he was not thinking of it. Lupin inspired him with a queer, complex feeling, made up of fear, hatred, involuntary admiration and also the vague instinct that he, Ganimard, in spite of all his efforts, in spite of the persistency of his endeavours, would never get the better of this particular adversary. He pursued him from a sense of duty and pride, but with the continual dread of being taken in by that formidable hoaxer and scouted and fooled in the face of a public that was always only too willing to laugh at the chief-inspector's mishaps.

This business of the red scarf, in particular, struck him as most suspicious. It was interesting, certainly, in more ways than one, but so very improbable! And Lupin's explanation, apparently so logical, would never stand the test of a severe examination!

'No,' said Ganimard, 'that is all swank: a parcel of suppositions and guess-work based upon nothing at all. I'm not to be caught with chaff.'

*

When he reached the head quarters of police, at 36, Quai des Orfèvres, he had quite made up his mind to treat the incident as though it had never happened.

He went up to the Criminal Investigation Department. Here, one of his fellow-inspectors said:

'Seen the chief?'

'No.'

'He was asking for you just now.'

'Oh, was he?'

'Yes, you had better go after him.'

'Where?'

'To the rue de Berne ... there was a murder there last night.'

'Oh! Who's the victim?'

'I don't know exactly ... a music-hall singer, I believe.'

Ganimard simply muttered:

'By Jove!'

Twenty minutes later, he stepped out of the underground railway-station and made for the rue de Berne.

The victim, who was known in the theatrical world by her stage-name of Jenny Saphir, occupied a small flat on the second floor of one of the houses. A policeman took the chief-inspector upstairs and showed him the way, through two sitting-rooms to a bedroom where he found the magistrates in charge of the inquiry, together with the divisional surgeon and M. Dudouis, the head of the detective-service.

Ganimard started at the first glance which he gave into the room. He saw, lying on a sofa, the corpse of a young woman whose hands clutched a strip of red silk! One of the shoulders, which appeared above the low-cut bodice, wore the marks of two wounds surrounded with clotted blood. The distorted and almost blackened features still bore an expression of frenzied fear.

The divisional surgeon, who had just finished his examination, said:

'My first conclusions are very clear. The victim was twice stabbed with a dagger and afterwards strangled. The immediate cause of death was asphyxia.'

'By Jove!' thought Ganimard again, remembering Lupin's words and the picture which he had drawn of the crime.

The examining magistrate objected:

'But the neck shows no discolouration.'

'She may have been strangled with a napkin or a handkerchief,' said the doctor.

'Most probably,' said the chief detective, 'with this silk scarf, which the victim was wearing and a piece of which remains, as though she had clung to it with her two hands to protect herself.'

'But why does only that piece remain?' asked the magistrate. 'What has become of the other?'

'The other may have been stained with blood and carried off by the murderer. You can plainly distinguish the hurried slashing of the scissors.'

'By Jove!' said Ganimard, between his teeth, for the third time. 'That brute of a Lupin saw everything without seeing a thing!'

'And what about the motive of the murder!' asked the magistrate. 'The locks have been forced, the cupboards turned upside down. Have you anything to tell me, M. Dudouis?'

The chief of the detective-service replied:

'I can at least suggest a supposition, derived from the statements made by the servant. The victim, who enjoyed a greater reputation on account of her looks than through her talent as a singer, went to Russia two years ago, and brought back with her a magnificent sapphire, which she appears to have received from some person of importance at the court. Since then, she went by the name of Jenny Saphir and seems generally to have been very proud of that present, although for prudence' sake, she never wore it. I daresay that we shall not be far out if we presume the theft of the sapphire to have been the cause of the crime.'

'But did the maid know where the stone was?'

'No, nobody did. And the disorder of the room would tend to prove the murderer did not know either.'

'We will question the maid,' said the examining-magistrate.

M. Dudouis took the chief-inspector aside and said:

'You're looking very old-fashioned, Ganimard. What's the matter? Do you suspect anything?'

'Nothing at all, chief.'

'That's a pity. We could do with a bit of showy work in the department. This is one of a number of crimes, all of the same class, of which we have failed to discover the perpetrator. This time, we want the criminal ... and quickly!'

'A difficult job, chief.'

'It's got to be done. Listen to me, Ganimard. According to what the maid says, Jenny Saphir led a very regular life. For a month past, she was in the habit of frequently receiving visits, on her return from the music-hall, that is to say, at about half past ten, from a man who would stay until midnight or so. "He's a society man," Jenny Saphir used to say, "and he wants to marry me." This society man took every precaution to avoid being seen, such as turning up his coat-collar and lowering the brim of his hat when he passed the porter's box. And Jenny Saphir always made a point of sending away her maid, even before he came. This is the man whom we have to find.'

'Has he left no traces?'

'None at all. It is obvious that we have to deal with a very clever scoundrel, who prepared his crime beforehand and committed it with every possible chance of escaping unpunished. His arrest would be a great feather in our cap. I rely on you, Ganimard.'

'Ah, you rely on me, chief?' replied the inspector. 'Well, we shall see ... we shall see ... I don't say no ... Only ...'

He seemed in a very nervous condition; and his agitation struck M. Dudouis.

'Only,' continued Ganimard, 'only I swear ... do you hear, chief? I swear ...'

'What do you swear?'

'Nothing ... We shall see, chief ... we shall see ...'

Ganimard did not finish his sentence until he was outside, alone. And he finished it aloud, stamping his foot, in a tone of the most violent anger:

'Only, I swear to Heaven that the arrest shall be effected by my own means, without my employing a single one of the clues with which that villain has supplied me. Ah, no! Ah, no! ...'

Railing against Lupin, furious at being mixed up in this business and resolved, nevertheless, to get to the bottom of it, he wandered aimlessly about the streets. His brain was seething with irritation; and he tried to adjust his ideas a little and to discover, among the chaotic facts, some trifling detail, unperceived by all, unsuspected by Lupin himself, that might lead him to success.

He lunched hurriedly at a bar, resumed his stroll and suddenly stopped, petrified, astounded, and confused. He was walking under the gateway of the very house in the rue de Surène to which Lupin had enticed him a few hours earlier! A force stronger than his own will was drawing him there once more. The solution of the problem lay there. There and there alone were all the elements of the truth.

Do and say what he would, Lupin's assertions were so precise, his calculations so accurate that, worried to the innermost recesses of his being by so prodigious a display of perspicacity, he could not do other than take up the work at the point where his enemy had left it.

Abandoning all further resistance, he climbed the three flights of stairs. The door of the flat was open. No one had touched the exhibits. He put them in his pocket and walked away.

From that moment, he reasoned and acted, so to speak, mechanically, under the influence of the master whom he could not choose but obey.

Admitting that the unknown person whom he was seeking lived in the neighbourhood of the Pont-Neuf, it became necessary to discover, somewhere between that bridge and the rue de Berne, the first-class confectioner's shop, open in the evenings, at which the cakes were bought. This did not take long to find. A pastry-cook near the Gare Saint-Lazare showed him some little cardboard boxes, identical in material and shape with the one in Ganimard's possession. Moreover, one of the shop girls remembered having served, on the previous evening, a gentleman whose face was almost concealed in the collar of his fur-coat, but whose eyeglass she had happened to notice.

'That's one clue checked,' thought the inspector. 'Our man wears an eyeglass.'

He next collected the pieces of the racing-paper and showed them to a newsvendor, who easily recognized the *Turf Illustré*. Ganimard at once went to the offices of the *Turf* and asked to see the list of subscribers. Going through the list, he jotted down the names and addresses of all those who lived anywhere near the Pont-Neuf and principally – because Lupin had said so – those on the left bank of the river.

He then went back to the Criminal Investigation Department, took half a dozen men and packed them off with the necessary instructions.

At seven o'clock in the evening, the last of these men returned and brought good news with him. A certain M. Prevailles, a subscriber to the *Turf*, occupied an entresol flat on the Quai des Augustins. On the previous evening, he left his place, wearing a fur-coat, took his letters and his paper, the *Turf Illustré*, from the porter's wife, walked away, and returned home at midnight. This M. Prevailles wore a single eyeglass. He was a regular race-goer and himself owned several hacks which he either rode himself or jobbed out.

The inquiry had taken so short a time and the results obtained were so exactly in accordance with Lupin's predictions that Ganimard felt quite overcome on hearing the detective's report. Once more he was measuring the prodigious extent of the resources at Lupin's disposal. Never in the course of his life – and Ganimard was already well-advanced in years – had he come across such perspicacity, such a quick and far-seeing mind.

He went in search of M. Dudouis:

'Everything's ready, chief. Have you a warrant?'

'Eh?'

'I said, everything is ready for the arrest, chief.'

'You know the name of Jenny Saphir's murderer?'

'Yes.'

'But how? Explain yourself.'

Ganimard had a sort of scruple of conscience, blushed a little, and nevertheless said:

'An accident, chief. The murderer threw everything that was likely to compromise him into the Seine. Part of the parcel was picked up and handed to me.'

'By whom?'

'A boatman who refused to give his name, for fear of getting into trouble. But I had all the clues I wanted. It was not so difficult as I expected.'

And the inspector described how he had gone to work.

'And you call that an accident!' cried M. Dudouis. 'And you say that it was not difficult! Why, it's one of your finest performances! Finish it yourself, Ganimard, and be prudent.'

Ganimard was eager to get the business done. He went to the Quai des Augustins with his men and distributed them around the house. He questioned the portress, who said that her tenant took his meals out of doors, but made a point of looking in after dinner.

A little before nine o'clock, in fact, leaning out of her window, she warned Ganimard, who at once gave a low whistle. A gentleman in a tall hat and a fur-coat was coming along the pavement beside the Seine. He crossed the road and walked up to the house.

Ganimard stepped forward:

'M. Prevailles, I believe?'

'Yes, but who are you?'

'I have a commission to . . .'

He had not time to finish his sentence. At the sight of the men appearing out of the shadow, Prevailles quickly retreated to the wall and faced his adversaries, with his back to the door of a shop on the ground-floor, the shutters of which were closed:

'Stand back!' he cried. 'I don't know you!'

His right hand brandished a heavy stick, while his left was slipped behind him and seemed to be trying to open the door.

Ganimard had an impression that the man might escape through this way and through some secret outlet:

'None of this nonsense,' he said, moving closer to him. 'You're caught . . . You had better come quietly.'

But just as he was laying hold of Prevailles' stick, Ganimard remembered the warning which Lupin gave him: Prevailles was left-handed; and it was his revolver for which he was feeling behind his back.

The inspector ducked his head. He had noticed the man's sudden movement. Two reports rang out. No one was hit.

A second later, Prevailles received a blow under the chin from the butt-end of a revolver, which brought him down where he stood. He was entered at the Dépôt soon after nine o'clock.

*

Ganimard enjoyed a great reputation even at that time. But this capture, so quickly effected, by such a very simple means, and at once made public by the police, won him a sudden celebrity. Prevailles was forthwith saddled with all the murders that had remained unpunished; and the newspapers vied with one another in extolling Ganimard's prowess.

The case was conducted briskly at the start. It was first of all ascertained that Prevailles, whose real name was Thomas Derocq, had already been in trouble. Moreover, the search instituted in his rooms, while not supplying any fresh proofs, at least led to the discovery of a ball of whipcord similar to the cord used for doing up the parcel and also to the discovery of daggers which would have produced a wound similar to the wounds on the victim.

But, on the eighth day, everything was changed. Until then Prevailles had refused to reply to the questions put to him; but now, assisted by his counsel, he pleaded a circumstantial alibi and maintained that he was at the Folies-Bergères on the night of the murder.

As a matter of fact, the pockets of his dinner-jacket contained the counterfoil of a stall-ticket and a programme of the performance, both bearing the date of that evening.

'An alibi prepared in advance,' objected the examining-magistrate.

'Prove it,' said Prevailles.

The prisoner was confronted with the witnesses for the prosecution. The young lady from the confectioner's 'thought she knew' the gentleman with the eyeglass. The hall-porter in the rue de Berne 'thought he knew' the gentleman who used to come to see Jenny Saphir. But nobody dared to make a more definite statement.

The examination, therefore, led to nothing of a precise

character, provided no solid basis whereon to found a serious accusation.

The judge sent for Ganimard and told him of his difficulty:

'I can't possibly persist, at this rate. There is no evidence to support the charge.'

'But surely you are convinced in your own mind, monsieur le juge d'instruction! Prevailles would never have resisted his arrest unless he was guilty.'

'He says that he thought he was being assaulted. He also says that he never set eyes on Jenny Saphir and, as a matter of fact, we can find no one to contradict his assertion. Then again, admitting that the sapphire has been stolen, we have not been able to find it at his flat.'

'Nor anywhere else,' suggested Ganimard.

'Quite true, but that's no evidence against him. I'll tell you what we shall want, M. Ganimard, and that very soon: the other end of this red scarf.'

'The other end?'

'Yes, for it is obvious, that, if the murderer took it away with him, the reason was that the stuff is stained with the marks of the blood on his fingers.'

Ganimard made no reply. For several days, he had felt that the whole business was tending to this conclusion. There was no other proof possible. Given the silk scarf – and in no other circumstances – Prevailles' guilt was certain. Now Ganimard's position required that Prevailles' guilt should be established. He was responsible for the arrest, it had cast a glamour around him, he had been praised to the skies as the most formidable adversary of criminals; and he would look absolutely ridiculous if Prevailles were released.

Unfortunately, the one and only indispensable proof was in Lupin's pocket. How was he to get hold of it?

Ganimard cast about, exhausted himself with fresh investigations from start to finish, spent sleepless nights in turning over the mystery of the rue de Berne, studied the records of Prevailles' life, sent ten men hunting after the invisible sapphire. Everything was useless.

On the 28th of December, the examining-magistrate stopped him in one of the passages of the Law Courts:

'Well, M. Ganimard, any news?'

'No, monsieur le juge d'instruction.'

'Then I shall dismiss the case.'

'Wait one day longer.'

'What's the use? We want the other end of the scarf; have you got it?'

'I shall have it tomorrow.'

'Tomorrow!'

'Yes, but please lend me the piece in your possession.'

'What if I do?'

'If you do, I promise to let you have the whole scarf complete.'

'Very well, that's understood.'

Ganimard followed the examining-magistrate to his room and came out with the piece of silk:

'Hang it all!' he growled. 'Yes, I will go and fetch the proof and I shall have it too ... always presuming that Master Lupin has the courage to keep the appointment.'

In point of fact, he did not doubt for a moment that Master Lupin would have this courage; and that was just what exasperated him. Why had Lupin insisted on this meeting? What was his object, in the circumstances?

Anxious, furious, and full of hatred, he resolved to take every precaution necessary not only to prevent his falling into a trap himself, but to make his enemy fall into one, now that the opportunity offered. And, on the next day, which was the 29th of December, the date fixed by Lupin, after spending the night studying the old manor-house in the rue de Surène and convincing himself that there was no other outlet than the front-door, he warned his men that he was going on a dangerous expedition and arrived with them on the field of battle.

He posted them in a café and gave them formal instructions: if he showed himself at one of the third-floor windows, or if he failed to return within an hour, the detectives were to enter the house and arrest anyone who tried to leave it.

The chief-inspector made sure that his revolver was in working order and that he could take it from his pocket easily. Then he went upstairs.

He was surprised to find things as he had left them, the doors open and the locks broken. After ascertaining that the windows of the principal room looked out on the street, he visited the three other rooms that made up the flat. There was no one there.

'Master Lupin was afraid,' he muttered, not without a certain satisfaction.

'Don't be silly,' said a voice behind him.

Turning round, he saw an old workman, wearing a house-painter's long smock, standing in the doorway.

'You needn't bother your head,' said the workman. 'It's I, Lupin. I have been working in the painter's shop since early morning. This is when we knock off for breakfast. So I came upstairs.'

He looked at Ganimard with a quizzing smile and cried:

' 'Pon my word, this is a gorgeous moment I owe you, old chap! I wouldn't sell it for ten years of my life; and yet you know how I love you! What do you think of it, artist? Wasn't it well thought-out and well foreseen? Foreseen from alpha to omega? Did I understand the business? Did I penetrate the mystery of the scarf? I'm not saying that there were no holes in my argument, no links missing in the chain ... But what a masterpiece of intelligence! Ganimard, what a reconstruction of events! What an intuition of everything that had taken place and of everything that was going to take place, from the discovery of the crime to your arrival here in search of a proof! What a really marvellous divination! Have you the scarf?'

'Yes, half of it. Have you the other?'

'Here it is. Let's compare.'

They spread the two pieces of silk on the table. The cuts made by the scissors corresponded exactly. Moreover, the colours were identical.

'But I presume,' said Lupin, 'that this was not the only thing you came for. What you are interested in seeing is the marks of the blood. Come with me, Ganimard: it's rather dark in here.'

They moved into the next room, which, though it overlooked the courtyard, was lighter; and Lupin held his piece of silk against the window-pane:

'Look,' he said, making room for Ganimard.

The inspector gave a start of delight. The marks of the five fingers and the print of the palm were distinctly visible. The evidence was undeniable. The murderer had seized the stuff in his blood-stained hand, in the same hand that had stabbed Jenny Saphir, and tied the scarf round her neck.

'And it is the print of a left hand,' observed Lupin. 'Hence my warning, which had nothing miraculous about it, you see. For, though I admit, friend of my youth, that you may look upon me as a superior intelligence, I won't have you treat me as a wizard.'

Ganimard had quickly pocketed the piece of silk. Lupin nodded his head in approval:

'Quite right, old boy, it's for you. I'm so glad you're glad! And, you see, there was no trap about all this ... only the wish to oblige ... a service between friends, between pals ... And also, I confess, a little curiosity ... Yes, I wanted to examine this other piece of silk, the one the police had ... Don't be afraid: I'll give it back to you ... Just a second...'

Lupin, with a careless movement, played with the tassel at the end of this half of the scarf, while Ganimard listened to him in spite of himself:

'How ingenious these little bits of women's work are! Did you notice one detail in the maid's evidence? Jenny Saphir was very handy with her needle and used to make all her own hats and frocks. It is obvious that she made this scarf herself ... Besides, I noticed that from the first. I am naturally curious, as I have already told you, and I made a thorough examination of the piece of silk which you have just put in your pocket. Inside the tassel, I found a little sacred medal, which the poor girl had stitched into it to bring her luck. Touching, isn't it, Ganimard? A little medal of Our Lady of Good Succour.'

The inspector felt greatly puzzled and did not take his eyes off the other. And Lupin continued:

"Then I said to myself, "How interesting it would be to explore the other half of the scarf, the one which the police will find round the victim's neck! For this other half, which I hold in my hands at last, is finished off in the same way ... so I shall be able to see if it has a hiding-place too and what's inside it ... But look, my friend, isn't it cleverly made? And so simple! All you have to do is to take a skein of red cord and braid it round a wooden cup, leaving a recess, a little empty space in the middle, very small, of course, but large enough to hold a medal of a saint ... or anything ... A precious stone, for instance ... Such as a sapphire..."'

At that moment, he finished pushing back the silk cord, and, from the hollow of a cup, he took between his thumb and forefinger a wonderful blue stone, perfect in respect of size and purity.

'Ha! What did I tell you, friend of my youth?'

He raised his head. The inspector had turned livid and was staring wild-eyed, as though fascinated by the stone that sparkled before him. He at last realized the whole plot:

'You dirty scoundrel!' he muttered, repeating the insults which he had used at the first interview. 'You scum of the earth!'

The two men were standing one against the other:

'Give me that back,' said the inspector.

Lupin held out the piece of silk.

'And the sapphire,' said Ganimard, in a peremptory tone.

'Don't be silly.'

'Give it back, or . . .'

'Or what, you idiot?' cried Lupin. 'Look here, do you think I put you on to this soft thing for nothing?'

'Give it back!'

'You haven't noticed what I've been about, that's plain! What! For four weeks, I've kept you on the move like a deer; and you want to . . . ! Come, Ganimard, old chap, pull yourself together! . . . Don't you see that you've been playing the good dog for four weeks on end? . . . Fetch it, Rover! . . . There's a nice blue pebble over there, which master can't get at. Hunt it, Ganimard, fetch it . . . bring it to master . . . Ah, he's his master's own good little dog! . . . Sit up! Beg! . . . Does'ms want a bit of sugar then? . . .'

Ganimard, containing the anger that seethed within him, thought only of one thing, summoning his detectives. And, as the room in which he now was looked out on the courtyard, he tried gradually to work his way round to the communicating door. He would then run to the window and break one of the panes.

'All the same,' continued Lupin, 'what a pack of dunderheads you and the rest must be! You've had the silk all this time and not one of you ever thought of feeling it, not one of you ever asked himself the reason why the poor girl hung on to her scarf. Not one of you! You just acted at haphazard, without reflecting, without foreseeing anything . . .'

The inspector had attained his object. Taking advantage of a second when Lupin had turned away from him, he suddenly wheeled round and grasped the door-handle. But an oath escaped him: the handle did not budge.

Lupin burst into a fit of laughing:

'Not even that! You did not even foresee that! You lay a trap for me and you won't admit that I may perhaps smell the thing out beforehand . . . And you allow yourself to be brought into this room without asking whether I am not bringing you here for a particular reason and without remembering that the locks are fitted with a special mechanism. Come, now, speaking frankly, what do you think of yourself?'

'What do I think of it?' roared Ganimard, beside himself with rage.

He had drawn his revolver and was pointing it straight at Lupin's face:

'Hands up!' he cried. 'That's what I think of it!'

Lupin placed himself in front of him and shrugged his shoulders:

'Sold again!' he said.

'Hands up, I say, once more!'

'And sold again, say I. Your deadly weapon won't go off.'

'What?'

'Old Catherine, your housekeeper, is in my service. She damped the charges this morning, while you were having your breakfast coffee.'

Ganimard made a furious gesture, pocketed the revolver, and rushed at Lupin.

'Well?' said Lupin, stopping him short with a well-aimed kick on the shin.

Their clothes were almost touching. They exchanged glances of two adversaries who mean to come to blows. Nevertheless, there was no fight. The recollection of the earlier struggles made any present struggle useless. And Ganimard, who remembered all his past failures, his vain attacks, Lupin's crushing reprisals, did not lift a limb. There was nothing to be done. He felt it. Lupin had forces at his command against which any individual force simply broke to pieces. So what was the good?

'I agree,' said Lupin, in a friendly voice, as though answering Ganimard's unspoken thought, 'you would do better to let things be as they are. Besides, friend of my youth, think of all that this incident has brought you: fame, the certainty of quick promotion, and, thanks to that, the prospect of a happy and comfortable old age! Surely, you don't want the discovery of the sapphire and the head of poor Arsène Lupin in addition! It wouldn't be fair. To say nothing of the fact that poor Arsène Lupin saved your life ... Yes sir! Who warned you, at this very spot, that Prevailles was left-handed? ... And is this the way you thank me? It's not pretty of you, Ganimard. Upon my word, you make me blush for you!'

While chattering, Lupin had gone through the same performance as Ganimard and was now near the door. Ganimard saw that his foe was about to escape him. Forgetting all prudence, he tried to block his way, and received a tremendous butt in the stomach, which sent him rolling to the opposite wall.

Lupin dextrously touched a spring, turned the handle, opened the door, and slipped away, roaring with laughter as he went.

*

Twenty minutes later, when Ganimard at last succeeded in joining his men, one of them said to him:

'A house-painter left the house, as his mates were coming back from breakfast, and put a letter in my hand. "Give that to your governor," he said. "Which governor?" I asked; but he was gone. I suppose it's meant for you.'

'Let's have it.'

Ganimard opened the letter. It was hurriedly scribbled in pencil and contained these words:

This is to warn you, friend of my youth, against excessive credulity. When a fellow tells you that the cartridges in your revolver are damp, however great your confidence in that fellow may be, even though his name be Arsène Lupin, never allow yourself to be taken in. Fire first; and, if the fellow hops the twig, you will have acquired the proof (1) that the cartridges are not damp; and (2) that old Catherine is the most honest and respectable of housekeepers.

One of these days, I hope to have the pleasure of making her acquaintance.

Meanwhile, friend of my youth, believe me

always affectionately and sincerely yours,
Arsène Lupin

12

The Secret of the *Magnifique*

E. Phillips Oppenheim

The man was awaiting the service of his dinner in the magnificent buffet of the Gare de Lyons. He sat at a table laid for three, on the right-hand side of the entrance and close to the window. From below came the turmoil of the trains. Every few minutes the swing doors opened to admit little parties of travellers. The solitary occupant of the table scarcely ever moved his head. Yet he had always the air of one who watches.

In appearance he was both remarkable and undistinguished. He was of somewhat less than medium height, of unathletic, almost frail physique. His head was thrust a little forward, as though he were afflicted with a chronic stoop. He wore steel-rimmed spectacles with the air of one who has taken to them too late in life to have escaped the constant habit of peering, which had given to his neck an almost stork-like appearance. His hair and thin moustache were iron-grey, his fingers long and delicate. The labels upon his luggage were addressed in a trim, scholarly hand:

> Mr John T. Laxworthy,
> Passenger to —,
> Via Paris.

A maître d'hôtel, who was passing, paused and looked at the two as yet unoccupied places.

'Monsieur desires the service of his dinner?' he inquired.

Mr John T. Laxworthy glanced up at the clock and carefully compared the time with his own watch. He answered the man's inquiry in French which betrayed no sign of any accent.

'In five minutes,' he declared, 'my friends will have arrived. The service of dinner can then proceed.'

The man bowed and withdrew, a little impressed by his customer's trim precision of speech. Almost as he left the table, the swing doors opened once more to admit another traveller. The newcomer stood on the threshold for a moment, looking around him. He carried a much-labelled dressing-case in his hand, and an umbrella under his arm. He stood firmly upon his feet, and a more thoroughly British, self-satisfied, and obvious person had, to all appearance, never climbed those stairs. He wore a travelling-suit of dark grey, a check ulster, broad-toed boots, and a Homburg hat. His complexion was sandy, and his figure distinctly inclined towards corpulence. He wore scarcely noticeable side-whiskers, and his chin and upper lip were clean-shaven. His eyes were bright and his mouth had an upward and humorous turn. The initials upon his bag were W.F.A., and a printed label upon the same indicated his full name as:

> Mr W. Forrest Anderson,
> Passenger to —,
> Via Paris.

His brief contemplation of the room was soon over. His eyes fell upon the solitary figure, now deep in a book, seated at the table on his right. He set down his dressing-case by the side of the wall, yielded his coat and hat to the attendant vestiaire, and, with the pleased smile of one who greets an old friend, approached the table at which Mr John T. Laxworthy sat waiting.

The idiosyncrasies of great men are always worth noting, and Mr John T. Laxworthy was, without a doubt, foredoomed from the cradle to a certain measure of celebrity. His method of receiving the newcomer was in some re-

spects curious. From the moment when the swing doors had
been pushed open and the portly figure of Mr Forrest
Anderson had crossed the threshold, his eyes had not once
quitted the heavy-looking volume, the contents of which
appeared so completely to absorb his attention. Even now,
when his friend stood by his side, he did not at once look
up. Slowly, and with his eyes still riveted upon the pages he
was studying, he held out his left hand.

'I am glad to see you, Anderson,' he said, 'Sit down by
my side here. You are nearly ten minutes late. I have
delayed ordering the wine until your arrival. Shall it be
white or red?'

Mr Anderson shook with much heartiness the limp fingers which had been offered to him, and took the seat indicated. His friend's eccentricity of manner appeared to be
familiar to him, and he offered no comment upon it.

'White, if you please – Chablis of a dry brand, for choice.
Sorry if I'm late. Beastly crossing, beastly crowded train.
Glad to be here, anyhow.'

Mr John T. Laxworthy closed his book with a little sigh
of regret, and placed a marker within it. He then carefully
adjusted his spectacles and made a deliberate survey of his
companion. Finally he nodded, slowly and approvingly.

'How about the partridges?' he inquired.

'Bad,' Mr Anderson declared, with a sigh. 'It was one
storm in June that did it. We went light last season,
though, and I'm putting down forty brace of Hungarians.
You see –'

Mr Laxworthy touched the table with his forefinger, and
his companion almost automatically stopped.

'Quite excellent,' the former pronounced dryly. 'Don't
overdo it. I should think that this must be Sydney.'

Mr Anderson glanced towards the entrance. Then he
looked back at his companion a little curiously. Mr Laxworthy had not raised his head.

'How the dickens did you know that it was Sydney?' he
demanded.

Mr Laxworthy smiled at the tablecloth.

'I have a special sense for that sort of thing,' he remarked. 'I like to use my eyes as seldom as possible.'

A young man who had just completed a leisurely survey of the room dropped his monocle and came towards them. From the tips of his shiny tan shoes to his smoothly brushed hair, he was unmistakable. He was young, he was English, he was well-bred, he was an athlete. He had a pleasant, unintelligent face, a natural and prepossessing ease of manner. He handed his ulster to the attendant vestiaire and beamed upon the two men.

'How are you, Forrest? How do you do, Laxworthy?' he exclaimed. 'Looking jolly fit, both of you.'

Mr Laxworthy raised his glass. He looked thoughtfully at the wine for a moment, to be sure that it was free from any atom of cork. Then he inclined his head in turn to each of his companions.

'I am glad to see you both,' he said. 'On the whole, I think that I may congratulate you. You have done well. I drink to our success.'

The toast was drunk in silence. Mr Forrest Anderson set down his glass – empty – with a little murmur of content.

'It is something,' he remarked, vigorously attacking a new course, 'to have satisfied our chief.'

The young man opposite to him subjected the dish which was being offered to a long and deliberate survey through his eyeglass, and finally refused it.

'Give me everything in France except the beef,' he declared. 'Must be the way they cut it, I think. Quite right, Andy,' he went on, glancing across the table. 'To have satisfied such a critic as the chief here is an achievement indeed. Having done it, let us hear what he proposes to do with us.'

'In other words,' Mr Anderson put in, 'what is the game to be?'

There was a short pause. Mr John T. Laxworthy was continuing his repast – which was, by the by, of a much more frugal character than that offered to his guests – without any sign of having even heard the inquiry addressed to him by his companions. They knew him, however, and they were content to wait. Presently he commenced to peel an apple and simultaneously to unburden himself.

'A great portion of this last year,' he said, 'which you two have spent apparently with profit in carrying out my instructions, I myself have devoted to the perfection of a certain scholarly tone which I feel convinced is my proper environment. Incidentally, I have devoted myself to the study of various schools of philosophy.'

'I will take a liqueur,' decided the young man, whose name was Sydney – 'something brain-stimulating. A Grand Marnier, waiter, if you please.'

'The same for me,' Mr Forrest Anderson put in hastily. 'Also, in a few moments, some black coffee.'

Mr Laxworthy did not by the flicker of an eyelid betray the slightest annoyance at these interruptions. He waited, indeed, until the liqueurs had been brought before he spoke again, continuing the while in a leisurely fashion the peeling and preparing of his apple. Even for some time after his friends had again offered him their undivided attention, he continued his task of extracting from it, with precise care, every fragment of core.

'In one very interesting treatise,' he recommenced at last, 'I found several obvious truths ingeniously put. A certain decadence in the material prosperity of an imaginary state is clearly proved to be due to a too blind following of the tenets of what is known as the hysterical morality, as against the decrees of what we might call expediency. A little sentiment, like garlic in cookery, is a good thing; too much is fatal. A little – sufficient – morality is excellent; a superabundance disastrous. Society is divided into two classes, those who have and those who desire to have. The one must always prey upon the other. They are, therefore, always changing places. It is this continued movement which lends energy to the human race. As soon as it is suspended, degeneration must follow as a matter of course. It is for those who recognize this great truth to follow and obey its tenets.'

'May we not hear more definitely what it is that you propose?' Anderson asked, a little anxiously.

'We stand,' Mr Laxworthy replied, 'always upon the threshold of the land of adventure. At no place are we nearer to it than in this room. It is our duty to use our energies to assist in the great principles of movement to which I have referred. We must take our part in the struggle. On which side? you naturally ask. Are we to be among those who have, and who, through weakness or desire, must yield to others? or shall we take our place among the more intellectual, the more highly gifted minority, those who assist the progress of the world by helping towards the redistribution of its wealth? Sydney, how much money have you?'

'Three hundred and ninety-five francs and a few coppers,' the young man answered promptly. 'It sounds more in French.'

'And you, Anderson?'

Mr Forrest Anderson coughed.

'With the exception of a five-franc piece,' he admitted, 'I am worth exactly as much as I shall be able to borrow from you presently.'

'In that case,' Mr Laxworthy said dryly, 'our position is preordained. We take our place among the aggressors.'

The young man whose name was Sydney dropped his eyeglass.

'One moment,' he said. 'Andy here and I have exposed our financial impecuniosity at your request. It can scarcely be a surprise to you, considering that we have practically lived upon your bounty for the last year. It seems only fair that you should imitate our candour. There were rumours, a short time ago, of a considerable sum of money to which you had become entitled. To tell you the truth,' the young man went on, leaning a little across the table, 'we were almost afraid, or rather I was, that you might abandon this shadowy enterprise of ours.'

Mr John T. Laxworthy, without being discomposed, which was almost too much to expect of a man with such perfect poise, seemed nevertheless somewhat taken aback. He opened his lips as though to make some reply, and closed them again. When he did speak, it was grudgingly.

'No successful enterprise, or series of enterprises, can be conducted without capital,' he said. 'I am free to admit that I am in possession of a certain amount of that indispensable commodity. I do not feel myself called upon to state the exact amount, but such money as is required for our journeyings, or for any enterprise in which we become engaged will be forthcoming.'

Mr Anderson stroked his chin meditatively.

'I am sure,' he said, 'that that sounds quite satisfactory.'

'I call it jolly fine business,' the young man declared. 'There is just one thing more upon which I think we ought to have an understanding. You say that we are to take our place among the aggressors. Exactly what does that mean?'

Mr Laxworthy looked at him coldly.

'It means precisely what I choose that it shall mean,' he replied. 'Any enterprise or adventure in which we may become engaged will be selected by me, and by me only. My chief aim – I have no objection to telling you this – is to make life tolerable for ourselves, to escape the dull monootony of idleness, and, incidentally, to embrace any opportunity which may present itself to enrich our exchequer. Have you any objection to that?'

'None,' Mr Forrest Anderson declared.

'None at all,' Sydney echoed.

'There are three of us,' Mr Laxworthy went on. 'We each have our use. Mine is the chief of all. I supply the brains. My position must be unquestioned.'

'For my part, I am willing enough,' Sydney remarked. 'It's been your show from the first.'

Mr Forrest Anderson, who had dined well and forgotten his empty pockets, laughed a genial laugh.

'I agree,' he declared. 'Tell us, when and where do we start, and shall our first enterprise be Pickwickian, or am I to play the Sancho Panza to your Don Quixote and Sydney's donkey?'

Mr Laxworthy regarded his associates coldly. There was a silence, a silence which became somehow an ominous thing. Around them reigned a babel of tongues, a clatter of crockery. Below, the turmoil of the busy station, the shrieking of departing trains. But at the table presided over by Mr Laxworthy no word was spoken. Mr Anderson's geniality faded away. His young companion's amiable nonchalance entirely deserted him. Either of them would have given worlds to have been able to dispel the strange effect of this silence with some casual remark. But upon them lay the spell of the conqueror. The little man at the head of the table held them in the hollow of his hand.

'It may be,' he said, breaking at last that curious silence, 'that no other occasion will ever arise when it will be necessary to speak to you in this fashion. So now listen. You are right to indulge in the urbanities of existence. Keep always the smile upon your lips, if you can, but underneath let the real consciousness of life be ever present. I do not claim for myself the genius of a Pickwick or the valour of a Don Quixote. On the other hand, we are not paltry aggressors against Society, failing in one enterprise, successful in the next, a mark for ridicule and contempt one moment, and for good-humoured sufferance the next. I do not ask you to embark with me as farceurs upon a series of enterprises carried out upon the principle of "Let us do our best and chance the rest." It is just possible that the fates may be against us, and that we may live together for many months the lives of ordinary and moderately commonplace human beings. I ask you to remember that no sense of danger would ever deter me from embarking upon any adventure which I deemed likely to afford us either diversion, wealth, or satisfaction of any sort whatsoever. We are not pleasure-seekers. We are men whose one end and aim is to escape from the chains of everyday existence, to avoid the humdrum life of our fellows. Therein may lie for us many and peculiar dangers. Adopt, if you will, the motto of the pagans – "Let us eat and drink, for tomorrow we die!" So long as you remember. Will you drink with me to that remembrance?'

Mr Laxworthy, as he grew less enigmatic in his speech, became, if possible, more whimsical in his mannerisms. He ordered the best Cognac, at which he himself scarcely glanced, and turned with a little sigh of relief to his book. In the midst of this hubbub of sounds and bustle of diners he continued to read with every appearance of studious enjoyment. His two companions were content enough, apparently, to relax after their journey and enjoy their cigars. Nevertheless, they once or twice glanced curiously at their chief. One of these glances he seemed, although he never raised his head, to have intercepted, for, carefully marking the place in his book, he pushed it away and addressed them.

'Our plans,' he announced abruptly, 'are not yet wholly made. We wait here for – shall we call it an inspiration? Perhaps, even at this moment, it is not far from us.'

Mr Forrest Anderson and his vis-à-vis turned as though instinctively towards the door. At that moment two men who had just passed through were standing upon the threshold. One was rather past middle-age, corpulent, with red features of a coarse type. His companion, who was leaning upon his arm, was much younger, and a very different sort of person. He was tall and exceedingly thin. His features were wasted almost to emaciation, his complexion was ghastly. He seemed to have barely strength enough to move.

'They are coming to the table next us,' Laxworthy said, in a very low tone. 'The address upon their luggage will be interesting.'

Slowly the two men came down the room. As Laxworthy had expected, they took possession of an empty table close at hand. The young man sank into his chair with a little sigh of exhaustion.

'A liqueur brandy, quick,' the older man ordered, as he accepted the menu from a waiter. 'My friend is fatigued.'

Sydney took the bottle which stood upon their own table poured out a wineglassful, and, rising to his feet, stepped across and accosted the young man.

'Do me the favour of drinking this, sir,' he begged. 'The service here is slow and the brandy excellent. I can see that you are in need of it. It may serve, too, as an aperitif.'

The young man accepted it with a smile of gratitude. His companion echoed his thanks.

'Very much obliged to you, sir,' he declared. 'My friend here is a little run down and finds travelling fatiguing.'

'A passing malady, I trust?' Sydney remarked, preparing to return to his seat.

'A legacy from that cursed graveyard – South Africa,' the older man growled.

Sydney stepped back and resumed his seat. In a few minutes he leaned across the table.

'The Paradise Hotel, Hyères,' he said under his breath.

Mr Laxworthy looked thoughtful.

'You surprise me,' he admitted.

'What do you know of them?' Anderson inquired.

Mr Laxworthy shrugged his shoulders.

'Not much beyond the obvious facts,' he admitted. 'Even you, my friends, are not wholly deceived, I presume, by the young man's appearance?'

They evidently were. Their faces expressed their non-comprehension.

Mr Laxworthy sighed.

'You must both of you seek to develop the minor senses,' he enjoined reprovingly. 'Your powers of observation, for instance, are, without doubt, exceedingly stunted. Let me assure you, for example, that your sympathy for that young man is entirely wasted.'

'You mean that he is not really ill?' Sydney asked incredulously.

'Most certainly he is not as ill as he pretends,' Mr Laxworthy declared dryly. 'If you look at him more closely you will discover a certain theatricality in his pose which of itself should undeceive you.'

'You know who he is?' Sydney asked.

'I believe so,' Laxworthy admitted. 'I can hazard a guess even to his companion's identity. But – the Paradise Hotel, Hyères! Order some fresh coffee. We are not ready to leave yet. Anderson, watch the door. Sydney, don't let them notice it, but watch our friends there. Something may happen.'

A tall, broad-shouldered man with a fair moustache and wearing a long travelling-coat had entered the buffet. He stood there for a moment looking around, as though in search of a table. The majority of those present suffered his scrutiny, unnoticing, indifferent, naturally absorbed in themselves and their own affairs. Not so these two men who had last entered. Every nerve of the young man's body seemed to have become tense. His hand had stolen into the pocket of his travelling-coat, and with a little thrill Sydney saw the glitter of steel half shown for a moment between his interlocked fingers. No longer was this young man's countenance the countenance of an invalid. It had become instead like the face of a wolf. His front teeth were showing – he had moved slightly so as to give his arm full play. It seemed as though a tragedy were at hand.

The man who had been standing on the threshold deposited his handbag upon the floor near the wall, and came down the room. Laxworthy and his two associates watched. Their two neighbours at the next table sat in well-simulated indifference, only once more Sydney saw the gleam of hidden steel flash for a moment from the depths of that ulster pocket. The newcomer made no secret of his destination.

He advanced straight to their table and came to a standstill immediately in front of them. Both the stout man and his invalid companion looked up at him as one might regard a stranger.

To all appearance Laxworthy was engrossed in his book. Sydney and Anderson watched and listened, but of all the words which passed between those three men, not one was audible. No change of countenance on the part of any one of the three indicated even the nature of that swift and fluent interchange of words. Only at the last, the elder man touched the label attached to his dressing-bag, and they heard his words:

'The Paradise Hotel, Hyères. We shall be there for at least a month.'

The newcomer stood perfectly still for several moments, as though deliberating. The young man's hand came an inch or two from his pocket. Chance and tragedy trifled together in the midst of that crowded room, unnoticed save by those three at the adjoining table. Then, as though inspired with a sudden resolution, this stranger, whose coming had seemed so unwelcome, raised his hat slightly to the two men with whom he had been talking, and turned away.

'The Paradise Hotel at Hyères,' he repeated. 'I shall know, then, where to find you.'

The little scene was over. Nothing had happened. Nevertheless, the fingers of the young man, as his hand emerged from his pocket, were moist and damp, and his appearance was now veritably ghastly. His companion watched, with a deep purple flush upon his face, the passing of this stranger who had accosted him. He had the appearance of one threatened with apoplexy.

'One might be interested to know the meaning of these things,' Sydney murmured softly.

Their chief looked up from his book.

'Then one must follow – to the Paradise Hotel,' he remarked.

'I begin to believe,' Anderson declared, 'that it is our destination.'

'There is no hurry,' Laxworthy replied. 'Grimes once told me that this room in which we are now sitting was perhaps the most interesting rendezvous in Europe. Grimes was at the head of the Foreign Department at Scotland Yard in those days, and he knew what he was talking about.'

A woman, wrapped in magnificent furs, who was passing their table, was run into by a clumsy waiter and dropped a satchel from her finger. Sydney hastened to restore it to her, and was rewarded by a gracious smile in which was mingled a certain amount of recognition.

'You seem fated to be my Good Samaritan today,' she remarked.

'It is my good fortune,' the young man replied. 'Can I help you to get a table or anything? This place is always overcrowded.'

She motioned with her head to where a maître d'hôtel was holding a chair for her.

'It is already arranged,' she said. 'Perhaps we shall meet in the Luxe afterwards, if you are going south.'

'You are travelling far?' Sydney ventured to inquire.

'Only to the outskirts of the Riviera,' she answered. 'I am going to Hyères – to the Paradise Hotel. Why do you smile?'

'My friends and I,' he explained, 'have met here to decide upon the whereabouts of a little holiday we mean to spend together. We were at that moment discussing a suggestion to proceed to the same place.'

She gave him a little farewell nod as she passed on.

'If you decide to do so,' she declared, 'it will give me great pleasure to meet you again.'

'I congratulate you,' Laxworthy remarked dryly, as Sydney resumed his seat. 'A most interesting acquaintance, yours.'

'Do you know who she is?' the young man asked, 'I only met her on the train.'

His chief nodded gravely.

'She is Madame Bertrand,' he replied. 'Her husband at one time held a post in the Foreign Office, under Fauré. For some reason or other he was discredited, and since then he has died. There was some scandal about Madame Bertrand herself, and some papers which were missing from her husband's portfolio, but nothing definite ever came to light.'

'Madame seems to survive the loss of her husband,' Mr Forrest Anderson remarked, looking across at her admiringly.

Laxworthy held up his hand. Almost for the first time he was sitting upright in his chair, his head still thrust forward in his usual attitude, his eyes fixed upon the door. The thin fingers of his right hand were spread flat upon the table-cloth.

'We have finished, for the moment, with the Madame Bertrands of the world,' he announced. 'After all, they are for the pigmies. Here comes food for giants.'

The light of battle was in Laxworthy's eyes. The greatest of men have their moments of weakness, and even Laxworthy, for that brief space of time, forgot himself and his pose towards the world. His thin lips were a little parted, the veins at the sides of his forehead stood out like blue cords. His lips moved slowly.

'You can both look,' he said. 'They are probably used to it. You will see the two greatest personages on earth.'

His companions gazed eagerly towards the door. Two men were standing there, being relieved of their wraps and directed towards a table. One was middle-aged, grey-headed, with a somewhat worn but keen face. The other was taller, with black hair streaked with grey, a face half Jewish, half romantic, a skin like ivory.

'The greatest men in the world?' Sydney repeated, under his breath. 'You are joking, chief. I never saw even a photograph of either of them before in my life.'

'The one nearest you,' Laxworthy announced, 'is Mr Freeling Poignton. The newspapers will tell you that his fortune exceeds the national debt of any country in the world. He is, without doubt, the richest man who was ever born. There has never yet breathed an emperor whose up-raised finger could provoke or stop a war, whose careless word could check the prosperity of the proudest nation that ever breathed. These things Mr Freeling Poignton can do.'

'And the other?' Anderson whispered.

'It is chance,' Mr Laxworthy said softly, 'which placed a sceptre of unlimited power in the hands of Richard Free-ling Poignton. It is his own genius which has made the Marquis Lefant the greatest power in the diplomatic world. It was his decision which brought about war between Rus-sia and Japan. It was he who stopped the declaration of war against Germany by our own Prime Minister at the time of the Algeciras difficulty. It was he who offered a million pounds to bring the Tsar of Russia to Germany – and he did it. There is little that he cannot do.'

'Is he a German?' Anderson asked.

'No one knows of what race he comes,' Mr Laxworthy replied. 'No one knows what country is really nearest to his heart. It is his custom to accept commissions or refuse them, according to his own belief as to their influence upon international peace. They say that he has English blood in his veins. If so, he has been a sorry friend to his native land.'

'We seem,' Sydney remarked, 'to have chosen a very for-tunate evening for our little dinner here. The place is full of interesting people. I wonder where those two are going.'

A maître d'hôtel, whose respect had been gained by the lavish orders from their table, paused and whispered confi-dentially in Mr Laxworthy's ear.

'The gentleman down there, sir,' he announced, 'the grey gentleman with his own servant waiting upon him, is Mr Freeling Poignton, the great American multi-millionaire.'

Laxworthy nodded slowly.

'I thought I recognized him by his photographs,' he said. 'Is he going to Monte Carlo?'

The attendant shook his head.

'I was speaking to them a moment ago, sir,' he declared. 'Mr Poignton has been here a good many times. He and his friend are going for a fortnight's quiet to the Paradise Hotel at Hyères.'

The maître d'hôtel passed on with another bow. The three men looked at one another. Mr Laxworthy glanced at the clock.

'Sydney,' he said, 'will you step down into the bureau and find out whether it is possible to get three seats in the train de luxe?'

'For Hyères?' Sydney asked.

Mr Laxworthy assented gravely.

'Certainly,' he said. 'You might at the same time telegraph to the hotel.'

'To the Paradise Hotel?'

Mr Laxworthy inclined his head.

A black cloud, long and with jagged edges, passed away from the face of the moon. The plain of Hyères was gradually revealed – the cypress trees, tall and straight, the shimmering olive trees with their ghostly foliage, the fields of violets, the level vineyards. And beyond, the phalanx of lights on the warships lying in the bay. The hotel on the hillside, freshly painted and spotlessly white, stood sharply out against the dark background. The whole world was becoming visible.

Upon the balcony of one of the rooms upon the second floor a man was standing with his back to the wall. He looked around at the flooding moonlight and swore softly to himself. Decidedly, things were turning out ill with him. From the adjoining balcony a thin rope was hanging, swaying very slightly in the night breeze. The young man gazed helplessly at the end, which had slipped from his fingers, and which was hanging just now over some flower-beds. He was face to face with the almost insoluble problem of how to regain the shelter of his own room.

From the gardens below came the melancholy cry of a passing owl. From the white, barnlike farmhouse, perched on the mountainside in the distance, came the bark of a dog. Then again there was silence. The man looked back into the room from which he had escaped, and down at the end of that swinging rope. He was indeed on the horns of a dilemma. To return to the room was insanity. To stay where he was to risk being seen by the earliest passer-by or the first person who chanced to look out from a window. To try to pass to his own veranda without the aid of that rope which he had lost was an impossibility.

It was already five minutes since he had crept out from the room and had let the rope slip from his fingers. The owl had finished his mournful serenade, the watch-dog on the mountainside slept. The deep silence of the hours before dawn brooded over the land. The man, fiercely impatient though he was to escape, was constrained to wait. There seemed to be nothing which he could do.

Then again the silence of the night was strangely, almost harshly broken, this time from the interior of the hotel. An alarm bell, harsh and discordant, rang out a brazen note of terror. Lights suddenly flashed in the windows, footsteps hurried along the corridor. The man outside upon the balcony set his teeth and cursed. Detection now seemed unavoidable.

The room behind him was speedily invaded. Madame Bertrand, in a dressing-gown whose transparent simplicity had been the triumph of a celebrated establishment in the rue de la Paix, her beautiful hair tied up only with pink ribbon, her eyes kindling with excitement, received a stream of agitated callers. The floor waiter, three guests in various states of déshabille, and finally the manager, breathless with haste, all claimed her attention at the same time.

'It was I who rang the danger-bell,' madame declared indignantly. 'In an hotel where such things are possible, it is well, indeed, that one should be able to sound the alarm. There has been a man in my rooms.'

'But it is unheard of, madame!' the manager replied.

'It is nevertheless true,' madame insisted. 'Not two minutes since, I opened my eyes and he disappeared into my sitting-room. I saw him distinctly. I could not recognize him, for he kept his face turned away. Either he has escaped through the sitting-room door and down the corridor, or he is still there, or he is hiding in this room.'

'The jewels of madame!' the manager gasped. 'I tremble in every limb. How can I know whether or not I have been robbed?'

'The pearls of madame,' he persisted – 'the string of pearls?'

'That is safe,' madame admitted. 'My diamond collar, too, is in its place.'

The manager and two of the guests searched the sitting-room, which opened to the left from the bedroom. Others spread themselves over the hotel to calm fears of the startled guests, and to assure everybody that there was no fire and that nothing particular had happened. The search was, of necessity, not a long one; there was no one in the sitting-room. The manager and his helpers returned.

'The room is empty, madame,' the former declared.

'Then the burglar has escaped!' she cried.

Monsieur Helder went down on his knees and peered in vain under the bed.

'Madame is sure,' he inquired, raising his head with some temerity but remaining upon his knees – 'madame is absolutely convinced that it was not an illusion – the fragment of a dream, perhaps? It is strange that there should have been time for anyone to have escaped.'

'A dream, indeed!' madame declared indignantly. 'I do not dream such things, Monsieur Helder.'

Monsieur Helder dived again under the valance. It was just at that moment that Madame Bertrand, gazing into the plate-glass mirror of the wardrobe, received a shock. Distinctly she saw a man's face reflected there. With the predominant instinct of her sex aroused, she opened her lips to scream – and just as suddenly closed them again. She stood for a moment quite still, her hand pressed to her side. Then she turned her head and looked out of the French windows which led on to the balcony. There was nothing to be seen. She looked across at Monsieur Helder, whose head had disappeared inside the wardrobe. Then she stole up to the window and glanced once more on the balcony.

'Madame,' Monsieur Helder declared, 'the room is empty. Your sitting-room also is empty. There remains,' he added, with a sudden thought, 'only the balcony.'

He advanced a step. Madame Bertrand, however, remained motionless. She was standing in front of the window.

'The balcony I have examined myself,' she said quietly. 'There is no one there. Besides, I am not one of the English cranks who sleep always with the damp night air filling their rooms. My windows are bolted.'

'In that case, madame,' Monsieur Helder declared, with a little shrug of the shoulders, 'we must conclude that the intruder escaped through your sitting-room door into the corridor. Madame can at least assure me that nothing of great value is missing from her belongings?'

Madame Bertrand, though pale, was graciously pleased to reassure the inquirer.

'You have reason, my friend,' she admitted. 'Nothing of great value is missing. The shock, however, I shall not get over for days. After this, Monsieur Helder, you will not banish my maid again to that horrible annexe. Whoever occupies the next room to mine here must give it up. Not another night will I sleep here alone and unprotected.'

Monsieur Helder bowed.

'Madame,' he said, 'the adjoining room is occupied by Mr Sydney Wing, an Englishman, whom madame will perhaps recollect. He is, I am sure, a man of gallantry. After the adventure of tonight he will doubtless offer to vacate his room for the convenience of madame's maid.'

'It must be arranged,' madame insisted.

Monsieur Helder backed towards the door.

'If madame would like her maid for the rest of the night –' he suggested.

Madame Bertrand shook her head.

'Not now,' she replied. 'I will not have the poor girl disturbed. After what has passed, she would lie here in terror. As for me, I shall lock all my doors, and perhaps, after all, I shall sleep.'

Monsieur Helder drew himself up upon the threshold. He was not a very imposing-looking object in his trousers and a crumpled shirt, but he permitted himself a bow.

'Madame,' he said, 'will accept this expression of my infinite regret that her slumbers should have been so disturbed.'

'I thank you very much, Monsieur Helder,' she answered graciously. 'Good night!'

Monsieur Helder executed his bow and disappeared. Madame paused for a moment to listen to his footsteps down the corridor. Then she moved forward to the door and locked it. For a few seconds longer she hesitated. Then she walked deliberately to the french windows, threw them open, and stepped on to the balcony.

'Good evening, Monsieur Sydney Wing – or rather good morning!'

The young man gripped for a moment the frail balustrade. It must be confessed that he had lost entirely his savoir-faire.

'Madame!' he faltered.

She pointed to the open doors.

'Inside!' she whispered imperatively – 'inside at once!'

She pointed to the swinging cord. The young man stepped only too willingly inside the room. She followed him and closed the windows.

'You will gather, Monsieur Sydney Wing,' she said, 'that

I am disposed to spare you. I knew that you were outside, even while my room was being searched. I preferred first to hear your explanation, before I gave you up to be treated as a common burglar.'

The young man's courage was returning fast. He lifted his head. His eyes were full of gratitude – or what, at any rate, gleamed like gratitude.

'Oh, madame,' he murmured, 'you are too gracious!'

He raised her hand to his lips and kissed it. She looked at him not unkindly.

'You will come this way,' she said, leading him into the sitting-room and turning on the electric light. 'Now, tell me, monsieur, and tell me the truth if you would leave this room a free man and without scandal. When I saw you first you were bending over that table. Upon it was my necklace, my ear-rings, a lace scarf, my chatelaine and vanity box, a few of my rings, perhaps a jewelled pin or two. Now tell me exactly what you came for, what you have taken, and why?'

The young man held himself upright. He drew a little breath. Fate was certainly dealing leniently with him.

'Madame,' he said, 'think. Was there nothing else upon that table?'

She shook her head.

'I can think of nothing,' she acknowledged.

'Tonight,' he continued, 'you were scarcely so kind to me. We danced together, it is true, but there were many others. There was the Admiral – the French Admiral, for instance. Madame was favourably disposed towards him.'

She was a coquette, and she shrugged her shoulders as she smiled.

'Why not? Admiral Christodor is a very charming man. He dances well, he entertains upon his wonderful battleship most lavishly, he is a very desirable and delightful acquaintance. And you, Monsieur Sydney Wing, what have you to say that I should not dance and be friendly with this gentleman?'

The young man was feeling his feet upon the ground. Nevertheless, he continued to look serious.

'Alas!' he said, 'I have no right to find fault. Yet two nights ago madame gave me the rose I asked for. Tonight – you remember?'

She looked at him softly yet steadily. Then she glanced at the table and back again into his face.

'You told me,' he continued, 'that the rose belonged to him who dared to pluck it.'

'It is a saying,' she murmured. 'I was not in earnest.'

Mr Sydney Wing sighed deeply.

'Madame,' he declared, 'I come of a literal nation. When we love, the word of a woman means much to us. Tonight there seemed nothing dearer to me in life than the possession of that rose. I told myself that your challenge was accepted. I told myself that tonight I would sleep with that rose on the pillow by my side.'

Slowly he unbuttoned his coat. From the breast pocket he drew out a handkerchief and unfolded it. In the centre, crushed, and devoid of many of its petals, but still retaining its shape and perfume, lay a dark red rose.

Madame Bertrand moved a step towards him.

'Monsieur,' she cried incredulously, yet with some tenderness in her tone – 'monsieur, you mean to tell me that for the sake of that rose you climbed from your balcony to mine, you ran these risks?'

'For the sake of this rose, madame, and all that it means to me,' he answered.

She drew a long sigh. Then she held out her hand. Again he raised it to his lips.

'Monsieur Sydney,' she said, 'I have done your countrymen an injustice all my life. I had not thought such sentiment was possible in any one of them. I am very glad indeed that when I saw your face reflected in the mirror of my wardrobe, something urged me to send Monsieur Helder away. I am very glad.'

'Madame.'

She held up her finger. Already the faint beginning of dawn was stealing into the sky. From the farmhouse away on the hillside a cock commenced to crow.

'Monsieur,' she whispered, 'not another word. I have risked my reputation to save you. See, the door is before you. Unlock it softly. Be sure there is no one in the corridor when you leave. Do not attempt to close it. I myself in a few minutes' time will return and do that.'

'But Madame –' he begged.

She pointed imploringly towards the door, but there was tenderness in her farewell glance.

'Tomorrow we will talk,' she promised. 'Tomorrow night, if you should fancy my roses, perhaps I may be more kind. Good night!'

She stole back to her room and sat on the edge of her bed. Very noiselessly the young man opened the door of the sitting-room, glanced up and down, and with swift, silent footsteps made his way to his own apartment. Madame, some few minutes later, closed the door behind him, slowly slipped off her dressing-gown, and curled herself once more in her bed. Mr Sydney Wing, in the adjoining room, lit a cigarette and mixed himself a whisky-and-soda. There were drops of perspiration still upon his forehead as he stepped out on to the balcony and wound up his rope.

It was the most cheerful hour of the day at the Paradise Hotel – the hour before luncheon. A swarthy Italian was singing love-songs on the gravel sweep to the music of a guitar. The very air was filled with sunshine. A soft south wind was laden with perfumes from the violet farm below. Everyone seemed to be out of doors, promenading, or sitting about in little groups. Mr Laxworthy and Mr Forrest Anderson had just passed along the front and were threading their way up the winding path which led through the pine woods at the back of the hotel. Mr Lenfield, the invalid young man, was lying in a sheltered corner, taking a sun-bath: his companion by his side smoking a large cigar and occasionally reading extracts from a newspaper. The pretty American girl, who was one of the features of the place, and Madame Bertrand, were missing, the former because she was playing golf with Sydney Wing, the latter because she never rose until luncheon-time. Mr Freeling Poignton and the Marquis Lefant were sitting a little way up among the pine trees. Mr Freeling Poignton was smoking his morning cigar. Lefant was leaning forward, his eyes fixed steadily upon that streak of blue Mediterranean. In his hand he held his watch.

'I am quite sure,' he said softly, 'that I can rely upon my information. At a quarter past twelve precisely the torpedo is to be fired.'

'Which is the *Magnifique*, anyway?' Mr Freeling Poignton inquired.

Lefant pointed to the largest of the grey battleships which were riding at anchor. Then his fingers slowly traversed the blue space until it paused at a black object, like a derelict barge, set out very near the island of Hyères. He glanced at his watch.

'A quarter past,' he muttered. 'Look! My God!'

The black object had disappeared. A column of white water rose gracefully into the air and descended. It was finished. Lefant leaned towards his companion.

'You and I,' he said, 'have seen a thing which is going to change the naval history of the future. You and I alone can understand why the French Admiralty have given up building battleships, why even their target practice here and at Cherbourg continues as a matter of form only.'

Mr Freeling Poignton withdrew his cigar from his mouth.

'I can't say,' he admitted, 'that I have ever given any particular attention to these implements of warfare, because I hate them all; but there's nothing new, anyway, in a torpedo. What's the difference between this one and the ordinary sort?'

'I will tell you in a very few words,' Lefant answered. 'This one can be fired at a range of five miles, and relied

301

upon to hit a mark little larger than the plate of a battleship with absolutely scientific accuracy. There is no question of aim at all. Just as you work out an exact spot in a
surveying expedition by scientific instruments, so you can
decide precisely the spot which that torpedo shall hit. It
travels at the pace of ten miles a minute, and it has a
charge which has never been equalled.'

Mr Freeling Poignton shivered a little, as he dropped the
ash of his cigar.

'I'd like to electrocute the man who invented it,' he declared tersely.

Lefant shook his head.

'You are wrong,' he replied. 'The man who invented that
torpedo is the friend of your scheme and not the enemy.
Listen. It is your desire – is it not – the great ambition of
your life, to secure for the world universal peace?'

Mr Freeling Poignton thrust his hands into his trouser
pockets.

'Marquis,' he said, 'there is no man breathing who could
say how much I am worth. Capitalize my present income,
and you might call it five hundred million pounds. Put a
quarter of a million somewhere in the bank for me, and I'd
give the rest to see every army in Europe disbanded, every
warship turned into a trading vessel, and every soldier and
sailor turned into the factories or upon the land to become
honest, productive units.'

'Just so,' Lefant assented. 'It may sound a little Utopian,
but it is magnificent. Now listen. You will never induce the
rulers of the world to look upon this question reasonably,
because every nation is jealous of some other, and no one is
great enough to take the lead. The surest of all ways to
prevent war is to reduce the art of killing to such a certainty
that it becomes an absurdity even to take the field. What
nation will build battleships which can be destroyed with
the touch of a finger at any time, from practically any distance? I tell you that this invention, which only one or two
people in the world outside of that battleship yonder know

of at present, is the beginning of the end of all naval warfare. There is only one thing to be done – to drive this
home. No nation must be allowed to keep the secret for her
own. It must belong to all.'

Mr Freeling Poignton nodded thoughtfully.

'I begin to understand,' he remarked. 'Guess that's where
you come in, isn't it?'

'I hope so,' Lefant assented. 'I have already spent a hundred thousand dollars of your money, but I think I have
had value for it.'

'Say, why don't you treat this matter as we should on the
other side?' Mr Freeling Poignton demanded. 'It's all very
well to bribe these petty officers and such-like, but the
admiral's your man. Remember that the money-bags of the
world are behind you.'

Lefant smiled faintly.

'Alas!' he exclaimed, 'the admiral belongs to a race little
known in the world of commerce. Money-bags which
reached to the sky would never buy him. There are others
on the ship who are mine, and with the information I have
the rest should be possible.'

Mr Freeling Poignton frowned. He disliked very much to
hear of a man who denied the omnipotence of money. He
felt like the king of some foreign country to whom a
stranger had refused obeisance.

'Well, you've got to run this thing,' he remarked, 'and I
suppose you know what kind of lunatics you've got to deal
with. Seems to me the most difficult job is for you to get on
the battleship at all without the admiral's consent.'

Lefant kicked a pebble away from beneath his feet.

'That is the chief difficulty,' he admitted. 'I was rather
hoping that Madame Bertrand might have been of use to
me there. She has been devoting herself to the admiral for
some days, and last night she got a pass from him, allowing
the bearer to visit the ship at any time, with access to any
part of it. This morning, however, she declares that she
must have torn it up with her bridge scores.'

'I suppose she can get it replaced?' Mr Freeling Poignton suggested.

Lefant hesitated for a moment.

'To tell you the truth,' he declared, 'my own belief is that the admiral declined to give it to her. Julie hates to admit defeat, however. Hence her little story. That does not trouble me very much, though. My plans are all made in another direction. Tonight is the night of the fancy-dress ball here, and the admiral is coming. When he returns to the *Magnifique*, the drawings of the torpedo will be in my possession.'

Mr Freeling Poignton laid his hand for a moment on Lefant's shoulder.

'Marquis,' he said, 'I've been a little led into this affair by you. Remember, these aren't my methods, and it's only because I see just how difficult it is to make a move that I'm standing in. But let this be understood between you and me. The moment those plans are in your possession, a copy of them is to be handed simultaneously to the Government of every civilized Power in the world, so that everyone can build the darned things if they want to.'

'Naturally,' Lefant assented. 'It is already agreed.'

'No favouritism,' Mr Freeling Poignton declared vigorously, 'no priority. We steal those plans, not to give any one nation an advantage over any other, but to put every country on the same footing.'

'It is already agreed,' Lefant repeated.

Mr Laxworthy and Mr Forrest Anderson passed along, on their way back to the hotel. Courteous greetings were exchanged between the four men. Lefant watched them with a faint smile: Mr Laxworthy with a grey shawl around his shoulders, his queer little stoop, his steel-rimmed spectacles; Anderson in his well-cut tweeds, brightly polished tan shoes, and neat Homburg hat.

'That,' Lefant remarked, inclining his head towards Mr Laxworthy, 'is exactly the type of English person whom one meets in a place like Hyères, at an hotel like this. One could swear that he lives somewhere near the British Museum, writes heavily upon some dull subject, belongs to a learned society, and has never had to make his own way in the world. He probably hates draughts, has a pet ailment, and talks about his nerves. He makes a friend of that red-faced fellow-countryman of his because he is attracted by his robust health and his sheer lack of intelligence.'

'I dare say you're right,' Mr Freeling Poignton remarked carelessly. 'What about luncheon?'

It was the night of the great fancy-dress ball at the Paradise Hotel.

Down in the lounge the tumult became more boisterous every minute. Automobiles and carriages were all the time discharging their bevy of visitors from the neighbouring hotels and villas. A large contingent of naval officers arrived from Toulon. The ballroom was already crowded. Admiral Christodor, looking very handsome, led the promenade with Madame Bertrand, concealed under the identity of an Eastern princess. There were many who wondered what it was that he whispered in her ear as he conducted her into the ballroom.

'It was careless of me,' she admitted softly, 'but I am really quite, quite sure that it was destroyed. It was with my bridge scores, and I tore them all up without thinking. You will give me another, perhaps?'

'Whenever you will,' he promised.

'Listen,' she continued. 'Tonight you must not leave me. There is a young Englishman – you understand?'

'Tonight shall be mine,' the admiral answered gallantly. 'I will not quit your side for a second for all the Englishmen who ever left their sad island.'

It was a gallant speech, but if Fritz, the concierge, could have heard it he would have been puzzled, for, barely half an hour later, a gust of wind blew back the cloak of a man who was stepping into a motor-car, and his uniform was certainly the uniform of an admiral in the French navy.

Through the windy darkness the motor-car rushed on its way to La Plage. The men who waited in the pinnace rose to the salute. The admiral took his place in silence, and the little petrol-driven boat tore through the water.

'The admiral takes his pleasure sadly,' one of them muttered, as their passenger climbed on to the deck.

'He has returned most devilish early,' another of them, whose thoughts were in the café at La Plage, grumbled.

The admiral turned his head sharply.

'I shall return,' he announced. 'Await me.'

Most of the officers of the *Magnifique* were in the ballroom of the Paradise Hotel. The admiral received the salute of the lieutenant on duty, and passed at once to his cabin. Arrived there, he shut the door and listened. There was no sound save the gentle splashing of the water near the porthole. Like lightning he turned to a cabinet set in the wall. He pulled out a drawer and touched a spring. Everything was as he had been told. A roll of papers was pushed back into a corner of this compartment. He drew the sheets out one by one, shut the cabinet quickly, and swung round. Then he stood as though turned to stone. The inner door of the cabin, which led into the sleeping apartment, was open. Seated at the table before him was Mr Laxworthy.

Lefant was a man who had passed through many crises in life. Sheer astonishment, however, on this occasion overmastered him. His savoir-faire had gone. He simply stood still and stared. It was surely a vision, this. It could not be that little old-fashioned man who went about with a grey shawl on his shoulders who was sitting there watching him.

'What in the devil's name are you doing there?' he demanded.

'I might ask you the same question,' Mr Laxworthy replied. 'I imagine we are both – intruders.'

Lefant recovered himself a little. He came nearer to the table.

'Tell me exactly what you want,' he insisted.

'First, let us have an understanding,' Mr Laxworthy answered, 'and as quickly as possible. For obvious reasons, the less time we spend here the better. The pinnace which brought you is waiting, I presume, to take you back. In this light you might still pass as an Admiral, but every moment you spend here adds to the risk – for both of us. My foot is on the electric bell, which I presume would bring the admiral's steward. You perceive, too, that I have a revolver in my hand, to the use of which I am accustomed. Am I in command, or you?'

'It appears that you are,' Lefant admitted grimly. 'Go on.'

'You hold in your hand,' Mr Laxworthy continued, 'the plans of the Macharin torpedo, the torpedo which is to make warfare in the future impossible.'

Then Lefant waited no longer. He flung himself almost bodily upon the little old man, who to all appearance presented such small powers of resistance. His first calculation was correct enough. Mr Laxworthy made no attempt to discharge the revolver which he held in his hand. In other respects, however, a surprise was in store for Lefant. His right hand was suddenly held in a grip of amazing strength. The fingers of Mr Laxworthy's other hand were upon his throat.

'If you utter a sound, remember we are both lost,' the latter whispered.

Lefant set himself grimly to the struggle, but it lasted only a few seconds! Before he realized what had happened, his shoulders and the back of his head were upon the table and Mr Laxworthy's fingers were like bars of steel upon his throat. He felt his consciousness going.

'You are content to discuss this matter?' his assailant asked calmly.

Lefant could only gasp out his answer. Mr Laxworthy released his grasp. Lefant breathed heavily for a minute or two. He was half dazed. The thing seemed impossible, yet it had happened. The breath had very nearly left his body in the grip of this insignificant-looking old man.

'Now, if you are willing to be reasonable,' Mr Laxworthy said, 'remember that for both our sakes it is well we do not waste a single second.'

Lefant's fingers stiffened upon the roll of papers, which he was still clutching. Mr Laxworthy read his thoughts unerringly.

'I do not ask you for the plans,' he continued grimly. 'You want them for your country. I am not a patriot. My country shall fight her own battles as long as they are fought fairly. These are my terms: put back those papers, or destroy them, and pay me for my silence.'

'You do not ask, then, for the plans for yourself?' Lefant demanded.

'I do not,' Laxworthy replied. 'They belong to France. Let France keep them. You have corrupted half the ship with Poignton's dollars, but it was never in your mind to keep your faith with him. The plans were for Germany. Germany shall not have them. If I forced you to hand them over to me, I dare say I could dispose of them for – what shall we say? – a hundred thousand pounds. You shall put them back in their place and pay me ten thousand for my silence.'

'So you are an adventurer?' Lefant muttered.

'I am one who seeks adventures,' Laxworthy replied. 'We will let it go at that, if you please. Remember that you are in my power. The pressure of my foot upon this bell, or my finger upon the trigger of this revolver, and your career is over. Will you restore the plans and pay me ten thousand pounds?'

Lefant sighed.

'It is agreed,' he declared.

He turned back to the cabinet, and Laxworthy half rose in his seat to watch him restore the plans. In a few seconds the affair was finished.

'Monsieur the Admiral returns to the ball?' Mr Laxworthy remarked smoothly. 'I will avail myself of his kind offer to accept a seat in the pinnace.'

They left the cabin and made their way to the side of the ship where the pinnace was waiting, and the lieutenant stood with his hand to the salute. Secretly, the latter was a little relieved to see the two together. Once more the pinnace rushed towards the land. The two men walked down the wooden quay, side by side.

'You will permit me to offer you a lift to the hotel?' Lefant asked.

'With much pleasure,' Laxworthy replied, drawing his grey shawl around him. 'I find the nights chilly in these open cars, though.'

Smoothly, but at a great pace, they tore along the scented road, through a grove of eucalyptus trees, and into the grounds of the hotel whose lights were twinkling far and wide. Lefant for the first time broke the silence.

'Mr Laxworthy,' he said, 'the honours of this evening rest with you. I do not wish to ask questions that you are not likely to answer, but there is one matter on which if you would enlighten me –'

Mr Laxworthy waved his hand.

'Proceed,' he begged.

'My little enterprise of this evening,' Lefant continued slowly, 'was known of and spoken of only between Mr Freeling Poignton and myself. We discussed it in the grounds of the hotel, where we were certainly free from eavesdroppers. I am willing to believe that you are a very remarkable person, but this is not the age of miracles.'

Mr Laxworthy smiled.

'Nor is it the age,' he murmured, 'wherein we have attained sufficient wisdom to be able to define exactly what a miracle is. Ten years ago, what would men have said of flying? Fifty years ago even the telephone was considered incredible. Has it never occurred to you, my dear Lefant, that there may be natural gifts of which one or two of us are possessed, almost as strange?'

Lefant turned in his seat.

'You mean –' he began.

Mr Laxworthy held up his hand. 'I have given you a hint,' he said; 'the rest is for you.'

Lefant was silent for a moment.

'Tell me at least this,' he begged. 'How the devil did you get on the *Magnifique*?'

They were passing along the front by the ballroom. Admiral Christodor and Madame Bertrand were sitting near the window. Laxworthy sighed.

'The greatest men in the world,' he said, 'make fools of themselves when they put pencil to paper for the sake of a woman ... Take my advice, Marquis. Destroy that uniform and arrange for an alibi. In a few hours' time there will be trouble on the *Magnifique*!'

Lefant nodded. His cocked hat was thrust into the pocket of his overcoat – he was wearing a motor cap and goggles.

'There will be trouble,' he remarked dryly, 'but it will not touch you or me. As regards Madame Bertrand –'

'She is innocent,' Laxworthy assured him. 'Nevertheless, a pass on to the *Magnifique* is a little too valuable a thing to be left in a lady's chatelaine bag.'

Lefant sighed.

'One makes mistakes,' he remarked.

'And one pays!' Laxworthy agreed.

13

The Murder at the
Duck Club

H. Hesketh Prichard

NOVEMBER Joe had come to Quebec to lay in his stores against the winter's trapping. He had told me that the best grounds in Maine were becoming poorer and poorer and that he had decided to go in on the south side of the St Lawrence, somewhere beyond Rimouski.

I knew that November was coming since two hours before his arrival a cable had been brought in for him, for when in Quebec, although he stayed at a downtown board-ing-house, he was in the habit of using my office as a per-manent address. I was therefore not at all surprised to hear his soft voice rallying my old clerk in the outer office. A more crabbed person than Hugh Witherspoon it would be impossible to meet, but it cannot be denied that like so many others he had a kindliness for November. Presently there was a knock at the door and Joe, his hat held between his two hands, sidled into the room. He was never quite at ease except in the open, and as he came towards me with his shy smile, his moccasins fell noiselessly on the polished boards.

I handed him his telegram, which he opened at once. It ran:

Offer you fifty dollars a day to come at once to Tamarind Duck Club.—*Eileen M. East.*

Joe whistled and characteristically said nothing.

'Who is Eileen M. East?' I asked.

Joe made no reply for a moment, then he indicated the telegram and said:

'This has been redirected from Lavette. Postmaster Tom knew I'd be in to see you. Miss East was one of an American party I was with, 'way up on Thompson's salmon river this spring.'

At this moment a clerk knocked and entered, bringing with him a second telegram. Joe read it:

You must come. Murder done. A matter of life and death. please reply.—*Eileen M. East.*

'Will you write out an answer for me?' asked Joe.

I nodded. Joe is slow with the pen.

'"Miss Eileen M. East." Please put that, sir, and then "arriving on 3.38," and sign.'

'How shall I sign it?' said I.

'Just write "November".'

I did so, and ringing again for the clerk I directed him to give the telegram to the boy who was waiting. There was a moment's silence, then –

'Can you come along, Mr Quaritch?'

I looked at the business which had accumulated on my desk, for, as I have had occasion to observe more than once, I am a very busy man indeed, or, at least, ought to be, for my interests, as were those of my father and grandfather, are bound up with the development of the Dominion of Canada and range through the vegetable and mineral kingdoms to water-power and the lighting of many of our greatest cities.

'Yes, but I must have ten minutes in which to give Witherspoon his instructions.'

Joe went to the door. 'The boss wants you right away, old man,' I heard him say.

Witherspoon shuffled into my room.

'I'll go and get a rig,' continued November, 'and have it

waiting outside. We haven't overmuch time if we're going to call at your country place for your outfit.'

A quarter of an hour later Joe and I were bowling along in the rig drawn by a particularly good horse. I live with my sister some distance out on the St Louis road, and thither we drove at all speed.

My sister had gone out to tea with some friends, but she is well accustomed to my always erratic movements, so that I felt quite at ease when I left a note explaining that I was leaving Quebec for a day or two with November Joe.

We reached the station just in time and were soon steaming along through the farmlands that surround Quebec City.

You who read this may or may not have heard of the Tamarind Duck Club. It is a small association composed chiefly of Montreal and New York business men, to which I had leased the sporting rights of a chain of lakes lying on one of my properties not very far from the waters of the St Lawrence. To these lakes the ducks fly in from the tide each evening, and in the fall very fine sport is to be obtained there, the guns often averaging ten and twenty brace of birds, the latter number being the limit permitted to each shooter by the rules. During the season there are generally two or three members at the clubhouse, which, though but a log hut, is warm and comfortable. In fact, the Tamarind Club has a waiting list of those who desire to belong to it quite out of all proportion to its capacity.

All these facts marshalled themselves and passed through my mind as the train rolled on, and at length I said to Joe:

'Murder done at the Tamarind Club! It seems incredible. It must be that some poacher has shot one of the guides.'

'Maybe,' said Joe, 'but Miss East said "a matter of life and death"; what can that mean? That's what I'm asking myself. But here we are! It won't be long before we know a bit more.'

The cars drew up at the little siding which is situated

within a walk of the Tamarind Club. We jumped down just as a girl, possessing dark and vivid good looks of a quite arresting kind, stepped from the agent's office and caught November impulsively by the hand.

'Oh, Joe, I *am* so glad to see you!'

November Joe always had a distinct appeal to women; high or low, whatever their station in life, they like him. Of course, his looks were in his favour. Women generally do find a kind glance for six foot of strength and sinew, especially when surmounted by a perfectly poised head and features such as Joe's. He had a curious deprecating manner, too, that carried its own charm, and he appeared unable to speak two sentences to any woman without giving her the impression that he was entirely at her service – which, indeed, he was.

'When I got your message from Lavette, I come right along,' said the woodsman simply; 'Mr Quaritch come, too. It's from him the Club holds its lease.'

Miss East sent me a flash of her dark eyes, and I saw they were full of trouble.

'I hope you will be on my side, Mr Quaritch,' she said. 'Just now I need friends badly.'

'What is it, Miss Eileen?' asked Joe, as she paused.

'Uncle has been shot, Joe.'

'Mr Harrison?'

'Yes.'

'I'm terrible sorry to hear that. He was a fine, just man.'

'But that is not all. There is something even worse! ... They say it was Mr Galt who shot him.'

'Mr Galt!' exclaimed November in surprise. 'It ain't possible!'

'I know! I know! Yet everyone believes that he did it. I sent for you to prove to them that he is innocent. You will, won't you, Joe?'

'I'll sure do my best.'

I saw her struggle for self-control; the way she got herself in hand was splendid.

'I must tell you how it happened,' she said, 'and we can be walking on at the same time, for I want you, Joe, to see the place before dark ... Yesterday afternoon there were five of us at the club. I was the only woman and the men settled to go out after the ducks in the evening, for though it had been wet all day, the wind went round and it began to blow clear about three o'clock. Four shooters went out; there was uncle and Mr Hinx, and Egbert Simonson, and – and Ted Galt.'

'Is that the same Mr Hinx who was salmon-fishing with us early this year?'

'Yes ... Most evenings I go with uncle, but yesterday the bush was so wet that I decided not to go, so the four men went, and at the usual time the others all came back. At half past seven, I began to get anxious, so I sent Tim Carter, the head guide, to see if anything was wrong. He found my uncle dead in his screen.'

'And what brought Mr Galt's name into it?'

She hesitated for a second.

'He and uncle had a good way to go to their places, which were next to each other. They walked together, and their voices were heard, very loud, as if they were quarrelling. Egbert Simonson complained about it when he came in – said they made enough noise to disturb the lake, and after that, of course, Ted was suspected.'

'Did Mr Galt own they'd had any words?' inquired Joe.

'Yes. Uncle was angry with him,' she admitted, and a colour showed for a moment in her cheeks. 'Ted is not a rich man, Joe; you know that.'

'Huh!' said Joe with complete comprehension. Then, after a pause, he asked : 'Who is it suspects Mr Galt?'

'It was Tim Carter who got the evidence together against him.'

'*Evidence?*'

'Uncle and Ted were placed next each other at the shoot.'

'And had Mr Harrison or Mr Galt the outside place?'

'Ted had.'

'Well, who was on the other side of your uncle? I suppose there must have been someone.'

'It was Mr Hinx.'

'Then what makes Carter so sure it was Mr Galt done it?'

'Ah! That is the awful thing. My uncle was killed with number six shot.'

'Yes?'

'And Ted is the only one who uses number six size. The others all had number four.'

Joe whistled, and was silent for some moments. Then he said:

'I think, Miss Eileen, I'd as soon you didn't tell me any more. I'd like best to have Mr Galt's and Carter's stories at first-hand from theirselves.'

The girl stopped short. 'But, November, you don't believe it was Ted!'

'I sure don't,' he said. 'Mr Galt ain't that kind of a man. Where is he?'

'Didn't I tell you? Some police came out on the last train. They have him under arrest. It is dreadful!'

*

Half an hour later November Joe was face to face with Carter, who gave him no very warm welcome, and added nothing to the following statement, which he had dictated to the police inspector and signed in affidavit form:

Last evening roundabout five o'clock, four members of the club, Harrison, Hinx, Simonson, and Galt, started out for Reedy Neck. Reedy Neck is near half a mile long by a hundred yards wide. It is a kind of promontory of low ground that sticks out into Goose Lake. The members walked to their places. I did not accompany them, because I had been ordered to take a canoe round to the north side of the lake, so as I could move any ducks that might pitch on that part of the lake over the guns. There are six screens on Reedy Neck. Before starting, the members drew lots for places as per Rule 16. Galt drew number one, that is the screen nearest the end of the Neck and farthest from the clubhouse. Harrison got number two. Number three was